THE LAWS OF MAGIC

TIME OF TRIAL

A Random House book
Published by Random House Australia Pty Ltd
Level 3, 100 Pacific Highway, North Sydney NSW 2060
www.randomhouse.com.au

First published by Random House Australia in 2009
This edition first published in 2010

Addresses for companies within the Random House Group can be found at www.randomhouse.com.au/offices.

National Library of Australia
Cataloguing-in-Publication Entry

Author: Pryor, Michael
Title: Time of trial / Michael Pryor
ISBN: 978 1 86471 865 2 (pbk.)
Series: Pryor, Michael. Laws of magic; 4
Target audience: For secondary school age
Dewey number: A823.3

Cover illustration by Jeremy Reston
Cover design by www.blacksheep-uk.com
Internal design by Mathematics
Typeset in Bembo by Midland Typesetters, Australia
Printed in Australia by Griffin Press, an accredited ISO AS/NZS 14001:2004 Environmental Management System printer

THE LAWS OF MAGIC

TIME OF TRIAL

MICHAEL PRYOR

RANDOM HOUSE AUSTRALIA

For the Centre for Youth Literature,
a national treasure.

Lili, Mike, Paula, Christine –
champions of the cause.

One

AUBREY FITZWILLIAM BRACED HIMSELF FOR THE NEXT attack from his young, tall and menacing adversary. Young and tall were manageable. It was the menacing part that was the problem.

Aubrey grimaced as sweat trickled from his brow and threatened to blind him, but he couldn't spare a hand to wipe it away.

His adversary advanced on him, murder in his eye, and launched a thunderbolt.

Aubrey played forward and had to jerk back when the ball leaped up off a good length, whistling past his gloves with nothing to spare.

The bowler stifled a groan and stood mid-pitch. He threw his head back as if to berate the gods for the injustice. Then he scowled at Aubrey before beginning his march back to his bowling mark.

Aubrey straightened and removed his batting gloves,

trying to give the appearance of someone who had so much composure that he could give the surplus away to those less blessed – while inside, his batting nerves jittered alarmingly.

The annual match between St Alban's College and Lattimer College was a carnival, the traditional event to mark the end of term. Surrounding the oval was a throng of vastly amused spectators, as well as a brass band, a coconut shy, sundry vendors of refreshments, assorted dogs and even a tethered hot air balloon for the amusement of those not entirely interested in the cricket. The day was bright and sunny, perfect weather for such an occasion.

Aubrey was batting much sooner than he'd expected. Coming in at number eight after a pitiful collapse by the higher order, he was attempting to gather the sixty-odd runs needed for victory. If he managed this improbable event, St Alban's would defeat Lattimer College for the first time in thirty-four years. At the moment, this was exceedingly unlikely, as it seemed to Aubrey as if Lattimer College was solely populated by six-foot-tall Adonises. Every one of their bowlers had shoulders so broad that he imagined Lattimer College was built with extra-wide doorways, to save these gargantuan athletes from having to turn sideways to enter rooms.

Aubrey's batting partner, by contrast, was a well-meaning, second-year magic student whose mind was mostly elsewhere. He had a disconcerting habit of blinking and saying, 'My word. Should I be running now?' when Aubrey was haring toward him, which hadn't helped matters at all.

The umpire cleared his throat. He was the professor of Jurisprudence, selected on the misunderstanding that a familiarity with the law meant he'd be a good umpire. His extremely thick glasses suggested otherwise. 'Are you ready, young man?' he quavered down the length of the pitch.

Aubrey sighed. 'Sorry, sir.' He pulled on his gloves. *Bat and pad close together*, he thought, *and if it's loose, lash it through the gap in the off side.*

Aubrey hadn't had a loose delivery in the four overs he'd faced, but he was doing his best to be optimistic.

The bowler pawed the ground impatiently. From where Aubrey stood he seemed small against the jollity of the spectators behind him. Parasols, straw boaters and striped blazers made a colourful backdrop, and Aubrey knew he'd lose sight of the ball as soon as the bowler hurled it.

He went into his stance and gripped the bat so tightly it hurt.

The bowler squared his shoulders, his shirt visibly straining not to burst at the seams. He grinned, then set off. At first he loped, easily and smoothly, like a steeplechaser. Soon, however, he accelerated, arms and legs pumping, a maniacal grin on his face.

Just as the bowler gathered himself for his huge final bound and delivery, Aubrey straightened. He smelled something – something more than the smell of mown grass, more than the tang of nervous sweat, something different from the aroma coming from the pie seller's barrow.

He smelled shrillness – and he knew magic wasn't far away.

Aubrey had noted, over the last few months, that his magical awareness had been developing. His lecturer in Magical Abilities had forecast such a thing. As the term had progressed, Aubrey and his fellow students had found that they could sense magic at greater and greater distances. Aubrey had also been intrigued to learn that as magical awareness matured, it could take on an odd cast, sometimes being experienced as a confusion of more ordinary senses. Hearing colours or tasting sounds, for instance. It was unsettling at first, and unpredictable, but Aubrey had quickly learned that he should be alert whenever it happened.

A chorus of delight brought Aubrey back to the here and now. With dismay, he realised the sound had followed the rattle of the stumps behind him. The professor of Jurisprudence peered down the pitch. 'Out?' he ventured.

Aubrey was on his way.

He trudged toward the pavilion, bat under his arm, but he was oblivious to the laughter from the crowd. The mix-up of sensory experience just before he was bowled was a tell-tale sign of strong magic. But where was it? He peered at the surroundings, the treetops, the river, the nearby colleges.

'Well done, old man,' George Doyle said as he hurried past to take up his post at the wicket. 'A nicely compiled six runs, that.'

Aubrey snorted. His friend was rolling his sleeves up as if he were heading for a paddle at the beach. 'So that would make me the second top scorer?'

'For now.' George grinned. He took off his cap and tossed it to Aubrey. 'Take care of this, would you? It'll only get in the way.'

'You're sounding confident for a number nine batsman.'

'They won't be expecting anything. I'll take them by surprise.'

George strode off, whistling, leaving Aubrey shaking his head. George had a habit of taking people by surprise, but he wasn't sure that cricket was the time for it.

Caroline Hepworth was waiting for him at the gate. She was dressed in a long skirt and blouse, fresh and white. The blouse was fastened at her neck with an onyx brooch. Her hair was pinned, or layered, or constrained in some way that Aubrey admired but would never have ventured an opinion on exactly how it was done.

Caroline's hair had been the cause of much thought on Aubrey's part. When he'd first met her, he'd thought it was the colour of chestnuts – deep, glowing brown with touches of burnished gold. But he was constantly revising his opinion. Sometimes it was more golden than brown, sometimes the other way around. And he'd never been able to work out how curly it was. It wasn't straight – at least, he thought not. But it wasn't crinkled like a Bedlington terrier. It was shoulder-length, give or take, and he'd settle for calling it wavy.

It was just that she did different things with it. Tied it. Rolled it up. Twisted it. Sculpted it. Constructed elaborate phantasmagoria with it. All depending on the occasion, and her mood.

'You should have played forward instead of back,' she said. She held a lace parasol. It dappled her face with shadow.

'I didn't play anything at all,' he said. 'I was distracted. Any chance of a drink?'

'Here.' A tall glass of cold lemon squash was thrust into Aubrey's hand. It slopped over the side. 'Ach, sorry!'

Aubrey shook off the sticky yellow liquid and wondered who his embarrassed benefactor was.

He was a tall youth, about Aubrey's age. He wore his striped blazer, white trousers and boater as if totally unfamiliar with them. His wild black hair surrounded a face that featured round spectacles and a beaky nose. He was all arms and knees, possibly the most stork-like person Aubrey had ever seen.

Caroline made the introductions. 'Aubrey, this is Otto Kiefer. He's says he's desperate to meet you.'

'Kiefer,' Aubrey said. He transferred his glass of squash to his left hand and shook. Kiefer was oblivious to the stickiness of the handshake, and performed his part of the transaction with considerable enthusiasm, pumping up and down as if he were trying to crank a stubborn motorcar.

'Fitzwilliam. Finally.'

Aubrey raised an eyebrow. Kiefer had a Holmland accent. While Albion and Holmland weren't at war – yet – Aubrey was always cautious when meeting Holmlanders. Albion was seething with Holmland intelligence operatives, espionage agents and straight-out spies. Aubrey often thought he couldn't turn around without tripping over one.

Being the son of the Prime Minister added a certain piquancy to this ubiquity. Holmland had never been above a spot of strategic assassination, so Aubrey kept his wits about him.

'Finally?' he echoed.

Kiefer nodded, furiously. 'I have been at this university for some time, but I couldn't find you. I searched many places until I saw Miss Hepworth.' He took a moment from his nodding to beam at Caroline. She smiled back serenely. 'From her mother, I know her. Painting exhibition. I had heard that she is your friend so I asked her where you were. Cricket, she said, so I am here.'

A cheer went up and Aubrey turned to see the umpire signalling four runs. 'George?'

'A remarkably fine cover drive,' Caroline said. 'Raced to the boundary.'

Kiefer tugged on Aubrey's arm. 'Fitzwilliam. I have something I must discuss with you. It is vital.'

Before Aubrey could respond, the sound of willow on leather was followed by more cheering. 'Another four,' Caroline observed. 'George is batting well.'

Aubrey wanted to see his friend's innings and tried to think how to put off the insistent Kiefer. 'I'm happy to chat.' He looked past the Holmlander's shoulder to where George took a mighty swing and dispatched the ball past point for another four. The crowd was in ecstasy, cheering for all it was worth.

'Good, good,' Kiefer said. He peered over the heads of the excited spectators. 'Where will we go?'

'Not now,' Aubrey said. 'What about –'

He broke off. Once again, a wrong-way-around smell came to him. This time, he wrinkled his nose at the bizarre sensation of roughness, something that his sense of touch should be bringing to him. He grimaced and looked around, searching for its source.

'Look out,' Caroline said.

'What?'

She didn't repeat herself. She simply took his shoulder, moved him aside, then darted out a slender hand. She caught the cricket ball easily, despite the solid *smack* it made.

She was immediately the heroine of the moment. A storm of applause erupted, and more than a few appreciative whistles, as she flung the cricket ball back to the panting fieldsman who was slumped on the fence. 'I didn't know George could bat,' she said. 'That was a fine six. Took it right off his nose.'

'Did he?' Aubrey said distantly. He looked upriver, past the dense line of willow trees, toward Canon's Bridge. The clouds, gathering in that direction . . .

George's next six landed ten yards away, right in the middle of a tea-set spread in front of an elderly clergyman, then rebounded into a refreshment tent before coming to rest in a bowl of ginger punch.

Aubrey didn't notice. He'd left the confused Kiefer behind and pushed through the crowd in the direction of Canon's Bridge. He wanted a better view of the unusual cloud formation, and he was tasting discordant music at the back of his mouth as he went. A small terrier cocked its head as he slipped past a betting tent (the odds on St Alban's College were tumbling as George cracked another boundary). The dog looked up at the sky and whined. 'You feel it too?' Aubrey muttered. He frowned at the cricket bat in his hand and the pads on his legs. It took him a moment to remember why they were there. The dog looked at the sky to the north, whimpered, then ran off through the crowd, tail between its legs.

Animals run away from danger, Aubrey thought. *Perhaps it knows something I don't.*

The river bent around the back of the cricket oval, making the sort of ridiculously picturesque scene that usually had a score of artists battling each other for easel space, the better to sketch the trees and ducks and Saturday afternoon rowing boats full of bright young things. Aubrey found it to be strangely quiet.

He came to Canon's Bridge and the road to the town. With his view clear of the willows he could see that the weather was turning alarmingly bad – a fact that would concern the spectators and cricketers, rain being the natural enemy of the game. Clouds had heaped up to the north like immense grey gunboats, a fleet of them stretched out across the sky and streaming toward the oval with malign intent.

He stared, and even though he was still in sunlight, he was suddenly chill.

There was no wind. Not a breeze, a zephyr, a fitful gust, nothing at all. *Air is never this still*, he thought, *not even in a tomb*. The thought made him shudder, then he blinked. *If there's no wind, what's driving those clouds this way?*

Realisation hit him, a solid punch to the chest. They weren't clouds that looked like battleships. They were battleships *made* of clouds, steaming toward him in the afternoon sky, dark-grey as thunderheads. Clouds made solid and menacing in a mighty show of magic.

Dizzily, Aubrey put a hand on the stone of the bridge to steady himself. He stared, and shaded his eyes, unwilling to believe what he was seeing. Battleships in the sky? He swallowed in a throat suddenly dry. He counted half a dozen or so cloud-built battleships, but they were accompanied by destroyers and cruisers, as well as tenders, troop ships and dozens of lesser craft. It was a skyborne fleet.

Even in his shock, Aubrey's mind was whirring, trying to work out the principles behind such a formidable, such a bravura, such a *showy* display of power.

A burly worker leading a horse and cart was coming along the road toward him. He smiled and tipped his cap to Aubrey. 'Make any runs?'

'A few,' Aubrey said faintly.

The man looked behind him, following Aubrey's gaze, and the grin faded from his face. 'My sainted aunt.'

Aubrey was glad. He wasn't the only one who could see the skyborne fleet. 'We're under attack.'

The worker swore. 'Don't stand there, son. Find cover.' He urged his nag on and hurried along the road out of town.

The cloud-built battlefleet surged nearer. They rose over the Torwell Hills to the north of Greythorn as if they were cresting huge waves, rolling down the other side in formation. Aubrey tried to count them, but lost track after four dozen when he realised a second rank of cruisers and destroyers was following the main line of battleships.

He could feel the magic even at this distance, like ice flung ahead of a storm.

He gripped the stone parapet of the bridge, then turned. No-one at the cricket match was looking to the north. All attention was on St Alban's spirited revival. The music played, dogs barked and the observers in the tethered balloon bobbed gently.

Alone on the bridge, Aubrey wished that a battalion of trained magicians stood with him.

It was up to him to do something, one of those moments that aroused equal parts terror and exhilaration. Sometimes he felt as if his entire life was a series of trials, each an opportunity to fail spectacularly or to succeed with glory. He preferred the latter and was deathly afraid of the former.

He twirled his cricket bat. He was dwarfed, outnumbered and unprepared. He was dressed in cricketing whites. He had lemon squash all down his arm.

Apart from a case of fright that'd choke a chicken, he thought, *I'm in fine shape.*

With a roar that set the church bells ringing, the battlefleet swept over the town.

Aubrey was knocked off his feet by the gale that accompanied the fleet as it thundered overhead. By the time he picked himself up, spitting road dust from his mouth, the ships had rumbled over the cricket ground. Pandemonium erupted. Tents were uprooted and whirled into the air. Spectators staggered every which way, some being flung off their feet as the stormfleet bore down on them. Dogs went berserk, running in circles and barking. The hot air balloon was wrenched from its moorings, and the last Aubrey saw it was streaking away to the south, white-faced passengers clinging for dear life.

With fumbling fingers, Aubrey unbuckled his pads and slung them away. He sprinted for an oval that had become a riot, feverishly flicking through his accumulated store of magic lore, trying to find something that could help.

The sun had disappeared, swallowed by the stormfleet as it circled, but the change in the weather had brought no rain. Instead, the cricket ground and its surrounds had become a howling cauldron. The wind was coming from all directions, so those seeking shelter could find no leeside on the pavilion or under the few trees that hadn't been shredded by the force of the storm. A plucky motorist drove off, heading for the main road, his motorcar crammed with passengers. He parped his horn as he passed Aubrey, but a few yards away, where the driveway to the cricket ground reached the main gate, the motorcar shuddered.

Aubrey stared. The motorcar hadn't just stopped – it had been slapped sideways, its front wheels wrenched into the ditch on the side of the driveway by an unseen force.

With some difficulty, the motorcar backed out of the ditch, then accelerated again toward the gate. This time, the vehicle was violently jerked to the right with the sound of breaking glass. The driver was flung out, but even as Aubrey hurried up, the young man had picked himself up and was dusting himself off. 'Oh, I say!' he shouted over the howl of the wind. 'My hat!'

His boater was a mess. Aubrey shrugged. 'What happened?'

The young man's passengers staggered out of the motorcar. They milled about uncertainly. 'No idea, old sport. Ran into the gatepost, I suppose.'

'I don't think so,' Aubrey shouted. 'Look.'

Just a few feet away, the air had taken on a greasy, shimmering aspect. As Aubrey peered at it, holding up a hand to shield his eyes from the upraised dust, he could make out that the air was moving, vibrating and rushing past at a dizzying velocity, enough to blur the scene on the other side. It made the trees and the town beyond look as if they were smeared with oil.

'Watch!' He bent and picked up a small stone. Squinting, he threw it at the barrier of moving air. Then he ducked as the stone shot back at them. It hummed past his head and smashed one of the headlights of the motorcar.

'Sorry,' he shouted, but he was apologising to no-one. The young man and his companions were scurrying back toward the pavilion.

Aubrey looked up to see that the stormfleet had blockaded the cricket ground, surrounding it in a swirling wall of cloud that extended from the heights right down to the earth. The magical warships were circling, patrolling the tight confines of this small area. The roar of their great guns punctuated the howling of the wind. Lightning tore at the dark grey, churning mass and made the gloom momentarily lighter with its ghastly, harsh radiance. The people trapped within the wall of cloud were starting to cluster in the middle of the cricket ground, near the pavilion. Anyone foolish enough to try to find a gap in the spinning cloud wall was twisted aside or knocked to the ground as soon as they touched it.

Aubrey decided he wasn't achieving anything where he was. He had to find Caroline and George.

He struggled toward the panicked crowd, battling the wind that tore at him. Each step was an adventure, for the wind was coming from all directions, but as he neared the building Caroline appeared. Even windswept, she was composed. 'Where did you disappear to?' she cried over the shrieking of the wind.

'I went for a stroll! Lovely day for it!'

The look she gave him plucked at his heart. He was acutely aware of her presence, even more so since their agreement to remain good colleagues and fellow adventurers rather than anything more. Her movements, her subtle grace, her laugh, were more irresistible than ever and yet he was honour bound to do nothing about it.

Keeping a friendly distance was the sensible thing to do, with their demanding studies and other commitments. Very rational, very sensible, and very, very difficult to endure when her presence was so intoxicating and frustrating. Sometimes he thought it would be better not to see Caroline at all. Then he'd be horrified by the prospect of not seeing her and he'd plunge back into his sea of indecision.

'The ships!' Her eyes were bright as they always were in times of high adventure. It was one of the things – one of the many things – that Aubrey adored about her. Her reaction to danger? Exhilaration! 'What are you going to do about them?'

Another thing about Caroline. She had confidence in him – at least, where things magical were concerned.

'We seem to be trapped!' Aubrey did his best to sound as if this were of no real importance.

A large picnic basket tumbled past. Caroline looked heavenward, then frowned, then she looked at Aubrey again. 'Why?'

Aubrey gaped at her. He'd been busy working on 'How' rather than 'Why'. He assumed that 'How' would give him a way to counter the stormfleet, perhaps a way to escape. 'Why' had slipped his mind.

A wave of dust made him close his eyes. When he opened them again, the cruising battleships were still there, the destroyers were still there, the tending craft still trailing in the skywake of the larger ships. 'Good question!' he shouted.

Around them, couples in what had been their outdoor finery were tottering, arm in arm, uncertainly. Knots of burly young men were hunched over, as if they could batter their way through the elements.

'You have a good answer?' Caroline shouted, obviously deciding that succinct communication was the order of the day.

By now a few others were milling around Aubrey and Caroline, no doubt through some primitive notion of safety in numbers. All were bedraggled, fearful, unkempt, a far cry from the carefree picnickers who'd been enjoying a sunny afternoon.

Aubrey quickly sorted through his options, limited though they were. Motorcars obviously had no hope of battering through the storm curtain. Communication with the outside world was impossible. Sitting tight and waiting for rescue was the most sensible thing.

Aubrey was about to recommend as much to Caroline when he glanced upward. The underside of the cloudy warships glided high overhead like sharks. He squinted, then stared. Something was falling from the largest of the ships. At first, he thought it was an anchor, which set his mind racing as to the implications of a threatening spectral fleet anchored in the middle of Albion's greatest university. Was it taking hostages? Trying to sabotage the nation's intellectual efforts?

Then the shape resolved itself and bone-melting fear muscled its way into Aubrey's consciousness. 'Depth charge!'

Caroline whirled. 'What?'

Aubrey threw caution to the winds – a simple task in the circumstances – and took her around the waist. Her eyes flew open wide and she automatically applied an agonising nerve hold to his elbow.

'High explosive!' Aubrey gasped. 'Submersible killer!'

The brick wall of the pavilion was the nearest possible shelter. He was about to gallantly throw himself on top of her – with the sole intent of protecting her – when the blast struck. A familiar wave of magic battered at him and ripped at the fragile bond that held his body and soul together.

Blackness, dark and terrible, swept him away.

Two

'**D**ASHED POOR TIMING, THAT STORM. I WAS IN GOOD FORM,' George said from where he was sitting at the foot of Aubrey's bed. Outside, the college clock struck five.

Caroline was there too, sitting on a rickety wooden chair dragged from Aubrey's desk, balancing a cup of tea on her knee. She hadn't touched it for some time; Aubrey was sure it was cold.

Otto Kiefer was standing at the window. He alternated between looking at Aubrey with an expression of satisfaction, and glancing uneasily through the drawn curtains. Aubrey thought he couldn't look more furtive if he'd tried.

Aubrey stretched and enjoyed the sensation. He realised he felt much better than he had any entitlement to. He ran a quick inner inspection and found no aches, no tender gums, no strained vision. A further check revealed that his body and soul were snugly united. Settled. As one. Which, again, was unexpected, given what he remembered.

He sat up and the room spun around him. He was perversely grateful and let himself sag again.

'Be easy, now,' Kiefer said. 'You still need rest.'

'It was a near thing,' Caroline said. 'If not for Otto, I don't know what would have happened.'

Aubrey had a fair idea. He shuddered. Carefully, he lifted himself onto one elbow. 'The stormfleet. What happened?'

'The depth charge exploded with a great deal of noise,' Caroline said. 'Then the clouds opened, the rain nearly drowned everyone, and lightning struck the pavilion, but suddenly it all stopped.'

'The clouds, the storm, everything just evaporated,' George said.

Caroline nodded. 'Everyone was dragging themselves away and George and Kiefer and I found you face-down in the mud.'

'Ah.'

'We thought you could tell us what all that was about,' George said. 'Rather dramatic as it was.'

Aubrey swallowed. 'It was Dr Tremaine. I recognised his magic.'

He recalled his first magical encounter with the ex-Sorcerer Royal, when he'd inadvertently established a tenuous magical connection with the magician. It was unpredictable but at times it provided an intimate appre-hension of the great sorcerer's magic. Occasionally useful, he was profoundly disquieted by it and the implications – which he was sure he hadn't fully determined.

Caroline stiffened. 'Tremaine.' She still had the ex-Sorcerer Royal fairly in her sights for causing the death of her father.

With his free hand, Aubrey patted himself to make sure he was unharmed. 'I seem to attract his attention, for one reason or another.'

'Nothing to do with foiling his plans more than once?' George frowned. 'I say. It's beginning to sound like he has a vendetta against the Fitzwilliams, isn't it? First he attempts something on your father, then your mother, and now you.'

Kiefer shook a fist. 'Tremaine!' he cried with such venom that everyone stared. 'He must be stopped.'

'You won't find any argument about that here, old boy,' George said after a moment's embarrassed silence. 'No Tremaine supporters in this room.'

'I know, I know,' Kiefer subsided. 'That is why I wanted to find you, Fitzwilliam.'

'I see,' Aubrey said. Only one conclusion could be drawn. 'What's he done to you, Kiefer?'

Kiefer slumped, almost comically, until he was sitting cross-legged on the floor. He put his head in his hands. 'He killed my father.'

Caroline gave an involuntary cry.

'I'm sorry to hear that.' Aubrey paused in the face of Kiefer's grief, but he needed to go on. 'How did this happen?'

'My father was a good man.' Kiefer's voice was muffled by his hands. 'He went to work for Dr Tremaine. He was promised much by the government – money, position, even a title.'

'Tremaine is a bad person to work with,' George said. Caroline nodded sharply.

Kiefer lifted his head. His eyes were rimmed with tears. 'My father was the finest industrial magician in

Holmland. The finest.'

Aubrey was naturally tender-hearted; he hated to see suffering. Whatever had happened to Kiefer's father was another score in the account against Dr Tremaine. 'I know what it's like to have a great father. It's an honour and a burden.'

Kiefer nodded. 'That is right. You understand, with a prime minister for a father.'

'I'm sorry for your loss,' Caroline said. Aubrey could hear the tension in her voice, the strain that was always there when the subject of Dr Tremaine surfaced. 'Can you tell us what happened?'

'My father was working on enhancing the action of catalysts in chemical processes.' Kiefer massaged his forehead with both hands. 'It is an area that I have also dedicated myself to. I aim to finish his work.'

'It's useful magic,' Aubrey said. 'Your father would have been an important man.'

'He was. He made great advances with osmium and platinum and the like. But Tremaine wanted more and more, faster and faster. He forced my father to experiment on other materials.' Kiefer paused and swallowed. 'Then, without telling my father, Tremaine removed the protective spells in the reaction chamber. Under pressure, it exploded.'

For a moment, the room was silent as they each contemplated the horror. 'I'm sorry,' Aubrey said again. He knew it was inadequate, but it was all he had.

'Thank you.' Kiefer cleared his throat, looked away for a moment, then he fixed Aubrey with a direct gaze. 'I know about you and Dr Tremaine, Fitzwilliam. In fact, I know many things.'

'You do?'

'He saved you, old man,' George said. 'After the depth charge thing. We thought you were *in extremis*, if you know what I mean.' He raised an eyebrow significantly.

Kiefer nodded. 'I brought that device with me all the way from Holmland. It is what saved you.'

'Device?'

'On your chest. I knew you would need it.'

Aubrey looked down, awkwardly, past his chin, but found it difficult to make out the object nestled on his chest. He sat up in the bed and took hold of it, to find that it was hanging from a fine metal chain around his neck. He stared at it dumbly.

It was a tiny wire cage in the shape of a sphere, perfectly round, wrought of silver or some other shiny metal, about the size of a small egg. Inside it was a solid metal ball, silver again. When Aubrey tilted it the ball rolled freely around inside the cage.

'And what is it?'

'It is a Beccaria Cage,' Kiefer said. 'A protective device that will keep your body and soul together.' He beamed. 'It is the cure for your condition.'

'My condition? What do you know about my condition?'

'We didn't say a word,' George said in response to Aubrey's accusatory look. 'He seemed to know all about it. After we carried you to your room, he produced this gadget from his pocket and it did the trick.'

'You were crying out,' Caroline said. 'In pain.'

'I don't remember,' Aubrey said softly, but he had a

dim impression of what he had endured. Somewhere, deep inside, part of him did remember, would never forget. Struggling, he remembered struggling, and an awful sense of separation.

'My uncle Maurice told me all about you,' Kiefer said, interrupting Aubrey's thoughts.

Aubrey frowned. 'I'm afraid I don't know anyone called Maurice.'

'He said he met you last year. At the Faculty of Magic. At the University of Lutetia?'

Aubrey couldn't have been more surprised if Kiefer had turned into a pig. In their recent escapade in Lutetia, they had spent some time in the decrepit Faculty of Magic. 'He was a caretaker.'

'He had been a caretaker there for a long time. He saw much.'

'I suppose he did.' Aubrey chewed on his lip. 'He knew about my condition?'

'He did. Two months ago, he wrote a letter and told me about it. He knew I was coming to Albion to continue my studies. He asked me to find this device at Fisherberg Academy, and bring it to you.'

Aubrey flicked the Beccaria Cage with a fingernail. 'So you stole this thing for him.'

Kiefer looked horrified. 'Stole it? No! It was in a basement, in a box with my name on it, just as Uncle Maurice said it would be.'

'And how did Maurice organise this, then?' George asked.

'He has many friends. He corresponds with people all over the world.'

'And he thought it could do me some good?' Aubrey

said.

'He wasn't sure. He said he wanted to do you a good turn, for what you did for the Faculty of Magic.'

Aubrey hadn't done much, apart from levitating the central tower and sending it across the city of Lutetia. He supposed that the faculty may have achieved some prominence because of it. Of course he'd heard about the renewed interest in magical studies at the University of Lutetia and how the department was undergoing a reinvigoration, but he wasn't sure that he could take all the credit. The study of magic was booming all over the world in these exciting and turbulent times.

'But he wasn't sure?'

'No. But I was curious. I undertook some research, which confirmed it. The device is powerful, emitting a soul-stabilising field of immense puissance.'

'I say,' George said, 'you wouldn't be studying magic, would you?'

'I began my studies in history, but I am studying industrial magic at the moment. I am taking some special classes here before resuming my studies at the Fisherberg Academy. Pressure containment and catalysts, mostly. I will be successful, you know.'

'A fine institution,' Aubrey said. The Magic Department at the Fisherberg Academy had produced many excellent magicians, especially those who worked with physical magic, hard-edged spell casters greatly prized by industry. Aubrey had no prejudice against industrial magicians, unlike many of his contemporaries. He admired their work and the way they improved many processes that were vital for the health and happiness of the entire community.

'You would have been lost,' Kiefer said, 'if not for my assistance. The device has restored your balance. Your body and soul are united as they should be.'

Aubrey couldn't argue. He felt as whole as he'd ever felt after the disastrous experiment at Stonelea School. He went to slip the chain from his neck so he could examine the Beccaria Cage more closely.

Kiefer's eyes flew open wide. 'Do not remove it! The cage is all that is stopping you from falling apart.'

The device was heavy in Aubrey's hand. He stared at Kiefer. 'I think you need to tell me more. Much more.'

Kiefer rubbed his palms on his trouser legs. With some effort, he untangled himself and stood. He took a deep breath and did his best to look dignified. 'I have come to seek your assistance, Mr Fitzwilliam.'

'I'm happy to give it.' Aubrey touched the Beccaria Cage. 'You've done a great thing for me.'

'Excellent.' Another deep breath. 'Now I want you to help me destroy Dr Mordecai Tremaine.'

An uncomfortable silence was a sudden visitor in the room. Aubrey pursed his lips, considering his options. 'Destroy Dr Tremaine?' he finally ventured. 'What makes you think we could help you achieve such a thing?'

Before Kiefer could answer, Caroline spoke up. 'Let's not dismiss such a request lightly.' Her voice was even, but Aubrey could see the effort this took. 'Dr Tremaine is a threat to the entire world.'

'He's the most dangerous man there is,' George said gloomily. 'And it's not exactly joyful to know that he has designs on people you care for.'

'I think we all agree on the peril that Dr Tremaine represents,' Aubrey said. 'He may be a madman, after all.

But he is also a genius.'

'Of that I am aware,' Kiefer said brightly. 'He is a most dangerous enemy.' He sighed. 'I risked much to bring that device to you. You must help me.'

Almost without his realising it, Aubrey's hand crept to cover the Beccaria Cage. 'This is sounding awfully like blackmail, Kiefer.'

For a moment, Kiefer looked old. He gestured – a jerky, ungraceful movement. 'It is as you Albionites say: a means to an end.' Before anyone could protest he climbed to his feet and went to the door. 'Rest, Fitzwilliam. Let the Beccaria Cage work on you. We will discuss mutual assistance tomorrow.'

Three

$\mathcal{D}$AWN HAD BARELY ARRIVED WHEN AUBREY WOKE. After he opened his eyes and saw the grey light that stole in around the curtains, it took him a moment to remember that he was in his college rooms. Then he touched the tiny Beccaria Cage and the events of the previous day came back to him.

Quietly, so as not to disturb the sleeping George on the other side of the room, he sat up and held the cage between his thumb and forefinger to examine it.

The metal ball rolled about as he tilted the cage from side to side. It glided smoothly, and Aubrey found himself entranced by its movements and the solidity of its contact with the fine wires. He was always impressed by clever construction, and the neatness of this device was captivating – but he needed to know more about it.

After a time, he reluctantly tucked the cage back inside his nightshirt. Then he eased himself out of his bed, found his dressing gown and slippers, and tiptoed to the door that led to the small study attached to their bedroom.

An hour later, Aubrey was deeply immersed in research. His collection of books covering the history of magic was proving useful, as he'd already found a dozen references to the Beccaria Cage. Even in its earliest eighteenth-century developments, when Giovanni Beccaria had proposed a device that used some of the principles of electrical conduction as well as aspects of the Law of Entanglement, it had been a cunning melding of magic and technology. Aubrey's particular device appeared to be a variation of the classical notion of a Beccaria Cage, however, with some embedded spells that he was having trouble identifying.

Intriguingly, none of the references mentioned a Beccaria Cage with a silver ball inside.

It was a mystery, but Aubrey loved a mystery.

He was reaching for Kuhn's *Magical Revolutions* when a tap came from the casement windows to his left. Aubrey automatically glanced in that direction to see a pigeon fluttering with some agitation. As he stared, it pecked at the glass again.

Aubrey went to shout, to shoo it away, assuming it was tricked by its own reflection, then he remembered that George was still asleep. He sighed, put down his pencil and crossed the room.

At the window, the pigeon continued fluttering and pecking at the glass. Aubrey stood there, waved his arms and made a fierce face, but the pigeon ignored him and tapped furiously at the window.

Shaking his head, Aubrey unlatched the windows and pushed them out. The pigeon tumbled backward in a flurry of wings but instead of flying off as Aubrey had expected, it rallied and darted at him.

He jerked his head back as the pigeon hurtled into the room like a feathery cannonball. He spun to see it career off the side wall, then gather itself with more intent than he thought a pigeon capable of before alighting on the desk where Aubrey had been researching. It immediately worried at an errant feather before fixing him with a beady stare.

Aubrey glanced at the door to the bedroom, but the steady drone that came from that direction told him that George was still asleep.

Aubrey stared back at the bird. No sense in trying to chase it out of the window. Small-brained as pigeons were, it would probably flap around in every direction but the one he wanted. It would be much better to throw a blanket over it first, then empty it outside.

Before Aubrey could move, however, the pigeon bent its head and pecked at a leg. Aubrey narrowed his eyes when he saw that this leg had something attached to it – a small metal capsule.

Aubrey's curiosity immediately scuppered his plan to get rid of the pigeon. At least, not before examining it. The bird must be a lost carrier pigeon, and who knew what message it contained in the capsule on its leg? If he could detach the capsule, he might be able to get the message to its owner.

Without looking, he reached behind himself and pulled the windows closed. Then he took off his dressing gown and held it in front of him, ready to stalk the pigeon.

Aubrey was glad no-one was around to see him as he advanced on the bird. He felt distinctly foolish, in nightshirt and slippers, holding a dressing gown as a net, inching toward a pigeon that was standing on his desk as if it belonged there.

He held his breath when the pigeon cocked its head, but it otherwise showed remarkable unconcern as he moved closer. He lifted the dressing gown, ready to cast it, then he peered around its edge. The pigeon was staring back at him with equanimity.

Aubrey lowered the dressing gown. He reached out, and the bird didn't show any signs of alarm.

Of course, he thought, *it must be accustomed to people*. A carrier pigeon would have been handled from an early age to get it used to having capsules strapped to its leg.

With as much gentleness as he could muster, Aubrey took the pigeon in both hands. It nestled there quite happily, and he found the capsule attached to the bird's leg with copper bands. He removed it easily.

The capsule was extremely light, made of thin aluminium, and only half an inch or so long. It didn't take Aubrey long to see that it was of two halves fitted tightly together. With a twist and a tug, the halves separated and a scrap of folded rice paper dropped to the desk.

His curiosity was circling as he carefully unfolded the paper. The capsule had no markings, but could it be military? Could the message contain secret information? He snorted. It was more likely to be a pigeon fancier taunting another pigeon fancier about how well his birds raced.

Finally, he had the paper unfolded. He smoothed it on the desk and stared at the words written in black ink.

Palaver. Gastropod. Snood. Philtrum.

Aubrey's brain turned to dust.

It was some time later when he realised that he was still standing at the desk. The pigeon was looking at him so he went to the window and opened it. After the pigeon flew out Aubrey threw the screwed-up scrap of rice paper out of the window and immediately forgot about it.

Quietly, with a nagging sense of urgency, he went into the bedroom and found his clothes. Without disturbing George, he dressed. Then the sense of urgency had him closing the door carefully behind him and sneaking down the stairs.

On the platform of Greythorn Station, Aubrey chafed while waiting with the morning passengers. He realised that he'd foolishly forgotten to bring a book, or even a newspaper, to fill in his waiting time, but soon found himself sitting on the hard wooden slats of a railway bench. He must have been more tired than he thought, for when the whistle announced the arrival of the train the station clock told him that nearly an hour had passed without his noticing.

While he searched for an empty compartment, this lapse of time gnawed at him. It was unlike him to be so unaware of his surroundings. His condition, balanced between life and death, had taught him about the value of every moment. Life was brief, a transient thing to be savoured, and even sitting on a station bench was something to be enjoyed.

It worried him, but the worry drifted away when he took his attention from it.

The train was crowded. Aubrey couldn't find an empty compartment but after he settled himself he scarcely noticed the other passengers. They were indistinct presences – collections of vague sounds and smells, blurred movements – as he sat fidgeting in the corner, right by the window. He spent some time watching one knee as he bounced it up and down, the jiggling movement soothing in its rhythm. At times, he thought someone in the compartment spoke to him, but by the time he'd gathered himself enough to reply it seemed pointless, unhelpful to his task at hand, so he didn't.

His earlier feeling of vigour had faded somewhat. He had a headache that was brooding right behind his forehead, a black presence that was threatening to grow. This concerned him, for he knew he had an important task – the responsibility was a fearsome jockey riding him with particularly sharp spurs – but he had trouble defining exactly what it was. It was as vague as the people in the compartment, shapeless as hunger, but just as demanding. He tried to concentrate, because he knew his task was important, but his attention had a tendency to wander and instead he found himself contemplating the wooden window frame. It was made of a mellow orange-brown timber, indifferently lacquered, and Aubrey spent a pleasant hour or two tracing the grain from one side to the other, a tricky task as the lines were fine and he often lost his place and had to start again.

He amused himself by rolling nursery rhymes in his head, repeating them until the words became nonsense collections of sound, but all the more hilarious for it.

Later, he understood that the train had stopped and that he was alone in the compartment. A figure was standing in the doorway and it occurred to Aubrey that responding to it would be a rather good idea. 'I'm fine, thank you, conductor. Just gathering myself before sallying forth into the city. Hat on, gloves on, and I'm ready to go.'

He stepped out of the compartment and strode whistling down the platform, even though it struck him that whistling was something he rarely did.

Outside the station, for once Aubrey didn't feel assaulted by the din of Trinovant traffic nor by the bustle of pedestrians as he joined the crowd. Even the slightly drizzly weather had no effect. His task now burned so brightly in him that everything else, really, was trivial.

It was a comfortable way to be, if a little foggy. Standing at the corner of Wye and Bank Streets, waiting for a chance to cross the busy road that would lead to the Palace, he wondered why life couldn't always be like this. It was a relief not to have to worry about things, knowing that every important decision had been made for him. All he had to do was carry out his task and everything would be perfect. He was well rid of such foolishness as ambition, duty, responsibilities.

First, of course, a detour to the Mire. It took two underground trips and a foot journey of indeterminate length, but he eventually came to the heart of this less than salubrious part of the city. Even at this early hour on a Sunday morning, it was busy. And once it became apparent that he was shopping for firearms, he was besieged by eager sellers – men usually, well fed and expensively dressed, with no sense of fashion but with a manner that said telling them as much would be a bad idea.

In a short time, he could have equipped a small army. Fleetingly, he felt that some of the more volatile nations on the Goltan Peninsula had perhaps done just that. Finally, he was able to purchase his desired weapon: a

Symons service revolver, the Mark V model, not the more common Mark IV. The shifty-eyed vendor – ocular unsteadiness another prerequisite of the trade, it seemed – assured him that it had only ever been used on the practice range. It was large: a .450 calibre, more than enough to punch a hole right through a wall, if needed. He had to chuckle when he considered something as silly as using the pistol to make holes in walls, but he stopped when he realised that the shifty-eyed man was looking at him strangely.

Aubrey declined an offer of heavy machine guns and mortars to go with the revolver, handed over the cash without counting it and was rewarded by a startled – and increasingly shifty – look from his new friend. It made him feel good.

After leaving the Mire, he bobbed along the pavement like a particularly content piece of driftwood. His feet knew his destination, and while he walked he spent some time looking at clouds as they moved across the sky, changing shapes as they were shepherded by the wind. He only became aware of his surroundings when the gates of the Palace loomed. It was a familiar sight and Aubrey's already cheery heart swelled to see it, even though the great rectangular bulk of a building was no-one's finest example of any sort of architecture. Because it was early, the Palace was quiet, with many windows still draped. The guards were in attendance at the gatehouse, of course, but otherwise the gardens, the paths, the parade ground were lonely, just as he had been led to believe.

The guards made Aubrey wait, but he didn't mind because the cobblestones were remarkably interesting. He absorbed himself in counting them and trying to estimate how many there were in the entire parade ground. He kept losing track and having to start again, but it didn't bother him. It was fascinating.

When Archie Sommers, Prince Albert's aide, appeared, Aubrey was irritated – in an abstract, blurry sort of way – that his counting was interrupted, but he soon remembered that Sommers was the easiest way to see the Crown Prince, and that was why he had asked the guards to fetch him. He put on a smile.

Archie Sommers was a young man, an ex-naval officer who had taken on the job after an accident at sea. Aubrey had always got on well with him as he had a devilish sense of humour and a keen interest in magic. One of his primary jobs was to screen Bertie from visitors, but Aubrey hardly thought that applied to him. After all, a cousin was a cousin.

Sommers hailed Aubrey. 'Fitzwilliam! What a surprise! Why didn't you telephone?' He shook Aubrey's hand.

Aubrey had no answer for that. In fact, it struck him as odd when he came to think about it, but the excuse came to him smoothly. 'Couldn't risk it, Sommers.' He coughed significantly. 'Sensitive matters.'

'I see.' Sommers looked pained. 'You know, I hate this carry-on. Secrets, spies, looking over your shoulder all the time.' He grinned. 'Not much we can do about it, eh? Come on, I'll get you a cup of tea. His Highness is talking with His Majesty's doctors, but won't be long.'

Aubrey paused and a passing thought made him frown. 'What time is it?'

'Just after eight. You've made an early start.'

He considered this for a moment. 'I suppose I have.'

He was left in one of the many drawing rooms in the Palace. He'd been in this one before, but he couldn't exactly remember when. It looked over Barley Park, green and lovely in the morning light, where the curve of Miller's Pond caught the sun and sparkled. It was a serene, beautiful sight and, gazing over it, he forgot all about the promise of tea. He tried to decide what the shape of the trees meant. They seemed mysterious and significant, so he used his forefinger to trace them on the window glass.

He could smell the furniture polish used on the table under the window. Eventually, he decided that it smelled like beeswax.

Dimly, he was aware of a voice, deep inside himself, that was doing its best to raise a hullabaloo. It was irksome, but only distantly, like a noisy neighbour in a district where the houses were five miles apart.

The business of the Palace went on around him, in the hushed and discreet way that the royal household staff had made a specialty. After someone placed a tea tray on the table by his side, he was left alone. Footsteps went past, soft conversations came from nearby, a muffled telephone rang. None of this bothered – or concerned – Aubrey. Periodically, he found he had to move position as his leg muscles were starting to cramp, and he had some notion that he was hungry, but these signs of physical discomfort were muted, as if they were happening to someone else.

The voice deep inside was doing its best to rattle the walls but it was easy to ignore.

One of the doors opened. Sommers entered. He was frowning, and Aubrey would have described him as looking troubled, if he'd been able to rouse enough interest to do so. Instead he smiled – something told him that smiling was good – and he stood.

'His Highness will be with you in a minute,' Sommers said in a tight voice. Aubrey saw his hand was hovering over the pocket of his jacket, and for an instant he wondered what the chap had there, but no sooner had the thought flitted into his mind than it left. The matter had no impact on his mission.

'Good, good,' Aubrey said. He bounced on his toes and realised that he was excited. His hands twitched, eagerly.

Sommers glanced over his shoulder, then toward the window. 'Why don't you take a seat, Fitzwilliam? His Highness won't be long.'

'I'll stand,' Aubrey said and had trouble smothering a laugh. What a time he was having! The way the light came in through the window, the sound of the motor traffic that echoed over the parade ground all made a delicious backdrop to his task.

A figure strode through the doorway. Aubrey's hand went to the inner pocket of his jacket only to realise, to his disappointment, that it wasn't the Prince.

'Hello, old man,' George said.

Before Aubrey could frame a reply, he had to disengage his finger from the trigger of the pistol. This took more attention that he thought. In the meantime, George was joined by someone else and Aubrey forgot everything in his astonishment.

'Caroline. What are you doing here?'

Caroline stood next to George. Her hands were clenched tightly together. 'Wrong question, Aubrey. You need to ask yourself what *you're* doing here.'

Aubrey's astonishment was whisked away and replaced by his consuming sense of purpose, the one he'd had since waking up. He grinned and once again his hand stole to the pistol in his pocket. 'What a ridiculous question.'

'Is it?' Caroline demanded. 'Think, Aubrey. Really think. Why have you come here at this hour? Why did you leave college so abruptly? Where have you been before you came here?'

Sommers coughed and looked significantly at Caroline. He was standing with his back against the wall, his arms folded on his chest, all friendliness gone. Aubrey would have been offended at this change, but he had other things to think about. 'Sommers,' he said. 'Where's Bertie?'

Sommers glanced at Caroline and George. 'His Highness is on his way. Your friends have been chatting with me.'

The pistol was really a fine piece of work, Aubrey decided. Compact, neatly machined. He liked the grip, particularly, with its neat cross-hatching. 'Sorry?' he said, realising that Somers had finished speaking. 'I missed that.'

Nodding, George strolled across the carpet, advancing on Aubrey. 'Time to go, old man. You're not yourself.'

This amused Aubrey. 'Not myself? Then who am I?'

Caroline, too, made her way toward Aubrey, moving a little to his right. George's broad shoulders blocked Aubrey's view of her, which was disappointing, but other matters were crowding for his attention.

'George was concerned about you,' Caroline said and he swung his head in her direction. 'He saw you leave college and he telephoned me immediately.'

'Lost you for a while,' George said, and Aubrey saw that his friend had moved to his left. He couldn't see both of them at once. He had to turn his head from side to side and was momentarily distracted by Sommers' scowling. 'Caught you near the Mire after one of Maggie's Crew told us where you were.'

'Maggie's Crew?' Aubrey frowned. This wasn't as much fun any more. Too many things to consider instead of the dreamy single-mindedness he'd enjoyed all morning.

'We saw where you were headed,' Caroline said. With a start, he saw that she was standing next to a large armchair, only a few feet away.

'How did you do that?' he asked.

'You're preoccupied,' George said and Aubrey started again. George had crossed the open space and was standing an arm's length away. 'You're having trouble focusing.'

'No I'm not,' he said automatically. 'I'm totally focused.'

At that moment, the door opened. Prince Albert stood there looking both shocked and angry, his distress showing in the way he straightened his jacket, then his tie, then his jacket again, a quick flurry of controlled, precise movements. 'Aubrey. What on earth is going on here?'

Rational thought abandoned Aubrey. His body went into action, independent of anything that he wanted, while a horrified, tiny voice screamed in horror, a cry only he could hear.

He flung back his jacket and wrenched the pistol from the inner pocket. Smoothly, he snapped off the safety catch and brought the firearm to bear on the heir to the throne. Finally, he felt whole and complete, his purpose fulfilled. A radiance filled the room. Prince Albert was outlined with an almost unbearably bright nimbus and shone like a beacon.

Aubrey almost sobbed out loud with joy as his finger tightened on the trigger.

George roared and tackled him, sending Aubrey reeling. It was momentary, for Aubrey caught himself and swivelled, his pistol-laden fist searching for the Prince in a room that was in uproar.

By then, Caroline had come close. In a flurry of silk and perfume, she caught his outstretched arm and clamped it to her side. Using both hands she seized his gun-fist, twisted just so, pressed right there and bent his wrist like that. Aubrey had never had red-hot iron spikes driven into his hand, but at that moment he would have preferred it as Caroline's knowledge of pressure points went to work. He let loose a heartfelt howl of pain and, despite his best efforts, he dropped the pistol. Caroline kicked it away. Sommers was ready, scooped it up, broke it, and emptied the cartridges on the floor. Then he took out his own pistol and snapped off the safety catch.

Someone was snarling. Aubrey searched for the source before realising – with some surprise – that it came from him. Caroline let go, edging away warily. Aubrey's arm hung limply at his side with bright points of pain throbbing away, little metal cymbals clashing in his temples, but it was unimportant. The pistol. He must have the pistol.

Strong arms seized him from behind in a full nelson. 'Easy, old man,' George growled in his ear.

Prince Albert approached, flanked by a grim Archie Sommers. 'Aubrey,' the Prince said, then he turned away, upset. 'You were right,' he said to Caroline. 'I didn't believe it when you said that Aubrey was coming to assassinate me, but you were right.'

Assassinate the Crown Prince? To Aubrey, it sounded like a fine idea, a natural and inevitable thing. If only he could get free from George's grip, he was sure he could wrestle the pistol away from Sommers.

He struggled, then howled again when Sommers hurried Prince Albert away, shutting the door behind them. That was wrong, so wrong that Aubrey felt ill, his stomach a curdled mass inside him. He threw himself from side to side, but George held fast.

'Steady, George,' Caroline said.

Caroline drew aside Aubrey's jacket. With her other hand, she held up a knife, right in front of Aubrey's eyes. It was small, barely as long as her hand, with a handle of mother-of-pearl and a pointed blade that looked sharp enough to slice steel.

She caught his gaze and held it evenly. Her eyes were calm, grey and icily determined. 'I can do this while you're moving. But it's probably better if you don't.'

Aubrey went to answer, but the knife flashed before anything intelligible made its way to his lips.

He looked down. His shirt gaped. Caroline picked the last button from its thread and let it drop on the floor to join its mates.

The Beccaria Cage lay on Aubrey's bare chest. He suddenly realised that it was heavy, pressing on his skin hard enough to leave a red mark. It seemed heavier. It was warm, too, but was that simply through contact with his skin?

The knife had disappeared from Caroline's hand. She seized the Beccaria Cage and yanked.

The chain parted. Aubrey's eyes flew open wide, then his head spun, the entire room shuddered, and all existence twisted, wrenched, swirled away.

Four

SOME TIME LATER, AUBREY BECAME AWARE THAT HE WAS in a room that resembled the drawing room at the Palace. Caroline and George were there, and the furniture was the same, so he conceded that it could possibly, actually be the Palace drawing room. At a pinch.

Even sitting as he was on a plush, overstuffed armchair, his legs felt like tubes of soggy clay. His skin was clammy. His chest hurt, but all this physical discomfort was the least of his concern.

He'd tried to shoot Bertie.

The enormity of what he'd nearly done struck him hard. Bertie, his friend, the heir to the throne of Albion? What had he been thinking? He wanted to shudder, but he wasn't quite capable of it yet.

He worked his mouth and tried to apologise, to explain the strange state he'd been in, but all he could manage was something that sounded like, 'Bleurgh.'

Caroline was sitting opposite, her hands clutched in her lap, and she was studying him closely. Blearily, he noticed that three armed guardsmen stood outside the window behind her. All of them were staring at him fixedly. He worked his jaw, then his mouth, until he was a little more confident. 'Were they there?' he croaked. 'All the time?'

George handed him a glass of water. 'The prince wasn't happy about it, but Sommers insisted. He swore they were all crack shots and would only maim you. If things went wrong.'

Aubrey nodded, as if he found that reassuring. It was really only because he found it easier than talking.

'It was the Prince who insisted that none of the agencies need be called,' Caroline said. She seemed balanced between anger and concern, and not quite trusting herself either way. 'Not the police, not the Special Services, not the Magisterium.'

'Come with us, old man,' George said. 'I think everyone except the Prince will be happy when you're well away from here.'

A stony-faced guardsman chauffeured them in a discreet Charlesworth motorcar. He drove as if it were a tank, ignoring most of the other traffic about. Wedged between Caroline and George in the back seat, Aubrey did his best to regain his faculties, while simultaneously feeling ashamed and furious.

I nearly shot Bertie.

His too-active imagination conjured up images of giant newspaper headlines: 'PRINCE SHOT BY PRIME MINISTER'S SON'. He saw grim police officers, handcuffs, magistrates, barred cells and judges. Judges with black caps, full of righteous wrath, condemning him to be hanged by the neck until dead.

He shuddered, successfully this time.

He saw his parents, grey and disbelieving, broken by the events. He saw Albion in turmoil as the Prime Minister resigned. He saw Holmland moving, the Continent at war with blood and flames and destruction. He saw one person, only one person, standing happy at the horror unleashed.

Dr Tremaine.

Hot anger slowly began to replace the sick hollow inside him.

'I was up early,' George was saying. 'Thought I'd dash off a few words about the affair at the old cricket game, mentioning the sterling work of a few individuals.' He looked pleased with himself. 'When I saw you sloping off without me, I thought it odd, especially after you asked me to spend today with you in the city.'

'George telephoned me at my college,' Caroline said. 'Despite your confidence that you'd made the Beccaria Cage safe, I had my doubts. So did George. He followed you.'

'How?' Aubrey's tongue still felt thick. Single words worked best.

'A combination of stealth and uncanny ability, old man. By the time I dressed and ran to the main gates, you were still in sight, not making much of an effort to cover your tracks either. Whistling, too, if I wasn't mistaken.'

'Ghastly?'

'Pretty much, yes.' George smiled a little. 'I was curious about your demeanour, so I decided to follow and observe you.' He shrugged. 'I've learned a thing or two about odd situations, you see.'

'Caroline?'

'I missed the train George and you took, but I managed to catch up with him when he lost you in the Mire. He telephoned from there and I immediately bicycled to join him.'

'We raced up and down the streets of the Mire looking for you,' George said. 'I was ready to give up when we almost stumbled on your little transaction.'

'George was very nervous,' Caroline said. 'Especially when you started waving that pistol around.'

George rubbed his chin. 'It became plain as day that you were heading for the Palace. We kept back until you were admitted, then we rushed over and managed to get to Sommers.'

'I was going to shoot Bertie,' Aubrey said slowly.

'So it appeared,' Caroline said. 'Whatever were you thinking?'

'Not much.' Aubrey remembered the blissful, purposeful state he'd been in. He closed his eyes as a wave of nausea rolled through him. 'Trigger words. I was sent trigger words. After that, I surrendered everything.'

Aubrey was both angry and ashamed. He liked to think that he was responsible for his own actions, for better and for worse. Successes and failures belonged to him, and he was prepared to take the good with the bad. But propelled on his deadly mission, he'd been turned into an automaton, a puppet controlled by . . .

'Dr Tremaine,' he said softly.

Caroline sat back and crossed her arms. 'You're sure?'

'Oh yes.'

He shivered, then the trembling seized his legs and quickly turned to cramp. He grimaced and massaged his calves, feeling the knots of muscle under his fingertips.

'Are you all right?' Caroline asked.

'No,' he said simply, for he could tell that – without the Beccaria Cage – his body and soul were once again at odds. The physical symptoms were dismayingly familiar: weakness, trembling, pain in his muscles and joints. He knew, if things went in their accustomed way, he'd soon start to feel feverish or experience double vision, or any one of a hundred bodily signs. If he couldn't stave off the disunification of his body and soul, the true death would soon draw closer.

George glanced at the driver and raised an eyebrow significantly. 'Ah. Your condition?'

Through recent experience, Aubrey had learned that everyone had ears. The driver, perhaps, was under no orders to report any conversations, but that was extremely unlikely. 'Indeed.' He grimaced. His feet hurt. 'Do you have that contraption? The Beccaria Cage?'

Caroline produced it from her handbag. She held it in her open palm where it nestled, strangely repellent. The broken chain hung limply. He shook himself, fighting with his weariness, struggling for his words. 'I think it works.'

'What?' George said, startled. 'Hold on a minute, old man. It turned you into a mindless assassin. If that's what you mean by "I think it works", then I suppose you're right, but . . .'

'It . . . it glued me together.' Aubrey struggled for words. 'I could feel its effect.'

'Dr Tremaine, remember,' Caroline said. 'The master of the hidden plot. Look inside the exterior.'

Aubrey cocked his head. Caroline was right. Dr Tremaine was the panjandrum of strategy, of the feint, of misdirection. Again and again, in Albion and in Lutetia, under the sea and under the city, he'd proved that his mind was capable of the most twisted, labyrinthine plots, where what was and what seemed to be swapped with such feverish regularity that one's own identity was seriously in question.

Aubrey took the Beccaria Cage and held it up to the window. Letting the light stream through it, he tilted it.

The tiny silver ball rolled and struck the edge of the cage. It made a dull, heavy sound, then it wobbled a little before it was still.

'I need to do some magic,' he said, not taking his eyes from the cage.

'Here?' George said. 'Now?'

'Can you manage it?' Caroline asked.

Aubrey swallowed. His throat was raw and painful. 'I think I must.'

Without a word, George reached over and slid the glass pane across, sealing off the rear compartment. Aubrey could see that the driver's mirror was artfully angled to ensure he could see what was going on in the back, but at least he couldn't eavesdrop.

The motorcar rumbled on. Outside, the business of the city streamed past. Carriages, cabs, motorcars, omnibuses. Shops, cafés, government buildings. Trinovantians, foreigners and some who were one pretending to be the other. *Appearances and reality*, Aubrey thought. *Let's take off the skin and see what lies beneath.*

With a sigh, he lifted the Beccaria Cage again in his left hand. His vision blurred, he squinted, then rubbed his eyes. His eyesight cleared a little and he decided it wasn't going to get any better than that.

He gripped the cage. The silver ball rolled then stopped dead and trembled, as if sensing something.

Concentrating gamely, Aubrey put the forefinger of his right hand up to the wire of the cage. The silver ball jerked and rolled to the far side, even though Aubrey was sure he'd held the cage level.

With an effort, he wedged the tip of his finger through the wire. It resisted, but he pushed until, with a grunt, he was through, bending the wire to allow access.

Inside, the silver ball began to roll about in erratic, wild movements, banging into one side of the cage and rebounding to the other like a mouse caught in a well with a cat.

Aubrey pushed his finger toward the silver ball. It froze for an instant, then quivered, before breaking left. Aubrey was ready for it, though, when it darted back to the right. He caught it against the wall of the cage, trapping it with his fingertip, and he hissed with satisfaction.

To his surprise, his fingertip sank into the surface of the ball as if it was a sponge. Before he could move, the ball clamped onto his finger with a razor-sharp grip.

Aubrey felt it sink into his flesh, but he didn't flinch – despite the pain. He pushed through the wire from the other side, with his left forefinger and thumb, and caught the ball from behind. Ignoring the pain in his right finger, he brought his left thumb and forefinger together like pincers. At the first sign of pressure, the ball let go of his finger, but Aubrey caught it, crushing the ball like a walnut.

Immediately, the motorcar was filled with a hideous smell. It swerved sideways and the driver glanced over his shoulder, his face screwed up. Not expecting such a stench,

Aubrey recoiled and threw up his hands, but because both hands were trapped in the cage all he succeeded in doing was hitting himself in the eye with it. He saw stars, blinked, let his hands fall to his lap and refused to look down – because he didn't want to see what the ball had done to his finger.

George held his nose and slid open the window on his side, then leaned across and did the same on the other. 'Good Lord,' he said with some reverence. 'You could use that smell as a weapon.'

Caroline frowned. She took out a handkerchief and dabbed at Aubrey's brow.

Aubrey knew the silver ball had attacked his finger. How badly, though, he wasn't sure. Still without looking, he tried to ease his finger out of the wire. Pain flared like a bright light. He drew in a sharp breath through his teeth.

Caroline was studying the cage dispassionately, but Aubrey knew her self-possession. 'How bad is it?' he asked.

'Blood everywhere. You've ruined your suit.'

'I knew it. I've lost my finger, haven't I?'

'I don't think so.'

A sharp tug made Aubrey straighten in his seat. Tears came to his eyes and he had a brand-new appreciation of the virtues of a lack of pain. 'Oh my.'

Caroline held up her hand. In it, she held his. Around the tip of his forefinger, just above the knuckle, was a thin band of red. A tiny trickle of blood was edging toward his knuckle. It looked as if he'd scratched himself with a fingernail.

'It hurt,' he said plaintively. 'I was sure it was working its way to the bone.'

'I'm sure it felt like that,' Caroline said. 'Here, wrap my handkerchief around it. It's already got blood on it. From your eyebrow.'

Aubrey gingerly touched his brow and winced. 'Hmm.' He prodded at the Beccaria Cage. The wires were a little bent, but there was no sign of the silver ball apart from the ghost of the eye-watering stench. He pushed the wires back into place so the mesh was regular again. Then he relinked the chain and slipped it around his neck.

Immediately, his fatigue disappeared like smoke on a windy day. He straightened and massaged the back of his neck with both hands. After he rubbed his eyes, his vision was sharp; when he took a deep breath, nothing caught or pinched.

'You've done something,' Caroline said. 'Your eyes are clearer.'

Aubrey glanced at the driver. His attention was entirely on the road ahead as they rolled past Barley Park, well on the way to Fielding Cross and Maidstone, the Fitzwilliam family home.

'The Beccaria Cage,' he explained. 'It works, but it was booby-trapped by Dr Tremaine. He knew I'd be keen to get my hands on something that would assist my condition. The silver ball must have been a concealed spell, lurking ready to entrap me.'

George shook his head. 'You were possessed.'

'Something like that. Not mindless, not like those poor lost souls we ran into in Gallia.' It was his turn to shake his head. The Soul Stealer of Lutetia had held the Gallian city in terror. 'I was aware of everything around me, but it was like seeing life through a lens that made everything warm and good, as long as I was moving toward my goal.'

'The Prince?' Caroline asked.

'Dr Tremaine hasn't given up on his plan to plunge the world into war,' Aubrey said. He put his hand over the Beccaria Cage as it lay against his chest. 'Imagine it. The death of the Prince, an assassin who – it would be shown – was ensorcelled by a Holmlander who had been the source of the infernal device.'

'Kiefer,' George muttered.

'Agreed.' Aubrey pursed his lips. 'Tomorrow, I think we need to pop up to Greythorn and have a chat with this Mr Kiefer.'

Five

THE NEXT MORNING, TILLY, ONE OF THE MAIDS, KNOCKED at the open door to Aubrey's room. 'Excuse me, sir. Telephone for you. It's Miss Caroline. She's ringing from her home.'

Aubrey had been assembling a few magical items in preparation for their trip to confront Kiefer but he immediately dropped everything. 'Thank you, Tilly,' he said as he bounded past.

'Aubrey,' Caroline said a split second before he spoke into the receiver.

'Caroline?' He made a mental note to himself: write down a list of clever greetings and store them by the telephone. That way he may have some chance of avoiding such a lame opening sally.

'I'm glad we've sorted out who we are,' she said. 'Now, we're not going to Greythorn.'

'We're not? What about Kiefer?'

'Aubrey, what are we using to speak to each other?'

'The telephone?'

'Exactly. Instead of racing pell-mell up to Greythorn, I've been using the telephone to make some enquiries.'

'I thought you were rearranging your schedule.'

'I've taken care of that. Professor Ainsworth wanted me to help him with some phylogeny research, but I've asked for a postponement. And Mother can make her own travel arrangements for a change.'

'Your mother is travelling?' Aubrey said and he punched himself on the thigh. 'Of course she is. That's what you just said. Where's she off to?'

'Holmland. Some sort of symposium next week in Fisherberg, but that's not important right now. I rang to tell you that Kiefer is no longer at Greythorn.'

'He must be somewhere else then,' Aubrey said and immediately awarded himself first prize in the Obvious Statement Stakes. He quickly went on. 'Fled, no doubt, after his machinations.'

'Not exactly, no. The porter at Kiefer's college happened to be an old friend of my father. A good man, a noted authority on Albion amphibians.'

'Kiefer's turned into a frog?'

'Try to keep up, Aubrey, I know you're capable of it. Kiefer was seen being bundled into a motorcar by a Holmland diplomat.'

'I see. And did the amphibian expert porter recognise this Holmlander?'

'No, but his assistant did, thanks to his special interest in international politics.'

'Well-educated staff at this college.'

'If you'd spent any time with the staff at yours, Aubrey,

you'd know that many of them are authorities in one field or another. They may not have formal degrees, but at Greythorn there are many opportunities to better oneself intellectually.'

'The diplomat?'

'Hugo von Stralick, Aubrey. Hugo von Stralick kidnapped Kiefer.'

Caroline's cab rolled into Maidstone just as Aubrey's father arrived in the prime ministerial motorcar. From the window of his room, Aubrey sighed as he watched Sir Darius leap to open the door of the cab. He didn't need to hear the ensuing conversation to know that his father's charm would be meeting Caroline's dogged demanding for more progress on the votes for women front.

They could be hours if he didn't do something about it.

He raced for the door, flinging a red velvet cushion over one shoulder as he went.

'Oof!' George toppled from the chaise longue where he'd been lying, doing his best to absorb Albion's best journalistic practices through the novel method of draping newspapers over his face while he snored.

'Caroline's here,' Aubrey said from the doorway. 'And so is Father.'

George blinked. 'Excellent. I think.'

'We may be off at any minute.'

'Good. Enough time for a nap, I'd say.' At Aubrey's expression, George held up a hand. 'Only joking, old man.' He rolled to his feet and made for the suitcase by the door. 'Here, let me unveil a little surprise I had sent down from Greythorn.'

'We don't have much time,' Aubrey said, eyeing the door.

'This won't take long. There.'

George straightened from fumbling through his luggage, beaming.

The garment he was holding looked like a sleeveless cardigan, but instead of buttons down the front it had two loose ties. This was all well and good, Aubrey decided. It was the way the entire object was covered with pockets that made it look bizarre.

'Interesting sort of vest,' he said carefully.

'It's for you, old man. Try it on.'

'Really, George, it's not the sort of thing I'd feel comfortable . . .'

'Nonsense. It's good, strong silk. And it's not a fashion item. It's an appurtenances vest.'

George thrust it at Aubrey. He ran his hand over it. 'Appurtenances vest?'

'For adventuring. You see, old man, you talk about planning and preparation, but lately I've noticed that you've been caught short, more than once. Without your magical wherewithal to do spells and the like.' He grinned. 'Stock up your appurtenances vest and you'll never be without a candle stub, or a bit of chalk or whatever. Just don't load yourself down too much. Wouldn't do to clank when we're trying to sneak up on a miscreant or two.'

Aubrey was touched. 'And where did you get this fine piece of equipment?'

'I made it.'

Aubrey stared.

'Took a while, but I think I'm a dab hand with a sewing machine, now.'

Aubrey shook his head in wonder. 'George, you're a marvel.'

'Correct. And don't forget to tell Sophie Delroy. She forgets sometimes.'

Aubrey went to his desk. He slipped a feather, two fingernail-sized mirrors, a pinch of gold dust and a number of other lightweight and potentially useful materials into the pockets of the appurtenances vest. He slipped out of his shirt, wriggled into the vest – making sure the Beccaria Cage hung freely – and then back into his shirt.

'How do I look?'

'Ready for whatever may come. How does it feel?'

Aubrey swung his arms. 'Very comfortable. Much more so than stuffing my pockets full of bits and pieces.'

'And that must be a good thing.' George yawned. 'Go, old man. I'll join you in a minute, once I've washed my face.'

Aubrey found Caroline and his father at the foot of the main stairs. They were talking earnestly – serious expressions, intense gesturing. He waited, judged the moment, then inserted himself into the conversation in a gap that made a split-second seem like a geological age.

'Caroline. Father. I'm glad you're here.'

'How long have you been standing there, Aubrey?' his father asked. Sir Darius was wearing his suit with the striped trousers, a sign that he'd been in Parliament. He stroked his moustache. 'We were talking about the suffragist movement.'

'And what the government is actually doing about the whole issue of votes for women,' Caroline said.

A voice came from further into the house. 'Bravo, Caroline. Don't let the discussion become sidetracked. The issue isn't the suffragist movement. The issue is what's happening in Parliament and in the party room.'

Lady Rose came to her husband's side and took his arm. She was wearing a loose green dress. Her hands were dirty and she had a basket over her arm from which a nose-tickling aroma arose.

'Darling,' Sir Darius said. 'How are the herbs doing? Sage and parsley and whatnot?'

'Splendidly. Especially the whatnot. I'm expecting a bumper crop of it. Hello, Caroline. It's good to see you.'

Caroline smiled and greeted Lady Rose with a warmth that Aubrey was pleased to see. He knew Caroline admired his mother and her scientific work. He did his best to facilitate Caroline's desire to help his mother, mainly because he did his best to do anything that would please Caroline, but also because it was likely to give him more opportunities to bump into her.

It wasn't manipulation, he assured himself. Then he looked at it again and promised himself he'd monitor his motives carefully. After the fiasco in Lutetia, he was doubly careful to be honest in his dealings with Caroline.

She deserved it.

'If you'll excuse me, Lady Rose, Sir Darius. I've actually come to see Aubrey. And George.' Caroline smiled and even at his distance at the top of the stairs, Aubrey felt it like a blow. A delicious, stupefying blow but one that nonetheless left his knees feeling weak as he tottered to join them.

Sir Darius looked doubtful. Lady Rose looked frankly sceptical. 'Well, if you must. Are you sure?'

'I am. We have matters to attend to.'

'Another threat to national security?' Sir Darius asked, then he winced. 'No, don't answer that. I don't think I want to know at the moment. Plenty enough to worry about.'

Aubrey caught the tension in his father's voice. 'International or home affairs?'

'The situation in the Goltans is precarious. Arnovia and Veltran are at each other's throats.'

Lady Rose gripped his arm hard. 'Holmland?'

'Behind it all, no doubt. I'm meeting their ambassador this afternoon to listen to another litany of disapproval and denial.' He scowled. 'To make matters worse, it appears as if the Muscovian political unrest is increasing. The analysts from the Foreign Office say that Muscovia could either collapse into revolution or sign a treaty with Holmland. I don't know which would be worse.'

The world was a powder keg. Aubrey felt sorry for his father, leading Albion in such times, but he was also grateful that the nation had such a leader.

'Sir,' he said, seizing the moment. 'Have you heard of any movements in the diplomatic staff at the Holmland embassy?'

Sir Darius pursed his lips for a moment. 'Anything in particular you're interested in, Aubrey?'

'Von Stralick. I've heard he may be in the country.'

'Ah. Tallis sent me a report yesterday. Special Services intelligence has indicated that this is a possibility. Not as a member of the official Holmland diplomatic staff, however. As a rogue.'

'A rogue?' Lady Rose echoed.

'A free agent,' Sir Darius said. 'If he's here, he's gone to ground. Probably with one of the refugee communities.'

'Ah.' Aubrey exchanged a glance with Caroline.

'And this is important in what way?' Sir Darius said.

'Von Stralick and I have unfinished business.'

'We live in a time of unfinished business,' his father said. 'But leaving well enough alone is a fine policy, although I find it hard to believe that either of you would take such advice.'

'Don't worry, Father,' Aubrey said. 'After what I've seen, I'd never underestimate Hugo von Stralick.'

'If that was meant to be reassuring,' Lady Rose said, 'then I'm afraid it failed by a considerable margin.'

'Mother –'

Lady Rose shook her head. 'Don't protest, Aubrey, you'll only back yourself into a corner. Caroline.'

Caroline blinked. 'Lady Rose?'

'Whatever it is that's going on, can I be assured that you and George are involved? That you're staying close to my son?'

Aubrey watched with fascination as Caroline sorted through the implications of those questions. Eventually, she nodded. 'Yes,' she said guardedly.

'My dear,' Lady Rose said to Sir Darius, 'I'm afraid that's about the best that can be done. If George and Caroline are part of this – whatever this is – then they'll temper the worst of Aubrey's excesses.'

The telephone rang. Aubrey noticed how his father stiffened, and how the four of them waited in silence while the butler answered it. It was with a sense of dread and certainty that they watched Harris approaching after he'd replaced the receiver.

'Sir? It was the Foreign Minister. You're needed at the Foreign Office.'

'My hat, Harris.' Sir Darius squeezed his wife's shoulder. 'I had been hoping we could lunch together.'

'I'm afraid not.' Aubrey thought his mother's attempt at indifference was half-hearted. 'Anyway, I have a meeting of my own. At the museum.'

'Good, good,' Sir Darius said absently. He was already on his way up the hall toward the front door. He took the hat and gloves that Harris offered him, then he looked up, sharply. 'Aubrey, I've had a report land on the desk about the incident with Prince Albert. I know you've told me everything, but I think you need to know that it's on the record now.'

'On the record?'

'An attempt on the life of the heir to the throne? Of course.' Sir Darius must have caught the dismay on Aubrey's face, for he went on. 'Don't let it worry you. My own dossier has some appalling things on it.'

'It has?'

His father smiled. 'As Prime Minister, I'm able to examine all top secret documents, my own dossier among them.' He stroked his moustache. 'Your case is different. You weren't responsible for what happened. My blunders, however, were all my own.' He turned to Lady Rose. 'I'm afraid I don't know when I'll be back.'

And he was off. Harris closed the door behind him, and Aubrey's determination to live up to his father's example was only increased.

Lady Rose put the basket of herbs on a hall table. 'I'm off. I shan't be back for the rest of the day.'

With more than a little disquiet, Aubrey watched his mother's brisk preparations to leave, noting the concern in her eyes that she attempted to hide. Like his father, she was extraordinarily capable, but she did pride herself on her self-reliance – to the extent that, at times, she found it difficult to confide her fears in others.

Caroline interrupted his thoughts. 'Aubrey, I'm assuming you have a plan?'

He never wanted to disappoint Caroline, even though he had no idea what she was referring to. 'Of course.'

'For finding von Stralick.'

'Oh.' An item rose from his back-of-the-mind ponderings. 'Refugee communities.'

'I'd been thinking along the same lines. So where do we start?'

Aubrey was inordinately pleased that they thought along the same lines. He filed it in his 'Reasons to be Optimistic' folder.

'South of the river,' he said, remembering their recent encounter with Count Brandt and his displaced Holmlanders.

'Which is half the city,' Caroline said gently.

Aubrey had an idea. 'Cook. I'll ask her where she gets her sausages. We had them last week and she was telling us how Holmland sausages are the best.'

'Woodley Lane in Little Pickling,' came a voice from the top of the stairs. 'Four of the best sausage-makers in one tiny stretch of street.' George stood at the top of the stairs, beaming. 'It's the centre of the Holmlander community in Trinovant.'

'I should have asked you first, George,' Aubrey said. 'Food is your business.'

'We all have our specialities, old man. Let's go. I might be able to pick up some of those delightful dumplings while we're there.'

Six

THE ISTROS COFFEE HOUSE WAS NAMED AFTER Holmland's most famous river. It was right in the middle of a small cluster of shops that seemed to be dedicated to recreating Fisherberg in the heart of Trinovant. The sausage makers fought for business, and the trade was brisk. Sweet pastries were piled high in the windows of Holmlander bakeries. Waltz music seeped through doors and open windows.

'This seems like a good place to start,' Aubrey announced after they'd studied the comings and goings for some time.

'It can't hurt to make some enquiries,' George said.

Caroline looked doubtful. 'I can imagine half a dozen ways this could go wrong.' She sighed. 'But I don't have any other ideas.'

Aubrey led the way. He pushed open the door and led the way into the warm, dark, splendidly aromatic interior.

It took his eyes a few moments to adjust, and he was relieved to see that their entrance hadn't excited any more than cursory glances from the patrons, who were far more interested in their refreshments. Aubrey's Holmlandish was good enough for him to hear half a dozen different regional accents in the room. It seemed as if the Istros Coffee House drew its customers from all over Holmland.

'Do you recognise anyone?' Caroline asked.

He shook his head. He'd been hoping that someone they'd met in their time with Count Brandt would have remained behind in Albion instead of joining their comrades in their ill-fated mission back to Holmland.

George nodded toward the back of the café. 'Sounds as if there's another room down there. I can hear accordion music.'

'Oh dear,' Caroline said. They both looked at her. 'I'm sorry. I have trouble with the accordion.'

'So does whoever's trying to play it.' George winced. 'Still, it's hard to tell the difference between an accordion played badly and an accordion played well.'

Bemused, Aubrey led them to a door just to the left of the entrance to the kitchen. A hearty Holmlandish dance tune came from it as the accordionist worked up a good head of steam. Caroline grimaced. 'I had a cat, once, who made that sort of noise when I accidentally stepped on his tail.'

'Steady, Caroline,' George said. 'Be brave.'

Aubrey edged through the doorway but his entrance wasn't discreet enough. A score of faces turned slowly to stare at the interlopers over their steaming coffee cups. The accordion player stopped mid-squeeze, much to Caroline's relief.

At the far end of the room, under the large portrait of the Elektor of Holmland, a lean, dapper man rose to his feet. He was dressed in a light grey suit, very stylish in a room full of heavy coats and scarves. He wore his hair long and over his ears. 'Fitzwilliam. You've brought Miss Hepworth and the other one to see us.'

Sitting on von Stralick's right was a young bespectacled man with a look of absolute horror on his face. He groaned, clutched both sides of his wild-haired head and let it fall forward until it hit the table with a thud.

Von Stralick looked down at him and sighed. 'You've met my cousin, Mr Kiefer, I take it?'

The inner sanctum of the Istros Coffee House was the meeting place of the Holmland intelligentsia in exile, von Stralick explained once the patrons settled and the accordionist resumed, to Caroline's irritation. Over the buzz of serious Holmlandish conversation and the gentle steaming of giant urns, Aubrey surveyed the room. Men and women, mostly middle-aged or older. The men had accepted that bald heads, beards and spectacles were essential if they were to be part of this gathering. Some, perhaps lacking confidence, took on all three. The women were less uniform in their dress and appearance, but were consistently intense in their participation in arguments ranging from, if Aubrey's Holmlandish was up to scratch, the role of free will, the purpose of life and the puzzle of collective unconscious to whether dogs have souls.

Von Stralick was relaxed, jovial and vastly amused at Aubrey's ordeal. Kiefer didn't look up. He had his head in his hands. 'Come, Fitzwilliam,' von Stralick said after Aubrey, George and Caroline had joined them at the table, 'tell me again about your buying a pistol. Most risible.'

Aubrey decided that von Stralick didn't look like a clandestine enemy agent keeping a low profile.

'It wasn't funny,' George said.

'No, of course not,' von Stralick said. 'Not from your point of view, anyway.' He nudged his silent tablemate. 'What do you say, Otto? Laughable, no?'

Kiefer groaned again, but still didn't lift his head.

'My cousin is distressed,' von Stralick said. 'Ashamed of what happened to you.'

'Wait,' Aubrey said. 'I've just run into a number of baffling things at once.' He counted on his fingers. 'Firstly, Kiefer is your cousin?'

Von Stralick beamed. 'Of course. My mother's sister's little boy. Ambitious, brilliant, but a little erratic.'

'So you didn't kidnap him from Greythorn?'

'Kidnap? Of course not. He telephoned me to say he needed to leave the university.'

Caroline leaned forward. 'But witnesses said you bundled him into a motorcar.'

Von Stralick glanced at his cousin. 'You've seen him, no? Sometimes his body and his brain seem to have only a passing acquaintance. He tripped himself while getting into the motorcar, I caught him, he became tangled. He was lucky not to dislocate a knee.'

'Compelling,' George said. 'But why was he fleeing?'

'I had to.' The muffled voice came from Kiefer, whose head was still buried in his arms. 'Because of what happened to Fitzwilliam.' He lifted a woebegone face. 'I turned him into a killer.'

'And I take it from your reaction,' Aubrey said, 'that this was not your intention?'

Kiefer straightened. His eyes were wide and he held up his hands, palm first, in abject surrender. 'Me? No! How could I? How could you believe I could? I would never do such a thing!'

Either he's the world's best actor, Aubrey thought, *or the poor fellow is genuinely mortified*. 'I see. So you're as much a victim here as I am?'

Kiefer beat at his chest with a fist. 'I suffered when I heard. As if my heart was torn from me and used to assault me about the head.'

Caroline tapped the table with a finger. 'And how exactly did you hear of Aubrey's plight?'

Aubrey turned and stared at her. Of course. This was crucial.

Kiefer still looked miserable, unaware of the intense scrutiny turned his way. 'Professor Glauber telephoned and told me what I'd done. It was he who suggested it was a good idea for me to leave.' He craned his neck and looked around the room. 'I wanted to thank him for his warning but they say he hasn't been here for some time.'

Von Stralick caught Aubrey's eye. 'Professor Glauber was lecturer in metallurgy at the Holmland Technological Institute. He has been in Trinovant for five years.'

'A regular customer here, is he?' Aubrey asked.

Von Stralick pointed at a vacant space at the table furthest from the door, right next to a hideously ornate vase. 'That's his place. No-one else would dare sit there.'

'You've met Professor Glauber before?' Aubrey asked Kiefer.

'He met me when I arrived in Albion and helped me find my feet.'

'A not inconsiderable task,' George pointed out.

'Exactly,' Kiefer said, then looked puzzled. 'I beg your pardon?'

'Never mind,' said Aubrey. 'The fact is that you know his voice.'

'Of course.'

'Even on the telephone.'

'It was him,' Kiefer said firmly.

'Or a good facsimile,' Caroline said. 'Aubrey, is there anyone you know who is expert at assuming other identities?'

Von Stralick hissed, a long, drawn-out breath. 'So you think *he's* responsible for this?'

'Dr Tremaine?' Aubrey said. 'It has every sign of his work.'

Aubrey could have sworn that no-one in the room had been listening to them. Conversations had been swirling in and out of the accordion music, waiters had been serving pastries and coffee, the fug of pipe smoke made a misty false ceiling. But immediately he mentioned the ex-Sorcerer Royal it was like dropping a crate full of china at a funeral.

Conversations ebbed to a halt. The accordionist stopped – again. A few heads turned their way but most gave every indication of straining not to do so. The affected nonchalance was so studied that Aubrey thought it could have passed the civil service examination with first class honours.

'Ach. It is as I feared,' Von Stralick said, ignoring the way everyone was ignoring them. 'Dr Tremaine has increased his power in Fisherberg, you know, so his plots are going to become more dangerous.'

'You are a bearer of good news,' George said. He turned in his chair. He searched the room for a moment, then plucked a tray of pastries from a passing waiter. 'Here. I think we're going to need these.'

Conversation gradually resumed until, once again, they were wrapped in the comfortable commerce of humanity, a plausible screen for their discussion.

Aubrey took one of the pastries. It was sugared and coiled like a snail. He was about to take a bite when he had a thought. 'Von Stralick, does Dr Tremaine know you're in Trinovant?'

'I hope not, but who knows what the villain knows?'

'And why exactly *are* you here?' George asked.

'Good question, George,' Aubrey said. 'Well, von Stralick? Last we heard, you were in Fisherberg, taking care of your career.'

Von Stralick suddenly found his empty coffee cup vastly interesting. 'I was. Then my career took care of itself.'

George harrumphed. 'Not a spy any more, is that what you're saying?'

'Intelligence work wasn't providing the opportunities it once had. Not with your Dr Tremaine so highly thought of.'

'Your superior in the Holmland Intelligence Department was not a Dr Tremaine supporter, I take it,' Caroline said.

'No. As a result, his influence declined markedly. Even more so after his unfortunate demise.' He looked up at the ceiling. 'Suicide, they said. He was a remarkable man, but I think that shooting oneself seven times in the back was beyond even him.' Von Stralick hardened. 'His name has been disgraced, his family ruined, thanks to Tremaine.'

Aubrey felt his stomach turn to ice. This was no game. 'So you were cast adrift? No-one to report to?'

'I have my superior's superior. He didn't answer my messages so I thought he may be in some difficulty. I decided to take matters into my own hands.'

'No wonder Albion seems like a more comfortable place,' George said. 'So if you're not spying, what's your game?'

Von Stralick rubbed his gloved hands together. 'Importing and exporting. A bit of this, a bit of that, I think the saying goes.'

'Nice and nebulous,' Aubrey said. 'Good-looking suit. Barber and Sons?'

'It is. I'm glad you like it.'

'A Barber and Sons suit means that you're not short for money.'

'Importing and exporting is doing well, in these troublesome times.'

Caroline sighed. 'Can you two finish posturing soon? Then we can move on to more important matters.'

'Such as the most dangerous man alive,' Aubrey muttered. The others looked at him. 'Sorry if it sounds melodramatic, but it's probably true. Someone who is dedicated to plunging the world into war, just to fuel his magical efforts at personal immortality? Sounds dangerous to me.'

'I agree,' Kiefer said. 'He must be stopped.'

'How?' George said. 'Easier said than done, it seems to me.'

'Flush him out,' Caroline said. 'Lure him to Albion and take him.'

Von Stralick lifted an eyebrow. 'Extraordinary.'

Caroline bristled. 'What do you mean?'

'Remember who we're talking about, Miss Hepworth. The most dangerous man alive and you want to confront him? Most people spend their waking hours hoping to avoid him.'

'We choose the place, the time, not him,' Aubrey said, picking up Caroline's suggestion. Slowly an idea was beginning to take form. 'Every other meeting we've had has been because of his planning. He's been prepared, with multiple escape routes, with backup resources. Let's turn the tables so that we're the ones who have traps within traps.'

Von Stralick sat back in his chair. 'You know, I think you could do this. At least, that's what the reports said.'

'Reports?' Aubrey said.

'Tremaine circulated a number of reports about the affair in Lutetia, then the failed plot to destroy your economy. He drew attention to you, particularly. He noted you as a potential threat, strategically and magically.'

For a moment, Aubrey felt absurdly pleased. Then he realised it may help to explain the attention he was receiving from Dr Tremaine.

The room suddenly felt much more exposed than it was.

A figure stood at the doorway. Once again, all heads turned in the direction of the newcomer – even Kiefer's, and he brightened noticeably. He stood and waved. 'Professor Glauber! Over here!'

Aubrey swung around to see a short, pear-shaped man rolling towards them. He wore round spectacles and had a peculiar, waddling gait, as if his shoes were much too long for his feet. His long, black coat hung to his knees and was buttoned to the neck. He wore black gloves. Several coffee drinkers hailed him as he passed, but he didn't respond, leaving a string of puzzled Holmlanders in his wake.

Despite Kiefer's entreaties, Professor Glauber didn't come to their table. He stopped and stared, making waiters edge around him. Aubrey shifted uneasily; he had the distinct impression that he was the object of the professor's scrutiny. Then, without a word or change of expression, Professor Glauber veered off and made for the far corner of the room, where a telephone was attached to the wall.

Kiefer sank, baffled. 'He must be busy.'

'Metallurgical crisis, no doubt,' George said. 'Happens when you least expect it, I imagine.'

Kiefer crossed his arms and did his best to look confident. 'When he's done, he'll tell you what happened.'

Aubrey studied the mysterious professor as he spoke into the telephone. The conversation was mostly on the other side, but the professor did glance constantly toward Kiefer, so Aubrey was sure the professor was aware that his protégé was in the room.

Aubrey was taken aback when the professor called him from across the room. 'Mr Fitzwilliam!' he bellowed, in a hoarse but commanding voice. 'Over here, if you please!'

The professor was so demanding that Aubrey was on his feet before he knew it. Kiefer looked hurt and Aubrey shrugged. 'I'll go and see what he wants.'

Caroline frowned and for a moment Aubrey thought she was going to say something, but the moment passed and she busied herself with her bag.

As Aubrey drew closer to the impatient Professor Glauber, he began to grow uneasy. The professor had him fixed with an impatient, glassy gaze and he was still clutching the earpiece of the telephone in one hand, almost as if it were a weapon.

'Hurry, Fitzwilliam.' The professor adjusted his grip on the earpiece. 'I have a message for you.'

'Is there someone on the other end?' Aubrey said.

'Yes,' Professor Glauber said. His face was leaden, with a greasy sheen to it. Aubrey wondered if the man were sick. 'It's important.'

Despite his misgivings, Aubrey stepped closer.

'Dr Tremaine wants you.' Glauber darted out a hand like a snake and clamped it on Aubrey's upper arm.

Instantly, Aubrey's eyes flew open wide. His teeth clicked together and his head snapped backwards. Every muscle in his body went rigid and it felt as if a bolt of white light had shot through his body. He started to shake, to spasm uncontrollably, his limbs flailing, his head jerking wildly. A scream sounded from nearby but Aubrey only heard it dimly as he shook, unable to speak or to tear himself away. All he could do was stare at the awful, impassive face of Professor Glauber.

Dosomethingdosomethingdosomething, he thought.

Then, if he'd been able to make his mouth work properly, he would have cried out with horror. Professor Glauber's hand, the one holding the telephone earpiece, had melted.

Even in the middle of his spasm, in a room suddenly thrown into chaos as Holmlanders bolted for the door, Aubrey managed to correct himself. *No, not melted.* Professor Glauber's hand had *fused* with the earpiece, reshaping and dividing until it disappeared through the holes. As he watched, helpless, the process continued rapidly, the professor's hand actually being drawn into the earpiece, right up to his wrist. Within seconds, the earpiece swallowed the professor's arm up to the elbow like a python swallowing a pig.

Aghast, Aubrey summoned all his strength. He struck at the hand clamped to his upper arm, but it was like hitting a sack of sand. The professor didn't even change expression. He pulled Aubrey closer, and grappled for a one-armed embrace while his other arm disappeared up to his shoulder.

His face showed no emotion.

He's going to disappear up the telephone line, Aubrey thought, heaving at the professor's grip. *And if he doesn't let go, he's going to drag me along with him.*

A metal tray skimmed past his startled eyes. It hit the professor edge-on, just above his nose, and made a musical ringing noise.

'Aubrey!'

Caroline came into view, swinging another metal tray, but she was seized by von Stralick. 'Do not touch them with metal!' he cried, but then he lurched backward to avoid Caroline's angry backswing.

The interruption gave George a chance. With a shout, he charged at Professor Glauber. If Aubrey had been able, he would have gaped, for George was wielding a wooden hatstand as a medieval knight would wield a lance. With a grunt, he smashed into the half-professor. Aubrey was thrown backward and, suddenly boneless, he slumped to the floor, striking his head hard enough that blackness threatened to swamp him.

No, he thought, and struggled with consciousness. Dizzy and feeling sick to his stomach, he sat up to see the aftermath of the affray.

All the customers had fled, as had the waiters. Von Stralick was standing with his back to the door, which was now closed. He had his wallet in his hand and he was counting bank notes.

Kiefer held a hand on his head, and was groaning.

Caroline was standing between Professor Glauber and Aubrey, twitching her attention to either side, as if daring either of them to do anything foolish.

George had thrown away the hatstand. 'Old man?'

'All present and accounted for,' Aubrey muttered. The room swam before his eyes, but he decided that was preferable to blackness.

The telephone had been ripped from the wall, but the earpiece was still attached. And half of Professor Glauber had disappeared into it. The telephone had swallowed his entire arm and part of his chest.

He was lying, eyes open, staring unseeing at the ceiling. His neck was twisted in a way that made Aubrey feel even sicker. 'He's not breathing.'

'I say,' George said. He nudged the professor with his foot. 'Look.'

The professor's coat had been torn away by George's hatstand attack. Underneath lay the real shock.

Professor Glauber was made of clay. His torso was dull brown, roughly formed, and Aubrey was both fascinated and repelled to see that copper wire peeped through.

George crouched and reached out a hand to the creature's face.

'Don't,' Caroline said.

'I think we have to.' George unbuttoned the collar, took a fold of skin, just underneath the creature's neck, and tugged.

It came away with the sound of old paper, dry and rustling, exposing more copper wire overlaid with clay. Wincing, Aubrey crept closer and examined the extraordinary creature.

He touched its cheek. It was remarkable. Extremely lifelike, it was starting to craze and harden – but Aubrey could see minute pores and blemishes in its surface. All its facial features were natural, down to small, ruddy veins on either side of the prominent nose. It was a work of art. Anything that was showing looked perfectly human. Anything that was hidden by clothing was rougher – clay over an armature of copper wire. Aubrey saw this as a blending of the magical animation of golem clay with the connective and conducting power of copper wire.

'Kiefer,' he said. 'How much does this look like Professor Glauber?'

Kiefer had been staring, wide-eyed. 'Look like? Are you saying this isn't him?'

'Not unless Professor Glauber was a golem.'

'A golem?' Caroline stared. 'Is that what a golem looks like?'

'Not usually. This is a kind I've never seen before.'

George helped Aubrey to his feet. A glass of water was pushed into his hand and he had a sense of déjà vu when he saw that it was Kiefer who had fetched it.

Aubrey nodded. A presence had lurked at the other end of the telephone and that presence was unmistakeable. 'Dr Tremaine.'

'Are you sure?' von Stralick said.

'He's the only one who could do this sort of thing.'
And I felt him there, at the end of the line.

Kiefer nodded. 'Do you have any hesitation about our course of action now?'

Aubrey felt at a juncture. With the world in such a precarious position, the actions of one powerful man could tip the balance. In Dr Tremaine's case, this was in the direction of war.

Kiefer wanted revenge, but could assisting Kiefer help stop the war?

The argument smacked of ends justifying means, an argument that Aubrey was automatically suspicious of, but in this case there was much to recommend such a course of action.

Not the least was helping Caroline achieve her goal.

For such a rational person, Caroline was single-minded about Dr Tremaine. Could Aubrey rise in Caroline's estimation by doing something about her obsession?

It's a pragmatic decision, he thought, but deep down, he was uneasy. He quashed the disquiet, nodding. 'All right, Kiefer. I'll help.'

Seven

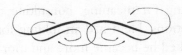

THE NEXT MORNING AT MAIDSTONE WAS AUBREY'S alone. After the incident at the Istros Coffee House the day before, von Stralick had claimed he had business to attend to. Caroline had gone home after making Aubrey vow that he would pursue this course of action. The proprietor of the café had glowered at them, only partly mollified by the cash von Stralick had tendered as they left. The arrival of black-uniformed Magisterium operatives had taken the sheen off the payment.

Aubrey had hesitated before contacting the Magisterium, but finally decided it was necessary. What were they going to do with a magical copper construct otherwise?

Rising early, George had accepted a lift from Sir Darius into the city. He had an errand to run for his father, investigating some new sort of agricultural machinery. He was excited about it, and Aubrey was pleased. Someone had to be excited about agricultural machinery.

This gave him some time, a valuable commodity in the world of Aubrey Fitzwilliam. He spent some of it working through his notes on the ancient tablet and script found in their underground adventures a few months ago, the tablet which had hinted that it was a cousin to the famous Rashid Stone.

The knottiness of trying to translate the mysterious ancient script absorbed him utterly. The world went away, time became irrelevant as he grappled with the arcane language, sifting for meaning, consulting old books of similar inscriptions. He'd had an inkling for some time, but as he worked he became more and more certain that tablet dealt with fundamentals of magic.

He wished that Professor Mansfield, his lecturer in Ancient Languages, would return from her sojourn in Aigyptos, but since he and his mother had played a considerable part in her secret mission to return the Rashid Stone to the Sultan of Memphis, the stone's rightful owner, he couldn't feel too affronted at her absence. He'd been corresponding with her, but the delay in the post made any serious discussion difficult.

Until she returned, he was on his own. So he surrounded himself with the best reference books and applied himself to the ongoing task of trying to decipher the mysterious script he'd found.

Research was, as usual, a seductive trap. He found himself following pathways and suggestions quite aside from his quest for decipherment. A hint about burial practices sent him reaching for a text on Etruscan rituals and he spent a good hour fascinated by these pre-Roman people.

Eventually, poring over details of urns and interment became mind-numbing. He stretched and decided he needed a break from the intensity of his research. He pushed back from the table then went to the safe which he'd had installed near one of his desks. It had been an item of some curiosity when he requested it, but he reassured his parents that it was necessary – and that he would share the combination with them.

At the back of the safe, past the collection of gold sovereigns and the gold tie pin given to him by his mother, he found the black velvet bag he'd been looking for. He straightened, shut the safe and tipped the contents of the bag into his palm.

The baroque beauty of the Tremaine pearl glowed softly and Aubrey remembered wresting it from the top of Dr Tremaine's cane. The ex-Sorcerer Royal had been furious, for the pearl had been given to him by his sister, and was his most precious keepsake.

Aubrey weighed in his hand. He'd always felt that pearls were warmer than other gems.

It was small, but could it be the way to stop a horrible war?

Aubrey was a student of history. He knew that wars were rarely caused by simple events. They were complex, chaotic affairs and were most often caused by the interplay of many, many incidents, some trivial, some significant, some outrageous. Economics, trade, deep-seated jealousies, misunderstandings, famines, intolerance, all played a part as nations lurched toward conflict. Wars weren't caused by one person, no matter how powerful, simply jumping up and saying, 'Right. This time I really mean it.'

But – and Aubrey's mind often threw up buts – perhaps it was different this time. Everyone thought war was inevitable. From the man in the street to the decision-makers in Parliament, Albionites were adamant that they didn't want war, yet were seized with a collective resignation that it was just around the corner – but was this the case? Holmland's ambitions, the tensions in the Goltans, all could be solved, perhaps, if it weren't for the machinations of one man.

Dr Mordecai Tremaine. He could be the pivot, the balancing point that the future of nations moved on. With his power, his influence and his maniacal vision, he could nudge the world into war.

Without him, could it be different? If he were removed, would that make the difference, slow things down so cool heads could prevail, so dialogue could ensue, so common sense could be given a chance?

He stared at the pearl. *I'm rationalising*, he thought.

He could use the pearl. He could use it to lure Dr Tremaine out of Holmland. Aubrey had been intrigued by the display of the Gallian crown jewels in Trinovant, and he imagined a similar display of unusual items, the centrepeice of which would be the Tremaine pearl. Plenty of publicity and Aubrey was confident that Dr Tremaine couldn't help himself. He'd vowed to regain the pearl and an opportunity like this would be irresistible.

For the beginnings of a plan, it was a good one. Some rough edges to be polished up, but it had the flavour of an idea with potential.

Then why did he feel uneasy about it?

He touched the pearl with his fingertip. The folds and wrinkles made it look like a miniature brain.

He bit his lip. He knew why he was uneasy. He loved his family.

Aubrey's mother and father were great puzzles to him

at times, and great sources of inspiration at others. He was proud of them, for all the exasperations they caused him. When his mother had herded him around the Albion Museum in the middle of the night, saving him from the gunmen he'd enraged, he'd been achingly proud of her. And his father? A man who had risked his life many times for others? The man who led the nation? Sir Darius Fitzwilliam was an impossible epitome, but the one man whose esteem and good opinion Aubrey was most desirous of.

So how could he use Dr Tremaine's familial love as the bait in a trap? Dr Tremaine loved his sister – Aubrey had heard it from the man's own lips. Aubrey felt that there was something grubby, something cheap about using such a feeling as a trick.

But then there was that chance to save the world from war . . .

Aubrey weighed his choices, felt the options, understood ends and means and how rationalising worked. He slipped the pearl back into the velvet bag and drew the string tight.

He'd go ahead with his plan, but that didn't mean he felt good about it.

It was hunger that brought Aubrey back to the world of Maidstone. Delicious aromas from downstairs had bypassed his brain and talked directly to his stomach. He stretched, taking his appetite as a good sign of his renewed constitution, and decided he deserved a bite to eat.

Michael Pryor

He'd clattered down the main stairs only to find Harris waiting for him. The butler held out the good silver tray, which meant that the envelope resting on it was important.

Aubrey read it, gazed at the ceiling for a moment as he worked through its implications, and then slipped it into his jacket pocket. 'Is the place neat and tidy, Harris?'

'Sir?'

Aubrey stifled a smile. Harris was capable of uttering that single word in a multitude of ways, as a master woodworker can turn a lump of wood into just about anything. This time, Harris pitched the word to tell Aubrey he was affronted at the question but confident that Maidstone was in tip-top shape. As it always was.

'Good, good. I wouldn't want the Prince to be presented with a smeary glass or an unpolished banister.'

'Sir.' *Not in this, or any other, world would such a thing happen. But I'll humour your little game.*

'Splendid. Three o'clock, the Prince will arrive.'

'Sir.' *I knew that, the butlers' network being what it is. The preparations are already well under way.*

Aubrey was surprised to find his mother at lunch. He'd expected her to be at the museum again.

She was picking at a fillet of fish in lemon butter. It was one of her favourite dishes, but she had hardly eaten any of it.

She looked up at his approach. 'Aubrey. Good.'

'I strive to please.' He took the seat opposite.

'Then you'll be a useful audience while I try to sort through something. Just nod and make approving sounds as I talk, will you?'

'With pleasure.'

A plate was put in front of Aubrey. His mouth actually watered at the appetising aroma that rose from the fish. A small bowl of green salad was placed nearby and the whole arrangement made Aubrey extremely happy to be united again so he could enjoy it.

His mother, dressed in light green, had her hair tied back loosely in the sort of absent-minded way that most women laboured for hours over, but without Lady Rose's confidence – or the scrap of old string she'd used. Although the room was the somewhat dark main dining room, her face caught the little light that filtered through the diamond-shaped window panes, and Aubrey, without any embarrassment, could see what made Lady Rose one of the foremost beauties in the land, and why so many tried hard to catch 'the Fitzwilliam Look'. But Lady Rose's combination of natural grace and innate scepticism about physical beauty meant that these efforts were doomed to failure. How can one use art to be artless?

He took his glass of ice-water and sipped at it while his mother found words to articulate whatever problem she was wrestling with.

Finally, she looked him in the eye. 'I have to go to Holmland.'

It was only with great effort that Aubrey didn't spray his mother with a mouthful of water. It took some time, and several napkins tendered by anxious staff, before he managed to control his choking. 'You have to go to Holmland?' he repeated as he dabbed his eyes. 'What? As head of an invading army?'

'Don't be silly, Aubrey. I've been invited to a symposium to give an address on the specimens I brought back from the Arctic.'

'Ah, yes. Seabirds.' Aubrey doubted he'd ever fully forgive himself for the actions that had precipitated that expedition. Or, more precisely, Caroline's accompanying his mother on it.

'The Holmland ornithologists are keen to hear what we found about albatrosses. They're a vocal lot and have agitated with the organisers of this gathering to include me.'

Aubrey ran his fingers through his hair. 'This is the thing in Fisherberg?'

'At the Fisherberg Academy. It's a prestigious occasion, a chance for Holmland to show the world that it isn't just a continental bullyboy. It's a home of arts, and sciences. Learning and culture.'

'I'm sure Chancellor Neumann is all in favour of it,' Aubrey muttered. He crossed his arms on his chest and stared at his fish. He wasn't as hungry as he had been. 'And what does Father have to say about this?'

'I imagine he won't be entirely pleased about it.'

'You haven't told him?'

'I haven't told him *yet*.'

'Ah. I see.'

Lady Rose glanced at Aubrey. 'I have a feeling I've slipped through the looking glass into Opposite Land. We seem to have swapped roles here.'

Aubrey gave a lopsided grin. He tried some of the fish. It was delicious and his appetite returned. 'You surprised me with your announcement.'

'So it seems.'

'But why are you telling me? Telling me before you tell Father, I mean.'

'To test your reaction. As a guide.'

'To how Father might react?' Aubrey thought about this for a moment while he savoured more of the fish. Then he frowned. 'Do you think it wise, going to Holmland right now?'

'We're not at war yet, Aubrey.'

'But Holmland has made at least two attempts on your life.'

'That was in the Arctic where their responsibility could easily be denied. They'd hardly let anything happen to the wife of the Albion Prime Minister, who would be a respected and invited guest at their showcase gathering of intellectuals and savants from around the world.' She took a sip of water. 'Besides, I'm sure that Tallis and Craddock will fight over whose service is best placed to supply me with an around-the-clock bodyguard.'

'Doubtless.' Commander Craddock as head of the Magisterium would claim that his operatives would be able to ward off any magical attacks, while Commander Tallis of the Special Services would insist that his agents were experts in foiling marksmen and crazed fanatics. In the end, Aubrey could see that they'd be forced to supply a composite squad, one that would do the job extremely well because each member would be striving to prove his service the better.

Lady Rose obviously considered her trial complete, for over the remainder of her fish and the subsequent fruit course, she steered the conversation to Aubrey's studies and his correspondence with Professor Mansfield. They'd been old friends at university, and Lady Rose was looking forward to renewing the acquaintance when Professor Mansfield returned.

While Aubrey was dawdling over an orange, Lady Rose stood. 'Excuse me, Aubrey, but I must be off.'

Aubrey climbed to his feet and dabbed his mouth with a napkin. 'To the museum again?'

'For a few hours. I need to organise shipment of some specimens to this symposium.'

Aubrey had a thought. 'Exactly when is this show?'

'It's not a show. Next week is the start of a progam of lectures and slide presentations by some of the brightest intellects in the world.'

'So soon?'

'It's been planned for some time. I'm sorry if they haven't been in constant communication with you. Now, after the museum, I'm meeting your father in the Parliamentary dining room for supper. We may be late.'

She left, and Aubrey lingered over his orange, making each segment last. He could imagine the supper might be a sticky one. Lady Rose was not a woman who felt she had to ask her husband's permission for her many and varied pursuits, something which had scandalised the nation at first. But when Sir Darius showed unquestioned support for his wife's career, it became a matter of some wonder, and inspiration for the suffragist movement. Despite Lady Rose having no formal role in the organisation, she was a model of the modern, free-thinking woman, one often used as an example by those pressing for Votes for Women.

So Sir Darius wouldn't argue about the propriety of the obligation. He would, however, have grave doubts about his wife's safety. And despite her confidence in the Holmlanders and the abilities of the Albion intelligence services, Aubrey was forced to agree with his father.

Professors, savants and academics from across the world cared little for politics. Many felt that national borders and the demands of patriotism shouldn't stifle intellectual commerce. It was a noble goal, and Aubrey supported it. Perhaps free and unfettered exchanges of views may help to break down the differences between nations.

But against that was the suspicion and hostility of the military and political factions of nations. At times, it seemed as if they had a vested interest in fostering suspicion. More suspicion meant it was only natural to build strong armies and to have strong leaders . . .

'Mr Fitzwilliam, sir?'

Tilly, the maid, hesitated at his elbow.

'Yes, Tilly?'

'It's His Royal Highness, sir. Prince Albert. He's here. In the library.'

Aubrey blinked. 'What time is it?'

'It's two o'clock, sir. His Highness apologised for being early.' Tilly dropped her gaze and Aubrey saw that she was blushing. Prince Albert was darkly handsome and this, combined with his status, tended to have an effect on women. Especially, but not solely, young women. He had a similar appeal to the mothers of unmarried young women, but the effect in that case was often laced with a tincture of calculation.

A serious-looking young man was on guard outside the library. He wore a dark, discreet suit. He made no secret of inspecting Aubrey before opening the door.

So I'm forgiven, but not forgotten. Aubrey couldn't really blame them. He thought he was lucky to have got off so lightly.

Prince Albert was reading a golfing manual and looked up as Aubrey entered. He replaced the book on the shelves and advanced, hand extended. 'Aubrey! You've recovered?'

They shook. Aubrey shrugged, glad that Bertie harboured no ill will. 'I seem right as rain. Better than ever, in fact.'

'I'm glad,' the Prince said and Aubrey saw that it was true and wholehearted. Prince Albert was genuinely relieved that Aubrey had come through the ordeal. His own peril was of little importance to him.

They each took one of the red leather armchairs in the centre of the library, and it was only then that Aubrey saw another serious-looking young man standing by the window. The Prince followed his gaze. 'Sommers' idea,' he apologised. 'He won't let me go anywhere any more, not without a squad or two of Tallis's Special Services operatives. Good people, all of them, but they rather damp the spontaneity. I visited the exhibition of the crown jewels from Gallia this morning, and I could hardly move, surrounded as I was by Albion's finest.'

'Doing your best for the alliance, I see.'

The Prince sighed. 'The President of Gallia thought a goodwill tour of their precious jewels would be helpful for our alliance. Splendid array, it is. Very popular.'

'And it's yours,' Aubrey said, 'by right.'

The Prince made a face. 'Don't, Aubrey, not even in jest.'

In their Gallian adventure, Aubrey, Caroline and George had found documentary proof that Prince Albert – through his mother's family – was the true heir to the crown of Gallia. The way the Prince had received this information told Aubrey that he'd suspected it for some time and that the ancient deeds were only confirmation.

Nothing had been made public about this. Gallia was a proud republic and had no need for kings since its revolution. Any move by the Albion royal family would undoubtedly fracture the alliance between the two nations.

Just another complicating factor in a complex world, Aubrey thought.

He leaned back in his chair and noticed how the Special Services agent had positioned himself so he could see the garden outside the window while keeping an eye on anything in the library. 'It's understandable you have protection. After all, I nearly killed you.'

'Not your fault, old fellow.'

Aubrey drummed his fingers on the armrest of the easy chair. 'I haven't actually apologised, have I?'

'Accepted and forgotten.' Prince Albert smiled a little. 'You know, I can't banish you from my presence. You'd be like a very large fog.'

Aubrey felt uneasy. 'Fog?'

'You'd be much missed.'

Aubrey groaned. The Prince looked thoroughly pleased. But despite the pain, Aubrey felt lucky to see this side of Bertie. His fondness for puns and wordplay was at odds with his public face, that of the serious, dutiful heir to the throne, hardworking in the stead of his father, whose periodic bouts of irrationality were getting worse.

'Have you come all the way over here just to subject me to that?' Aubrey asked.

'I was on my way back to the Palace after the Gallian commitment, but I couldn't resist. It was your, how can I put it . . . *pun*-ishment?'

Aubrey put his head in his hands. 'I'm appalled.'

'Good. You need appalling every now and then.' The Prince chuckled. 'I actually did want to see how you were. It must have been dreadful, being taken over like that.'

Aubrey shuddered. 'Being out of control? A nightmare.'

'I'm glad you weren't successful. It'd make it hard to take up cousin Leopold on his invitation.'

The misgivings Aubrey had felt before Bertie launched his pun assault were nothing to the misgivings that pricked him now.

'I only know one Leopold,' he said slowly. 'One Leopold who'd be your cousin, anyway. We're talking about the Elektor of Holmland, aren't we?'

'Cousin Leopold, that's what I said.'

'Ruler of the most powerful nation on the continent? The country that's looking to expand its borders? The country that's likely to be our greatest enemy if this war breaks out?'

'Leopold is most upset about that,' Prince Albert said. 'He says Chancellor Neumann and his government are getting out of hand.'

Aubrey rubbed his forehead. 'You're not going, are you?'

Suddenly, it was as if the Prince had taken off one set of clothes and put on another. He straightened, nodded solemnly, and the punning young man was gone. In front of Aubrey was the heir to the throne of Albion, the one who'd been born and raised knowing his duty. 'Aubrey, I don't want the world to go to war, and that's what's going to happen if something isn't done about it.'

'And your visiting Holmland is going to stop the war?'

Bertie rubbed his hands together and stared at them. 'That's not the public reason for my visit, no. But while I'm there I want to see what I can do. It might be a step in the right direction. I can't overlook a chance to bring our nations closer together. It may help ease tension.'

'Of course. But you must have considered that this invitation could be a plot.' Aubrey had a thought. 'If you're shown to be a Holmland sympathiser, it may diminish your reputation here.'

'It may be. But I'm willing to risk that for the chance to speak face to face with Leopold.' He frowned. 'I have doubts over the veracity of some of the public pronouncements that he's said to have made.'

'This visit wouldn't be based around a symposium or anything, would it? Next week?'

· A small smile. 'Leopold always did like a show. He adored visiting the Great Exhibition here when he was small.'

Aubrey glanced at the Special Services operative. 'I can see that you've made up your mind. You'll have protection?'

'Tallis and Craddock have insisted on it. As has your father.'

'You've discussed this with him?'

'Of course. He wasn't happy, but he understood my reasoning.' The Prince pursed his lips. 'I want to ask you to come along. Having such a useful chap as yourself in my entourage might help reassure your father.'

Aubrey was ready to agree, but then he remembered his promise to Caroline and Kiefer. His face fell. 'Sorry, Bertie. Other commitments.'

Bertie stood. 'Don't trouble yourself, old fellow, just thought I'd see if you were available. If there's anything I understand, it's commitments.' He shook Aubrey's hand. 'Now, to another of those commitments.'

Aubrey walked with him to the front door. 'What is it this time? Dedicating a new bridge? A meeting of an excruciatingly dull committee?'

'A new battleship is being launched at Imworth. I have to be there. Show of support and all that.'

'Of course.'

Aubrey saw the Prince out. When the door closed, he stood for a moment, admiring his friend. It couldn't be easy being the heir to the throne – not to mention that Bertie could rightfully claim the throne of Gallia as well if he chose. *There's someone who knows how to keep a secret.*

Eight

EVENTS WERE BUMPING TOGETHER LIKE THUNDER-
clouds before a storm. After the Prince left, Aubrey
abandoned his plans for more research. He decided to
go looking for Hugo von Stralick, but not before taking
a special item from the safe and replenishing George's
appurtenances vest with a variety of possibly useful
items.

Holmland was at the heart of things, he decided as the
underground train made its way toward Little Pickling. Dr
Tremaine, the symposium, the appearance of Otto Kiefer
and his Beccaria Cage. He needed to talk to someone
about Holmland's intentions, and Hugo von Stralick was
the one whose brain he could pick.

The train took him across the river and he waited
impatiently, fingering the Beccaria Cage through his
shirt, until he alighted at Laidley Grove Station. After that
it was a fair hike to get to the Istros Coffee House.

From the outside, the café looked none the worse for the fracas the previous day. The proprietor didn't look overwhelmingly happy to see him, frowning as Aubrey made his way through the warm and exotic front room.

The inner room was equally warm, but as Aubrey stood just inside the doorway he couldn't help but feel that something had changed. Gone was the excited argument, the chatter. The tables were well populated, but heads were bowed, conversations guarded. His arrival sent a ripple of surprised glances around the steamy, smoky room, but no-one would meet his gaze.

He scanned the café but couldn't see von Stralick. He was about to give up when Kiefer wandered through the front door. He looked relieved, and twisted his cloth cap between his hands as if he were trying to wring it dry. 'Hugo said you'd be looking for him.'

'And where is he?'

'He asked me to find you. Find you and take you to him.'

Aubrey didn't like being at von Stralick's command. 'Where?'

'I'll take you.'

'Cab?'

Kiefer looked blank and Aubrey could see him trying to remember how much money he had in his wallet. 'We will walk.'

Kiefer's long legs set a cracking pace, but Aubrey found it easy to keep up, thanks to his reconstituted self. This meant he had enough energy to question Kiefer and, after some initial resistance, the youth became almost garrulous, telling Aubrey a long, rambling tale of the way his father had been exploited, his tragic death and the subsequent struggles of the family. Kiefer walked with his head down and his hands clutched behind his back as he kept up his monologue of money problems and how these had made him careful with every penny, even after he'd been sponsored in his studies by one of Holmland's more generous nobles. On more than one occasion, Aubrey had to steer him around lamp posts and fellow pedestrians, and he had to take him by the arm whenever it came time to cross a road.

After fifteen minutes of this erratic journey, Kiefer stopped suddenly and peered around. They were approaching a busy intersection, near a flower market, if Aubrey's nose was any judge.

Kiefer turned his gaze to Aubrey. He was calm and serious. 'Your Dr Tremaine took all my father's notes, you know. After the laboratory explosion.'

Aubrey stared, then realised that Kiefer was simply continuing the earlier conversation. 'I'm sorry to hear that.'

'I wanted them,' Kiefer continued, desolate. 'Not just because of the findings.'

'Catalytic magic. Much work is going on in this area.'

Kiefer shrugged. 'This is so. The notes will help my career, that is true. But I wanted them because they belonged to him. My father.'

'Of course.'

Kiefer pushed his spectacles back on his nose. 'I will have my revenge, you know. With your help or without it.'

Kiefer's quiet determination was impressive, but it also had a brittle edge, as if he'd fired his revenge for too long and while it had become hard, it had also become breakable.

'Dr Tremaine is no ordinary enemy,' Aubrey advised. 'Don't do anything rash.'

'Rash? Rash is not my way. I am here after much planning, much pondering.' His face fell. 'My plans did not go as I had hoped, it seems. Tremaine must have intercepted the letters from Uncle Maurice, found the Beccaria Cage and prepared it for you.'

'Perhaps.' Aubrey had come to a different conclusion. While Dr Tremaine wasn't above making the most of an opportunity, he was the great instigator of schemes. Aubrey could see him tinkering with a Beccaria Cage, secreting his mind-controlling spell, and then sending a bogus letter to Maurice alerting him to the presence of the artefact. The arch-manipulator, setting the wheels in motion, then moving on to his next scheme.

Aubrey couldn't help but feel for the despairing Holmlander. 'Don't worry, Kiefer. I understand what you want. But we must be cautious.'

'You have reasons to bring him down?'

'I do.'

'Then let us work together.' Kiefer held up a hand. 'But please do not mistake me. I am no traitor. I love my country and I will do nothing to harm it.'

'I see.'

'I am glad.' He scowled. 'Your Dr Tremaine is not good for Holmland. The sooner he is out, the better.' Kiefer set off again, but after a few steps he stopped and turned around. 'That way,' he said, leading back the way they'd come.

A few minutes later, he clapped his hands together and rubbed them, his bony elbows posing a hazard to passing traffic. 'We are here.'

They'd left Little Pickling and come to a neat, orderly street in nearby Crozier. The street was lined with townhouses, four or five storeys tall, all made of clean red brick. At the end of the street was the imposing bulk of the Showellstyle Station.

'Von Stralick has rooms here?'

'He owns the whole building.' Kiefer pointed at the townhouse in front of them.

'Really? The importing and exporting business must be doing well.'

Kiefer looked thoughtful for a moment, then shrugged. He mounted the stairs and clattered the brass doorknocker.

Aubrey was still gazing upward, trying to count windows and rooms, when the door opened and von Stralick stood there. 'Ah, Otto. You've found him. Very good.'

Aubrey climbed the stairs. 'Von Stralick. You want something?'

Von Stralick looked pained, then ushered Aubrey and Kiefer inside. He closed the door before answering. 'I want to help you stop Dr Tremaine.'

Aubrey was immediately suspicious. Hugo von Stralick was both opportunistic and self-interested. An offer of help like this, unasked for, was something to be approached very, very carefully. 'For purely altruistic reasons?'

'I could say that getting rid of Dr Tremaine would be good for Holmland, but that all depends on how you see the future direction of our country.' He coughed into his hand. 'I know you may find this hard to believe, but I have a personal reason for stopping him.'

'Go on.'

'My late superior, the man I reported to, was more than a colleague. He was an old friend and a good man. A family man. He didn't deserve what happened. I help you stop Tremaine, I will get great satisfaction.'

It sounded plausible. *Perhaps too plausible?* Aubrey wasn't about to accept such a declaration at face value. He needed time to think. 'Er. What about a cup of tea first?'

Von Stralick raised an eyebrow, then chuckled. 'Tea. A standard Albionite delaying tactic. Otto?'

'Of course. And what about some of those tasty Albion scones? I can make some if you like.'

He rushed down the dimly lit hall.

Von Stralick glanced at Aubrey and shrugged. 'He does try to be useful.'

'So I see. I hope he knows his way around the kitchen.'

'Do not underestimate him, Fitzwilliam.' Von Stralick winced at a crash that came from the direction that Kiefer had gone. 'He is very talented, in a number of fields. And he is determined to succeed.'

'In gaining revenge on Dr Tremaine?'

'Yes. But Otto is ambitious in a more practical sense. He wants wealth and position and feels that he has missed out on it. That is why he came to study in your country, in hopes of the advancement he desperately wants.'

'He thinks it's owed to him,' Aubrey said softly, 'because of the unfulfilled promises made to his father.'

Von Stralick glanced sharply at him then smiled. 'You are quick, Fitzwilliam.'

Aubrey shrugged. 'Do you mind if I use your telephone while the water is boiling?'

The door knocker hammered while they were enjoying Kiefer's surprisingly excellent scones.

Von Stralick left the drawing room, frowning, and returned, frowning. 'I would have appreciated it if you'd asked me before you extended an invitation to my home.'

Aubrey stood and felt immeasurably better to see Caroline and George. 'I thought I needed to even the odds.'

Von Stralick nodded his head. 'Of course you did.' He bowed. 'Miss Hepworth. Doyle.'

Caroline was dressed in a grey outfit and she carried a small leather bag. She looked puzzled, but didn't say anything.

George was in tweeds, as if he were off for an afternoon in the country. 'Von Stralick. Nice place you have here. Who did you steal it from?'

'Very droll, Doyle,' von Stralick said. 'You should consider a music hall career.'

He led them to the dining room. A large oval table took up the middle of the room, while windows looked over a small courtyard with hydrangeas. The dining room had sideboards and glass-fronted cabinets. On inspection, Aubrey could see that none of them were cheap.

They arranged themselves around the oval table. Aubrey and von Stralick faced each other at the ends, while Aubrey had Caroline on his left and George on his right. Von Stralick had Kiefer on his right. The balance was in Aubrey's favour, which was how he preferred to begin an encounter.

Aubrey opened. 'Before we were set upon at the café, I suggested that we move against Dr Tremaine. Together.'

Von Stralick raised a finger. 'Point of order, Mr Chairman. Before *we* were set upon? It seemed to me that the telephonic assassin singled you out, Fitzwilliam.'

Caroline cut in. 'Be that as it may. Dr Tremaine needs to be stopped, the sooner the better.'

Von Stralick turned to Kiefer. 'Dr Tremaine was responsible for her father's death. She seeks vengeance.'

Caroline clasped her hands in front of her and Aubrey saw that the quicks were white. 'I seek justice.'

Von Stralick chuckled. 'And isn't it fortunate for you that justice and vengeance coincide, in this case?'

Aubrey could see Caroline making a mental note of von Stralick's condescension, for later. *Not a good start to our alliance*, he thought. 'Von Stralick,' he said hurriedly. 'What has Dr Tremaine been up to lately? Surely you have recent information.'

Von Stralick folded his hands on the table in front of him and stared at them. 'He is well enmeshed in the Chancellor's government. Very impressed with his work, they've been. Even though his plots in Gallia and Albion didn't fully come to fruition, the disruption they caused was useful. After all, sometimes it's just as good to have your enemy jumping at shadows, expending energy on things that aren't there.'

'Commander Tallis told me he was a sort of special adviser,' Caroline said, 'working with many different departments.'

'Mainly with the army and the navy,' von Stralick said. 'They like his ideas.'

Aubrey shuddered, but he was still thinking about Caroline's remark. How often had she been reporting to Commander Tallis? 'So Dr Tremaine works to prepare their armed forces, advise their magical researchers, creating havoc wherever he can. And he's shown he can reach out to strike here.'

'Papers were full of the stormfleet descending on Greythorn,' George put in. 'Dashed effective of him. People are watching the skies and raising the alarm whenever a flock of sparrows swoops overhead.'

'Showy, theatrical, effective,' von Stralick said. 'That sounds like him, doesn't it?'

'Enough is enough,' Caroline said. 'We must neutralise him.'

'The best plan seems to be that we lure him here,' Aubrey said, conscious that an idea had graduated to an altogether firmer status, 'to Albion, to our home ground. We trap him, and hand him over to the authorities.'

Aubrey noted how Caroline looked away at that, but before he could question her, von Stralick held up a finger. 'This depends on having something to lure him with.'

Aubrey was conscious that all eyes were on him. He took a deep breath and put both hands on the table. 'We do,' he said. 'His late sister.'

The reactions were as varied as the people around the table. George leaned forward and looked thoughtful. Caroline stiffened. Von Stralick opened his mouth, but was cut off by Kiefer, who raised a hand and waved it wildly. 'Sylvia Tremaine? Dead. No, this isn't so.'

Aubrey had the sequence of events all organised in his head – he'd suggest a plan, it would be pooh-poohed, then discussed, then modified, then discarded, then resuscitated, then banged into shape and then applauded – but Kiefer had derailed this neatly.

'I beg your pardon?' he said. His hard-learned tact kept him from the first response that came to his mind, which was, 'Are you stark, raving mad, Kiefer?'

'Dr Tremaine's sister,' Kiefer said, with rather less certainty now everyone was looking at him. 'She is lost, not dead. She vanished and has never been found.'

General mayhem ensued as everyone spoke at once. Everyone, except – for once – Aubrey. He was too stunned.

Dr Tremaine's past was shrouded in mystery. He cultivated this and never denied a rumour, no matter how outlandish. He seemed to have come from nowhere – although gossip had it that he was born on the Continent, in Antipodea, the Americas or to a disreputable peer – and proceeded to cut a swathe through society with his riches and through academia with his intellect. He also wrestled, sang, painted and shot with the best of them.

The only family he ever mentioned was his sister, Sylvia, and he always spoke of her as if she had passed away a long time ago. It garnered him much sympathy, especially among tender-hearted women.

He told me his sister had died, Aubrey thought, *but truthfulness isn't Dr Tremaine's strongest suit*. 'Kiefer, where did you get this information?'

'I heard it,' Kiefer mumbled, 'in Fisherberg.'

'In Fisherberg?' George said. 'This is useful stuff, Kiefer. Did you hear it from someone in the Chancellor's government?'

'No,' Kiefer said in a small voice. Then he actually blushed. Two bright spots of red rushed to his cheeks and he dropped his head. The hands he'd clasped in front of him were suddenly fascinating.

Caroline tapped the table. 'Where did you hear it, Otto?'

Kiefer sighed and lifted his head. He spread his hands. 'Gossip. Coffee house gossip.'

His gaze darted around the table and his face fell at the reception this revelation received. He rallied and went on. 'You see, among students, Dr Tremaine is a topic of much fascination. Where he is from, what he's up to, where he gets his clothes . . . A few items are accepted fact. That his sister survived her illness is one of them.'

George snorted. 'Are we going to rely on gossip?'

Von Stralick coughed. 'I too, have heard this. I understood it to be common knowledge in Fisherberg.'

Aubrey rubbed his face with both hands. 'Perhaps there's a way to find out if she is alive.'

'I suppose we could ask Dr Tremaine,' von Stralick said, 'but I don't know if he'd be forthcoming.'

Aubrey smiled. He took the velvet bag from his appurtenances vest and shook it into his palm. He held up the Tremaine pearl. 'She gave this to him. I was going to suggest we put it on display, a public display. George could work on getting publicity in the papers, Dr Tremaine would hear about it and then . . .' He rubbed his chin. 'But first, I think I can use it to see if Sylvia is still alive.'

Kiefer started. 'Of course! The Principle of Familiarity!'

Aubrey nodded, saw the mystified expressions and explained. 'Inanimate objects can form connections with people, if they're in contact with them for long enough. The human consciousness impinges itself on the object, as it were.'

'Yes,' Kiefer said. He leaned forward and slapped his hands on the table in front of him in a rapid drumbeat. 'Yes. And if the object is removed from the person, from their consciousness, the separation is hurtful to it. The object yearns for its owner, longs to be reunited.'

'A trifle more anthropomorphic than I'd put it,' Aubrey said, 'but the principle remains. It's one we can use, with the correct preparation, to point the way to Sylvia Tremaine.'

'Just like we used the brick from the tower of the Magic Faculty in Lutetia to point the way to the Heart of Gold?' George said.

'I used the Law of Constituent Parts there,' Aubrey said and he noted the look of intense interest on Kiefer's face. 'That's for connections between inanimate objects. The relationship between people and objects is more complex.'

And the spell will be more complex, he thought, running through the possibilities in his head and feeling the rising of his pulse that signalled a challenge was in sight.

Caroline and George exchanged a glance. 'You're going to do some spell casting here?' she said. 'Is that wise?'

Aubrey steered a course and only answered the first question. 'Yes, right here. But let me do a little probing, first, just to make certain.'

Kiefer rubbed his hands together, eagerness itself. 'I'm keen to see your magic at work. The new style Albion rationalism is all the talk in Fisherberg.'

Aubrey suddenly felt self-conscious. He wondered if it was because of von Stralick's noting every move. Or perhaps it was Kiefer's extreme attention, as if he were observing an operation. He focused on George and Caroline instead. He wanted to let them know that he felt stronger than he had in ages, much more able to undertake complex magic.

He flexed his shoulders. A simple probing spell. Even though all magical observation affected the object observed in some way (the Principle of Conscious Scrutiny), he felt it was worth it, especially if he could construct his observation spell to have the lightest of touches, a mere feather brush so Aubrey could detect anything unusual about the pearl before he proceeded further. It was wise, judicious spellcraft.

Feeling all eyes upon him, he reached for the notebook and pencil he had in his jacket pocket. Kiefer grunted with approval, then suddenly swore, thrust back his chair and stood. 'Don't do anything. I think I left the kettle on.'

'Don't wait for him,' von Stralick said sourly as Kiefer galloped out. 'He could be a long time. Difficult places, kitchens.'

Aubrey hesitated. *A simple spell*, he thought and then tucked away the notebook. *No need to scratch out anything.*

A tiny cautious voice insisted otherwise, but with Caroline and George watching, he found it easy to ignore it. 'Right. Let's see what's going on with this pearl.'

He decided to use Tartessian, a difficult ancient language he'd been studying at university. He told himself he wasn't showing off. His decision was based solely on his need to practise it. The simple matter of not having used it before in an active spell didn't seem dreadfully important.

He placed the velvet bag in the centre of the table. Then he settled the pearl on it. He adopted what he hoped was a commanding pose – arms extended, brow furrowed – while trying to ignore Caroline rolling her eyes. Striving for a deep, thrilling timbre, he started with terms outlining the direction of the spell and the vicinity, then rolled out the variables for intensity and duration, emphasising the lightest possible touch. The plosives of the Tartessian language caused him momentary alarm, but he thought he managed them well as he brought the spell to a conclusion. A tiny flourish of a signature, and it was done.

The pearl exploded.

Nine

AUBREY SHOOK HIMSELF AND SAT UP, RUBBING THE BACK of his neck. *I see*, he thought, looking around and steadfastly refusing to be surprised. *We're in a dungeon.*

They were all in various aspects of disarray. George was sprawled against the rough stone block wall, groaning. Eyes closed, von Stralick was on his back on one of the four straw mattresses. The only one who didn't look distressed was Caroline. Aubrey was greatly relieved to see that she was unharmed, standing at the door – heavy wood, massive iron hinges, a single peephole – with her ear to its surface. She saw him looking at her and she held up a finger, demanding his silence.

He was happy to comply. It gave him a chance to make sense of the waves of magic that were rolling over him from . . . where?

Such was the enveloping nature of the magic, he didn't have to concentrate or extend his magical senses. The *weight* of it pressed on him from all directions. It made his skin tingle, his bones itch, and sent a play of contradictory tastes flickering across his tongue. Odd sensations that weren't smells slid through his nostrils, making him wrinkle his nose and paw at it, trying to dislodge the birdsong that was caught there.

The overwhelming effect was disconcerting, to say the least, but Aubrey – strangely – didn't find it unpleasant. The magic had been shaped and wrought, it had a single-mindedness of purpose. But for what?

'Nothing,' Caroline said as she descended the three stairs that led to the door. She shook her head in disgust and wiped her hands together.

'Nothing?'

'No sounds. We've either been forgotten or the guards are asleep.'

'Guards?'

Caroline gave him a pitying look. 'We're in a dungeon, Aubrey. What's a dungeon without guards?'

Aubrey considered this for a moment. He glanced at the others. George had levered himself up and was leaning against the wall looking dazed. Von Stralick was still unconscious.

'Caroline,' he ventured. 'How did we get here?'

'Really, Aubrey, that blow on your head must have been worse than I thought. You shouldn't have struggled so when they burst in.'

Aubrey stood. He did it slowly, distracted for a moment by the bizarre sensation of tasting tartan. 'I shouldn't have struggled when they burst in?'

'You argued at first, as usual, then you struggled.'

'With whom?'

'With . . . With . . .' Caroline frowned. 'They came to get us and brought us here.'

'Of course they did. We were abducted. How else would we wind up here?' Aubrey went to the wall and put his palm against it. He bit his lip. The magic was coming from the walls. Or through them? 'Do you remember the journey?'

'What are you getting at, Aubrey?' Caroline came close, glancing at the others. It was not an altogether unpleasant situation, Aubrey decided, Caroline's deciding to come nearer to him.

'The journey,' he said in a hushed voice and had the pleasure of her leaning closer. 'How did it take place? How did we get from von Stralick's place to here? Motorcar? Omnibus? Airship?'

'Don't be silly,' she said, but a frown creased her perfect brow.

'Humour me.'

'I . . .' She shook her head and looked angry, fetchingly angry, rather than frightened. 'What's going on here?'

'We're trapped in a metaphor, I think.' He slapped the stone wall. 'Although I think this one has gone right through the other side of metaphor into the realm of cliché.'

'You're being obscure again. I warned you about that.'

'The pearl, Caroline. Remember the pearl?'

'Oh.' Caroline's eyes opened wide. 'I'd forgotten. We were gathered around the table. You were posturing, ready to do your magic, and then . . .'

Aubrey winced a little at the 'posturing'. 'And then we were here.' He swept an arm around. 'This place is reeking with magic of the Tremaine sort. We've been transported here. I must have triggered something.'

'Kiefer isn't here because he wasn't close enough to be swept up?'

At that moment, von Stralick sat up and rubbed his eyes. 'Where am I?'

'And the cliché is complete,' Aubrey said.

Von Stralick scowled. 'If this place is a metaphor, as you say, then shouldn't we approach it on that level? Shouldn't we look to escape? Trick the guards? Tunnel out of here? Bend the bars and squeeze through?'

George turned from looking out of the barred window. 'I'm not sure if that would be a good idea.'

Aubrey had to stand on tiptoes; he wasn't really surprised at what he saw.

The window looked onto a shaft. It was square, some ten yards across. Across from their window was an identically barred window. Aubrey looked up and he groaned. The shaft stretched up as far as he could see. Thousands, tens of thousands of barred windows disappeared into infinity. He looked down and saw the same depressing scene.

A tap on the shoulder. 'Make a stirrup, Aubrey.'

He blinked as Caroline slipped off her shoes. She held her dress up over her ankles while Aubrey fumbled to lace his hands together. It was no effort to lift her, and soon she was gripping the bars and staring at the improbable sight that lay outside.

Aubrey found his head resting against her knee. Solely to retain balance, he told himself, but he wished that her inspection would go on forever.

'You can let me down now,' Caroline said.

'Are you sure? Take your time. I mean, there are a lot of windows out there.'

'I've seen enough.'

He lowered her reluctantly. She took his shoulders to help herself down. 'Thank you, Aubrey. You're very useful, sometimes.'

Lost for words, and lost in the moment, he nodded. Then he straightened a tie that he felt must have deviated by at least half a degree from the vertical.

'Please,' von Stralick said with a knowing smile, 'if you'll step aside, I too would like to see this amazing sight that has rendered you speechless.'

Aubrey backed away and stumbled into George, who was hunched over and attacking the wall with a penknife. He grinned at Aubrey. 'If I have my clichés right, the mortar should be weak around one of these blocks.'

Caroline peered at George's efforts. 'And on the other side will be a grey-bearded prisoner? The one who knows all the secret escape routes?'

Aubrey shrugged. 'I'm not sure we can rely on every aspect of the cliché. What if the originator of this place grew up with different clichés? Like one with the pit of boiling oil on the other side of the loose stone block?'

'We'll just have to be careful,' George said. 'Ah.'

'That sounded like an "ah" of satisfaction, George,' Aubrey said.

'Satisfaction and discovery, old man.' George straightened and dusted his hands together. 'We do, indeed, have a loose block of stone. With a bit of an effort I think I can drag it out.'

'Rather than pushing it in and losing it?' von Stralick said, joining them after his introduction to the ominous shaft. 'We don't want to leave an obvious hole in the wall if we have picky gaolers, do we?'

It took George only a few minutes – and plenty of needless suggestions from his onlookers – before he'd managed to free enough mortar to get a grip on the sides of the stone block. Grimacing with effort, he inched the block forward. It grated, nearly stuck, then it was finally balanced ready to come out.

'If it's too much for you,' von Stralick said to George, 'I'm sure I can lend a hand.'

'Appreciate the offer, von Stralick,' George said, 'but I think I have it under control.'

Aubrey wished that George and von Stralick would stop sparring, but it seemed as if they were in a drawn-out battle of niggling, like a pair of five-year-olds in a sandpit.

George leaned against the block with his shoulder, wiped his hands on his trouser legs and nodded. 'All right, everyone. Stand back.'

He switched position and grasped the underside of the block. Gritting his teeth, he edged it forward until he was taking its full weight. He grunted and moved backward, slowly, knees bent. 'Nothing behind me, is there?' he asked, the strain in his voice evident. The tendons in his neck stood out.

'All clear,' Aubrey reported. He knew his friend was strong, but this was an impressive display.

'Good.'

George shuffled back, then sank at the knees. With care, he moved his grip until he was holding the sides again, then gently lowered the block to the floor.

He straightened, sighed and massaged the small of his back. 'There. Easy as you like.'

'Liar,' Aubrey said.

'True.' George flexed his hands. 'I was just doing my best to keep up the cliché count.'

Aubrey went to reply, but his attention was caught by the hole in the wall and the words died in his mouth. He stared, then moved closer – carefully – to confirm what the removal of the stone block had revealed.

White. The hole opened onto pristine white.

George looked quizzically at Aubrey. Von Stralick narrowed his eyes and took a small step back. 'What is it?'

Aubrey squinted, then frowned. What he'd thought was a blank, white space was anything but. It had a lustre, a subtle, shifting sheen that looked as if it was composed of a thousand different shades of white, shifting as he moved his head.

He reached into the gap. George caught his arm. 'I was going to say "be careful", old man, but I realised who I was talking to. What about "try poking it with something first"?'

Aubrey patted the appurtenances vest through his jacket, then he looked around.

Von Stralick, with a solemn face, handed him a long straw. 'From the mattress. It was the best I could do at short notice.'

Aubrey thanked him. He edged his makeshift probe into the hole. When it reached the whiteness, the straw buckled. 'It's hard.' Then he shrugged. *In for a penny, in for a pound.*

Before anyone could stop him, he put his hand into the gap, forefinger extended. He tapped the white surface with his fingernail. 'Quite hard.'

'Pearl usually is,' Caroline said.

Aubrey straightened. 'Pearl?'

'Pearl,' she repeated. Then she gestured, encompassing the dungeon and its surrounds. 'We're trapped in Dr Tremaine's pearl.'

Of course. Immediately before waking in the dungeon, what had he been doing? Probing the pearl. He must have triggered a defensive spell and it had caught them all.

Von Stralick nodded. George peered into the hole. 'Makes sense to me.'

'Brilliant notion,' Aubrey said to Caroline.

'I'm glad you're impressed,' she said, offering him a smile.

The door to the cell suddenly swung back with a satisfyingly melodramatic creaking, and crashed against the wall with enough force to shake dust from the ceiling.

'Ah. More have been sent.'

Framed in the doorway was a young woman and Aubrey was actually relieved. He'd half-expected to see a guard – hunchbacked or otherwise – leering at them, and was thankful that this wasn't the case. His active imagination had provided fleeting visions of being asked questions while keepers enjoyed working the various means of extracting information. He wasn't overjoyed at the prospect.

Their visitor was a striking figure, nonetheless, as she stood at the top of the stairs, studying them. She wore a long velvet gown the colour of old blood – a crimson so deep it was almost black. Her hair was thick and black, hanging past her shoulders. Aubrey had the distinct impression that she wasn't well, for her skin was pale and her dark eyes sparkled with fever one moment, then lapsed into dullness the next. On top of this he had the creeping sense that she had a close resemblance to someone he knew well.

'Sylvia?' he said.

She inhaled sharply and turned her attention to him. 'Why do you call me that?'

'Because you look like Dr Mordecai Tremaine.'

'Mordecai?' She put a hand to her throat.

Caroline was grim. 'What has he done to you? Imprisoned you here?'

She shook her head and her black hair danced. For a moment, animation came to her face and her eyes glinted with vigour. 'No, never imprisoned,' she said, but the energy fled and once again her face was almost a doll-like mask. 'This is my home. I belong here.'

'In a pearl?' Aubrey said.

'A pearl?' Her brow wrinkled. 'What a strange notion you have.'

'Then what is this place?' George asked.

'Come with me,' she said. 'I'll show you.'

'We're free to go?' Von Stralick asked.

She shrugged, as if this was unimportant. 'You're free to come with me.'

Aubrey had more than a few misgivings. Her demeanour didn't inspire confidence. 'You *are* Sylvia Tremaine, are you not?'

'I like the name.' She turned away, back toward the corridor outside the doorway. 'But it's unimportant.'

'No it's not. What happened to you? Why are you here?'

She sighed. It was an expression of despair and desolation such that Aubrey's heart went out to her. 'That sort of thing doesn't matter. I am here. It is where I belong.'

She left the cell, but the door didn't close behind her. Aubrey looked at the others. 'Well?'

George shrugged. 'I'd rather follow her than be stuck here.'

Caroline came close. 'What's wrong with her, Aubrey? She seems . . .'

'Not quite there?' von Stralick offered. 'Either that or she's very ill. Some sort of wasting disease?'

'I don't think it's anything like that,' Aubrey ventured. 'It doesn't seem natural.'

'So it's something unnatural,' Caroline said. 'That's a cheery prospect.'

'In an unnatural place like this,' George said, 'it makes sense.'

'Let's see where she leads.' Aubrey mounted the stairs and stepped into the corridor. Caroline, George and von Stralick came right behind him.

At least the metaphor is consistent, Aubrey thought as they marched along the corridor. The stonework was weighty, gloomy and with the requisite amount of moss and spider webs in the corners overhead. Wall sconces held burning torches at intervals sufficiently spaced to ensure plenty of shifting shadows. They passed other cells, the doors of which were heavy timber, bound with iron. Several of the doors were open and Aubrey peered in as they passed, but the cells were empty.

He caught up to Sylvia. 'Is there anyone else here? Any other prisoners?'

She walked in silence for some time; Aubrey took her head nodding as a sign she was considering the question. Eventually, she made a vague gesture with a hand. 'I have had other guests here. I don't know what happened to them.'

She looked at him with eyes that were pieces of night, and then she looked away. Aubrey shuddered.

Caroline sidled up to him. 'Aubrey,' she said softly. 'How long have we been walking?'

Aubrey blinked. 'I've no idea.'

'Have you noticed how we haven't turned a corner? This is the longest corridor I've ever been in.'

'No cross-corridors either,' von Stralick added.

George scratched his chin. 'I wonder, if we keep going, whether we'll end up back at our cell.'

Aubrey glanced at him sharply. Then he took a few brisk steps to Sylvia's side. 'Where are we going?'

She considered this while they walked on. 'I'm not sure.'

'You're not sure?'

'I like walking.' She nodded, once. 'I want to show you where I spend my time.'

'Is it close?'

'Of course. Here it is.'

Aubrey looked in the direction she was pointing. With a chill, he saw the corridor coming to an arch that he was sure hadn't been there a moment ago. He looked back over his shoulder to see intense wariness from the others.

Well, he thought, *we could go back to the cell*. But then he wondered if it would be that simple.

Sylvia waited at the arch. 'This way.'

Even though he was alert, Aubrey found himself stumbling with surprise when they crossed under the arch. George made a noise as if he'd been struck in the stomach.

We've left the prison, Aubrey thought as he gazed around. *Or if we haven't, penal theory has undergone a radical change.*

They were – suddenly, shockingly – in a charming, sunny drawing room. The scent of roses came in through the open windows, which looked out onto masses of garden colour. Daisies and columbines grew thickly underneath the standard roses, which were the rich, dark red that is only seen in dreams. A stretch of lawn as flat as a bowling green led to an avenue of cypresses which screened off any further view.

The room was airy and pleasant, free of overcrowding knick-knackery. Four easy chairs and a sofa in cheery floral chintz, a glass-fronted bookcase, a tall clock against the far wall, three small tables. A tall vase of irises stood on one of them.

'This is my favourite room.' Sylvia stood gazing through the window, hardly even seeming to breathe. 'It always was.'

Aubrey, without realising it, had spread his arms, as if he'd dropped from a height onto a surface of uncertain footing. Embarrassed, he brought his hands together and rubbed them.

Caroline and von Stralick stood just inside the arch. Caroline's gaze was darting around the room, obviously looking for danger. Von Stralick was equally tense. The only one who looked at ease was George. He stuck his hands in his pockets, sauntered into the room and dropped into one of the armchairs. 'No sense in letting these go to waste,' he said as he made himself comfortable. 'I say, Sylvia. Any chance of a cup of tea? And a bite to eat?'

Sylvia turned around and stared at George as if this was the most remarkable thing she'd ever heard. 'Eat?'

'You know. A scone, a slice of seed cake, something to make the tea go down.'

Aubrey shared a glance with Caroline and von Stralick. Caroline nodded slowly and advanced into the room.

Sylvia didn't notice this unspoken conversation. She was absorbed with George's suggestion. 'That sounds like a good idea.'

She crossed the room and left through a door on the right-hand side of the room.

Aubrey swallowed. 'That door wasn't there before.'

Caroline nodded. 'Before what?'

'Before ever, I'd say. A seat?' he asked Caroline.

Von Stralick watched them, then followed, not without a few backward glances.

Aubrey was pleased to see that Caroline had taken a position on the sofa. He battled with himself for a split-second before he managed to cut off von Stralick and take the seat next to her. She smiled at him tolerantly. He'd have preferred her smiling at him with admiration, or respect, or awe, but tolerance was acceptable.

Sylvia appeared. She drifted in carrying a large silver tea tray piled high with delights, which she placed on a small round table that was between the sofa and George's chair.

That table wasn't there earlier either. Aubrey sat back, frowning, and scanned the room, trying to catalogue every item in it.

He had a puzzle on his hands. Trapped, perhaps in danger, he still couldn't help feeling the thrill of a challenge. His curiosity and his intellect were humming – probing, noticing, appraising, calculating.

He was willing to accept they were trapped inside Dr Tremaine's pearl – the observations fitted with that hypothesis. Finding Dr Tremaine's sister would be too much of a coincidence otherwise. But how were they to get out? Especially if the surroundings changed and flowed with Sylvia's needs.

Sylvia sat on one of the chairs and poured the tea. Aubrey noted how her movements were slow, as if she were moving through something denser than air. George sipped his tea and made a face. His waggling eyebrows alerted Aubrey in time so that he wasn't taken by surprise when he sampled it.

The tea was tasteless. *No, not quite tasteless*, he corrected himself. It had a faint tea taste, as if it had been diluted a hundred times, a memory of tea flavour lingering. And it was barely warm, too.

He put a hand on Caroline's arm, stopping her from raising her cup to her lips. She frowned at him, but quickly saw the lie of the land. She put the cup back on the saucer and balanced it on her lap.

Von Stralick had his eyes on Sylvia and missed the unspoken warnings. He took a mouthful and grimaced. With the aplomb of someone who had been a diplomat, he managed to swallow it instead of spitting it out. He held the cup away from him and stared at it with disgust. Then he glared at Aubrey, who shrugged.

'Cake, George?' Aubrey passed the platter. It was piled with dark-brown slabs, but Aubrey couldn't smell a thing. He felt a little guilty, but decided that George was the right man for any job concerning food.

George snorted, but took a slice. His expression and the shudder after taking a bite was enough for Aubrey to guess that it, too, was not what it appeared.

The awkward silence continued, only broken by von Stralick's stubborn stirring of his tea. The 'tink-tink-tink' of the spoon on the fine china was loud in the room until Aubrey coughed. 'Sylvia. Was it your brother who put you here?'

Sylvia was gazing at the garden. Slowly, she turned her head to Aubrey and, once again, he had the feeling she wasn't all there. 'My brother? Mordecai?'

'That's the one,' Aubrey said.

'Have you seen him?' she said, with a touch of animation – the most feeling Aubrey had seen in the strange, wan woman. 'I miss him so.'

She went to the window and stood, unmoving, gazing at the garden.

Aubrey motioned to von Stralick and George, while keeping a good eye on her. 'We have two ways out of this room,' he said in a low voice, 'if we don't count the garden windows. Caroline and I will try to get some more information from her while you two see what you can find.'

Von Stralick rubbed his chin. 'Reconnoitre and report?'

'Exactly.'

George dropped the cake on a side table. 'Glad to be rid of it. Tasted like ashes.'

Once George and von Stralick had gone, Aubrey and Caroline went to Sylvia at the garden window. Aubrey almost felt as if he were intruding, but the urgency of their situation pressed him forward. 'Forgive me, Sylvia, but I need to ask. Can you remember how you came to be in this place?'

Again, she took her time before she answered and Aubrey had the distinct sense that she was weighing every word he'd uttered, testing them for sense and meaning. 'I thought I had always been here, but your question makes me think.' She paused and the garden drew her gaze again. 'I seem to remember a time when I was elsewhere.'

'With your brother?' Caroline asked.

Sylvia nodded. 'He isn't here so it must have been somewhere else.'

'What can you remember of it?' Aubrey pressed.

'I remember that I wasn't well.' She paused. 'Most grievously ill. Mordecai was at his wits' end.'

Aubrey had a premonition of what was to come. Dr Tremaine wasn't one to admit defeat. The man who was manoeuvring the whole continent to war in his quest for personal immortality wasn't about to let something as trivial as a mortal illness thwart his will.

'He worked magic on you,' he said. 'He's locked you in here, preserved, until he finds a cure for your condition.'

Finding a cure for a condition, Aubrey thought. *I'm not the only one in that pursuit, it seems.*

Without any reaction at all, Sylvia turned back to the garden. Aubrey found her lack of curiosity frustrating. Then he added it to his other observations. Her flatness, her lack of vitality. Her reactions – emotional and otherwise – were slow. It was as if she was missing something essential . . .

She's only living half a life.

The thought was teasing, suggestive, but he needed to know more. 'And why are *we* here?' he asked Sylvia. 'Do you know?'

'To keep me entertained.' She didn't look at him. 'People have appeared, now and then. Perhaps Mordecai sent them.'

'Perhaps he did,' Caroline said carefully. 'And what happened to the other visitors?'

'I think they wore out.'

Aubrey stared. 'Wore out?'

She glanced at him, but her gaze slid across his face, never fixing, never lingering. 'I like watching. But it's sad when they finish.' Her mouth turned down – but maddeningly slowly. 'It will be sad when your friends finish.'

George. 'Where are they?' Aubrey demanded.

Sylvia gestured at the arched entry. 'Out there. I'm sorry.'

Aubrey didn't like the sound of that, but Caroline almost beat him to the door.

'It's probably better to stay here,' Sylvia said. 'This is the safest place.'

Aubrey cursed himself for sending George and von Stralick exploring. He should have been more careful. 'You stay, Caroline. Keep an eye on her.'

Caroline was already at the arch. She grinned fiercely at him. 'You're suggesting we separate and see what happens? How many ghost stories have you read, Aubrey?'

'Right. Let's stay together. As close as possible.'

'Aubrey.'

'It was your idea.'

She sighed. 'The corridor is now going both ways. Choose a direction.'

The archway now opened onto a corridor that stretched into dim distance, both right and left. Both directions were identical – duplicates of the prison corridor, disappearing into infinity. He cocked his head but all he could hear was a thin whistling. Wind? A drift of scent came to him, alternating between dank and dusty, as if it couldn't make up its mind. *Or as if it were being made up on the spot.* 'I don't think it matters.'

'Right is right, then.'

Ten

CAROLINE MARCHED OFF, AND AUBREY HAD TO HURRY to catch up.

'Can you do anything?' Caroline asked him when he'd reached her. 'Anything magical. Can you find them? Or can you stop this place getting us as well? Either would be useful. Both would be best.'

'Ah, yes. Of course.' He walked with arms behind his back, chewing his lip. 'Do you have anything belonging to George or von Stralick?'

'No.'

'Neither do I. There goes any hope of using a location spell.'

'Perhaps you should list the other spells you can't do, to save time thinking about them.'

'I have another idea.'

'I hope so.'

Aubrey cupped his hands to his mouth and shouted. 'George!'

The corridor echoed beautifully and his voice rolled away into the distance. 'Simple. Straightforward. Direct.'

'And not terribly effective. I don't hear any answers.'

'That's because you've given up too early. We have to keep trying.'

So they pressed on, along the hypnotically straight corridor, shouting and listening, shouting and listening, until their voices were hoarse. Eventually, he leaned against the cool stone of the wall and held up a hand. 'Rest stop. Please.'

Caroline nodded, absently. 'Perhaps they went the other way. We should go back.'

'Or they might be just ahead and we should go on.'

Caroline consulted her wrist watch. She was one of the few females of Aubrey's acquaintance who carried a watch, and the only one whose watch was a wrist watch. She did have most elegant wrists, he decided, and it did suit her.

She saw him looking at her. 'We've been going for fifteen minutes.'

'It seems longer.' Aubrey rubbed the bridge of his nose and took a deep breath. Then he frowned and took another. 'Can you smell that?'

Caroline studied him, judged that he wasn't joking, then sniffed, delicately. 'Bread. Freshly baked. And bacon.'

Aubrey wet a finger and held it up. 'It's coming from up ahead.'

'Mmm. Smells like heaven.'

Aubrey went to set off then froze, mid-step. 'That's what I'm afraid of.'

Caroline looked at him with alarm, and he took it as a good reason to look back – which he enjoyed. Then she shook her head with exasperation. 'Can't you keep your mind on our task?'

'Of course. Sorry.'

Which he was. And wasn't. And he didn't know quite what to say about his most mixed of mixed feelings, so he lurched off in a random direction, away from her.

Suddenly, a wave of dizziness struck him and he had to reach out and steady himself against the wall. It was as if his sense of perspective had undulated for an instant, the entire corridor swelling like a balloon before snapping back into place.

Caroline's face was pale.

'You felt it too?' he asked.

She nodded. 'Something changed.'

Aubrey looked back the way they had come, but the corridor was the same as before. He thought about taking a few steps in that direction to find out if they'd passed through something unseen, but the queasiness in his stomach convinced him otherwise. Besides, the smell of freshly baked bread still beckoned.

Ahead, the corridor looked indistinct, slightly misty. 'Do you see that?'

'It's wavery. Foggy.'

'Press on or turn back?'

'I say we press on.'

'Very well.' Shoulder to shoulder, they edged forward. Aubrey could feel the magic on all sides, the subtle background prickling that reminded him that they were inside a pearl.

The corridor rippled again and this time all its dimensions wavered. Height, width and depth stretched and contracted all at once in a movement that made him sick to his stomach, so offensive was it to his innate notion of the solidity of things. Like most people, he'd grown up accepting that buildings just don't warp themselves at random. Dizziness piled on top of his nausea, so much so that he stumbled and clutched at Caroline's arm, but she was quicker and had already gripped his hand. He had the profound sense of a dream transition, where one moment he'd be in a classroom but then a sudden shift would find him in a park, all without any real in-between state.

'Aubrey.' Caroline's grip on his hand was almost painful, but no force in the world would have made him relinquish it. The contact meant nothing, he knew that, apart from the natural human desire for comfort when in danger. But he wasn't going to be the first one to let go.

They found themselves in a gallery, a rectangular walkway looking down on a well-lit room. He took a deep breath. 'All right, so we're somewhere else now.'

'I'm glad you said that,' Caroline whispered. 'I thought I might have been dreaming.'

Aubrey clutched an ornately carved pillar nearby with his free hand, partly for extra steadiness, and partly to reassure himself that this place was real and solid. *Insofar as that means anything around here*, he thought.

Another deep breath. He did his best to take in the new surroundings, nailing down the new reality through empirical observation, doing his best to be a rational, intelligent being.

Four doors, evenly spaced, opened onto the gallery, halfway along each side. They were elegantly set with six glass panes, ruby red. Aubrey nominated the doors as north, south, east and west and felt better for it. The orientation had a settling effect.

A waist-high rail ran around the gallery. It was a rich, red-brown wood, polished smooth. He ran a hand along it and enjoyed the satin touch. The rail surmounted a carved wooden screen made of the same red-brown wood. It was a repeating vegetative pattern, undulating vines alternating with large rosettes.

When Aubrey leaned over the rail he was looking down on a library. The room was lined with bookshelves. Two long tables – covered with books – were arranged in the middle of the room, running along the long axis. A chair stood with each table, while a large red leather armchair took up most of the gap between one of the tables and the north end of the room.

The room smelled of leather and paper, with just a hint of dust. It was the perfect place to enjoy a book, Aubrey decided. Quiet, comfortable, a place to immerse oneself in the world of the written word.

Which is what Hugo von Stralick was doing. With every appearance of bliss, he was reading, standing in front of a wall of books and sampling them with an expression of deep and utter contentment.

It would have been a restful sight, but Aubrey stared, disbelieving, because von Stralick was moving like lightning, picking up books, flicking pages, replacing and extracting another, every movement done with supernatural rapidity.

Agog, Aubrey watched while the Holmland spy sped through a green-bound book he'd plucked from the shelves only seconds earlier. His face was both thoughtful and delighted as he read, his eyes flicking from side to side, his fingers turning pages almost in a blur. His other hand was holding open the gap on the shelf, obviously where the book had come from, with the intention of returning it to its space soon.

Von Stralick was browsing, but it was the browsing of a creature made of pure speed. In seconds, he'd worked his way through a dozen books.

Aubrey met Caroline's wonder-filled eyes. 'What on earth . . .?' she said before words failed her.

'Magic,' Aubrey said simply. The magical power of their prison was propelling von Stralick at breakneck speed. Aubrey shook his head. No, that wasn't right. Von Stralick didn't seem strained or hurried. He was simply moving at a different rate. A phenomenally faster rate.

Aubrey gnawed at a lip. Or could it be that *time* itself was moving at a different rate down there?

He hissed as the implications hit him. If time were speeding away, how much time did von Stralick have left?

'Hugo,' Aubrey called, but von Stralick didn't look up. With eye-watering swiftness, he simply nodded and chuckled – high-pitched – before replacing a fat book. Immediately, he sought another, a slim black volume.

Aubrey called again, but von Stralick was oblivious. 'He's either gone deaf or . . .'

'He can't hear,' Caroline finished. 'What's he doing here? And what happened to the food smells?'

'Food?' Aubrey sniffed. 'It's gone.'

'Library smell only.' Caroline dropped his hand, causing him a momentary pang, and leaned over the railing. 'Let's go down and see what's going on.'

'It would help if there were a staircase.'

Caroline straightened. 'Ah. Rather a glaring omission.'

'It seems as if we're not meant to get down there.'

'Well, if there's no stairway, we'll have to find another way down.' She frowned slightly as she measured the drop by eye. 'It's not that far. Twenty feet from this rail. Less from the floor.'

'It's too far to jump.' Aubrey drummed his fingers on the rail and hummed a little. 'I don't suppose there are any bed sheets lying around? Nothing we could tie together to lower ourselves down?'

'No.'

'Didn't think so. So perhaps it might be better to attract his attention.' He bent and unlaced a boot. 'I'm sure he won't be able to ignore this.'

'I'm glad you wore your good socks.'

'Socks?' He looked down. 'So that's where they went.'

'Aubrey.'

'Of course. I'll get on with it.' He hefted his boot, measured the distance, paused for dramatic effect, then threw it at von Stralick.

The boot sailed in an arc, but Aubrey's jaw dropped when, mid-way and in mid-air, it bounced once, then settled, bobbing slightly like a cork on a pond, well above von Stralick's head.

Caroline tutted. 'I don't think you should try the other boot, not even for balance.'

'Right. Good idea.' Trying to make sense of this impossible spectacle, Aubrey leaned over the rail. He grunted, reaching down as far as he could, but couldn't feel anything. He straightened and then went to climb over the rail.

Caroline put her hands on her hips. 'What on earth are you doing?'

'Testing. I need more data, more observations before I can work out what's going on.'

'It's something invisible, something that's keeping us from von Stralick and something unknown. Isn't that enough?'

'It's a good start, but I need more.'

Aubrey stepped over the rail, balanced on the narrow ledge, held onto the rail with both hands and stretched out a foot – his booted foot.

Ah.

Not far below the level of the gallery he struck a surface. It was spongy and giving, like a balloon filled with water. He pressed, and his foot sank. He pressed harder and the invisible material resisted, pushing him back.

'I wonder if he can even see us,' Aubrey muttered, while eyeing his boot, stranded in the middle of the unseen barrier. Von Stralick looked as if he was trapped in a bubble – a bubble where time flowed differently.

And if he spends much longer in it, Aubrey thought, *he'll start to age*. With a growing hollowness in his chest, he wondered how long a lifespan was in such a place. It must be shorter, but how short? Sylvia had mentioned others, but had also mentioned that they had worn out . . .

Caroline helped him scramble back over the rail. 'It's as if he's on display.' She gazed around the gallery. 'Like a zoo.'

'Mmm. For Sylvia?'

'She's the only one here. I have the impression that this whole place is for her benefit.'

'To spy on someone in a library?' Aubrey rubbed his temples. 'It seems rather excessive.'

'Craddock and Tallis would love a facility like this. If they could observe suspects in their normal surroundings, they might learn a thing or two.'

'Learn a thing or two.'

'Aubrey, when you repeat my words like that, it means I've said something that made you think.'

'Perhaps.'

'If so, and if you come up with something clever, I want to register that I was the one who started the whole thing.'

'Done. Due credit will be given to you in the playbill when this little drama hits the stage. "From an original idea by the redoubtable Caroline Hepworth."'

'Redoubtable.' Caroline flashed a quick smile. 'I like that. It makes a change from "capable" or "competent".'

Aubrey had a thousand other words he could use to describe Caroline, but he refrained, lest she see that his feelings hadn't disappeared. They were hidden, put aside, honouring her request to stay at arm's length.

The sudden opening of the gallery's north door made Aubrey whirl. He felt absurdly vulnerable, with one boot on, one boot off. So it was with relief that he realised that it was the wraith-like Sylvia who was drifting through the doorway.

She glanced mildly at von Stralick, who was so absorbed in a weighty volume that he turned the pages only every few seconds, then she walked slowly toward Aubrey and Caroline. 'You found him,' she said, with the barest trace of surprise. Aubrey realised that this was her way. She had ghosts of emotion, hints, suggestions, nothing that took hold of her, no passion or intensity – apart from the memory of her brother.

'I watch them,' she said, interrupting his thoughts. 'My guests. I watch them once they're appropriately housed.'

Aubrey studied her face. It moved in slight, hesitant ways, as if feelings were strangers.

'What about us?' Caroline said.

'Oh, you'll be housed soon. Don't worry.'

Aubrey swallowed. 'In a library?'

'That's his dream, not yours.' Sylvia lay a finger along her cheek. 'I suppose you could end up in a library, but it would be different. Yours, not his.'

Caroline stiffened. 'Are you saying that you'll put us somewhere like von Stralick? But it will be our dream?'

'So it seems.' A suggestion of an anxious frown flitted across Sylvia's mask-like face but it evaporated in an instant. 'I don't do anything, you know. I just watch. It's hard to learn when I don't have anyone to watch.'

'Wait,' Caroline said. 'You're learning? Learning what?'

A flicker of confusion crossed Sylvia's face before she was, once again, serene. 'I'm not sure.'

'Von Stralick,' Aubrey said, pointing. 'What's he doing?'

'What he likes to do, what he does best.'

Aubrey was surprised. He hadn't imagined von Stralick's idea of heaven was being surrounded by books. 'Does he know you're watching?'

'No. He thinks it's real.'

'Like a convincing dream,' Aubrey said. Caroline glanced at him. She could see the danger, too. 'So we'll be in a place like that, unaware that it's not real, and just going about our business for your entertainment.'

A hint of shock; her hand almost went to her mouth before it dropped, once again, to her side. 'No. Not entertainment. Learning.'

It was Caroline who leaped to the conclusion this time. 'And his life goes faster in there, the better for you to watch and learn?'

Sylvia peered over the rail, her expression dreamy. 'It appears so. It gets faster, too. Especially toward the end.'

Aubrey wasn't enchanted by this. 'You said you had other . . . visitors. Ones who aren't here now. They were in places like this?'

'Not libraries,' Sylvia murmured. She rested her chin on one hand as she propped an elbow on the rail. 'I remember one was in a laboratory, a magical laboratory. She loved it. Another, one of my favourites, was living in a forest among the pines.'

'They're gone.' Caroline's face was determined, but Aubrey could see that the ghastly fate of those who had gone before was haunting her.

He found he had to steel himself as well, and he concentrated on noting how callous Dr Tremaine was, how careless of the lives of others. He had some sympathy for Sylvia's plight, and he'd even thought he'd detected Dr Tremaine's humanity in trying to save her – but in the end he was essentially as selfish as ever. He'd sacrifice others without a thought to achieve his ends.

And you're preparing to sacrifice Sylvia to serve your ends, a voice whispered. *Are you so different?*

He shook his head. Conscience. Imagination mixed with empathy.

'Gone,' Sylvia murmured. 'One day, they were near their end, and the next I couldn't find them or their happy place.'

Aubrey had a new definition of nightmare. Trapped in a make-believe place, imprisoned but never knowing it. But his inner contrariness pointed out that being granted heaven couldn't be a bad thing . . .

Living a hoax would be, though, Aubrey thought and he shuddered, thinking of the ant farm he'd kept as a young lad. The ants had been well fed and watered and he had watched their busy industry for hours, convinced that they were much better off than they would be out in the wild.

Unfeeling manipulation. It was an easy frame of mind to slip into, and rewarding in its sense of power. Aubrey vowed never to succumb to it.

'Where's George?' he asked Sylvia. 'And how do we get them out of here?'

'Get them out?' She looked at him as if he'd asked her to draw a four-sided triangle. 'It's where they belong.'

'Not us.' Caroline pushed past the pale woman, heading for the north door. 'Aubrey, time to follow our noses.'

Aubrey looked back to see Sylvia with one elbow on the rail, leaning over, studying the scene below as if she were on a riverbank on a lazy summer's afternoon.

On the other side of the door was the stone prison corridor again – and the tantalising smell of food. The smell of bread was overlaid with other aromas – bacon, coffee, and something fresh and fruity. 'Food,' Aubrey said, staring at the doors stretching out on either side of the corridor. His stomach growled.

'Real food.' Caroline peered ahead. 'And where there's food . . .'

'We should be able to find George.' Aubrey set off, trying not to limp with his unbooted foot. Of course George's idea of heaven would involve good food, and plenty of it.

'This one, I think.' Caroline drew up in front of a door. Aubrey sniffed and had to agree. It was like standing in front of the world's best pastry shop during the morning baking. She pushed the door, it swung open and they stepped out onto another gallery.

Aubrey stopped short. 'That's not what I imagined.'

He'd expected George to be sitting back at a table laden with delicacies, being waited on, new dishes being thrust upon him, sampling, grazing, appreciating good food and drink. Instead, his friend was speeding about a kitchen – working like a whirlwind. One look at his white jacket, hound's-tooth trousers and the tell-tale puffy white hat and it was obvious that George's heaven was food-related – but as a chef, not as a gourmand.

'Hidden depths, perhaps,' Caroline murmured as she leaned over.

Aubrey knew he shouldn't have been surprised. George was the most generous person he knew. His idea of heaven wouldn't be selfish, pleasing himself, it would be providing goodness for others.

The kitchen was spotless. The floor was made of gleaming white tiles, while the great cast-iron stove that took up one side of the room was black. It beat out heat that Aubrey could feel from the gallery. He could also smell the baking bread smell from the man-sized oven on the opposite wall.

Which made him think and, without realising it, he began to hum as he drummed his fingers on the rail and pondered the situation. Heat, smell, and light obviously passed through the barrier – at least, in one direction. Was it permeable in both?

He took in the rest of the scene with a glance while he was thinking feverishly. Fresh wooden benches, a large trough, shelves and a servery window ledge where George was a blur, arranging plates of gorgeous-looking food. Breakfast, from the look of it, with bacon, eggs, mushrooms and neatly grilled tomatoes. George was managing to keep plate after plate moving through his kitchen and onto the ledge of the servery window, topped with piping hot toast with nary a sign of burning. The plates disappeared, whisked away, but try as he might, Aubrey couldn't see how. One instant they were waiting, the next they were gone.

George was sweating, red-faced, and grinning as he shook pans, cracked eggs and slapped bacon on a large griddle, cooking up a storm. He moved with smooth economy of effort but with the same prodigious speed that had infected von Stralick. Aubrey was impressed, but not surprised. He knew George's large frame made people think he was clumsy, but George had a natural fluency of movement that would be called grace in another person. His sporadic efforts with the cornet showed that he was dextrous, and once he realised that dancing was a good way to meet young women, he had become very accomplished on the dance floor.

Aubrey took a sixpence from his pocket and spun it into the air. It glittered and arced toward where George was busily working. Then it struck the invisible barrier and hung in the air, gently moving up and down like a cork on the sea. 'The barrier is selective,' he said to Caroline. 'We can see him, he can't see us.'

'But smells are getting out. And sounds,' Caroline said as George dumped a pan into the sink. It clattered against a collection of dirty utensils.

'Or is it that nothing is getting in from this side? Light isn't getting through, that's why he can't see us. No sound, so he can't hear us. That makes it a one-way barrier.'

'You're trying to think of a way to get in.'

'Of course. Before our turn comes.'

Aubrey felt as if he were wrestling with a dozen ideas and possibilities at once. He was hard-pressed to deal with them all as they grappled, pulled and gouged at him. He'd worked with scores of spells and had knowledge of hundreds more. But if he was dealing with Dr Tremaine, he knew that he'd be up against very special magic. This whole place was magically constructed, and it also had an ongoing responsibility. It preserved Sylvia, and provided the environment that supported and protected her, as well as snatching outsiders and imprisoning them.

First question: could anything pass through the barrier both ways? If he could determine that, it may give him something to work with.

Air, that was for certain. Neither George nor von Stralick showed any signs of gasping for breath. He shook his head, violently, and scowled.

'No answer yet?' Caroline asked.

'No.' He was acutely aware of his sock-clad foot. He tried to curl it around his leg. 'I thought air was the answer, but the whole floor below is isolated from the gallery. It could have its own source of air.'

'True.' Caroline joined him. She, too, gripped the rail and scowled over George's busy domain. Aubrey decided that a scowl, on her, was decidedly becoming.

She turned to him. 'You said the barrier felt spongy.'

He nodded. 'Springy, definitely not a rigid barrier.'

'Your boot was bobbing up and down. It would tend to indicate that the surface undulates.'

'It wasn't liquid, if that's what you're thinking,' Aubrey said, but Caroline had set him thinking in a different direction. 'More like a rubbery blanket, held at four corners but not drawn taut.'

'Allowing room for expansion? This whole place must be adaptable, from what we've seen.'

The solution was close, hovering just beyond reach, Aubrey knew it. Talking aloud, working with Caroline was a definite help – another good reason to keep associating with her. 'I couldn't push my way through it. It resisted effectively enough.'

'If you can't push through it, why not try to pierce it?'

He smacked himself on the forehead. 'Of course. Or we could slice it.' He looked around, then patted his pockets. 'Of all the days to forget my sword.'

'I was thinking of that scythe you left behind,' Caroline said, keeping a straight face. 'Rather short-sighted of you.'

'You're right. Next time before we head off for a spot of adventuring, could you please remind me to take some sort of large, sharp-edged implement? Agricultural or military, doesn't really matter.'

For a moment, swept up in the banter, they caught and held each other's gaze. In a heartbeat, Aubrey felt a wave of emotion so intense that it almost made him stumble. His affection for her, his desire to be near her shook him – and he thought he saw it mirrored in her eyes. *No*, he told himself sternly, the voice of duty coming to the fore. *It's wishful thinking. Don't deceive yourself.*

'Aubrey,' she said. She looked away, briefly, then she brought her gaze to bear on him, steady, luminous and all-enveloping.

It took all his strength, but with a great effort he coughed and took a tiny, shuffling step back, unsure if it was the right thing to do but feeling it was the *only* thing to do. 'No sharp objects?' he said lightly. He wiped his face with a hand. 'Right, then it'll have to be magic.'

She paused a moment, then hooded her eyes. 'Of course. That's your department.'

Was it his imagination, or did her voice catch a little? 'Indeed.' He cudgelled his brains, but no ready-made spell summoning large, sharp blades immediately sprang to mind.

So it's back to first principles, he thought, glad of the distraction of wrestling with spell elements.

Slicing, piercing, bisecting, dissecting. Could he conjure up some sort of force to cut the barrier? The Law of Division had some useful applications when it came to chopping up substances, but ensuring that each bit still retained the characteristics of the whole . . .

He stared at where the barrier must be. Perhaps he was thinking about this the wrong way.

Just as it was a necessary part of many applications to limit the time of a spell's effect using the Principle of Duration, many spells limited the spell's range by including a component based on the Principle of Range of Effect. A restraining diagram was another magical way of achieving the same thing.

Which was, Aubrey realised, just like putting a barrier around a spell.

If he could take this principle and invert it, it might be a way to *remove* a barrier instead of putting one in place. With a snort, he remembered the old Arabian fairy story where a simple 'Open Sesame!' was enough to open a magically sealed doorway. He wondered if it was the 'sesame' that did it, or if naming any aromatic seed would have done the trick – and he wished things were that simple in the real world.

If he were to make this work, he needed to construct a spell that would cover extent, duration, physical parameters, intensity and range of effect, as well as dealing with the time differential. His spell would need to manipulate time, space and also the intricacies of another's magic, all without creating channels where the intersecting magics would feed upon each other, perhaps creating ferocious confluences which could run out of control.

And, of course, he was mindful of Ravi's Second Principle: the more complex the spell construction, the more effort is required from the spell caster. Unconsciously, he fingered the Beccaria Cage that lay against his chest. After the late Lanka Ravi's masterly exposition, Aubrey understood its significance in an intensely personal manner. Performing magic was perhaps the most taxing thing he could do, and it was the act most likely to stress the bond between his body and soul. The so-far useful magic of the cage would likely be tested most when he performed complex magic as he was about to do now. Would it hold? Or would it collapse, sending him into a crisis?

And did he have any options?

'It's dangerous,' Caroline said, watching his face.

'Perhaps,' he said, with a fair stab at calmness. 'We'll soon find out.'

He decided to use Danaan, a language he'd been immersed in. With the efficiency of effort he'd learned since beginning university ('Don't re-invent the wheel!' Professor Fortescue was fond of saying in his Aspects of Spell Construction lectures. 'Reuse parts of spells that have worked well in the past!') he plucked components from spells he'd hammered out for temperature stabilisation, light intensity and controlled acceleration of distant bodies. Of course, none of these were in Danaan, so he had to translate them in his head, but luckily none of the numerative determinants were outlandish.

'You might like to stand back,' he said to Caroline when he was ready.

She nodded, gripping her hands tightly in front of her. 'No theatrics. Just get the job done.'

He threw her a quick grin. 'Bare-bones magic this time, I assure you. I want to get out of here quickly.'

He cleared his mind and then drummed his fingers on the rail while he gathered himself. Then he lifted his hands and rubbed them together to find that they were sweating, a sign that his body knew it was nervous, even if he denied it.

He coughed, clearing his throat, and tried to ignore the fact that Caroline was watching him like a hawk – and the fact that he was wasting time.

He settled, then began, every muscle in his body taut. The first component (delineation) came smoothly, then the spell was under way.

A small part of Aubrey's mind monitored his performance, the inner critic ready to carp, but each element unfolded with the clarity, the certainty of purpose of a master mason building a wall.

The inner critic, however, had a proviso. It was bricklaying of the sort where a mason builds a wall by standing ten yards away and lobbing the bricks into place one by one, blindfolded.

Eleven

A SOFT 'POP!' SIGNALLED THAT THE SPELL HAD BEEN successful. The floating sixpence tumbled to land at George's feet. Aubrey had a moment's alarm when he felt, through his magical senses, a fleeting examination, a distant awareness turned his way, but then it was gone.

George was looking up, startled. He held a frying-pan in one hand. It had an omelette in it. 'I say!' he said in a voice that was completely normal in pitch and pace. 'What are you two doing there?' Then he looked at the frying-pan, his clothes and his surroundings. 'More to the point, what am I doing here?'

Caroline looked to Aubrey, but he didn't answer. 'Magic, George,' she said. 'Best not to dally. Can you climb out of there?'

George looked around, bewildered. 'It's not a dream?'

'No.' Aubrey was a little dazed himself, but it was a minor cost for such a complicated spell. Then he realised that something warm was nestled against his chest.

The Beccaria Cage.

He fumbled under his shirt and found the wire mesh was warm to the touch. Warmer than could be explained just by skin contact. He wanted to inspect the artefact to see what was going on, but a metallic crash shook him out of his introspection.

'Here, old man, what about a hand?'

George was balanced on an huge upturned stock pot that he'd placed on one of the benches. Cookware was still bouncing on the hard tiled floor, the result of his making room, but Aubrey saw that George had removed all the pans from the stove top to keep their contents from burning. Thoughtful to the last.

George grasped Aubrey's proffered hands, but Aubrey immediately found himself slipping until Caroline came to his rescue. She anchored him delightfully, bracing his shoulders while George clambered over the rail. 'What is going on?' George said as he brushed himself down. He plucked his chef's hat from his head and regarded it curiously.

'What do you remember?' Caroline shepherded both George and Aubrey to the western door.

'I went to explore, as agreed.' George frowned, flapped a hand. 'That's about it.'

'You were sucked into your dream,' Aubrey said. 'You were given a place where you'd be happy, and you were going to stay there.'

'A velvet prison, eh?' George glanced over his shoulder. 'Never really thought about cooking like that.'

'Did you enjoy it?' Aubrey asked. Caroline opened the door.

'It all seems a bit distant now. But it strikes me that I did.' He looked thoughtful and stroked his chin. 'I thought it was real.'

'You would have been happy. Deceived but happy.'

'Forever?'

'It would have been a lifetime, at any rate.'

They found von Stralick's library prison with only one false start. Sylvia wasn't there.

Von Stralick was less philosophical than George. After Aubrey and Caroline shared the explanation, he was angry. 'She was going to watch me? Like a zoo creature?' he burst out after a pile of books on top of a table had provided his escape.

'There you go, von Stralick,' George said. 'You're a specimen.'

Von Stralick shot George a look, but restrained himself. He straightened his lapels and brushed his jacket. 'Now, let us get out of here.'

Easier said than done, Aubrey thought as he laced up his retrieved boot. He studied the four doors.

'We should find Sylvia,' Caroline suggested. 'She's at the heart of this.'

George grimaced. 'Our keeper? I'd have thought it was a good idea to stay away from her.'

'If anyone has answers, it will be her,' von Stralick said, automatically taking up a contrary stance from George. They eyed each other steadily. Aubrey could see the tension. Much of it could have come from being wrenched from a happy dream, but some of it went back to their simmering antipathy.

'I have an idea,' he said abruptly. The other three swivelled and locked on him. It was like walking out onto the stage and having the spotlight find him, solo, the centre of attention.

He never minded that.

He adopted a pose designed to inspire confidence – shoulders back, feet apart just so, one fist on a hip and the other hand on the chest. It had worked well in the production of *The Barber and the Berber* and he was a little disappointed at the uniform scepticism that faced him, but he ploughed ahead. 'This whole place, the prison in the pearl, is a magical construct. She said that she doesn't do anything here – it's all done for her. This suggests that to keep his sister safe, Dr Tremaine provided the place with a guardian spell, one that would bend the place to her whim – and provide her with opportunities for learning.'

'That's you, von Stralick,' George pointed out.

'And you too,' von Stralick said. 'Although what she could learn from you, I have no idea. How to be a buffoon, perhaps?'

'I felt something earlier,' Aubrey continued, 'when I freed George. I think it could be this guardian. It lies inward, at the heart of this place, like a control room in a foundry. If we can find it, I might be able to manipulate it to free us.'

As long as it's a passive watcher spell, he thought. The possibility of it being rather more aggressive did cross his mind, but he thought it wiser not to raise this.

Aubrey asked Caroline to choose a door. Without hesitating, she took them through the northern door; once again they were in the stone walls of the prison corridors.

Caroline raised an eyebrow at Aubrey. 'Well?'

'Let me see what I can do.'

Caroline adopted an alert attitude, doing her best not to look at Aubrey. George and von Stralick, too, were on guard.

Which left Aubrey to ply his magic.

This should be straightforward, he thought, and his hand brushed the bump of the Beccaria Cage under his shirt. It no longer felt warm, but now was not the time to investigate.

Straightforward. All he wanted to do was use his magical awareness to sense the density of the surrounding magic, hoping to trace it to its source. Since this whole place was a magical construct, it was imbued with power, every wall, every stone positively dripping with it. If he concentrated he hoped to be able to detect differences, quite unlike trying to trace magic in the ordinary world, where its faintness was easily swamped by the vigour of the everyday.

He wasn't trying to cast a spell. It shouldn't arouse the interest of the guardian. Using his magical awareness was passive, like a radio antenna catching messages crossing the ether.

He closed his eyes and concentrated, extending his awareness to the surroundings, and immediately gasped. To his magical senses, the walls of the prison corridor were dull, glowing blocks, beating ruddily like coals in the heart of a fire. When he turned, he could also feel the floor and ceiling, radiating magic with the same muted intensity.

He took a step, eyes still closed, and bumped straight into someone. Immediately, he knew it was Caroline. His eyes flew open and he apologised, but Caroline shook it off. 'Didn't you see me?' she asked.

'I had my eyes closed.' He thought about it. 'I can sense the walls, but not you.' He shut his eyes and extended his awareness again. He swivelled his head. The construction of the prison corridor was clear, if dim, but all he could sense with his pseudo-sight was the structure. He couldn't see Caroline, or George, or von Stralick. And when he looked down, he couldn't see himself. The only things that registered were those imbued with magic.

'It helps to keep my eyes closed, but I need to keep moving,' Aubrey said to them after he opened his eyes again. 'That way I can detect the fluctuations in the magic field and steer us in the right direction.'

'Here.' Caroline offered her arm. 'I'll lead you.'

It was all Aubrey could do not to jump at the opportunity.

He took Caroline's arm gently. She drew him close, and he sternly told himself that made good sense, the better to guide him past any obstacles. He refused to linger on her perfume (violets) or the fact that her forearm was slim but strong under the crepe de chine.

They walked on, Caroline leading with firm confidence, murmuring the occasional warning when it seemed he was veering too close to a wall. Soon, however, Aubrey was lost in the magical radiance about him. At times, he had the impression of layers, hinting at the expanses that lay beyond the nearer walls. This double-sense was unsettling at first, experiencing the magical world so pressing, smouldering with subdued power, while other senses reported the real world. He heard the footfalls of his friends, their breathing.

Gradually, he was able to sense differences in the magic. Mostly, the walls, floors and ceilings were a dim red, almost brown. But sometimes patches of wall glowed more urgently, a brighter red, almost shading into orange. He stopped at one of these and placed his palm on it to test his judgement. He felt a tingling on his skin that confirmed his growing feeling that when the phantom colours were brighter, the magic was more intense.

Gradually, the changes in field intensity began to resolve themselves. Aubrey was sure he was looking at interlocking pieces, as if the whole place were a gigantic, shifting puzzle, one of those wooden ones where the configuration could be changed – with the right will and the right intent.

'On and on it goes,' von Stralick muttered. 'A lack of imagination is present here, I fear.'

'A lack of imagination, perhaps,' Caroline said, 'but not a lack of determination. I think we're being followed.'

Aubrey winced. 'Sylvia?'

'I imagine so,' Caroline said.

'If it's not her,' George said, 'I don't think I want to find out who it is.'

'What could she want?' von Stralick said.

'She might be wondering where her new exhibits have gone,' Aubrey said. 'She might want them back.'

'Back in her terrarium?' George said. 'I'm not enchanted with that prospect. How far have we got to go?'

'It goes on forever,' von Stralick said.

'Not forever,' Aubrey said. 'This way.'

According to his sensing, they'd turned three left-hand corners and crossed four intersections. Each time, he'd briefly opened his eyes and found that the real world did not mirror his magical senses.

Nevertheless, he was sure they were headed in the right direction. The background glowing was increasing in intensity and the walls were now a dark cherry-red, with highlights of orange and yellow where a corner or intersection appeared.

He noted that each corner was in the same direction. When faced with a choice of direction, the increasing intensity was always to the left, even if his friends didn't notice it.

And he was sure they were going inward.

This impression was nothing to do with his magical awareness. It was a suspicion, nothing more. Were his feet, his calves telling him that the floor was sloping? Was the floor subtly grading downward? If so, with the left-hand turns that were coming more frequently, did that mean they were spiralling inward?

To the heart of the place?

He only realised that he had tensed his grip when Caroline spoke. 'Is something wrong?' He admired her self-possession. She had no trace of alarm or even tension in her voice. If there was something wrong, she was looking to do something about it rather than to panic.

'We may be getting nearer to our goal,' he said. They reached a three-way intersection. Aubrey led them to the left-hand branch.

'Good. You have a spell ready?'

Aubrey nodded. 'Just in case.'

'We may not need it. But better to have something ready and not use it than to need something and not have it available.'

Good sense, Aubrey thought. But then again, Caroline was nothing if not sensible.

He did enjoy it, though, when she wasn't. The sensible, dutiful Caroline often overwhelmed the carefree, cheeky Caroline, the one that was only seen in glimpses. But he couldn't quibble. Duty tended to rule his life as well. With such prominent parents, with such expectations from society, what choice did he have?

It could be worse. They took another left-hand turn. *I could be Bertie. Now there's someone where duty comes first, middle and last.*

Aubrey absently took another left-hand turn while he pondered the thorny issue of duty and individual dreams. This meant that he didn't notice the blazing wall of magic until Caroline nudged him.

'Aubrey. What are we going to do?'

He lifted his head, eyes still closed, and gasped. 'Good Lord!' Automatically, he flung up a hand to protect himself.

Their path was blocked by a burning wall of fire – at least, that's what it looked like to his magical pseudo-sight. Bright orange-white, it seared, a crackling, potent magic barrier.

Confronted by such an outpouring of raw magic, he staggered and opened his eyes.

And gaped at a featureless stone wall.

'A dead end, it looks,' von Stralick said. 'I hope you've brought us here for a reason.'

'Aubrey never does anything without a reason,' George said. He paused. 'Well, he does sometimes but then it turns out that he had a reason after all. After the fact, if you know what I mean.'

Aubrey shook himself. The difference between his magical apprehension and what confronted them in the real world was so extraordinarily vast that he was having trouble coming to terms with it. They both reinforced each other – one was a magical barrier, the other an equally effective material barrier – but as he dealt with the overlapping double-sensed impressions he realised that it was what lay on the other side that was important.

Though the wall itself was highly charged with magic, he could feel even more forceful magic coming from the other side and it made him extremely nervous. It was like hearing a tiger behind a closed door and wondering how strong the timber was.

Despite this, there was only one way to go.

'We have to get through,' he said. 'What we're seeking is on the other side.'

He inched closer to the wall. He felt as if he were walking into a stiff breeze as the magical power pushed against him and he had to lean into it. He placed a hand on its surface and felt a prickling, a tingling. Drawing back, he sensed that the surface of the barrier wasn't as uniform as he had first thought. In his pseudo-sight, it actually rippled with power, shimmers of brighter colour streaking across it, forming patterns, a subtle, lace-like tracery. He took a step back and tried to take in the whole wall, tried to apprehend the delicate weaving and twisting of magic, but he found it difficult. The further away he was, the harder it was to make out as it merged and blurred into one fiery whole.

Then, just a pace or two away to his left, he noticed a fine silvery-orange line that was suspiciously straight and well-defined against the branching rivulets of magic that ran across the wall. He moved closer and, with some difficulty, was able to discern that the line turned at right-angles. He sighed with relief.

'I think we have a door.' He touched the surface to make sure. He opened his eyes and rubbed his hands together. The tingling persisted, turning into a fading sense of pins and needles.

'Where?' Caroline asked.

'Here.' Aubrey stepped back when the stone wall swung inward.

George steadied him with a hand. 'Good show, old man!'

'Wait. Can you hear something?'

Von Stralick frowned. 'Voices. Many.'

'But they're whispering,' George said. 'Whatever for?'

'I have no idea,' Aubrey said, 'but I think we need to find out.'

Aubrey waited for a moment, giving anything lethal a chance to lunge out at them. He was grateful when it didn't. Finding secret doors into areas of great magic only to have something ravenous and many-toothed swarm out wasn't one of his favourite pursuits.

He eased through the doorway, his blinding light spell on his lips and every nerve alert. Then he stopped, gaping, as the others entered. George and von Stralick stifled oaths, while Caroline's eyes were wide with astonishment.

The space was too grand to be called a room, and too outlandish. It was a white ovoid twenty yards or so in diameter, softly shimmering with the lustre of . . .

Pearl, he thought, but it was more than that. The

walls, the ceiling were curved and the sheen captured all the subtle iridescence of nacre and magnified it a thousandfold. It was the *heart* of the pearl.

The entire space was filled with ghosts – and all of them were Sylvia Tremaine. Murmuring, whispering, vacant-eyed replicas of their host.

Aubrey prided himself on being a rationalist. A modern magician couldn't be anything else, since contemporary magic insisted on empirical observation, measurable evidence and reproducible results.

He may have known that, but deep in his primitive self didn't. He backed against the gently curving wall, his skin feeling two sizes too small. His stomach knotted as fear took hold.

The ghosts ignored him. A score or more of them, transparent, insubstantial, drifted around the room whispering to themselves, their voices combining to fill the room with the sound of moth wings.

Aubrey's breathing slowed as he began to sort through what he was seeing. It wasn't a conscious decision, it was simply an extension of the way he saw the world. It was a place that could be made sense of – with enough thought, intelligence and insight.

The insubstantial figures were indeed replicas of Sylvia, and they didn't seem to notice him watching them. With interest, he saw how they disregarded each other even when their gliding, erratic paths brought them close to another ghost. His eyes widened as two of the insubstantial figures actually intersected, passing through each other as if neither was there.

Observation, he thought shakily. *More data needed*. He signalled to the others, taking them from their silent amazement, and indicated that they were to be ready to act. He steeled himself and held out a hand, right in the path of one of the wanderers.

Blank-eyed, hands clutched at breast level, the transparent Sylvia replica didn't pause in her step. She simply passed straight through Aubrey's hand, leaving him wringing it and frowning.

It had felt as if he'd dipped his hand in ice water, but that was all. The Sylvia replica had drifted through him as if he wasn't there. Aubrey could make out her whisperings, but the words made no sense to him: 'Lost, lonely, lost and lonely. Lost, lonely, lost and lonely.'

He trotted alongside, but the words didn't vary. Over and over again: 'Lost, lonely, lost and lonely. Lost, lonely, lost and lonely.'

Curious, he turned and followed another only to hear a similar nonsense. 'Far away, far away, far away.'

He shuddered when he listened into a third – 'It hurts so, make it stop. It hurts so . . .' – delivered with what he could only call a deadpan expression, and he hoped Bertie would forgive him for that.

He'd only ever seen one thing that had any resemblance to these apparitions – and that was his own soul, once it had been disrupted from his body. These were similar. More insubstantial, less *real* – if that made any sense in this sort of thing – but there was definitely a similarity.

A hand fell on his shoulder and he yelped, the noise cutting through the echoing susurrus of whispers and echoing around the pearl chamber.

'Steady on, old man,' George said. 'We've got to get out of here.'

'What? Why?'

'Sylvia says so.' George pointed at the ghostly figures in their endless promenade around the pearl chamber. 'They mustn't be let out.'

'I am a larger piece than those poor things,' Sylvia said. 'They are tiny splinters, hardly holding themselves together.'

Once again, they were in the sitting room. Outside, it appeared to be later afternoon, shadows creeping over the garden.

'We are all made of many parts,' Aubrey said carefully, unsure what she meant.

'So true. So true.' Sylvia pondered this for a time. She stared at the wall over Aubrey's left shoulder for so long that he turned to see what was so interesting. *Unless she's fascinated by flat, pale blue paint*, he thought, *then she's lost her train of thought.*

'Now then, Sylvia,' George said, taking advantage of what was proving to be a very large gap in the conversation, 'd'you think you could help us get out of here? We'd like to go home, you see.'

'Home.' Sylvia lingered over the word. 'I had a home, once.'

'Of course you did,' von Stralick said. 'Now, about getting us out of here . . .'

'They spoke like you, there.' She looked at him with a flicker of interest. 'They sounded like you.'

'Holmlanders?' Aubrey jumped in. He wanted to keep that flicker alive. 'Did you once live in Holmland?'

'I was born there,' she said simply. 'And so was Mordecai. I seem to remember we were happy.'

Aubrey sat back in his chair. This was a remarkable piece of information: the first hint Aubrey had ever heard that the great Dr Tremaine was actually a Holmlander.

'Now,' Sylvia said. 'You must go back in your places. You have been so inventive, so elusive, that I'm sure I have much to learn from you.'

George coughed. 'Look here, Sylvia. I think I'm speaking for everyone here when I say that's not what we'd prefer.'

'I agree with Doyle,' von Stralick said, without a trace of irony. 'We must leave. Now.'

'I don't think so.' A touch of a frown wafted across Sylvia's brow. 'You will stay here.'

Even though her voice was soft and wan, Aubrey could hear the surety in her voice – and it was the absolute certainty of her brother. To Dr Tremaine, the universe was simply how he saw it, nothing more complicated than that.

Occasionally, Aubrey found himself admiring such unswerving self-belief, but more often he found himself wondering what such an attitude *missed*. He felt it could lead to overlooking things, ignoring things that were only ever thought of if one bothered to reflect.

It doesn't seem to have stopped Dr Tremaine, though.

His thoughts were interrupted by George standing up and pacing the room. His friend didn't look happy. 'Sylvia, I don't mean to be rude, but we don't belong here. It was an accident that brought us inside your place.'

'It doesn't matter.' Sylvia brushed the cushion of the settee with her hand, even though it looked perfectly clean. 'You'll be happy here.'

'That's not the point,' Caroline said. 'We don't want to be here.'

'That doesn't matter either.'

Aubrey tried another tack. 'Sylvia. What were those things in the pearl chamber? Why shouldn't they be let out?'

'The pearl chamber?' Sylvia tilted her head back and studied the ceiling. 'I remember.'

'Of course you do. You said we had to keep the door closed.'

'Yes. Or else they'd find the open door and wander. It took so long to find them all last time.'

'Last time?'

'When we came here. After Mordecai's spell.'

'Wait. You said you were a larger part than those things in the chamber.'

Sylvia nodded. 'Mordecai. To save me from my sickness. He said he was manipulating the Law of Separation.'

Aubrey saw it immediately. 'Oh.'

'What is it, Aubrey?' Caroline asked.

He chose his words carefully. 'The Law of Separation states that a whole can be divided and reunited again without any harm, as long as all the correct limitations are placed on the constituent parts.'

When Sylvia spoke again it was as if it was from a long way away. 'He wanted to separate me. He said he would divide me into my constituent parts, thus separating my illness from the rest of me.' She paused. 'After that, he said he would bring me back together without it.'

'But that's not the way the Law of Separation works,' Aubrey said. 'That'd be like disassembling a clock, putting it back together and then expecting it to work with a few gears and springs left out.'

'Mordecai knew what he was doing. He told me so.'

The conclusion was inescapable. 'The spell would have rebounded,' Aubrey said. 'Horribly.'

Sylvia put a hand to her cheek. 'Our soul shattered into fragments.'

An icy trickle ran down Aubrey's spine. His experience with the dissociation of his body and soul had led him to find out as much as he could about the condition. He'd learned much about disunification – and he'd heard hints of souls being shattered. The prospect wasn't a cheery one. 'What happened?'

'Our soul was shredded and all the pieces were on the verge of being scattered, irretrievably. But Mordecai managed a preservation spell. Our body was left behind, alive but not alive. Then he caught what soul fragments he could.'

'And you ended up here?' Caroline asked. 'Trapped in a pearl?'

'He would have used what was close at hand,' Aubrey murmured. 'Quick thinking.'

'Preserved in a pearl,' Sylvia said. 'Mordecai swept up the fragments of our soul that he could find and put them all here. I was the largest. Once inside, I searched until I found the others, and put them in the heart of the place. Safe.'

'Very safe. He put a guardian spell in place, didn't he?'

'To watch over us. To protect our sanctuary.'

'By trapping any intruders,' Aubrey said absently. He was having his doubts about the thoroughness of Sylvia's account. What if Dr Tremaine actually wasn't aware of everything that had gone on? Complex preservation spells could have unexpected effects. It could explain why he was angry about losing the pearl, but not desperate to get it back. He may not have realised how much of his sister was actually trapped inside it.

He chewed his lip. Something Sylvia had said had snagged his curiosity. He couldn't let it pass – it was like a white piece of lint on a dark suit. 'You said that when the spell went wrong, your brother swept up the fragments that he could find.'

'Poor Mordecai. He did his best, but he didn't realise that he hadn't gathered up all of them.'

Aubrey tried to keep the tension out of his voice, but he saw how both Caroline and George had noticed. They were watching the exchange very closely. 'Some of the fragments are still missing? Out there somewhere?'

'One is still lost. We will never be whole again until it's found and brought to us.'

Aubrey had some sympathy for this. 'What if we find it for you? Would you let us go to do that?'

Aubrey thought he saw a slight widening of the eyes. 'Of course.'

'All of us?'

Sylvia turned to George and von Stralick. 'Wouldn't one of you like to stay?'

The hurried declinings of the offer were heartfelt. Sylvia – or the main Sylvia fragment – shook her head. 'A pity.'

Aubrey put his hands together and clenched them. This was a delicate game. 'So we can all go?'

'Are you all needed?'

'Yes. Most certainly. It is difficult out there.'

'I thought it might be.' She stood, took a few steps, then turned to face them. 'Yes, you can all go, since you're needed.'

The expressions of relief – rubbing of foreheads, exhalations of breath – were muted, guarded, but unmistakeable. 'Now,' Aubrey said, 'you wouldn't have any idea where this other fragment is, would you?'

'We may be disunited, but we still have a connection. I know where it is.'

'You do?'

'It's gone home.'

'Where?' Aubrey asked, but like the tiny 'click' a clock makes just before its alarm rings, he had a premonition what she was going to say.

'Holmland.'

Twelve

𝒜 WILD YELL GREETED THEIR REAPPEARANCE. AUBREY whirled, and – heart thundering, every nerve taut – saw Otto Kiefer staring at them, telephone in hand.

'What?' The Holmlander was wide-eyed. 'Where? What?'

Aubrey didn't answer. He propped himself up against the table with both arms. Triggered by Kiefer's startling shriek, his whole body had decided it should get ready to defend himself against a horde of demons – or to run away at a speed that would see him in serious consideration for a spot in the national athletics team.

They were back in von Stralick's parlour. Afternoon light was coming through the curtained windows. The chairs were in disarray around the table. Four were pushed back, one was lying on the floor.

In the middle of the table was the Tremaine pearl.

Caroline had returned, to his relief, as had George

and von Stralick. All of them had adopted poses of fight or flight and Aubrey found time to be amused that the 'Fight' option was a 2–1 winner. Von Stralick was the exception, being halfway to the door before he realised that Kiefer was the source of the extraordinary noise. Within two steps, however, he had slowed, resumed an appearance of calm, and was brushing off his lapels. 'We are back, Otto.'

Kiefer was gaping at them, moving his head slowly from side to side, as if he thought it was all some sort of trick. Then he caught sight of the telephone in his hand and he flinched. 'I was about to call the police.'

George stepped over. He took the earpiece and replaced it. 'No need.'

Caroline dropped her hands and relaxed from her fighting pose. She moved to Kiefer and guided him to a chair. 'We're safe, Otto.'

He sagged with a huge exhalation of air. He mopped his brow with a handkerchief he extracted from his pocket after some fumbling. 'Thank goodness. But where did you go? When I came back, you were nowhere.'

'How long ago was that?'

The question perplexed Kiefer for a moment. 'A minute or two?' he hazarded.

'It seemed like more,' muttered von Stralick.

'That's what happens when you mess around with magic,' George said, affecting a pose of someone who encountered the outlandish every day. Aubrey nearly laughed.

'But what happened?' Kiefer repeated, and Aubrey launched into an account of their time inside the Tremaine pearl. By the time the story had finished, with interjections, corrections and asides offered by Caroline, George and von Stralick, Kiefer was aghast. He shook himself all over, like a dog emerging from a river, and he held up a single, long finger. 'So we now have the way to our revenge, then?'

This time it was the turn of Aubrey, Caroline, George and von Stralick to be taken aback. Aubrey scratched his chin. 'I suppose you're right. If we can find the missing part of Sylvia in Holmland, and unite her, then we will have the perfect lure for Dr Tremaine. He won't be able to resist.' Not with the sense of guilt he must feel about his sister, Aubrey decided.

He looked at the others. Caroline's expression was grim, as if she'd fastened her will on a course of action. George looked uneasy, unconvinced, and he glanced at Aubrey. Von Stralick and Kiefer, however, were eager, hounds who'd just scented a fox within easy reach.

Aubrey wasn't obsessed with revenge. He'd come to terms with his antipathy for Dr Tremaine. He was happy to work against the ex-Sorcerer Royal, but he wasn't about to sacrifice everything in a headlong pursuit of the rogue magician. He was prepared to wait, to plan, to find the best opportunity to strike.

But Kiefer, von Stralick and Caroline were different. He wondered if their enmity burned too brightly and was blinding them to the realities of their situation, the dangers they faced.

'Come now,' von Stralick said, seeing Aubrey's indecision. 'This is a chance. You said yourself that she was his weakness.'

'She is. I have no doubt about that.'

Caroline touched him on the arm. It was light, almost

hesitant, but he would have noticed it in the middle of an artillery barrage. 'Let us take our chance.'

Aubrey ran a hand through his hair. 'Anyone fancy a trip to Holmland?'

Late afternoon was sliding into evening when Aubrey, Caroline and George left von Stralick's residence. A fine carriage went past with two charming, grey-haired ladies taking in the gentle end of the March day. Aubrey smiled and received a warm nod for his trouble.

Kiefer had hurried off immediately. He was bubbling with the possibilities presented by Aubrey's resolution, but he claimed he had some important research to undertake on pressure containment. Von Stralick didn't make any effort to question him about his plans. Aubrey thought that watching over his erratic relative was proving to be more onerous than von Stralick may have expected.

When von Stralick shepherded them out in a polite but firm manner, Aubrey decided that some communication with Holmland was about to take place behind the closed door.

They walked off in silence.

'You seem distracted,' Aubrey said to Caroline.

'I've just remembered I promised to help Mother with a few things.'

'I see. And how is this is a problem?'

'It's not a problem at all. I simply must be off.'

'Ah.' With mixed feelings, Aubrey saw a motor cab trundling their way. It responded to his wave and drew up smartly. He was pleased he'd been able to help Caroline with such alacrity, but disappointed to be deprived of her company.

She slid back the window of the cab. 'Now, don't do anything without me.'

'Anything?' Aubrey said. 'That's rather all-encompassing. I mean, breathing, for a start . . .'

'Don't do anything about going to Holmland.' Caroline glowered at him, then spared George a glare as well. 'If I know you two, you'll be off on the morning train.'

It sounded appealing, striking while the iron was hot, but Aubrey put a hand on his heart. 'We won't.' He gave a dramatic sigh. 'It's a shame. I was sure I heard of a band of itinerant puppet players who were heading toward Fisherberg. I thought George and I could join them, in disguise. Or was it a troupe of freestyle Morris Dancers?'

'Not Morris Dancers, old man.' George shuddered. 'You know I'm scared of Morris Dancers.'

A tiny dimple appeared in Caroline's cheek and her eyes were merry. 'As long as we understand each other.'

With that, she was off, leaving Aubrey thinking that that was the last thing he'd ever claim.

Aubrey watched the cab round the corner, and then he turned to George. 'Now, I *didn't* know you were afraid of Morris Dancers. How did this come about? You were frightened by a particularly horrible Morris Dancer when you were small?'

George put his nose in the air and sniffed. 'It's not something I like to talk about.'

Aubrey loved a mystery but he currently was in a position where he had to prioritise them. 'You know, George, I think it could be time to drop in on my father.

He might be able to help us with some background on the Holmland situation.'

George brightened. 'Just in time for dinner, I'd say. At his office?'

'We can be there in fifteen minutes. Mother will be there too, you know.'

'Jolly good. They say he has a fine table there.'

'And a fine appreciation of what's going on in Holmland,' Aubrey replied. *Which is just what I need*, he thought.

The Prime Minister's Offices was a deceptively bland name for one of the most important buildings in the realm. A short walk from the Houses of Parliament – for convenience – No. 4 Credence Lane was a four-storey sandstone building in a short cul-de-sac that had once been a salubrious neighbourhood, but now all the houses had been converted to various departmental warrens by the innumerable parts of the Civil Service. Aubrey remembered the place well from when Sir Darius had last been Prime Minister. He knew that the tenants of the buildings in Credence Lane were constantly in flux as the departments rose and fell in importance. Numbers 2 and 6, for instance, were currently occupied by shadowy sections of the Foreign Office. They'd displaced the Ministry of Trade and an influential section of the Department of Inland Revenue. When a taxation department was considered unimportant, Aubrey reflected, times were strange indeed.

Two police constables were on patrol at the entrance to Credence Lane, where it opened off busy Playford

Street. Another sign of the times, Aubrey decided, and he nodded cheerfully to them as they passed.

Aubrey used the brass knocker to hammer on the door to No. 4. The door opened. He'd been expecting one of the Prime Minister's staff to answer, as in the past, but this time it was another police constable. Tall, broad-shouldered, with a small toothbrush moustache, he filled the doorway and stared down at Aubrey with professional scrutiny. 'Yes? Can I help you?'

Aubrey recovered and didn't show his surprise, even though he could make out the figure of another police office standing in the hall behind the door-filler. 'I'd like to see the Prime Minister.'

'You have an appointment?'

'I'm his son.'

The constable grinned a little and relaxed. 'You'd be Mr Aubrey, then? Come along. The PM has left orders that if you were ever to turn up, he'd see you straight away.'

Aubrey gestured at George. 'This is . . .'

The constable nodded. 'George Doyle. The PM said he was likely to be with you.' The constable leaned out of the doorway and peered down the street. 'And he said a Miss Hepworth may be with you. Not today?'

Aubrey was a little flustered by this. 'No.'

'A pity. I'm right in assuming she's the daughter of Ophelia Hepworth? I wanted to chat with her about her mother's work. Doing great things with redefining the relationship between perspective and meaning, she is.'

A voice came from over the constable's shoulder. 'Don't forget that we could have asked about the incisive nature of her social commentary, Stan, mediated as it is in playful manipulation of artistic conventions.'

'Oh, right, there is that too.' Stan the constable nodded at Aubrey. 'We would've appreciated that.'

'I'll try to bring her next time,' Aubrey said faintly. The quality of the city constabulary was apparently climbing.

They were shown to a waiting room off the entrance hall. It was a serious space with four leather armchairs and a solid-looking clock on the mantelpiece over the sombre, unlit fireplace. The room was comfortable and afforded a fine view of the street outside.

Ten minutes by the clock and a door banged shut somewhere in the interior of the building. The sound of footsteps hurrying down stairs, then a well-dressed gentleman strode past the open doorway and left the building. Aubrey barely had time to realise who it was before his father appeared, looking spruce and well polished as always. 'Aubrey. George. Excellent.'

'Hello, Father. What were you doing talking to Stafford Bruce?'

Sir Darius looked pained. 'There isn't actually a law forbidding the Prime Minister from talking to the shadow minister for defence, you know.'

George stared at Sir Darius then toward the street, as if wondering whether he could run after Stafford Bruce to question him. 'Dashed interesting, though, Sir Darius, don't you think? Especially in these times.'

'If you could take your journalistic hat off for a moment, George, I need to talk to you. Both. To ask a favour.'

Aubrey enjoyed it when his father asked him to help. He appreciated the tangible proof that his father trusted him – and that he was useful. And he also appreciated the peek behind the scenes of the operations of government. His father's willingness to use unusual channels was something Aubrey noted, sure that it would come in handy when he eventually made his way into the world of politics.

Besides, it put him in a useful bargaining position.

'Happy to help, sir,' he said to his father. 'What is it you want?'

'Not here,' Sir Darius said, glancing around. This startled Aubrey. If the waiting room in the Prime Minister's own office wasn't a safe place for discussion, what was?

Sir Darius led them deeper into the warren of rooms that the humble façade of No. 4 concealed. Most of the doors were closed. Those that were open showed rooms that reeked of bureaucracy and paperwork – filing cabinets, manila folders, piles of papers overflowing from in and out trays. Harried-looking clerks didn't even look up as they passed, frowning at ledgers or speaking earnestly into telephones.

Sir Darius took them through a door next to the rear stairs. Inside, it was windowless, but otherwise comfortable, with four of the same leather armchairs as in the waiting room. A low table took up the space in the middle of the room. On it was a large red book. A door on the right led further into the building and the walls were heavy with sporting prints: hunting dogs, racehorses.

Sir Darius waited until Aubrey and George had taken a seat. He stood easily, hands behind his back. 'Fancy an overseas trip?'

Over the last few days, Aubrey had found that his anticipatory sense was humming on all cylinders. Looking at his father, he had a distinct sense what was coming. 'I always enjoy travel,' he said carefully.

'Broadens the mind.' George frowned thoughtfully. 'Deepens it, too, I shouldn't think, but I don't know about lengthening the mind. Doesn't sound right.'

'Quite,' Sir Darius said. 'But I wasn't thinking about an aimless outing. I need you to accompany your mother to Holmland.'

Aubrey blinked. 'You know about the symposium?'

'Don't worry, Aubrey, I haven't been spying. Something came up at the museum, so she couldn't come to dinner. We had afternoon tea instead.'

Aubrey was already seeing an opportunity. After all, they'd just been planning a trip to Holmland. What did they say about two birds and a stone? 'I'd be happy to.'

Sir Darius sighed and ran his hand through his hair. Aubrey then saw his father instead of the Prime Minister desperately doing what he could to avoid war. 'A Holmland symposium. All open and above board. At least, that's what they want us to think.'

'And you think that it's otherwise?'

'It's actually part symposium, part trade exhibition, and mostly a chance for the Chancellor to show how wonderful Holmland is.' He touched his immaculate moustache with a finger. 'A few token exhibitors will be there from Albion and other countries. Plenty of shady customers will be on the lookout for the latest developments. Bound to be an interesting place.' He frowned. 'If I didn't take precautions and something happens, I wouldn't forgive myself. If I take precautions and nothing happens, then nothing is lost.'

'But you don't want to make an issue of it,' George said suddenly. 'Not wanting to give the Holmlanders a chance to get offended.'

'Precisely. I could send a troop of bodyguards. I could demand a Holmland military escort. I could insist on around-the-clock protective spells from a squad of never-sleeping, all-seeing oriental mystics. Any of which would enable the Chancellor and his government to display enormous huffiness and then refuse to appear at the talks we've invited them to in September.'

Aubrey straightened. 'I hadn't heard of any talks.'

'I'm glad. I was starting to think that this office was leaking like a rusty sieve.'

'Diplomatic talks aimed at anything in particular? Averting a war, for instance?'

Sir Darius's face grew solemn. 'We've stood up to their posturing over the Goltans. We've refused to be cowed by their bluster over the Marchmaine question and their designs on south Gallia. But it's not enough to act as a bulwark against Holmland aggression. This is the modern era. Surely civilised people can sit down and talk through differences. And if talking is going to stop carnage on the Continent, I'm prepared to talk until the cows come home.'

'But you're still worried about Mother and this symposium.'

Sir Darius sighed. 'I don't like your mother going to Holmland. Not at this time.'

'You could forbid her from going,' Aubrey suggested, then he realised what he'd said. He nearly fell off his seat with horror. Both Sir Darius and George stared at him. 'Er. I'll deny that I ever said that, you know.'

'I've already erased it from my memory,' Sir Darius said. 'Thank goodness.'

'I don't think anyone could stop Lady Rose from doing something she'd set her mind on,' George pointed out.

Sir Darius clicked his tongue. 'I don't think he's recovered yet, the last fellow who tried.'

The three males contemplated the awesome magnificence of Aubrey's mother in silence for a few moments, looking at the floor and nodding, before Sir Darius clapped his hands together. 'You'll do it, then?'

'Glad to.'

'George?'

George glanced at Aubrey. 'Sounds like a wheeze.'

'Excellent.' Sir Darius looked pleased. 'Now, what was it you wanted to ask?'

Having had his wishes granted and his questions answered without having to offer anything in return, this question left Aubrey unprepared, but he rallied. 'Stafford Bruce. What's he up to?'

Sir Darius raised an eyebrow. 'Now, you didn't come here to ask that because you didn't know about him until you saw him pass the waiting room, but I'll let that pass.'

'He's on the outer with his party leadership,' George said. 'Is he thinking of crossing the floor?'

Aubrey was flabbergasted. 'You're becoming a political pundit, George. All that newspaper reading?'

George smiled smugly. 'That and a naturally enquiring mind.'

Sir Darius chuckled again. 'He's a good man, is Bruce, so naturally he wouldn't see eye to eye with Rollo Armitage. I've simply left the door open to him. If he can't stomach the Royalists any more, the Progressives would be pleased to have him. Someone who has the steel to cross the floor on a bill so important to the party leader as the Security Intelligence Reorganisation bill is the sort of person we'd value.'

Rollo Armitage was one of Sir Darius's oldest political foes. At one time he'd been second-in-command to Sir Darius when he was Royalist party leader, but had shown his true colours in a series of dastardly alliances, deals and betrayals that saw Sir Darius stripped of party leadership and the Prime Ministership.

Aubrey was about to ask more about the bill when the other door was flung open. An angry-looking Commander Tallis, head of the Special Services, marched in. Hard on his heels was an equally unsettled-looking Commander Craddock, head of the Magisterium. Tallis was wearing his usual black topcoat and trousers, while Craddock wore a long coat, almost sweeping the floor. He had a broad-brimmed hat in one hand. 'Prime Minister,' Tallis barked. 'We need one of your constables to follow someone.'

Craddock surveyed the room and narrowed his eyes when his gaze lit on Aubrey. 'No need, I think, Tallis. We have someone here for the job.'

Tallis scowled. 'Fitzwilliam? You think so? Begging your pardon, Prime Minister.'

Sir Darius frowned. 'I take it this is urgent? So urgent that it can't wait?'

Craddock nodded. 'We were waiting for your meeting. Through the window, Tallis saw Bruce leave. He was immediately met by one of his underlings.'

'Gave him something,' Tallis growled. He was a compact, almost solid man, especially when he stood at parade rest, hands behind his back, legs slightly spread, as he was now. 'Papers.'

'And this is an issue in exactly what way?' Sir Darius asked.

'The underling is a known Holmland agent,' Craddock said. 'A magical operative. We've had our eye on him for some time.'

'Joint operation,' Tallis growled again. 'His being a spy and a magician meant Special Services had to inform the Magisterium.'

'Luckily, we knew about him first and we were the ones to alert Special Services to his existence,' Craddock said.

For something that's urgent, Aubrey thought, *inter-service rivalry seems to be much more important*. He stood. 'Which way did this underling go?'

'Right at Playford Street,' Tallis said.

'And what did he look like?' George asked.

'Small, striped trousers, bowler hat,' Craddock said.

That narrows it down to a few thousand civil servants in this part of the city, Aubrey thought. 'Anything else?'

'He was carrying an umbrella. Black.' Tallis snorted. 'No sign of rain.'

Aubrey turned to his father. 'Sir?'

'Go. Be careful.'

Thirteen

THE POLICE CONSTABLES STARED AT AUBREY AND GEORGE as they scampered out of the doorway. Breathing fast, flushed, Aubrey pounded along the pavement until they reached Playford Street.

'Right,' George panted, and they were off.

The street was busy. Motorcars and lorries rumbled along with dour intensity. The pavements were thick with people who all had the focus of those who wanted to be somewhere else. *Probably home, eating supper*, Aubrey thought as he came to one of those awkward impasses with a woman wearing a large, flowery hat. He moved left, and she moved in the same direction. He went back the other way just as she did. She pursed her lips and frowned, as if he were deliberately playing games. Aubrey took half a step back just as she lurched in the same direction but he was ready and shifted his weight back, slipping around her and hurrying to catch up to George. 'Any sign?'

'Other side of the street,' George said. 'Just passing the tobacconist.'

Aubrey stuffed his hands in the pockets of his jacket. A tall man wearing a cloth cap obscured him for a second, then he saw their quarry. He was just as Tallis and Craddock said: small, bowler hat and carrying an unneeded umbrella. He had a buff envelope in one hand.

Aubrey kept his gaze on the shop windows they were passing, using them to keep track of the umbrella-carrying spy, so he wouldn't have to directly look at him as he navigated the busy pavements.

He blinked and stared at the wavy reflection in the gentleman's outfitters they were passing. Then he whipped his head around to scan the other side of the street.

The spy had disappeared.

'There.' George prevented himself from pointing with an almost physical effort. 'Down those stairs.'

They crossed the street, slipping between lorries, motorcars and a dignified open carriage. The stairs led to a narrow shop below street level, the bottom floor of a tall building. Warm yellow light spilled from its windows, a sign that evening was asserting itself.

Thomson and Sons, the sign over the door read. *Fine and Rare Books. Bibliographic Antiquities.* Aubrey had a moment's hesitation, wondering if this was a dodge and the spy was exiting through a rear door, but decided they had no choice. He pushed in and a cheery bell over the door announced their entrance, much to his disgust. George reached up to still it, but it was too late.

A tall, spindly man appeared from a darkened doorway behind the counter. He stood for a moment, polishing his spectacles, before slipping them on and nodding.

'Welcome to Thomson and Sons. I am Mr Thomson. Can I help you?'

He had long grey hair, parted in the middle and pushed back on both sides in waves. He was smartly dressed in dark green topcoat and well-knotted tie from one of the better clubs in the city. On either side of him, the counter was laden with books in neat piles.

'Early Latin magic,' Aubrey said briskly. 'What do you have?'

Mr Thomson raised an eyebrow. 'I'm afraid we have very little on magic here, young sir. If that's what you're looking for, you'd be better off trying Fletcher's, in Cook Street.'

'Ah. Of course.' Aubrey flapped a hand and looked about vaguely. 'Isn't this Fletcher's?'

George took his cue. 'I told you it wasn't, Richard. Now, come on, let's go.'

'There's no hurry, Horace. Now I'm here, I'd like to look around. This seems a delightful place.'

Aubrey wandered off, but not before seeing George roll his eyes at Thomson the Bookseller.

Now, to find our quarry.

The bookshop was deeper than Aubrey had thought, and it opened into a number of separate rooms, all teeming with bookshelves. The whole place smelled of must and dust, while tiny hand-written signs pointed out that this shelf was devoted to Comparative Religion, while this one was full of Eastern Religions, and another was simply the home of Food.

With a nod and a tilt of the head, Aubrey and George split up, strolling though the bibliophile's paradise. At any other time, Aubrey would have been fascinated by what surrounded him. The books were old and intriguing, from all over Albion, from the Continent and even further afield, if he recognised a row of handsome Nipponese volumes correctly. In his guise of a book fancier he picked several books from shelves to maintain his pose, but had to be firm with himself otherwise he was going to get immersed in an old Holmlandish hunting text.

At the sound of George clearing his throat nearby, Aubrey raised his eyes from the delightful engraving of a three-horned beast that seemed to be slightly affronted at the lance a mounted hunter was jabbing in its rump. The throat-clearing sounded too definite to be just book dust, so Aubrey wandered to the end of the shelf in search of its source.

There, right at the rear of the shop, under a narrow, barred window, was their quarry.

The spy looked up at their appearance and then did something that let Aubrey know that the man wasn't a polished operator. He quickly slipped an envelope into the book he was holding, snapped it closed and rammed it back on the shelf.

Then he stood there and tried to look innocent.

Amateur, Aubrey thought. Of course, the best thing to do when revealed was *not* to pretend to be doing nothing, but to pretend to be doing something much less serious than what one was really doing.

Then Aubrey realised he was behaving in an equally amateurish fashion. He was staring at the suspect, thereby breaking his cover and drawing attention to himself. George, too, was goggling and the result was something like a meeting of three people where someone has just done something embarrassing and no-one is willing to draw attention to it.

Aubrey recovered. He turned to George. 'You said that Architecture was up here.'

George rallied splendidly. 'I did not, Richard. You just didn't listen.'

Aubrey smiled at the rat-like man, who was frozen to the spot in his efforts at innocence. 'Sorry to disturb you. You haven't seen Architecture, by any chance?'

He shook his head, and Aubrey could see tiny beads of sweat on his forehead. 'It's History here,' he croaked.

'There's a pity.' Aubrey caught George by the arm and they retreated. 'Can you follow him when he leaves?' he whispered as they gathered themselves in a corner near Epic Poetry and Medicine.

'I think so.'

'I'll retrieve the documents after he's gone.'

'He's leaving them here?'

'It's a drop. He's obviously arranged with a confederate who'll arrive here soon and pick them up.'

Furtive footsteps on the other side of the bookshelf signalled that their quarry was on the move again. George scratched his head. 'I don't like separating.'

'It's the only thing to do. We need to know if he has any other assignations. I'll take the documents and then contact Craddock so that this place can be watched to see who arrives for them.' Aubrey could hear the congratulations already. 'I'm not taking any chances by leaving the documents here. They're better off with me.'

A flicker of doubt crossed George's face, but he nodded and set off in the direction of the front of the shop.

Aubrey hummed to himself a little, then slipped around to where the spy had done his clumsy sleight of hand.

It took Aubrey a few minutes. He had to picture where the spy had been standing, how far he'd been reaching up (or was it down?) and the size and colour of the book in his hand. It didn't help that the books in this section of the shop were almost uniform. Old, some hundreds of years, they were all bound in dull, age-darkened brown leather. The sizes did vary, as did their extent, but Aubrey had to try half a dozen before he struck gold.

The book was heavy when he slipped it from the shelf and he needed both hands. He hefted it, smelled the foxy smell of mould. When he opened it, the spine creaked, but the pages fell open to reveal an envelope.

Buff, heavy bond, it was unaddressed. The spy wasn't *that* much of an amateur. For an instant, Aubrey considered opening it, but – with an effort – he refrained. His curiosity was fierce – he desperately wanted to see what the spy was handing over. Such a well-placed agent could get his hands on all sorts of things. And what was Bruce's involvement? It would be a blow to Aubrey's father if the man was a Holmland dupe. If Bruce's office was found to be leaking secrets to foreign powers, he'd have no choice other than to resign, and with him would go Sir Darius's chance to solidify his party's position in Parliament.

Aubrey replaced the heavy old book on the shelf and almost laughed aloud. *Gallian Royalty*. He should really buy it for Bertie. Perhaps it could shed some light on the tangled tree that the Crown Prince's family had become. It might be a useful sort of apology for trying to kill him . . .

Aubrey replaced the book and slapped the envelope in his other hand. *Now*, he thought, *a quick trip back to No. 4 and Craddock can't help but be impressed*. A mission taken up with no warning, successfully achieved – especially if George returned with news of the spy's destination.

A job well done. Aubrey would be happy with that – especially if his father was the one who said it.

Craddock finished reading. He nodded significantly at Sir Darius, then handed the letter to Tallis on the other side of the desk, but Aubrey took note of Craddock's expression. His gaze was on the ceiling. His lips were pursed – not tight with anger, but thoughtfully, as if he was considering a number of options. Aubrey glanced at George, but his friend merely shrugged then sat back in the leather armchair.

The room was silent until Tallis snorted like a hippopotamus. 'Dung.'

Aubrey blinked. 'Dung?'

'Bird droppings. What do you call it? Guano.' He held the papers by one corner and handed them back to Craddock.

'From San Martin, the Andean republic,' the head of the Magisterium said. 'Fascinating.'

'It's a shipping manifest,' Tallis said.

Sir Darius was standing with his back to the closed door. He narrowed his eyes. 'Or is it a list of arrivals and departures?'

'Could it be a code?' George asked, keen to contribute after returning to No. 4 with the disappointing news that he'd lost the spy.

'We'll test it,' Craddock said, 'but it doesn't appear so. We'll also probe it for hidden writing, for magical imprints, the whole panoply.'

'Guano,' Sir Darius repeated. He touched his moustache. 'It's not just for fertilizer, you know.'

Tallis frowned. 'Eh?'

Craddock was up to the mark. 'When guano is refined, it's a vital source of nitrates – what we used to call saltpetre. For fertilizer. And explosives.'

'Munitions,' Sir Darius said. 'Every bullet, every shell is dependent on nitrates for its power. Albion companies have a monopoly on shipping San Martin guano. And San Martin guano supplies most of the world.'

'Including Holmland?' Aubrey asked.

'At the moment, yes,' Sir Darius said. 'But if it comes to war, Holmland's supply would be cut off, with disastrous consequences for its armaments.'

'So no wonder they're sniffing around the guano.' George made a face. 'Makes me feel quite ill, that thought.'

'All this doesn't put Stafford Bruce in the clear,' Sir Darius said. 'Unfortunately.'

Tallis grunted. 'We'll make a copy of this document, alter the sensitive parts, and replace it in the bookshop. Then we'll monitor the place to see who arrives to pick it up.' He smiled. 'And if this agent is foolish enough to return to Bruce's office, we'll nab him there. If not, we'll have to work harder.'

'We'll find him,' Craddock said. 'And then we'll know what he's up to.'

'And who will be overseeing this?' Sir Darius said. 'Is this the domain of your department, Craddock, or yours, Tallis?'

Aubrey watched the reaction of the two men with interest. Both seemed unhappy with his father's words, but neither wanted to say as much. Tallis scowled, his heavy eyebrows almost threatening to meet the moustache on his upcurled top lip. Craddock, on the other hand, merely stiffened, his mouth slightly tensing, his nostrils constricting by the tiniest amount as if to ward off a nasty smell.

'We have a reorganisation under way,' Sir Darius said to Aubrey. 'And it affects you, and your irregular status with the Magisterium.'

'Magisterium no more,' Craddock said. 'I am now in charge of the Magic Department of the Security Intelligence Directorate.'

'Which is part of the Ministry of Defence,' Sir Darius said. 'Two departments, Special Services and Magic, working together instead of at odds. It's what we need in these times.'

'Of course, Prime Minister,' Tallis said, but Aubrey could see from the sidelong look he gave to his colleague that Tallis was already imagining himself in charge of the entire Security Intelligence Directorate.

It made sense, uniting the two squabbling intelligence agencies. Aubrey, though, wondered if it would be a happy arrangement.

'If you gentlemen are finished,' Sir Darius said, 'I need to talk to my son.'

'Another time then, Prime Minister,' Craddock said. 'I still have some items to discuss regarding our new arrangements.'

Tallis looked at him sharply. 'If we're finished, Prime Minister, I have matters to attend to. National security matters,' he added, just to emphasise that he, for one, was more concerned with the fate of the country than with playing internal power games.

It was a ruse that failed simply because it was so transparent.

Once the two warring power-seekers left, Sir Darius slumped in a chair. 'Good men, both of them. But they'll be the death of me.'

'Taylor will take care of them,' Aubrey said without much confidence. The Minister of Defence was competent, but he had a feeling that more than mere competence would be needed to keep those two in check.

'Let's hope so.' Sir Darius rubbed his face with both hands and Aubrey saw how weary he was. He felt sorry for his father, but he knew that this fatigue wouldn't abate unless international tensions miraculously ebbed, a situation about as likely as Caroline saying she really liked staying home and knitting instead of adventuring.

He nearly slapped himself on the forehead. Caroline. She'd be furious if he didn't take her along on a Holmland adventure. But she couldn't come with them, not unchaperoned. While she didn't care a fig for such outdated things, Aubrey was sure that – reluctantly – his mother would insist on utter propriety in her troupe. She wouldn't want the Holmlanders to have any excuse for offence.

He put that knotty problem aside for later.

Sir Darius drummed his fingers on the armrest of the chair. 'Aubrey, in Fisherberg, I want you to be my eyes and ears. Keep an eye on the Prince. And on your mother.'

'She knows that the Prince is going?'

'I told her. That's when I suggested your going with her.'

'And her reaction?'

'I was surprised. She quite liked the idea – but she didn't want to inconvenience you.'

'Happy to do it,' George said, then he blushed. Both Aubrey and his father knew about George's infatuation with Lady Rose and had, with commendable restraint, never spoken of it. It lingered, a source of mild unspoken amusement, between Aubrey and his father and – perhaps – his mother.

'Good,' Sir Darius said, 'but I'm asking you to keep your wits about you. About Holmland in general. I'd be interested, in particular, to hear your impressions of Chancellor Neumann.'

'Have you met him?'

'Once. Forceful chap. Ex-military, which is only to be expected in a Holmland politician.' Sir Darius looked thoughtful. 'He spent time in their Second Rifle Brigade as a sharpshooter, of all things.'

'The Chancellor?' George said. 'I thought he would have been an officer type.'

'He was, but not straight away. Apparently he insisted on seeing life as the ordinary infantryman did. Interesting fellow. I look forward to getting your observations directly.'

Aubrey saw it immediately. 'You want us to report to you, rather than have reports filtered through Craddock and Tallis.'

'That's part of it. The other part is that you have shown that you have a knack for the – how shall I put it – unconventional? I'd feel much better knowing that the outlandish is being taken care of as well as the obvious.'

'Unconventional?' Aubrey repeated, feeling strangely unoffended.

'And outlandish,' George added.

'I see.'

Sir Darius grinned. 'Perhaps I should call you my insurance against the unexpected. The others can handle the straightforward security matters, but with you on the spot, the Prince – and your mother – will be much safer.'

'I'm sure we can do it between the two of us,' Aubrey said and George nodded his agreement. 'Is there anything in particular we should be aware of?'

Sir Darius frowned. He sat back and uncrossed his legs. 'Nothing concrete. But there is chatter.'

Aubrey nodded. Chatter was intelligence talk. Intercepted communications. Overheard snatches of conversations. Vague rumours. Information bought from those willing to sell. None of which was definitive, but added together chatter sometimes gave a flavour, a sense of something in the wind. When the sheer amount of chatter rose, peaking like a wave, it was enough to give intelligence chiefs sleepless nights, being aware that something was afoot, without knowing exactly what it was.

'Any names being mentioned in this chatter?' Aubrey asked with an attempt at nonchalance.

'Our friend Dr Tremaine has been whispered about. But then again, his progress through the ranks of Holmland has been the source of much gossip for some time now.' He grimaced. 'And there appears to be brigand trouble on the Holmland–Gallia border – they may be rebels, one never knows – and some oddness going on in Fisherberg itself.'

'Oddness?' Aubrey asked.

'Magical oddness. Should be your cup of tea, Aubrey.'

Fourteen

AUBREY ENJOYED TRAVEL. IT DIDN'T MATTER IF IT were by train, boat or horse and cart, he loved the anticipation of arriving in a different place. The perspectives that were granted a traveller were special and changing, always being glimpsed and left behind, with something new just ahead.

Aubrey had one substantial regret: he'd been unable to contact Caroline by telephone. He'd tried for two days, with increasing feverishness, but in the end he'd had to write a letter advising her of the sudden change of plans. He'd spent a whole morning trying to find the words to explain that she wasn't being left behind – it was simply unfortunate circumstances and he'd do his best to make up for it and he'd make sure it wouldn't happen again and . . .

It sounded feeble even as he wrote it, and he could imagine her disappointment only too well.

In his mind, he could see a graph of Caroline's estimation of him. When they first met at Prince Albert's estate, he hadn't made a good impression – the graph would begin at a very low level. In the adventure of the Prince's near-assassination, he could imagine the graph sloping upwards. Not rapidly, and with a few dips where he managed to put his foot in things, but the trend would have definitely been upward, to a high point just after his father's election as Prime Minister.

Then the Gallian imbroglio. Aubrey winced, because after a reasonably positive series of escapades where he thought he'd conducted himself quite well – graph heading upward again – he'd made a disastrous miscalculation in manipulating Caroline's plans for his own ends. When his mother – his own mother – had taken Caroline on a polar expedition with the express point of putting some distance between Aubrey and her, the graph must have plunged, crossing the neutral axis, he imagined, with Caroline's attitude actively negative toward him.

From this nadir, however, thanks to some painful humility and hard work, Aubrey hoped that the graph had been inching its way into positive territory. The underground pursuit of Dr Tremaine and the affair with the Bank of Albion had been a chance for him to show his capabilities, which he hoped weren't unimpressive. Their rapprochement after these affairs may not have restored matters entirely, and their agreement to remain colleagues meant that a limit was placed on how far the graph could climb, but surely it had peeped into positive territory. Surely.

Now? Caroline would be affronted at being left out of this Fisherberg trip, and unhappy at the lack of communication. The graph was about to dive again.

He sighed. If only human matters worked like mathematics. A mathematical function was crisp, clear and open to understanding – with enough effort. To Aubrey's mind, human affairs were just the opposite – opaque, baffling and profoundly difficult.

The trip to Fisherberg had been planned as a cross-continental train journey, much to the displeasure of the navy. The Admiralty was mightily miffed when Lady Rose declined the offer to sail on the HMS *Invulnerable*, one of the latest class of cruisers that the navy was taking to Fisherberg to show off to the Holmlanders. While Aubrey would have enjoyed the chance to spend a few days exploring the most modern ship in the Albion fleet, he thought his mother's decision was wise. Entering Fisherberg by train would be far more discreet than steaming into harbour aboard a warship. Lady Rose was visiting Holmland as a scholar, not as a symbol of national power.

The boat train crossed south-east Albion with steely efficiency. The special carriage allocated to Lady Rose at the end of the train was plush and comfortable, but before they left, Aubrey – taking his job seriously – inspected it to make sure that it was secure, even though this had already been done by some of Tallis's operatives. He approved when he found it had only two entrances. One opened directly into the carriage and the other was the interconnection between it and the second-last carriage. This interconnection included an alcove constantly manned by one of Tallis's operatives.

Lady Rose was equally well guarded on the ferry across the channel, while the train that was waiting for them in Gallia had another reserved carriage at the rear, and Aubrey could see the work of the friendly Gallian government in the squad of police who surrounded it at Legras Station, the departure point for the train to Lutetia. They postured and preened when Lady Rose approached, and Aubrey thought a fist-fight was going to break out on the platform to see who was going to have the honour of opening the door for her.

The train sped across the countryside toward the capital of Gallia. While clean and comfortable, it rattled in disconcertingly erratic ways. Aubrey generally enjoyed the regular clicketty-clack rhythm of trains. This one, however, had nothing regular about it. It groaned up gentle slopes, protested around the mildest of corners, made hard going over bridges and was reluctant to enter tunnels, as if afraid of the dark.

All the while, it shifted between a clicketty-clicketty and a clacketty-click-click as it ran over the rails, at intervals that were gratingly and irritatingly random.

George, however, was immune to this. He had spread a newspaper on one of the mahogany tables near the windows and was poring over it, frowning, as if he meant to memorise every word. After an hour or so, Aubrey had become so edgy from the non-rhythm of the train that he stood and began pacing the length of the carriage. His mother was at one end, writing in a large notebook, consulting one of the many volumes she'd plucked from the trunk she'd brought with her. He tried to start a conversation, but the voice dried in his throat when she held up a hand without looking up. He knew that gesture. She was in the middle of something important and didn't want to be interrupted. He went to look at what she was writing, but as soon as he leaned over her open hand turned to a single, admonitory finger.

It was enough. He left her in peace. He'd sighted enough to see that she was working on another draft of her symposium presentation. Why she'd be doing this baffled him. He thought each of the previous nine drafts had been fine.

That left only one source of distraction. 'Anything interesting in the paper, George?'

Aubrey inserted himself into the bench seat on the opposite side of the table from his friend. Outside, the afternoon sun beat on the cosy fields of northern Gallia. It was almost like a picture book, with well-behaved flocks of sheep staring at the train as it whistled past. In the distance, a thick forest marched up the side of a modest hill. To one side, a church stood, as if happy to be there.

George didn't look up. 'Always interesting things in the paper, old man. You should know that.'

'You're applying yourself to this one with special intensity, though. What is it? The world of sport in uproar over a race-fixing scandal?'

'Not much, apart from some sort of commotion on the border with Holmland.' George shook his head. 'This is just the last newspaper I'm bound to enjoy for some time. I wanted to make it last.'

'I knew your lack of languages would come home to roost. You should have paid more attention in class.'

'I did. Just didn't understand a thing, that's all. Was all foreign to me.'

George's inability to come to terms with anything beyond the most basic niceties of foreign languages had never concerned him. He was convinced he could get by anywhere in the world with a firm handshake and a sunny smile. It generally worked, but it seemed as if newspapers were immune to this approach.

'So you're going to devour the last of good old Albion's newspapers, then.'

'It's all I can do. Every last little word, I'll read.'

'No matter how trivial, how boring?'

'Advertisements for bootblack will be like religious texts to me. Details of shipping consignments I'll ponder as if they hold the mysteries of the ages.'

Aubrey cocked his head. 'Are you sure you can't spend your time any more usefully?'

'Not really. Especially since by doing this I've just learned that Caroline is on her way to Fisherberg.'

Aubrey straightened so quickly that he banged his knee on the underside of the table – but he hardly noticed. 'Caroline?'

'A small article in the Arts section. It seems as if Ophelia Hepworth is on her way to this Fisherberg symposium, just like your mother.'

Aubrey remembered that Caroline had told him this. At the time, it was a two he hadn't put together with another two and so missed out on coming up with four. 'And Caroline is going with her?'

'"Accompanying the influential artist on her Holmland sojourn is her daughter, Miss Caroline Hepworth." Sounds like her, doesn't it?'

'It certainly does.' Aubrey sat back, bruised knee forgotten. Caroline in Fisherberg? Excellent. Some time ago, he'd been surprised when she'd mentioned, quite offhand, that she'd visited Fisherberg before. But he could see this being extremely useful. If she could be persuaded to overlook his not asking her along, then persuaded to show them around, it was the sort of thing that could make a difference to their time in the Holmland capital. Of course, that would mean spending time together, which would be a fine thing. Enjoyable. Friendly. Most splendid.

'I say,' George said. 'D'you think it might be time for a spot of early lunch?'

'George, straight after breakfast is your notion of time for a spot of early lunch. I think we might wait until after we've joined the Transcontinental Express.'

'In Lutetia?' George thought for a moment, and Aubrey could see him weighing up having some solid, uninspiring food now, or waiting for the legendary offerings of the Transcontinental's board of fare. 'It's not more than an hour away, you'd say?'

Aubrey glanced at the scene outside the window. 'At the most.'

His estimate was almost exact. Fifty-five minutes later saw the train pull into St Remy Station and when it finally stopped the release of steam sounded like a sigh of relief.

Aubrey had never taken the fabled Transcontinental Express and, despite his misgivings about leaving Caroline behind, and despite taking his bodyguarding duties seriously, he was looking forward to it. Tales of intrigue and mystery had sprung up almost as soon as the Express completed its first journey, late last century, from Lutetia to Constantinople, the gateway to the Orient. Winding its way through a dozen countries – although that number was currently in flux with the shifts in national makeup – the Transcontinental Express was reputed to play host to smugglers, arms dealers, tragic refugees and dispossessed nobles. Plans were hatched in corridors, assignations made in corners, revolutions decided on platforms while waiting for stationmasters – who may or may not be counter-intelligence operatives – to give the all clear.

Aubrey couldn't wait.

At St Remy Station, Lady Rose left Aubrey and George to wrangle with the Gallian porters and their plans to decant the luggage onto the Transcontinental. There was no shortage of willing hands, but Aubrey could see that actual organisation was thin on the ground. Each of the porters had his own idea of the best way to do things, and each of them had a different idea where the Transcontinental Express actually was. It took a giddy few moments before he and George were able to round up all the porters and herd them into a line. With this leadership, they then transported the bags to the next platform, a mere twenty yards or so away, and into the specially prepared carriage on which they'd spend the next twenty-four hours.

Aubrey lingered. He wanted to inspect the magnificent Transcontinental locomotive.

Gallian locomotive engineering was substantially different from Albion work, but he admired their approach. The locomotive was a 2-6-4 with a tapered boiler, beautifully suited for racing across flat country, but well able to cope with the steep mountain passages that were a major part of the journey. The engine cowling was a highly polished deep blue, with 'Transcontinental Express' emblazoned along its length. Near the driving wheels, he squatted to peer at the coupling rods and nodded in approval at the sound anti-hammering magic that he detected. It was a clever solution.

When Aubrey finally stepped into their special carriage, he removed his hat with some reverence. This was opulence more at home in a palace than in locomotive transport. It was like entering a lavish living room, rather longer and narrower than most, but impressive all the same. The windows were shaded with blue velvet curtains. Oriental screens, potted palms, gas lights on the walls, a discreet but thick Overminster carpet, a heavy sideboard and an absurdly comfortable sofa and chairs were closest to him, while the far half of the carriage was blocked off by what looked like a set of folding doors in strikingly grained ebony.

'Four individual sleeping compartments at the rear,' came a Gallian-accented voice at Aubrey's shoulder. He jumped and whirled to see a dapper attendant, white coated, thinly moustached, reserved and ready. 'A bathroom with full-sized bath – no shortage of hot water, piped directly from the locomotive – and a small library. Small, but well stocked.'

George appeared behind the attendant. 'I say. This is just the ticket!'

'I dare say,' said the attendant, as if he had such approbation from every passenger. On reflection, Aubrey decided he probably did. 'Is there anything you young sirs need before we leave the station?'

Aubrey shook his head. 'I don't think so. It seems as if you've catered for everything.' He had a thought. 'Is there a door at the rear of this carriage?'

'Indeed. But your security men have made sure that it's locked, bolted and chained.'

'Good.'

'Will there be anything else?'

George raised what was obviously a pressing question for him. 'Lunch?'

'Will be available as soon as we leave the station. Fifteen minutes.'

'Excellent.'

It took some time to stow the appropriate luggage, dispatching the rest to the box car, and then it was a matter of setting up Lady Rose so she could continue her work. Absorbed in her presentation, she spoke little as Aubrey and George steered her toward a table in a corner of the carriage, near one of the large windows. She didn't stop working for a second, reading from her papers, frowning and scribbling on them with a well-worn pencil.

Eventually, she was set up just as the train began to glide from the station. The whistle, when it sounded, was smooth and well modulated, far from the usual brazen shriek of a locomotive signal.

So Gallian, Aubrey thought. 'Should we order you some lunch, Mother?'

'Of course.' His mother dashed something on the page she was reading, then she screwed it up and flung it at the waste paper bin that stood near the grand piano. It lobbed in perfectly.

'Anything you'd like?'

He had to wait for some time before he had a reply: 'I'll leave it up to you.'

As they left, Aubrey wondered if she even knew they were there.

Fifteen

THE RESTAURANT CAR WAS TWO CARRIAGES TOWARDS the front of the train. Aubrey and George passed compartments which were sparsely populated; Aubrey amused himself by trying to tell the spies from the saboteurs from the international criminals. Most of them looked like solid business travellers with dark suits and glasses, and briefcases bulging with soap catalogues, but he consoled himself with the knowledge that that was a measure of their craft, adopting such a perfect disguise for crossing countries. Who would suspect a soap salesman of plotting international intrigue?

They also had to make their way through a lounge car, dimly lit even in the middle of the day thanks to the shades pulled down on most of the windows. Conversations here were studiously furtive, as if the few denizens were making a point of their raffish notoriety. A central bar stretched almost the entire length of the lounge car and had attracted a handful of determined-looking travellers, all of whom seemed to be experts at avoiding eye contact.

The restaurant car was another long, narrow oasis of opulence. An aisle ran down the middle with tables under the windows on each side. All was compact but luxurious, with fine china and silverware in place on the starched white linen cloths. Fresh flowers – in low, stable vases – graced every table. They were greeted by a waiter who took them to a vacant table.

For a lunch, it was both substantial and grand. Four courses, from soup through to dessert, with the sort of service that Aubrey had only experienced in the most exclusive of restaurants. His appetite was hearty and he thoroughly enjoyed the experience of appreciating fine food while the train pulled smoothly through the outskirts of Lutetia before gathering itself and racing through the countryside.

Through his shirt, he touched the Beccaria Cage in silent thanks for its good work.

Eventually, George touched his napkin to his lips. 'Superb. That strawberry mousse was the best I've ever had.'

'After your third helping, I guessed as much.'

George sighed with great inner satisfaction. He gazed through the window with a happy smile on his face. 'This is the way to travel. Scenery, good food, comfort.'

'You know, I hear that one of the Holmland dirigible companies is starting passenger flights. That could be spectacular.'

'Good food?'

'They promise it will be first class.'

George nodded. That was enough for him.

Aubrey grinned. 'Let's go to the lounge car for a while.'

'Shouldn't we be getting back to your mother?'

'She's well protected. We can play cards, or backgammon, or chess.'

George put a finger to his nose in a gesture that Aubrey guessed was meant to look conspiratorial. 'You want to spend some time watching the other passengers, don't you?'

'Of course. Call it a spot of covert surveillance, but it really boils down to a bit of poking about.'

'Discreet poking about.'

'Naturally.'

It was also a chance to study the train's journey. Aubrey had chosen a table which had a map on the wall between the windows. It showed the Continent, from Lutetia to Constantinople, with the Transcontinental's passage picked out in blue. After leaving Lutetia, it climbed through the mountains in an almost straight line to the border with Holmland. The border crossing at the dual city of Teve-Grodenberg was the major stop before Fisherberg. A tense city in these times, Aubrey had hoped to have time to do some intelligence gathering around there.

Aubrey sat with his back to the window, the better to keep an eye on the half dozen patrons who were seated at the bar. A waiter brought mineral water and, when asked, a pack of cards. Aubrey admired the stylised representation of the Transcontinental locomotive on the back of the cards and then dealt a hand of Goltan whist. They'd both been introduced to bridge, by Caroline, and enjoyed the fashionably new game, but when there was only the two of them, they always returned to the game of their childhood, Goltan whist.

They had played the game so often, over so many years, that they knew each other's habits extremely well. The two-handed game, in any case, was simple and straightforward, so that the enjoyment didn't come from the play, it came from the company.

While shuffling between hands, he tried a showy single-handed cut. The cards sprayed all over the table.

George raised an eyebrow. 'You've been practising.'

Aubrey scrabbled around on the floor, picking up the cards. 'Almost ready to go on the stage, I'd say.' He barely avoided banging his head on the table as he straightened.

'Stick to magic, old man,' George suggested and, as luck would have it, his voice fitted neatly into one of those silences that fall in a crowded room, so that his words hung in the air like an unusual cloud, the sort that brings people to windows to stare, point and consult books about rare meteorological phenomena.

Aubrey dealt the next hand. 'Well, we didn't set out to draw attention to ourselves, but we've managed it beautifully.'

'Any arms dealers rushing over to try to make a sale to us?'

'No. But a startlingly attractive woman looks as if she's coming this way.'

'She is?' George put down his cards and straightened his tie. 'How do I look?'

'Complex.'

'Complex?'

Aubrey didn't have a chance to answer. The woman had arrived at their table. 'I am Zelinka. You have magic?'

She was tall, taller than George, and dressed entirely in black. Her dress and tight-fitting jacket had the sheen of expensive silk. Aubrey couldn't clearly make out her features for she wore a hat with a veil, but he had the impression of large, dark eyes.

Her voice was husky and undeniably foreign, although her Albionish was good. Aubrey found it hard to guess her origin. Somewhere on the east of the Continent, most probably, although nationalities in that region were often a matter of opinion. Depending on the year of one's birth, one's home town could belong to half a dozen different nations.

When she pushed up her veil, Aubrey swallowed and tried to catalogue a description, both to steady himself and because the authorities might find it useful.

She was only a few years older than he was, middle twenties at the most. Black hair framed her face and her eyes were large and dangerously dark. Exotically beautiful, she had high cheekbones and when she frowned, small, even teeth caught the edge of her dark-red lips.

Aubrey stood, slowly. 'Madame Zelinka.' After gaping for a moment, George also managed to get to his feet.

She turned her head from Aubrey to George and back to Aubrey again. She stared into his face. 'You are the one I was to meet, no?' She dropped her veil. 'I can feel that you have the magic. Where do we talk?'

Aubrey made a split-second decision. She'd obviously mistaken him for someone else, but he was intrigued as to who that was. Who'd be waiting to talk magic on the Transcontinental Express? If he could play along and learn the answer, it could be very useful.

Besides, it was thrilling.

'I am Mr Black,' he said. 'This is my associate, Mr Evans.' He glanced around the lounge car. 'That booth in the corner. It's private enough.'

She followed his gaze, then nodded.

Aubrey endeavoured to convey his intentions to George by way of gestures and facial expressions. George rolled his eyes, but signalled his acquiescence with a shrug. Aubrey was thankful for their long friendship, which meant that words were sometimes unnecessary. This silent dialogue, however, was cut off when the stranger reached the booth and turned. 'I will sit nearest the door.' She slipped into the booth with a rustle of fabric.

'We were going to insist you did,' George said, rallying to his role. She glanced at him sharply, and George smiled the smile of someone who knows a great deal more than he's willing to let on. It was a useful expression, especially for when he didn't have a clue what was going on.

'You're younger than I expected, Mr Black.' She shrugged, minutely. 'It is no matter. I deal with people who seem to be all ages. I make no judgement.'

Aubrey smiled slowly. 'I'm older than I look.'

George coughed into a closed fist. 'And that's old enough.'

Aubrey just restrained himself from kicking George under the table. There was such a thing as over-egging a pudding. 'What do you want?' he said abruptly, trying to catch her off guard. 'Time is short.'

Her expression hardened. 'You are meeting someone else, aren't you?'

'Who we are meeting next is of no concern to you.'

'It's Guttmann, isn't it? I thought I saw him earlier.'

Aubrey made a note of the name and was already congratulating himself for his decision to go along with the pretence. 'I haven't seen Guttmann for years.'

'Don't be a fool. Guttmann will cheat you and then kill you.'

'It's a dangerous business we're in,' Aubrey said, doing his best to hide the fear that woke in his stomach. 'Guttmann and the others.'

Cryptic though his utterances were, they seemed to convince her.

'Your company can supply the magic we need?'

More intelligence gold. Aubrey rubbed mental hands together with delight. 'Provided we're given the right parameters.'

'Parameters? No-one said anything about parameters.'

Aubrey held up a placatory hand. 'You can't do magic without parameters. I'll need to know area of effect, duration, that sort of thing.'

She considered this then nodded. 'I'll need to contact my people.'

'Of course.'

'Your reputation says that you have access to some sort of magical suppression. Is this true?'

Aubrey stared. Had she worked out who he really was? He sought for time. 'It depends. It's difficult to know without some idea of the type of magic we're dealing with.'

'Of course, of course.' She clicked her tongue. 'I need more information from my colleagues.' She stood. 'You will wait to hear from me?'

Aubrey and George were on their feet, and Aubrey took a chance. He sensed that she was keen to do business. 'I have other clients, you know.'

She stiffened. 'I will contact you in Fisherberg.'

'Tomorrow?'

'Yes.'

Aubrey looked at George. He took his cue and nodded. 'Very well,' Aubrey said.

She left without saying goodbye. Aubrey and George resumed their seats. 'Now, old man,' George said. 'Would you mind telling me what that was all about?'

'I'm not entirely sure. I was extemporising.'

'Ah. Making it up as you go along.'

'Exactly. I thought it a lark to see if we could pick up some titbits which could be useful to our spymasters.'

'It seems as if we've stumbled into more than that,' George muttered. 'Striking-looking woman, she was, wouldn't you say?'

'She's too old for you, George. And probably too dangerous.'

'Who is she, anyway?'

'No idea. She didn't give away much, so she's certainly an experienced hand at this.'

'At this? At what?'

'Subterfuge. Clandestine plots. Trans-national schemes.' Aubrey crossed his arms and sat back. 'She's a mercenary, perhaps, or a member of some partisan group or other, resisting something they think needs resisting. The Continent is swarming with such at the moment.'

Aubrey knew that Holmland wasn't alone in its territorial ambitions. The hotbed that was the Goltan Peninsula was a mass of seething malcontent and brooding grudges. Borders moved around as if they were made of rubber. And on the other side of Holmland, even though the Central European Empire was thrashing around in the last days of its viability, Emperor Wolfgang was looking for any excuse to prove it wasn't so.

Riding roughshod over local history, culture and sensibilities was a way of life for those with lofty ambitions and fat heads, and it resulted in resistance leagues and underground movements springing up like mushrooms after autumn rain. All of these groups had axes to grind and there were plenty of shady business people ready to sell them bigger and better axes – at a price.

Aubrey knew that Albion's intelligence agencies were doing what they could to keep informed about these groups. Part of this was defensive, but part of it was strategic. He was sure there was a sub-department somewhere in the Ministry of Defence devoted to working out just which of these groups may be useful in distracting Holmland from war with Albion – or which could be handy allies in the war that was to come. If he could garner any information along these lines, it could be valuable.

George sat up. 'I say. Shouldn't we be getting that lunch to your mother? We promised.'

It had slipped Aubrey's mind. He summoned a waiter and explained his situation. The waiter was happy to organise a luncheon for Lady Rose. Aubrey was sure she wouldn't notice the lateness of the arrival of her meal. When she was immersed in a knotty task, the end of the world could come and go and she wouldn't be aware of it.

They passed the rest of the afternoon in their special carriage. George went back to his newspaper and was making a determined effort to reach his goal of being able to recite its contents by heart. Lady Rose scowled her way through her lunch of soup and a beautifully constructed salad, without leaving a table that had become a city of book towers. Aubrey was left to his own devices and applied himself to reading something he'd found in the small library, a collection of Holmland folktales featuring the unlikely hero of Hans the Cheesemaker, who waddled his way through a series of increasingly bizarre dairy-related adventures.

As evening drew in and the shadows crept across the countryside, the attendant was escorted in by one of the guards. He lit the gaslamps and took away the remains of Lady Rose's meal, which made Aubrey sit up. 'I think I'll go back to the restaurant car,' he announced, 'and book a table for us. We don't want to miss out.'

Lady Rose waved a hand. He had the impression he could have declared he was going to sprout wings and fly to Antipodea and he would have had the same reaction. George grunted. 'You want me to come along, old man?'

'No need, no need. Not when you're making such splendid progress.'

George had already lowered his head. He grunted again.

The lounge car was more crowded at this time of the day. Aubrey wondered if it was the darkness that brought them out, making the furtive ones feel more secure in the shadowy corners of the car. He listened for any details of assassinations or bombings as he eased his way through the well-dressed crowd, but caught nothing except complaints about the water.

A first-class sleeping car separated the lounge car from the restaurant car. It would be a favoured position, Aubrey decided, not far from the amenities of life. The corridor ran alongside the compartments, each closed discreetly. The train was navigating a long curve, for Aubrey found himself leaning outward. Through the windows, he could see they were well into the mountains. The solemn pines were thick and close to the tracks.

The train rocked back the other way and, as it did, the compartment door just in front of Aubrey burst open. A man staggered out. He had blood streaming from a cut on his forehead, but he hardly seemed to notice. He barked a guttural oath, then waded back into the compartment, from which came the unmistakeable sound of a fracas.

Aubrey rushed over. He stood in the doorway, holding onto the frame as the train chose this moment to shudder and jerk.

The compartment was small and compact. The beds had not been pulled down and the two bench seats faced each other. In this cramped space, the bloody-browed man was throwing punches at someone whose presence astonished Aubrey into immobility.

It was Manfred, the erstwhile stage performer, the sleight-of-hand artist who had been revealed as a double agent – and who had led a cadre of Holmland rebels to their deaths.

Manfred looked the same as when Aubrey had last seen him – tall, well groomed, neat pointed beard – but his composed stage persona was a million miles away from what Aubrey was presented with here. Manfred was absorbing the battering from Bloody Brow while keeping one arm flung out to prevent a woman from leaving the corner where he'd trapped her. He stood unflinching, taking the punches on his body and face as he concentrated on keeping the woman confined. She wasn't helpless, either. She was hammering at the back of his head with cold fury.

Then she saw Aubrey and she froze. She pointed at him. Bloody Brow turned and gaped, letting his fists fall to his side. Manfred didn't move.

'That's him, Guttmann, he's your competitor,' the woman said, and Aubrey saw that it was Madame Zelinka, his mysterious contact from the lounge car. She didn't have a veil this time and her exotic beauty was on full display.

Manfred stared, and appeared as astonished as Aubrey. 'You?' He looked over his shoulder at her. 'That's him?'

In two steps, Bloody Brow crossed the compartment and seized Aubrey by the shoulders. He smiled, and the effect was disturbing. As well as the rivulets of blood coursing down his face, Bloody Brow had very bad teeth.

'Well,' Aubrey said. 'It looks like you have this all under control. I'll just be going.'

'I don't sink zo,' Bloody Brow said. He yanked at Aubrey and stuck out a foot. Aubrey tripped and stumbled into the compartment. Before he knew it, Manfred had grabbed him and pulled him closer. He squinted, staring at Aubrey, studying his face as if he had writing on it that was small and hard to read. Then a gust of cold air whipped over his shoulder and he smiled.

Aubrey saw that the outer door had been flung open. He flailed, but all he managed to grab was a feather from Madame Zelinka's hat. Then, suddenly and awfully, Manfred heaved and Aubrey was sailing through the air.

He had time to see that the train was crossing a steel bridge before he began the long arc to whatever lay below.

Sixteen

UBREY WAS FALLING. HE WAS RELATIVELY HAPPY about this state of affairs; it meant that he hadn't yet reached the sudden stop at the bottom.

Wind tore at him. A yell was wrenched from his throat as he flailed uselessly. Every fibre of his being wanted him to be perched cosily on solid ground instead of falling free and heading toward certain death.

It made rational thought difficult, but in the middle of his terror, his attention was taken by what he had in his left hand.

An ostrich feather. Long, black, flapping wildly, it was indisputably an ostrich feather. Dimly he remembered snatching for something solid as he was hurled from the compartment. He saw his hand seizing the most flimsy handhold imaginable – the feather in the hat of Madame Zelinka.

Suddenly, a spell wrote itself across his mind in blazing

letters a dozen feet high. Like to like, the Law of Sympathy, the ostrich feather. He barked out syllables that were torn from his throat by the wind. He finished, sought desperately for any sign of taking on featherlike floating, then he hit the ground.

That's a good sign, Aubrey thought groggily as he lay on his back and gazed at the branches overhead. *I can open my eyes.*

He groaned. He felt as if a herd of elephants wearing concrete boots had wandered over him on the way to a meeting, then come back to look at the lumpy patch they'd stumbled over. He closed his eyes and waited while the thundering in his head abated. In the painful interim, he scrabbled at the ground and his hands came back full of pine needles. He stared at them numbly. They must have helped cushion his fall. Then he felt the rocks under the pine needles and he decided that his hasty feather spell must have worked.

Slowly, with every movement revealing a new bruise – but nothing more serious – he sat up. A few deep breaths and he felt rash enough to attempt to stand. When he did, he swayed on rubbery legs, glad he could feel anything at all. He checked, and the Beccaria Cage was still around his neck, and it was undamaged.

He heard the sound of water nearby. Limping and shuffling like a crab, he winced his way to the edge of a stream, silver in the moonlight. He stood watching the ripples for a moment, then he looked up at the dark sky. He stared for a moment, then all the strength went from his knees and he sat, heavily, on the soft, muddy bank.

Some time later, he realised that the stream lay at the bottom of a gorge. The railway bridge stretched across it. It was high above the tallest trees and Aubrey's head spun as he tried to work out how far he'd fallen. Two hundred feet? More?

He looked back to where he'd landed, half-expecting to find an Aubrey-shaped outline imprinted in the ground. Then he crawled over and searched the area until he found the ostrich feather. He held it up and laughed. Just a little. It hurt too much otherwise.

After tucking the feather inside his jacket, he trudged to the stream again and washed his face. The water was icy cold and took his breath away. He drank a sip or two, not because he was thirsty, but for something to do while he thought.

His body must have taken on just a little of a feather's lightness before he struck the ground. He still had momentum, but that last instant transformation may have saved his life.

Giddy with relief, he stood and pushed back his hair. He was alive, and that at least gave him a chance to try to work out what had happened. The mysterious Madame Zelinka had obviously been having a disagreement with Manfred and another equally mysterious man. A deal gone wrong? An old grudge? Three people – who was allied with whom? Or was it a triangle of mistrust, each of the other two?

And why was Manfred here? He'd disappeared after betraying Count Brandt and his people, but Aubrey doubted that he'd gone to an idle retirement. A Holmland spy like him could be involved in a hundred different plots.

Aubrey had admired Manfred's stage skills, and had been assured of his loyalty to the exiled Holmlanders' cause during the Brandt episode. When the truth of Manfred's treachery became known Aubrey had been outraged. The notion of that sort of betrayal offended him in a deep and affecting way. It wasn't just the loss of life, it was the baseness of the act, the calculated, cold-hearted ability to doom others for personal gain.

It made his head hurt all over again. All that was clear was that the instant Aubrey arrived, at least two of the people in that compartment had suddenly decided he was more important than their disagreement. United against him, they pitched him out of his train.

To his death.

He shuddered, then took a deep breath. George would miss him soon, and his mother would too. Eventually. It wasn't that she didn't care for him, he added to himself. It was simply that when she was busy, little things like food and missing offspring tended to slip by her.

George would realise something was wrong, but Aubrey could imagine it taking some time before he could convince the authorities on the train of this. Then there would have to be a search of the train. And after that? How far away would the train be by then? Could George, and his mother, make it stop?

He shook his head. He was on his own in the shadowy wilderness. He had to do his best to get to civilisation. The border crossing was only a few hours away. If he could get word to an Albion consul by telegraph, then all would be well.

Now. Which way to the nearest telegraph station?

A breeze made its way down the course of the stream. The trees lining the banks sighed; the sound spread across the night like a chorus of disapproving librarians. The landscape was alive with motion – shadowy, half-glimpsed movements as branches swayed, leaves bent and dipped. Aubrey could hear nothing artificial, not a sign of humanity. No machinery, no voices, no music. He may as well have been the only person on the face of the planet.

He rubbed his hands together. Twenty or thirty of his bruises demanded his attention but he ignored them and studied the water. *Right*, he thought. *If I follow it downstream, it's bound to reach a bigger stream. If I follow that, I'll come to a river. And so on.*

All he had to do was keep working in the direction of the current. Eventually he'd find a settlement, or a town, or something that took advantage of the waterway. If he were in luck, it would be big enough and well connected enough to have a telegraph station.

He found his wallet was still in his inner jacket pocket. Failing a telegraph station, he'd hire a local to drive him to the border, or ferry him. He'd even buy a horse if he had to.

He touched the Beccaria Cage for luck, then set off.

Aubrey had camped out enough not to be spooked by the noises of the night. As he slogged along the bank, pushing through reeds and skirting huge thickets of blackberries, he tried to reconstruct the map of the area in his mind. Dense forest was what he could remember, and he couldn't argue with that level of accuracy. The Stallaard River was the main waterway in the region, but he thought that it was rather north of the train line. He tried to work out from the moon's position which direction he was heading, but he couldn't remember the formula. Was it forty degrees right of the moon at midnight or left of the moon at some other time he couldn't remember anyway?

This poser kept him occupied for some time as the land fell way steadily and the stream on his left-hand side grew noisier and noisier. Without noticing it, he'd picked up a handy stick. When the way underfoot became rocky, he was grateful for it, using it as a staff to help his passage.

Footing and direction kept him busy enough so that he didn't notice the man standing in his way until he almost bumped into him.

Aubrey stopped dead and stared. The man was gigantic. In the moonlight and shadow, it looked as if he were carved out of rock, roughly, with great slabs for a face. *If ever I've seen a brigand*, Aubrey thought, *this is one*. In fact, he decided this was such a good example the man deserved to be stuffed, mounted and put on display in a museum with a neatly lettered card saying 'Brigand' underneath.

'What kept you so long?' the giant growled in rough Gallian. 'We've been waiting for you.'

Aubrey almost laughed. Being mistaken for someone else was becoming almost commonplace. 'I had a fall.'

The giant looked down at him. 'A fall? You seem all right.'

'It could have been worse.'

The giant decided that this was an appropriate response. 'This way.' That was the last Aubrey heard from him for some time.

The noise of rushing water grew louder as the giant guided Aubrey through what had become a rough and ready path between clefts in the rock. The stream had grown up into a wild and rushing river. Soon, they were deeper in the gorge, a chasm where the night sky far above was a narrow sliver, its darkness considerably lighter than the blackness around them. The giant picked his way carefully but confidently, pausing and extending a massive hand to help Aubrey in tricky sections. He kept his silence, only breaking it with a grunt now and then to draw Aubrey's attention to a slippery section, or loose shale underfoot or any one of a hundred perils concealed by the shadows that didn't seem to inconvenience him in the slightest.

After five minutes, they began to climb up the side of the gorge. Aubrey divided his time between concentrating on his guide's broad back, making sure he was secure on the narrow ledge, rehearsing a few spells that might be useful, and trying not to think about the fall that was waiting for him on his left. He'd had quite enough near-death plummeting for one night.

Caves, he thought glumly when he glimpsed a flicker of light in the rock wall. *I should have known we were going to end up in a cave.*

He shrugged, nearly overbalanced, steadied himself against the rough rock on his right. He hoped that the caves were the dry and cheery sort, well ventilated, with none of the dankness that made grottoes so depressing, despite what the poets say.

The entrance was four or five yards wide, and tall enough for the giant to enter with only the slightest bowing of his head. He stood just inside and beckoned Aubrey forward.

For a moment, Aubrey was indecisive, then he stood straighter. It wouldn't do to appear hesitant. He reminded himself that the brigand's friends – whoever they were – were expecting someone, so he needed to be that someone. Someone bold enough to turn up in the middle of nowhere for a rendezvous. Someone confident enough to be out in the wilderness alone. Someone to be taken seriously and not dispatched immediately.

Having decided all that, he strode into cave looking right and left, and stood, hands on hips. 'Now, who's in charge here?' he demanded into the murky firelight, while his eyes adjusted.

The cave smelled not of damp, but of the soot and ash that came from the large fire in the middle and from the lanterns and torches that were sitting on rock ledges or jammed into crevices. This gave the effect of a marquee filled with party lights, but those assembled, staring at Aubrey, scowling and suspicious, looked as if they'd be rather out of place at a summer evening soiree.

He could make out a dozen, maybe a score of them. Dark haired and dark eyed, they had a wild and abandoned look about them. He cast his gaze around the cave – slowly, confidently, with a touch of impatience – and they studied him with weather-beaten faces. Their clothes were a mixture of browns and greens, looking remarkably durable. Each one of them had firearms, cudgels or knives close at hand – tools of the trade, Aubrey guessed. The brigands were sitting on rough stools or benches, a few standing and leaning against the cave walls as smoke whirled past them and up into the black heights, drawn by a natural chimney that was no doubt one of the attractions of the place.

The only ones without extravagant black moustaches were the three women. Their eyes were just as flinty as the men and Aubrey had no desire to cross them, not the way one of them was honing a long and obviously much-used knife. She looked at him speculatively and he wasn't reassured. It made him feel like a Sunday roast just before carving.

These had to be the brigands his father had mentioned, and Aubrey's situation became more than simple survival. He now had a duty to observe, investigate and report.

'In charge?' came a voice in rough Gallian that was overlaid with a Goltan accent. It was followed by the sound of spittle sizzling in a fire. 'I am in charge, for my sins. Who did you expect?'

Aubrey bit his tongue. He'd had an overwhelming impulse to say, 'No-one, really. I'm a stranger here and you've got the wrong person entirely,' but he managed to clamp down on it. 'And you are?' he said with what he hoped was professional wariness.

The man stalked out of the shadows. He was tall and rangy, with a neatly pointed beard to complement his drooping moustache, and with a melancholy, brooding aspect about him. 'Rodolfo.'

'Just Rodolfo?'

'Rodolfo is enough.' Rodolfo pushed back his wide-brimmed hat and studied Aubrey. 'You're younger than I expected.'

'I'm not responsible for your expectations,' Aubrey said, 'and I can't do much about my youth.' He eyed the cavern sceptically. 'But I'm old enough to find this place disappointing.'

The brigands muttered at this. Aubrey felt a trickle of sweat slide down the back of his neck as he heard the sound of knives being drawn. And did that 'click' come from the safety catch of a Tolmeyer Military Pistol?

Rodolfo squinted at him. 'You are Castellano?'

Aubrey was exquisitely aware of the number of hand weapons in the immediate vicinity, but he knew that he had to stake his claim to being taken seriously. So he went for something that he imagined would be impressive to a band of brigands. He couldn't pretend to be Castellano – he knew nothing of the man and would be tripped up in seconds. Reaching for an alternative, he remembered playing the part of Captain Green in *Those Darkest Hours* at Stonelea School. Green was a mercenary and a bully, but a highly intelligent one. He was perfect.

'Of course I'm not Castellano.' He did his best to bristle with indignation. 'What sort of unit are you running here? If you don't know what Castellano looks like, you could be fooled by anyone!'

'You're not Castellano?' Rodolfo's eyes were steady. 'What happened to him?'

'I killed him,' Aubrey said in his best Captain Green voice. Menacing and authoritative were the keys to getting that character right. 'He was a careless fool. When the train slowed down before the bridge, it was obvious that he was about to leave. I followed him.'

'He's dead? What about his body?'

'It won't be found. Not with the spells I used.'

To judge from the hush that fell, this was appropriately demonstrative of a ruthless nature. Rodolfo studied him with what Aubrey hoped was respect. 'So. And you are?'

'Call me Mr Black. I represent certain interests. Interests that are old rivals of Castellano.'

'He mentioned nothing of this.'

'Did he represent his company as a leading supplier?' *Of what*, Aubrey desperately wanted to know. 'Did he say he could help you?'

'He did.'

'Hah. He was lying. He was a fly-by-night operation. He would have taken your money and that would have been the last you saw of him.'

'I don't think so.' Rodolfo thoughtfully fingered the bandolier of bullets that ran across his chest. 'We have ways of making sure we get what we want.'

And what do you want? 'My colleagues and I do not like competitors, even ones so puny as Castellano and Co. Especially those that do not deliver. It is bad for business.'

'So you can supply the weapons that Castellano could not?'

Weapons! 'Of course. What are you looking for?'

'Magic. If we are to stop Veltran from destroying itself, we want some of the compressed spells we hear so much about.' He nodded. 'Of course, we may use such to continue causing havoc in Holmland as we make our way home.'

This brought various expressions of enthusiasm from the brigands – throaty cheers, assent, and a few voices struck up the Veltranian national anthem, but it petered out and became an argument about the actual words.

Aubrey now was in a different situation from the one he had thought. Instead of facing instant death at the hands of a band of itinerant bandits, he was facing instant death at the hands of some sort of partisan underground political organisation from the Goltans that had relocated into Gallia. Admittedly, the outcome could be the same, but the complexion of this encounter had changed abruptly.

Initially, it had been a case of bluffing his way out of the clutches of outlaws. Now he had to do that – or escape any way he could – and report back to the Albion intelligence agencies about this development. Rogue elements operating out of Gallia and attacking Holmland installations could be just the excuse Holmland needed to advance into Gallian territory, precipitating who knew what response from Gallia. Or would Holmland just assume the attackers were Gallian? The result would be the same. And, naturally, Albion would have to come to the aid of their Continental ally and the whole ghastly business would be on in earnest.

And their expressed desire to stop Veltran from destroying itself? He knew that Veltran, like many of the Goltan States, was torn by factions. Some of these factions had links to Holmland and welcomed stronger ties with the dominant state on the Continent. Not Rodolfo's crew, from the sounds of it.

Aubrey was in a dangerous situation. Adventures were all well and good, but right at this minute he would have preferred being on the train with a warm cup of cocoa.

'Compressed spells are dangerous,' he began.

'Dangerous?' Rodolfo said. He rubbed at his forehead. With his sad eyes, Aubrey thought he looked more like a priest than a revolutionary. 'We've grown accustomed to danger, Mr Black. In Veltran, heart of the Goltans, danger is when your friends become your enemies overnight.'

More muttered approval from the shadows. Rodolfo didn't have the swagger that went along with being a brigand chief, but his followers seemed devoted to him. A reluctant leader, was Aubrey's summation.

'I can get my hands on compressed spells,' Aubrey admitted, seeing the way the negotiation was headed. These people weren't about to be dissuaded by doubts about safety. More muttering came from the brigand chorus, rather more cheery this time as they considered the possibility of new implements of mayhem. 'What sort of thing are you after?'

'Thunderstorms.' Rodolfo studied him closely. 'We heard of a compressed weather spell that exploded in Albion, recently. It did much damage.'

'It flattened a whole building,' Aubrey said, hiding his surprise. He remembered the destruction of St Olaf's church hall, one of the series of events leading up to Dr Tremaine's attempt to turn Trinovant into a living creature. Count Brandt had nearly been killed. Weather magic was awkward – dangerous, difficult to manage, but spectacular.

'Your people have access to such things?'

'Oh, certainly,' Aubrey said, thinking of the resources of the Magisterium, or whatever they'd become. He was sure that Craddock would be able to supply a weather spell if he thought cultivating these people might be useful.

Rodolfo gestured to the giant at the entrance of the cave. 'We have a list, what we want.'

Aubrey had to keep up appearances. 'Not so fast,' he said as a sheaf of tattered paper was thrust on him. 'We need to discuss payment.'

Rodolfo smiled wryly. 'Of course. You are a businessman, not a patriot.' He dragged a stool from underneath a protesting brigand and sat on it himself. He put his elbow on his knee and his chin in his hand. 'Tell me what you want. I will protest, of course, but we will eventually reach an understanding. It is the way.'

'Gold. Deposited in a Helvetica bank.'

Softly, he whispered a spell he'd been rehearsing and snapped his fingers. A bright green flame shot upward from them, an intense jet that reached the rocky ceiling before disappearing, leaving an unexpected smell of mothballs.

Rodolfo didn't move, but a few startled oaths came from his followers, and some dark mutterings. Rodolfo sighed. 'Gold in a Helvetica bank? I can arrange that. Now, let's haggle over price.'

Aubrey shook his head. 'We never haggle.' He glanced at the sheaf of papers and he plucked a figure out of the air. 'Ten thousand pounds.'

'Done.' Rodolfo raised his eyebrow sardonically and caught Aubrey's eye. Immediately Aubrey knew he'd come in too low. It galled him, not because he had anything at stake, but he hated losing even when he had no personal interest.

When Rodolfo gestured and the hospitality phase of the negotiations began, Aubrey was torn. He knew it was dangerous to refuse food and drink offered like this – and he was ravenous after his trek through the woods – but he knew the train was getting further and further away.

But there was no stopping Rodolfo's band. While their leader brooded, leaning against the wall of the cavern with his arms crossed on his chest, a brace of pheasants roasted on a spit. A cask of wine was broached and soon the cave was full of lusty singing.

Someone pushed a mug of wine on Aubrey. He nodded his thanks but only pretended to drink.

He worked his way around the cavern, weaving among the happy band, making mental notes for his report. The origination of the boxes that most sat on. The calibre and make of the rifles. The makeshift radio equipment at the rear of the cavern. The maps unscrolled on the table. A ragtag bunch they might look, but they were reasonably well equipped, and deadly serious.

Aubrey was having trouble labelling them. Were they brigands? Freedom fighters? Revolutionaries? He decided that this would only be known in hindsight, when all was done, and the histories were being written by the victors. It gave him pause, the shifting nature of things, the uncertain times in which he lived. Belief could lead to great deeds or it could lead to horror – the line was a delicate one and again hindsight was the only way to know when one had stepped over it.

Sizzling pheasant meat, mushrooms, sliced roast potatoes and fresh bread on a tin plate appeared in front of him. 'Eat, eat,' Rodolfo said. 'You are too skinny. Eat.'

Aubrey's stomach insisted that Rodolfo was right. He took the plate, sat on a coil of rope, and, while the singing around him redoubled, its contents vanished with surprising speed.

He wiped the plate with the crust of bread, wondering where it came from. A nearby village friendly to their cause? An elderly man staggered past, roaring what could be considered a song, even if it was a completely different one from that the rest of them were trying to sing. It was as if he'd taken a tune, gutted it, stuffed it with random notes while preserving the words and then decided that volume was more important than tune anyway, dammit.

Aubrey looked for their leader, and found him away from the centre of activity. He was still sitting on his stool, still brooding, watching his band enjoy themselves. 'They're happy,' Aubrey said.

'Happiness passes, but it is good while it lasts.'

'You've been out here long?'

Rodolfo glanced sidelong at Aubrey. 'Long enough.'

'It must be difficult, fighting for your cause.'

Another sidelong glance. 'Fighting is difficult at any time.'

'You're not a soldier then?'

This time, Rodolfo turned to face Aubrey squarely. 'I was a school teacher, Mr Black. When Holmland sympathisers murdered the president of my country, I was appalled but did nothing. When anti-Holmland agitators killed the man who led our army, I was aghast. When the government began to round up people to stop the killing, I lost track of who was who. When my brother was seduced by those who claimed that Veltranians were historically a Holmlandish people and joined a group who wanted to blow things up, I wrote a letter to the newspaper denouncing such things.' His face hardened. 'I was called in by the headmaster, told that I no longer had a job. When I went home to my flat, the landlord threw me on the street. A band of men then assaulted me and as I lay in the gutter I realised that being appalled and aghast and affronted wasn't enough. I knew I had to fight.'

Rodolfo's voice was soft, but Aubrey heard every word, despite the carousing that was going on. He felt the man's pain, his anger, his loss, but he had to ask. 'And you're certain you're fighting for the right cause?'

Rodolfo's dark eyes were intense. He leaned forward. 'Certainty is a fool's crutch.' He stood and stretched. 'Now, Mr Black. You seem to be still here.'

'That's what I wanted to talk about.' Aubrey brushed off his trousers. His stomach was full; he felt warm and strong. 'What's the best way to get back to my train?'

'You want to rejoin it?' Rodolfo made a gesture as if it were a matter of little importance, something of the order of an annoying fly. 'This is no problem. Carlito will take you. Carlito!'

A scrawny figure stumbled out of the unruly choir, nearly tripping on the outstretched sleeping form of a replete outlaw. He wore a stocking cap over greasy, greying hair. He was small and ferret-like, with a prominent nose. He looked inquiringly at Rodolfo, who gestured at Aubrey. 'This man wants to get to the Transcontinental Express.'

Carlito screwed up his eyes. 'Now?'

'As soon as possible,' Aubrey said.

'Carlito will get you there,' Rodolfo said.

'How?'

'Raft, signor. Raft,' Carlito said, grinning in a gap-toothed way that made the word sound like the equivalent of 'death trap'.

It was.

Seventeen

*T*HE RAFT TRIP WAS MADNESS. WITHIN MINUTES, AUBREY was convinced that Carlito was the man for the job.

The raft itself was a ramshackle assemblage that looked more like an accidental coming-together of flotsam than a water-tight, navigable vessel. Some of it was made of barrels, some of it was sheet metal, some of it was rope and netting, a fair proportion of it was prayers. Branches were woven in and out of the chaos, but most of the raft was still open space. Carlito had to steady Aubrey as he boarded because his feet found gaps more easily than solid construction. The raftman's grin didn't waver as Aubrey wobbled, lurched and eventually threw himself at the spot Carlito indicated with a blackened finger. Then, picking a rope somewhat at random, Aubrey thought, Carlito cast off and they were whipped into the maelstrom.

Aubrey's first reaction, after a faceful of icy spray, was that the river had more than grown up. He'd first encountered it as a wild mountain stream, wayward, but still young and with a chance to reform. Now, it was a hardened villain of a waterway, carving its way through solid rock at the bottom of the perilous gorge. In seconds, Aubrey's breath was driven from him in a series of plunges that jarred his bones and drenched him in water he was sure would have frozen if it had stayed still for even an instant. His teeth chattered; his hands hurt from gripping whatever structural component was closest and least likely to detach itself.

The darkness at the bottom of the gorge was almost complete, so Aubrey couldn't anticipate the wild changes in direction and the plummeting, swerving passage of the raft. Flashes of white foam made him jerk his head left and right but imminent death was on every side, only interrupted by the towering darkness of immense rocks that even the thunderous river couldn't shift.

As they were flung through the watery violence, Aubrey was constantly battered by the roar the river made as it sped along, madcap and unbridled. The noise filled the narrow space and assaulted them as if it were alive and malicious. It was an all-consuming sound, a head-filling sound. It hissed and bellowed, and underneath was the grinding of boulders being dragged along the riverbed.

Carlito's navigation was eccentric. He stood, swaying, at the rear of the craft, with a heavy wooden pole under his right arm which he used to fend off the rocks that threatened to bring their journey to an abrupt end, although how he saw them Aubrey had no idea. This was a rational, even sensible course of action, but it wasn't consistent. At times Carlito simply grinned as the raft slammed into the sides of the gorge or into a fang of rock, and allowed the raft to career away down the gorge. How he chose which to fend off and which not to defeated Aubrey. He gave up trying to work out the raftman's method. Instead he concentrated on hanging on.

He had no idea how long the passage took. The ride took a few seconds or a few lifetimes, one or the other.

Carlito left the jelly-legged Aubrey on the outskirts of Agoulle, where the river burst from the chasm, widened and lost most of its violence. Behind them was the dark cleft of the gorge, which Aubrey was sure had a charming local nickname like 'the Widowmaker'. Any description of it would be accompanied by the opinion that only lunatics would attempt passage through it.

Carlito, apparently a professional lunatic, steered the raft under some willows. He pointed to the lights of the houses and to where the railway line ran alongside the main street. For a moment, Aubrey sat on the raft and stared upward, enjoying the stars and the way they'd stopped wheeling crazily across the sky. Then he took a deep breath and launched himself onto the river bank. It was soggy and evil-smelling from what Aubrey suspected was animal droppings, but it had the immensely wonderful benefit of not being the raft.

With some reluctance, he looked over his shoulder. 'How will you get back?' he asked Carlito.

Carlito glanced at the raft he was standing on. It was noticeably smaller than the vessel in which they'd begun their journey. 'I will walk. A few days, I will be back with Rodolfo.'

'What about your raft?'

He shrugged. 'They only last one journey.'

Aubrey understood. He shook the man's hand and Carlito disappeared back upriver.

Aubrey straightened his dripping jacket and staggered toward the lights. A few minutes later, the Transcontinental Express rumbled into the town, slowing for the tiny village. Aubrey ran hard as it rattled through a series of switches. He sprinted alongside, sure-footed in the dark, and swung up with the sort of cavalier deftness that comes after staring utter annihilation in the face and surviving it.

The rocking of the train and the warm blanket nearly made Aubrey nod off. With an effort, he listened to George and his mother take turns in explaining how worried they'd been.

'I'm sorry,' he said again after they ran out of ways to make him feel guilty for having been thrown off the train.

'Good,' George said and he sat back, arms crossed.

'And what do we do now?' his mother asked. 'Are those people still on the train?'

Aubrey yawned, stifled it. 'Send one of Tallis's people to see. He can liaise with the conductors and train officials.'

'You're not worried about them?' George asked.

Aubrey thought that he'd had a surfeit of worry in the last few hours. 'All I really want to do is sleep.' His fatigue-muffled brain lumbered through a number of thoughts. 'No. Must compile a report first. Get it to Craddock. Or Tallis. Or whoever it is today.' He looked at his mother. 'Or should I go straight to Father?'

'You'll go straight to bed.'

'I agree, old man,' George said. 'Any report you try to write tonight is likely to be three parts nonsense. Plenty of time for clear thinking in the morning. We're not due to arrive in Fisherberg until eleven o'clock.'

'Code,' Aubrey mumbled. His head suddenly felt very heavy. Or had it somehow turned to iron, attracted to the magnet concealed in the armrest of the chair? 'I'll have to work up a code to use.'

'I'm sure the embassy in Fisherberg will be able to help,' Lady Rose said.

Aubrey studied her for a moment, the time it took for him to make sense of her words. Finally, he nodded, which was a mistake, one that sleep had been waiting for. It enfolded him and he didn't resist.

Aubrey woke feeling groggy, but a fine breakfast revitalised him enough to spend an hour feverishly writing an account of the bizarre encounter with the Veltranian rebels. George and Lady Rose both wisely left him alone, retiring to the lounge car and only returning when the train reached the outskirts of Fisherberg.

Fisherberg was a fine old city that was making a determined effort to be a dominant modern city. Aubrey put the finishing touches on his account – folding it up and patting it into an inside jacket pocket – in time to see that the train had slowed and was making its way along the bank of the Istros River. The riverbanks here seemed to be totally devoted to factories which were competing to see who could belch out the most smoke, with a subsidiary competition in foulest-smelling waste-water discharge.

He wished Caroline were with him. Not for her company, he quickly reassured himself. Her knowledge of Fisherberg would be useful, that was all. She'd know if the factories were a recent development or not. She could be a handy guide. Helpful, in a practical way. And he couldn't be chided for seeking her company on that basis, could he?

Having convinced himself of this – and he told himself he was hard-headed and rational on this score – he tried to estimate how many factories they were passing. It was heavy industry here, obviously, and no doubt it was part of the Chancellor's grand plan for Holmland. He wondered how many of them were making arms and weapons.

George strolled in. 'Remind me never to play whist with your mother again, old man.' He peered out of the window.

Aubrey stretched. 'Ah, yes. I should have warned you.'

'She's a demon. Wiped me out conclusively. Would have been embarrassing, if anyone had have been watching.'

'The lounge car was empty?'

'A veritable ghost car.'

'Hmm. It makes me wonder how many people have managed to slip off this train en route.'

'Very mysterious. Now, where are we staying in Fisherberg? Somewhere with a good table, I hope. Lunch is just around the corner.'

'Father insisted we stay at the embassy. And don't worry, Quentin Hollows has assured us that he has an excellent Lutetian chef on staff.'

'Hollows? He's the ambassador? Good chap?'

'He's one of Father's old friends, from the early days in the House. He can be trusted.'

Quentin Hollows had been one of his father's earliest appointments after he won the election last year. He'd recalled the previous ambassador – Sir Wallace Bannister, a notorious timeserver and crony of Rollo Armitage – and replaced him with someone who could actually speak Holmlandish. Apart from that useful skill, Quentin Hollows was an outstanding political strategist who had helped Darius Fitzwilliam in his campaigning. He was the sort who was useful to have in the capital of the most warlike nation on the Continent, the nation that was shaping up to be Albion's foe. He was also a natural diplomat; Quentin Hollows was not about to put his foot in anything.

'Excellent, excellent.' George rubbed his hands together. 'I'll help you then. I enjoy packing.'

George's packing was instructional. Mostly it consisted of roaming around Aubrey's sleeping compartment and slinging items at the trunk in any order, as they came to hand. After that, it was simply a matter of sitting on the lid of the trunk until it could be latched shut. 'That's why trunk lids are built so solidly,' George explained as they stood to one side and let the porter ease his trolley under the edge of the compacted luggage. Aubrey thought that if the trunk did give up and disgorge its contents, the result could be dangerous, as well as embarrassing. He wasn't looking forward to explaining how the porter's head injury was caused by flying underwear.

In the hustle and bustle of the Central Fisherberg station, Albion embassy officials were waiting on the platform. A tall, distinguished-looking man dispatched officials to take over from the porters who were grappling with the luggage. Then he approached Aubrey's mother, who was thanking the attendant who'd taken care of them on the train. The official wore a dark blue suit in the modern style, with a striped tie that Aubrey thought belonged to one of the better squash clubs in Trinovant. He took off his hat and gloves and handed them to an obviously less important official. 'Lady Rose?'

Aubrey's mother immediately brightened. 'Quentin! It's good to see you. How is Fisherberg treating you?'

He took her hand in both of his and held it for a moment. 'Fisherberg is a fine town,' he said. 'Holmlanders are naturally generous, you know, and hospitable.'

'I've always thought so. If it weren't for politics . . .'

She left the thought unfinished, but Aubrey could see the guarded expression on Hollows's face. 'Now,' he said, plainly changing the subject. A train on the next platform screeched a warning whistle and started to pull out in a cloud of steam. 'I haven't seen your son for years.'

Lady Rose made the introductions. Hollows had done his homework, for he asked cheerful questions about St Alban's College and university life that left both Aubrey and George impressed. 'I should make introductions myself,' he said eventually. 'Some new members of my staff: Mr Todd and Mr Stevens. Cultural attachés.'

Two figures had been hovering nearby, discreetly, and at the mention of their names they eased themselves through the crush. One murmured polite excuses, while the other did his best not to knock anyone over.

Aubrey stared. George started to laugh but it was cut off when Hollows stepped on his toes with some force.

Mr Todd and Mr Stevens were Hugo von Stralick and Otto Kiefer wearing disguises.

Aubrey looked at Hollows, who raised his eyebrow, minutely. He turned back to his new cultural attachés. He stared at the false beards and dark glasses. 'Mr Todd,' he said in a strangled voice. He held out his hand to von Stralick.

'I'm Stevens,' he said sharply.

'Of course you are. And that would make you Mr Todd?'

Kiefer nodded decisively, as if he'd been preparing himself for this moment. 'I am Todd. I am an inexperienced cultural attaché, but I am willing to learn.'

George shook hands mutely.

I hope the explanation for all this is a good one, Aubrey thought.

'That's a good explanation,' Aubrey said, 'but it isn't actually explaining anything I wanted explained.'

'I'm sorry.' Hollows eased himself back into the embrace of the leather armchair. 'I thought a quick précis of the political situation was in order.' The inner drawing room in the Albion Embassy was extremely comfortable. It was high-ceilinged, with duck-egg blue walls and elaborate eighteenth-century cornices. Landscape paintings of idyllic Albion countryside hung on the walls except over the wedding-cake of a fireplace, where a vast gilt-framed mirror took up residence and reflected with all its might.

Lady Rose was sitting in a red velvet easy chair, regarding the ambassador with some sympathy. Von Stralick and

Kiefer were sitting side by side on a leather sofa. They'd discarded their disguises. Kiefer looked uncomfortable, but that was such a customary attitude that Aubrey thought no more of it. Von Stralick was far more composed, but Aubrey thought he was on edge, despite the easiness of his manner.

'*I* appreciated it, Quentin,' Lady Rose said. 'Don't be so ungracious, Aubrey.'

'I'm sorry,' Aubrey said. 'I am grateful, please don't think that I'm not.' He was. Hollows had confirmed that Dr Tremaine had embedded himself firmly as the Chancellor's most trusted adviser. 'But what I'd really like an explanation for is these two.' He pointed at von Stralick and Kiefer, who had remained silent during Hollow's briefing.

Hollows glanced at the two Holmlanders with a touch of amusement. 'Our helpful friends? Of course.'

Lady Rose made an impatient noise. 'I gather that this is some sort of intelligence tomfoolery, but I don't like being kept in the dark. Everyone here except me seems to know something about these two, apart from the fact that they like wearing disguises.'

Von Stralick stood to attention. A moment later, after a subtle kick, Kiefer did as well. 'I'm sorry, Lady Rose,' von Stralick said. 'Todd and Stevens were assumed names, as you've gathered. I am Hugo von Stralick, at one time a junior functionary in the Holmland Embassy in your country. This is my cousin, Otto Kiefer.'

'Hugo is the Holmland spy I've told you about, Mother,' Aubrey said.

Von Stralick looked pained, but this disappeared as he and Kiefer sat again. ' "Spy" is a word I do not like using, even at the best of times.'

'What about "failed spy"?' George suggested.

'Thank you, Doyle. I am indebted to you for your unflinching honesty.'

Hollows coughed. 'Von Stralick is working for me at the moment. He has no official role with the Holmland intelligence services, but I find his understanding of the Holmland situation to be valuable.'

'What about your superior's superior?' Aubrey asked von Stralick. 'You'd hoped he may be able to help you.'

'Ah yes, Baron von Grolman. He apparently saw the writing on the wall and resigned from the Chancellor's government. Withdrawn from public life, I understand.' He looked unhappy. 'Whatever has gone on, I'm having trouble contacting him.'

'Dr Tremaine's doing?' Aubrey asked.

Hollows nodded. 'It wasn't long after Dr Tremaine assumed his new role in the inner sanctum of Holmland decision-making that Baron von Grolman was accused of embezzlement. It was a trumped-up charge. The baron is so wealthy he doesn't need to stoop to anything as sordid as embezzlement.'

'I will try to contact him again today,' von Stralick said. 'The baron is a good man, but perhaps too independent in his thinking for the Chancellor's liking.'

'And now he's out of the picture,' Hollows said. 'When von Stralick contacted us with an offer to help us, we verified a number of things and welcomed him aboard, especially since he told us of his acquaintance with you.'

'So you see,' von Stralick said, beaming, 'we are now on the same side, officially!'

Aubrey was less than overjoyed. He'd been prepared to work with von Stralick, but on his own terms, with his own safeguards in place.

Kiefer looked at him anxiously. 'So we are united in our mission?'

Hollows frowned. 'Yes, quite. We're glad to have you both aboard.' He nodded at Aubrey. 'Von Stralick has given us some useful insights into the way Dr Tremaine has been operating. I've coded them and sent them to . . .' He paused. 'The Directorate, is that what it's called now?'

'The Security Intelligence Directorate, sir.'

'I really can't keep up sometimes,' Hollows muttered.

The ambassador's mention of coding reminded Aubrey of his run-in with the Veltranian rebels. 'Who's your chief intelligence operative here, sir? I need to get something back to Albion.'

'Major Vincent.' Hollows reached over for the bell pull. 'You had an incident on the train? Dashed exciting mode of transport, but somewhat wearying, with all the comings and goings.'

Comings and goings. Aubrey could see how being flung off a moving train could be put into that basket. 'I met some brigands. Not on the train, though. Near the Bramantine Gorge.'

'Eh?' Hollows sat forward. 'Brigands? What happened?'

Aubrey gave an account of the brigands who turned out to be Veltranian rebels. After he finished, he spent an hour or so of coding and the job was done. Major Vincent promised that the report would go in the next dispatch bag.

Aubrey wandered back to the residential section of the embassy, deep in thought. The ambitions of the rebels added another wrinkle to a situation that was already well furrowed, but it seemed as if its consequences weren't as urgent as some of the others.

Such as finding Caroline.

He brightened at this prospect, rounded a corner, and ran into von Stralick and Kiefer.

They were waiting for him on the landing above the main entrance, right under a large stained-glass rendering of the Albion flag. 'Fitzwilliam,' said von Stralick. 'We must find this fragment of Dr Tremaine's sister before anyone else does.'

Aubrey stopped dead, took stock, backed up a little, then took another run at his words. 'Anyone else?'

Kiefer glanced at von Stralick, then answered. 'I ran some experiments. Talked to some people. Ghost hunters are abroad.'

Aubrey had a fleeting longing for simple times. Then he remembered his father's hint that there was oddness in Fisherberg. 'Ghost hunters. You're joking, aren't you?'

'I do not joke.' Kiefer looked thoughtful. 'Not that I know of.'

Von Stralick nodded. 'That's right. Totally devoid of humour is Otto.'

'But ghost hunters? It sounds like something from a fairytale.'

'Holmland has always had ghost hunters,' Kiefer said. 'They're part of our history.'

'A bit of an embarrassment in this day and age,' said von Stralick. 'But they seem to have had a resurgence recently. Especially here in Fisherberg, where people are complaining that ghosts have been harassing them.'

Aubrey had the itchy uneasiness of a mystery presenting itself, but he wanted to throw up his hands. His plate was currently full of mysteries drenched in mystery sauce, with a mystery side salad. Enough was enough. 'And where have these ghost hunters come from?'

Von Stralick spread his hands. 'Rural areas, I expect. Until recently, I didn't think we had any left. I thought they went the way of the fletcher and the reeve.'

'Ghosts.' Aubrey shook his head. 'What exactly are ghosts?'

'Are you unwell, Fitzwilliam?' von Stralick said. 'Ghosts are not real. They are fairy stories, something to scare children.'

'A fairytale that's given rise to an occupation dedicated to finding them.'

'Charlatans.' Von Stralick snorted. 'Like fortune tellers, they prey on the gullible.'

'Most likely,' Aubrey said, 'but what if they aren't? What if they really can find ghosts? Or something they call ghosts, anyway.'

Kiefer frowned. 'My friends say that people are reporting transparent figures wandering about, passing through walls, things like that. They sound like ghosts.'

'Wait,' Aubrey said. 'Haven't we recently seen transparent figures wandering about, passing through each other?'

'So you told me,' Kiefer said. He touched his spectacles and added to the tapestry of smears Aubrey could see on the lenses. 'In Dr Tremaine's pearl.' He smiled. 'So it could be that the ghost hunters are detecting the same sort of thing: fragments, splintered souls.'

In that instant, Aubrey saw it. 'That piece of his sister's soul. It's out there.'

'And someone might be hunting it as we speak,' von Stralick said.

'Perhaps we need to talk to some of these ghost hunters,' Aubrey said.

Von Stralick sighed. 'You can't trust them. They will tell you what you want to hear.'

Kiefer put a hand on his cousin's arm. 'It can't hurt to talk to them. They gather at the Blue Dog, do they not?'

'They do.' Von Stralick glanced at Aubrey. 'You are free tomorrow, Fitzwilliam?'

Aubrey winced. He'd been hoping to find where Caroline was staying. 'I'll see what George is up to.'

'Splendid,' von Stralick said. 'That way we'll be well prepared if we need someone to act as a sack of potatoes.'

Eighteen

THE NEXT MORNING, AUBREY DECIDED THAT THE BLUE Dog was well named, because the sign hanging out the front of the tavern was as blue a dog as he'd ever seen. Not grey, not a delicate seal colour, but an eye-watering, startling blue, the sort of blue that tropical fish adopted as a warning of their extreme toxicity.

The tavern lurked in an old district of Fisherberg that rejoiced in the attractive name of Thart, near the river. At first, as they made their way down the hill towards the bridge that bisected the tiny locale, it appeared to Aubrey as if Thart was composed entirely of taverns, inns, hotels and grog shops. When they drew closer, however, he was able to make out that a few eateries had squeezed in between the rowdy, low-slung bars, and a pawnbroker had a prominent position on the crossroads, ready to buy, sell and loan day and night.

From the top of the hill, Aubrey had seen how Thart was

turned inward, resisting the tide of modernising that had enveloped the rest of the city. Its buildings were all low – none more than two storeys – and built in a combination of wood and stone that reeked not just of age but of smoke, dirt, grease, oil and other, mostly inflammable, substances. It was only a few city blocks, perhaps two or three streets wide and the same again across.

Kiefer gestured vaguely at the bridge. 'Many of the ghost hunters sleep under there, when they're in the city.'

'They come from the countryside?' Aubrey asked as George surveyed the scene.

'Hmm?'

Aubrey sighed. Kiefer had been even more absent-minded than usual this morning, his thoughts quite obviously elsewhere. Aubrey had never realised that catalytic magic was so fascinating.

Von Stralick snorted. 'Usually, the people in the city are not näive enough for the ghosthunters' business. In the country, though, they can ply their trade, make their money by preying on the peasants.'

Aubrey had no time for frauds who deliberately preyed on the insecurities of people – hopes, fears, losses – but he didn't like the way that von Stralick lumped all country dwellers as simple-minded dullards who were just as culpable as the shysters.

Aubrey understood how von Stralick could be sceptical about the ghost hunters, but he wasn't about to leap to that conclusion. While great strides had been taken in rational magic in the past few decades, most of that was the result of work done in universities and other academic institutions. The results had found their way into industry and life in general, but this didn't mean that all traditional folk practices had ended overnight. Many had been shown to be worthless but others had demonstrable results that kept them in circulation. At the farm on Prince Albert's estate – Penhurst – Aubrey knew of a worker who could reliably cast a spell that would lead him to a lost lamb. As Aubrey's own magical talents had developed, he could sense the man's magic and he had no doubt that it was real, not just some combination of luck and local knowledge. It was the only spell the man could cast, and it was an erratic, fugitive talent, so it was fortunate that he was a cheery fellow with a broad back and an almost unlimited ability to work hard.

Aubrey wasn't willing to discount the ghost hunters. If they had any insights into what was happening in Fisherberg, he was happy to glean what he could.

The Blue Dog's entrance was below street level. He and George followed the two Holmlanders, and together they found themselves in a place that looked as if it was designed to deter strangers.

Whatever light the windows let into the tavern – and it wasn't a great deal – was instantly turned grey and tired by the build-up of noxious exhalations and fumings from the patrons and the huge open blazes that filled the fireplaces on either side of the single large room. The air, thus, took on a character of its own and became a feature of the place. Aubrey, accustomed as he was to air that was mostly transparent, was intrigued by the smoky indistinctness. For a moment, it was as if he were looking through gauze.

The room was entirely constructed of dark wood, grimed and blackened by the same miasmas that had done the job on the windows, lack of diligent cleaning apparently being a prerequisite for owning the Blue Dog over the centuries. Directly in front of him was the bar, a long counter that looked solid enough to withstand a siege. On reflection, Aubrey decided that this was probably a good thing. Behind the bar were empty shelves where, in a more genteel establishment, bottles may have stood.

Two mighty wooden pillars held up the ceiling. They were scarred, slashed, carved and burned but looked as if they wore these marks as trophies.

Long tables and benches, arranged with almost military precision, filled the room. Aubrey had trouble seeing this array at first, because the benches were packed with customers. They were sitting shoulder to shoulder, a solid lattice of squat, silent, broad, fur-clad people.

Aubrey stared from the doorway. For a moment he thought that they'd stumbled into a meeting of a fraternity of extremely well-behaved bears.

Kiefer sniffed, then – quite obviously – regretted it, for it meant that he inhaled more than he needed to of the rich aroma that fought with the light for possession of the air.

Von Stralick took charge. He strode between the tables, looking straight ahead, and confronted the barman. Aubrey, feeling that in unity there was strength, hurried along behind, with Kiefer, who was still struggling for breath, and George – who was doing his best to look formidable.

The barman was short, but he was as broad as two men. He had shaggy, shoulder-length hair. His hands were spread on the bar in front of him, ready, as it were, for anything.

'Are you gentlemen lost?' the barman said, making a fair stab at civility. As long as he didn't make a fair stab in any other way, Aubrey was satisfied with this.

'I don't think so,' von Stralick said. 'This is the Blue Dog?'

The barman turned this over, let it brown for a moment or two, then judged it was done. 'Could be,' he allowed.

'Well, we're looking for ghost hunters.'

'A pity,' the barman said, only missing a verse or two of beats, 'there's no ghost hunters around here.'

Aubrey sighed. He knew evasion when he saw it, being somewhat of an expert. Even without turning around, he had the sense of dozens of pairs of ears listening to every word. He had the distinct feeling that they were getting the preliminaries to a very long run-around. It was time to change the game, he decided, so he stepped forward. 'A pity indeed,' he announced in his clearest Holmlandish, 'because I have a hundred marks for the best ghost hunter in Fisherberg.'

Aubrey hadn't meant to start a brawl, but he was proud that having initiated one it became such a good brawl. Once von Stralick, Kiefer, George and he were safely on the same side of the bar as the barman, he watched in wide-eyed wonder as the furry men hurled themselves about the tavern in an attempt, presumably, to be the last standing and thus the only one able to claim the role as best ghost hunter in Fisherberg.

Seeming to defy the laws of physics, and most of the laws of Fisherberg, they howled, bit, kicked, wrestled, headbutted, punched and flung each other in all directions until the bar room was full of flying furry bodies filling all available space. Benches and tables were pressed into service, splintered, abandoned, cursed at and then forgotten as it got down to hand-to-hand assault. Aubrey saw ghost hunters hurled against the giant uprights with such force that – if correctly harnessed – it could power entire cities; he stared in amazement as the flungees simply staggered to their feet, shook themselves in furry outrage and waded back into the fray.

When he saw a ghost hunter thrown against one of the large windows and simply bounce off he shrugged, accepting that the glass had transmogrified over the years due to its exposure to the air of the room into something only remotely glasslike.

Gradually, it became apparent that little actual damage was being done in the fracas. The heavy furs that swaddled the ghost hunters acted not just as insulation and homes to entire species of insects, but as padding. Equally apparent was that this expenditure of energy in mayhem had a ritual aspect about it, as if it had been done many times before. Singly, then in twos and threes, the ghost hunters reached some sort of understanding of their place in the great pecking order of ghost hunters. After picking themselves up and dusting themselves off, the lesser ghost hunters sauntered off, leaving the tavern with the air of people who just remembered an appointment. Not an important appointment, just a mildly diverting one, like a chance to see a man about an interesting dog.

Once this part of the process had begun, things moved quite swiftly. Dozens became scores became tens became a handful. Then it was two ghost hunters facing off, snarling oaths that sounded blood-curdling but were incomprehensible to Aubrey's ear. They circled each other, arms outstretched, like giant fuzzy crabs. Then, in a perfect pantomime that could have been seen by a short-sighted audience member in the rearmost of the back stalls, one of the two – they were quite indistinguishable – straightened, snapped his fingers, spun on his heel and limped toward the doorway.

The remaining ghost hunter rubbed his hands together for a moment then ambled to the bar. 'You have a hundred marks?'

Fleetingly, Aubrey wondered what would happen if he said no. Pushing the impulse aside, he took out his wallet. 'Are you a ghost hunter?'

The triumphant warrior beat his chest with the flat of a hand. 'Bruno Fromm is the best in Fisherberg.' Pause. 'Best in Holmland.'

George took this carefully. 'You're certainly the only one still here, at any rate.'

'Those others? Impostors. Cheats. Fools.'

'You know them well?' von Stralick said.

'Fromm should. They are Fromm's cousins.'

Bruno Fromm peered at them from the narrow gap between the brim of his furry hat and the start of his woolly beard. His eyes were dark and shiny, glinting through the steam of the coffee cup in front of him. 'You want to find a ghost.'

Aubrey, George, Kiefer and von Stralick were on the other side of the righted table. At Fromm's insistence, they'd been supplied with coffee as well. Aubrey had sniffed his, but not tasted it since he had an aversion to sipping anything that promised to dissolve his teeth. 'A special ghost.'

'Ah.' Fromm stared at his coffee. The movements of his cap made Aubrey realise that he was wrinkling his brow underneath all that fur. 'Fromm thought you were just sightseers.'

'Sightseers?' George said.

'Rich folk. Want to see a ghost. Plenty of them about.'

'Rich folk or ghosts?' von Stralick asked.

'Both, lately. Lots and lots of ghosts, lots of work for ghost hunters.' Fromm grinned with a mouthful of startlingly good teeth. 'But finding what you're after, something special, that's different.'

'You can't do it.' Aubrey made motions to rise.

Fromm shook his head. 'Fromm didn't say that. Fromm just said it was different.'

'How?'

'Costs more.'

'How much?'

'How much is it worth?'

'What if I offer you fifty? After which you'll get all offended and demand two hundred, and I'll get up to leave only to hear you suggest a hundred.'

Fromm looked nonplussed, then suspicious. 'You're making fun of Fromm?'

'Not all. I don't mind haggling. I just don't like the time it takes, so I sped through it. For both our sakes.'

'A hundred?' Fromm brightened. 'Must be important. Someone close? Relative? A friend?'

'A friend of a friend,' von Stralick said. George snorted.

Fromm drained his coffee and rose. For a moment, he stood there and examined his hands. 'They're not really ghosts, you know.'

Aubrey was alert. 'What do you mean?'

'Fromm can see you're not stupid. Not just looking for cheap thrills, you. So Fromm doesn't want to lead you astray.'

'If they're not ghosts,' Aubrey said carefully, 'what are they?'

The ghost hunter groped for words. 'Ghosts are meant to be what some people leave behind when they die.'

'That's the story,' Aubrey said. The room had become tense. George, Kiefer and von Stralick were silent. Kiefer had grasped the edge of the table and was leaning forward as if that would make him remember better.

'Good story. Not good truth,' Fromm said. 'When we die, souls don't linger here. They go somewhere else.'

Aubrey was very still. Could the crude magic of the ghost hunters shed some light on his condition? When his soul had been wrenched from his body, it had immediately been drawn to the portal that led to the true death. No chance of loitering, ghost-like, haunting anyone or anything.

He tapped the Beccaria Cage under his shirt. 'That's my understanding, too.'

Fromm peered at him. 'Fromm was right. You aren't stupid.' He huffed for a moment, then he groped in a hidden pocket. Aubrey tensed, and felt George stir at his side, but relaxed when Fromm merely took out the hundred-mark coin, the reward Aubrey had already given to him. He turned it over and over in his hands. It sparkled, golden. 'Ghosts aren't souls. Not whole souls.'

At this confirmation of his suppositions, Aubrey clenched his fists. 'Explain.'

'Ghosts are pieces of souls.' Fromm tossed the gold coin in the air and caught it again. 'Sometimes, it happens. Souls get shivered apart. The splinters get scattered. Sometimes, the biggest piece clings to the body, hard. The rest wander off, but they're not quite right.'

'Missing something?' Kiefer asked.

'Missing more than a few somethings. If ghost hunters can smell them, we can round them up and . . .' He shrugged. 'After that, it's not up to us.'

Aubrey could imagine the grateful relatives receiving the fragmented souls and then having to find a way to reunite the pieces. This was a branch of magic he'd never heard of, never suspected. Was it just a Holmland specialty, a way of looking at things that was peculiar to this country, or was it the sort of backwoods thing that existed in Albion but had never been thought worth serious study?

He knew one university that would soon be pursuing this area, as soon as he got back to Greythorn. 'And you can find a particular ghost? Splinter?'

'Fromm can. If Fromm can sniff something that the person owned.'

Aubrey felt in his pocket. 'I have just the thing.'

He held out the Tremaine pearl. He'd expected Fromm to snatch at it, but instead the ghost hunter sat back and regarded the pearl with narrowed eyes. He licked his lips nervously and held out a hand. 'Here.'

With some reluctance, Aubrey placed the pearl in Fromm's grubby palm. The ghost hunter grimaced, then cocked his head to one side and squinted at it. Then he surprised Aubrey by growling deep in his throat.

Slowly, the ghost hunter raised his hand. He brought the pearl up to his prominent nose and sniffed, like a man taking snuff. The pearl actually rolled closer to his cavernous nostrils before rocking back to the middle of his palm.

Fromm hissed and closed his fist on the pearl. 'There are ghosts in here, already.'

Aubrey was both impressed and relieved at this confirmation of the ghost hunter's power. 'Sorry. I forgot to tell you about that.'

'This ghost you want Fromm to find. It's another one like these? Part of the same soul?'

'That's right.'

'Ah.' Fromm rolled the pearl between his thumb and forefinger. 'If you want to make her whole again, you'll need her body as well as the pieces.'

Aubrey glanced at George and von Stralick. 'And what makes you think we want to do that?'

'It's what people do. Not easy, though.'

'Let us worry about that,' von Stralick said. 'Can you find the ghost out there using this?'

'Plenty to work with, here. She's in the city, for sure, and Fromm will find her.'

'He will?' George said. 'I mean, you will?'

'Of course. Meet here tomorrow, noon.'

Aubrey had more than a few misgivings, and not the least was seeing Fromm tuck the Tremaine pearl into a pocket. 'Do you need to keep that?'

'How can Fromm do his work without it?'

'It's magic, you know.'

'Fromm knows. That is why Fromm doesn't want to keep it. As soon as all is done, you can have it.'

Aubrey settled for that.

They made arrangements to meet the next day. He gave the ghost hunter a twenty-mark piece as a token of good faith. The ghost hunter gave him a clap on the back as a token of his.

Fromm left, vowing to find his cousins and treat them to a meal.

They followed, after paying their bill. The sun was getting low, barely above the rooftops. A wind was coming from the river. It was fitful, but decidedly chilly.

Kiefer stuck his hands in his pockets. 'I must go. I have important preparation for the symposium.'

'You're helping at the symposium?' Aubrey said.

'Helping?' He smiled. 'This morning I heard that I have won the inaugural Chancellor's Prize. I will be presenting an important paper.'

'Congratulations,' Aubrey said and he had the explanation for Kiefer's distraction. 'I didn't know they were giving prizes for catalytic magic.'

Kiefer was dismissive. 'Nothing as straightforward as that. Much more interesting, but I still need to meet someone who is helping me work through some documents.'

'Good, good.' Mention of the symposium made Aubrey think of Caroline. Where would she be staying? In Lutetia, her mother had a flat. Would she have one here?

'I should go as well,' von Stralick said. 'I have things to do.'

'A ghost hunter's reputation to check?' George said.

'Among other things. I will be in touch.'

Aubrey watched the Holmlanders march off, deep in conversation. 'Do you trust him?'

'Von Stralick? Not really. He bears watching.'

'Agreed.'

Aubrey always enjoyed getting to know a new city, and he and George took the opportunity to walk to the embassy rather than catch a cab. He looked back at the centre of the city a mile or so away, toward the Assembly Building, where the Chancellor was no doubt holding sway at this very moment, and the bulk of the Freestein Arch, the monument to Holmland's military past. The Academy, the site for the symposium, was north of the centre of the city, only a short tram ride away. The streets were busy and if it weren't for the Holmlandish signs he could have believed he was in Trinovant. Tobacconists, shoeshops, bookshops all tended to emphasise how similar the folk of Holmland were to the folk of Albion. Aubrey took some heart at this, but shuddered at the thought of war coming to these bustling, ordinary streets.

Clean streets, too. The pavements were well swept and the glass in the shop fronts sparkled. After they bought pies from a roaming vendor as a quick lunch, they wandered through more streets full of shops. After a time, Aubrey had an itchy feeling. He stopped and peered at a collection of hats. 'I think we're being followed,' he said to George.

'How can you tell?' George put his face closer to the glass. 'I think Sophie would like that yellow one.'

'Reflection,' Aubrey said. 'That man. The one inspecting flowers at the barrow. That's the third time I've seen him.'

'I see. What do we do?'

'We could evade him easily enough.'

'Which sounds like a good idea.'

'Or we could see what he wants.'

'Which sounds like a potentially dangerous idea.'

'But productive.' Aubrey frowned at the shop display. 'Do you really think Sophie would like that yellow one?'

'Certain of it, old man.'

Aubrey shook his head at George's confidence. 'Let's see how much it is, then.'

'Excellent.'

'We'll go in. You engage the shop assistant, talking hat talk and whatnot. I'll take up a position just inside the doorway and accost this stranger, not allowing him to leave.'

'First-class plan, that. Apart from one thing you've forgotten.'

'What's that?'

'I don't speak Holmlandish.'

Aubrey winced. How could he forget? George approached foreign languages in the same way a bull approached a china shop – plenty of energy, unfortunate results.

Aubrey sidled along the pavement until he could see through the glass of the door. 'Strikingly attractive shop assistants they have in these Fisherberg shops.'

George took his hands out of his pockets. 'Eh? Let me see.' He peered through the glass. 'Look, Aubrey, I always say that language is overrated as a means of communication. I'm sure I can get through to her.' He peered again and his smile broadened. 'To them. Come now, mustn't give up so easily, old man.'

What's a plan without a hiccup? Aubrey thought as he followed his beaming friend into the refined enclosure of the hat shop.

After that, all went smoothly. George threw himself into the task of engaging the two charming blonde shop assistants with gusto, pointing, sawing at the air with his hands, somehow getting one of them to try on the yellow hat.

The whole performance was so ludicrous and engaging that Aubrey was taken by surprise when their quarry slipped in, glancing in irritation at the bell above the door.

Aubrey was fortunately well hidden behind the door as it swung back and was able to flip the card on the door to 'Closed', turn the key in the lock and then stand with his back to the door after the man had taken a few steps into the headgear wonderland.

'Who are you working for?' he said in Holmlandish and was pleased at the startled hunching of the man's shoulders. George and the shop assistants were too busy in their language-free frenzy of miscommunication to even notice.

When the man turned, he'd managed to compose himself. Aubrey automatically noted his thin, clean-shaven features, his pinched mouth, his well-made clothes. Not expensive, but well made nonetheless. 'I work for someone who has been looking for you.'

Hmm, Aubrey thought, *that narrows it down to a few hundred*. 'Why didn't your employer send me a letter instead of dispatching someone to follow me?'

The man adjusted his cuffs, glanced at the shop assistants, who still hadn't noticed him, and shrugged. 'She prefers not to commit herself to writing on this matter.'

She? For an infinitesimal moment, Aubrey wondered if Caroline had been seduced by the cloak and dagger world in which they found themselves, but he immediately rejected this notion. Caroline was far too level-headed to participate in such nonsense.

He mentally riffled through the possibilities and an intriguing prospect presented itself – the mysterious foreigner from the train. 'I've been waiting for her to make contact. You'll take us to her?'

Another glance. 'I'm not sure if your friend wants to come.'

'Let me worry about that.' Aubrey had a thought. 'Why were you following me if she wanted me to meet her?'

A small, rather nasty smile. 'She wanted to know what you're up to.'

Really? 'Nothing important, as you've seen. George, are you finished?'

With some reluctance, George disengaged himself from his pantomime negotiations. 'May have to come back here soon,' he said. 'Excellent stock they have.'

'Shall we go?' their newly acquired guide said.

Aubrey stood back from the door. 'By all means.'

He took them to an apartment building, five storeys of completely new accommodation all done in a style that combined Holmlandish efficiency with décor that was rich, comfortable and discreet.

When the lift stopped on the fifth floor, their guide paused for a moment before opening the doors. Then he took his time, peering to his left and right before exiting. 'This way.'

He slowed as they approached the end of the corridor. 'What's wrong?' Aubrey asked.

'I . . .'

Raised voices came through the last door on the right. Even though the words were unclear, the anger wasn't. Two people were shouting – a man and a woman, both trying to talk at once. Then came the sound of breaking glass and the woman screamed.

Their guide stopped. 'She didn't pay me for the physical stuff,' he muttered and took off, barging past Aubrey and George.

Aubrey hardly noticed. His lips were already moving, rehearsing a spell to smash down the door. He fumbled under his shirt for some matches he'd packed in his vest, ready for a quick application of the Law of Intensification.

'No time for spells now,' George growled over the crash of splintering furniture. He backed up, lowered his shoulder, and charged the door.

It burst open. Aubrey was right behind his friend but they both pulled up short at the frozen tableau that confronted them.

Tumbled furniture. Broken glassware. A spilled bottle of wine.

And two people Aubrey had seen before. The man was standing behind the woman, an arm around her throat.

Aubrey was immediately taken back to the Transcontinental Express, and the brawl in the compartment. 'Madame Zelinka,' he said. 'Manfred.'

'Fitzwilliam!' Manfred said. With his free hand, he flung something at Aubrey and George.

Aubrey felt the magic, saw that it was a compressed spell, pushed George to one side and dived after his friend, hoping that the overturned sofa would provide some protection.

Then the room exploded.

Nineteen

UBREY WAVED AN ARM, TRYING TO FIND SOME CLEAR air in the billows of choking plaster. Behind him, the wall that separated the room from the corridor had mostly disappeared, thanks to the shaped magical explosive charge that Manfred had hurled at them.

George rolled over and coughed. 'Good Lord,' he said with some reverence after he saw the hole in the wall. 'Unfriendly greeting, wouldn't you say, old man?'

The sound of fist on flesh came from the other side of the room and Manfred cursed. Out of the dust cloud, a figure dived over the top of the sofa and landed on top of them.

'Madame Zelinka!' Aubrey gasped after a few seconds of desperate untangling.

She rubbed her knuckles and glanced at him, then she attacked the cushions and extracted a large revolver. She peeped over the sofa and quickly pulled the trigger three times. Aubrey stared, open-mouthed.

The revolver hadn't made a sound.

'Magical noise suppression, Mr Black,' she snapped, noticing his astonishment. She squinted toward the far side of the room but the air was still almost opaque. Aubrey lifted his head, cautiously, but could only make out dim shapes of furniture and the more brightly lit rectangles that must have been windows. Then, to add to his flabbergastedness, Madame Zelinka stabbed a finger at George. 'You have no magic. Blow.'

George blinked. 'I beg your pardon?'

'Quickly. Put your lips together and blow.' She pointed at the other side of the room. 'In Guttmann's direction. Now.'

George did as she bid. His cheeks bulged, and he blew. Immediately, without lowering her revolver, Madame Zelinka barked out a torrent of Achaean syllables which Aubrey, astonished, recognised as components of an intensification spell. When she finished, the room was rocked by a gust of wind. It was strong enough to send books flying from a nearby bookcase and to topple a pair of ornamental potted palms, but it did achieve what Aubrey assumed was Madame Zelinka's aim. The air was cleared of dust as the wind herded it all out through a broken window. They could see Manfred standing, peering, on the other side of the room.

The shortfall in the plan was that it meant he could see them. With a grin that Aubrey didn't like at all, backhanded, he slung a glittering ten-mark piece at them.

And the man who Aubrey thought had no magical ability followed it with a short, hard, Chaldean spell.

Magnification, Aubrey thought, and even though he hadn't heard the spell before he immediately grasped its purpose. Manfred aimed to expand the coin, but such a thing was impossible to maintain for any length of time – which wasn't important. The coin rapidly grew until it was as big as a dining table. All it had to do was maintain those dimensions for a few seconds and it would crush them like beetles.

It was Aubrey's turn. He spat out a tiny spell, one he'd been thinking about since the experience in the pearl prison. It was a temporal spell, using some of the principles that had been in play accelerating time in the cells in which George and von Stralick had been trapped. If he could cast the spell on the falling coin, make its time go quickly, then . . .

'Ow!' George rubbed his forehead, then plucked the ten-mark piece from his chest. He shrugged and tucked the coin into his pocket. 'Ten marks is ten marks,' he said when he saw both Aubrey and Madame Zelinka staring at him.

A crash. Aubrey poked his head up to see that Manfred had dragged down the tall bookcase. Books scattered across the floor and Aubrey winced. Manfred vaulted lightly over the bookcase, using it as a screen. He poked up his head and Madame Zelinka pulled the trigger again. Manfred jerked his head sideways and then stared at the hole in the wall right next to him. He ducked, but not before a vase flung by George hit him. Heartfelt cursing from behind the bookshelf signalled that the Holmlander would be sporting a black eye tomorrow, if nothing else.

Madame Zelinka glared but didn't pull back behind the sofa.

'That's Guttmann?' Aubrey asked.

She glanced at him suspiciously. 'I thought you knew Guttmann.'

'I know him as Manfred. And I didn't know he was a magician,' Aubrey said. 'Look out.'

A black shape, the size of an orange, darted out from behind the bookcase and flew straight at them with evil intent.

Aubrey dived left, Madame Zelinka dived right, and George ducked. The black shape sped past and went straight through the hole in the wall behind them before it managed to pull up and flit back at them. By that time, George had seized a large chunk of plaster in two hands. He swung lustily, connected, then staggered and dropped the plaster.

Aubrey scrambled to his friend. 'George?'

George raised himself. Carefully, he edged his fingers under the plaster and lifted.

On the other side was an irregular black splotch. It looked like a giant inkblot from the world's messiest writer.

'Crude. He must have been in a hurry.' Aubrey poked it with a finger. 'Clay. Maybe a hunter golem of some kind?'

'It doesn't matter.' Madame Zelinka dragged Aubrey back behind the sofa. George scuttled to join them. 'Can we take him?'

'Who? Manfred?' Aubrey rubbed his chin and slipped back into the mercenary role. 'What's in it for us?'

'Not being killed?' George suggested.

Aubrey ignored him. 'What does he want? And just who are you?'

'He wants magic. A particular sort of magic'

'But you were trying to buy magic from my firm.'

She frowned. 'Of course. We purchase what we need to complement our expertise. And it's our special expertise that Guttmann wants.'

'Of course,' Aubrey said hastily. This commerce in magic was new to him. He was working in the dark; he needed more information. 'What sort of magic is he after?'

She gave him another suspicious look and Aubrey felt that this was her standard mode. 'Does your firm deal with industrial magic?'

If I say yes, she'll consider me a threat. 'No. We specialise in weapons.'

'I thought as much. Otherwise Guttmann would have approached you already to find his catalytic intensifiers and pressure chamber reinforcing spells.'

'Not our business line at all,' Aubrey said but something pricked at him. Manfred was after heavy-duty industrial magic of a very specific kind. Who was he working for?

Madame Zelinka went to reply, but before she could, a high-pitched whine came to them from Manfred's hiding place. 'What is that?' she said.

Aubrey reached out. 'Magic.' As he hadn't heard the spell, he didn't know exactly what was going on but he could tell it was powerful and localised.

The whine became a hissing crackle. Then a blast of heat struck them. Aubrey closed his eyes and threw up an arm. A rending groan was followed by the sound of timber giving way, then a mighty crash.

George poked up his head. 'Your bookcase is gone.'

Aubrey joined his friend. Then he leaped to his feet and raced across the room.

Manfred had escaped. Behind the bookcase a rough oval had been burned right through the floor. Aubrey found himself peering into the room underneath this one. It was a scene of destruction, with a mound of plaster and timber burying any furniture unlucky enough to be directly below.

'And Manfred has gone as well.' Aubrey straightened. 'I hope he enjoys his black eye.' He rubbed his forehead and found it was gritty. He peered at fingers that were brown with dust and white with plaster. 'Any chance of freshening up a little?' he asked a fierce-looking Madame Zelinka, who had joined him to peer through the hole in the floor.

She unbent and studied him carefully. 'Perhaps. But not here.'

'Why not?'

George pointed at the window. 'Listen.'

The ringing bells of approaching police motorcars was the same in every country, Aubrey decided. 'Agreed. Best not to be found here. Any suggestions?'

Madame Zelinka hurried for the door. 'Follow me.'

Aubrey admired her preparations. She took them up three floors in the lift to a rooftop suite. 'I always have a retreat nearby,' she said before she opened the door. 'One never knows when it may be useful. As today.'

Aubrey was grateful, and to judge by George's sigh when he threw himself into the nearest chair, so was he.

After they'd each spent some time in an impressive bathroom, cleaning off the worst of the dust, Aubrey found that the mysterious Madame Zelinka served excellent coffee. Aubrey was willing to accept that any coffee in the world would seem good after the horror brew he'd nearly drunk in the Blue Dog.

'I am pleased that you came,' she said after they'd settled. The plush armchairs were a cunning combination of wood and velvet that looked dreadfully uncomfortable but defied that expectation by being supremely restful. 'I would have had trouble without you.'

Aubrey nodded, but he had something on his mind. 'You let me be thrown off the train.' He inhaled the coffee tang and closed his eyes for a moment.

'I had to. I would have been killed otherwise.'

'Difficult decision,' George said. He'd stowed away three small cakes in quick time and was eyeing another.

'Not really,' Madame Zelinka said. 'I would not be any use to the cause if I were dead.'

Aubrey sat back and groaned, internally. *Another devotee to a cause.* But he couldn't help himself – he was curious about the strange, suspicious woman. She was restrained, competent, and her inscrutability made him want to know more. He drummed his fingers on the armrest and glanced out of the window. It had a view out across the city. He could clearly see the Academy with its grey buildings interrupted by a surprising amount of greenery, making it look like a park where someone had lost some government offices.

Should he tell Madame Zelinka that the man she knew as Guttmann was actually the Great Manfred, stage performer and Holmland agent? He gnawed on this, but decided to keep it to himself until he knew more about her. 'Your cause has enemies,' he said.

She shrugged. 'Sometimes business causes enemies. Sometimes it is politics that causes enemies. Guttmann is trying to do some deals with industry, and industry is full of enemies.'

Aubrey was puzzled. He'd only known that the Holmlander had been a double agent working for a different branch of Holmland intelligence from von Stralick, not someone involved in industrial espionage. 'You want to continue business with my firm?' he said, trying to keep up his guise. He hoped that his pause had made him appear imperious, aloof, even mysterious himself, but he had suspicions that he may have come across as dull.

'That's what I wanted to talk to you about. Your offer sounded good, but I'm not sure if we can continue on the same basis.'

'Because I was thrown from a train?'

'No. Because you appear to be staying at the Albion Embassy.'

'Of course.' No point denying it. Madame Zelinka had obviously had him followed for some time. Aubrey glanced at George, who shrugged, selected a pistachio-adorned morsel and took a bite. No help there.

'Of course?'

'The Albion government is one of our best clients,' he said, spinning the story as it came to him. 'At least, the army is.'

'Not the navy?'

'They couldn't afford us. It causes some friction between them, but that is no business of ours.'

'So you should be in a position to supply us with the magical apparatus we need.'

'I need more information.'

Madame Zelinka's mouth tightened. She studied him for some time and he was forced, professionally of course, to meet her exotically beautiful gaze. Finally, she gave a tiny shake of her head. 'I told you that we need some of your Albion magic suppressors. I've spoken to my colleagues. It appears as if we may need several.'

Aubrey managed to nod in what he hoped was a knowledgeable way. The magic suppressors, the devices that Clive Rokeby-Taylor's company had perfected, were currently on Albion's 'not to be exported' list. While Rokeby-Taylor had wanted maximum commercial exploitation of the revolutionary magical technology, after his demise caused his nest of companies to collapse the government had clamped down on the devices, realising that they may have a useful role to play in the armament build-up. A few devices, it was rumoured, had made their way to the Continent – which was not surprising, with Rokeby-Taylor's Holmland connections – but they apparently were not the fully functional version.

The magic suppressors had a thousand possible uses. Mostly defensive, neutralising spells and spell casting, they could be used to surprising offensive effect. If a foe was depending on spells to enhance artillery, say, and suddenly the spells failed, then a counter-attack could be devastating.

With countless skirmishes in the Goltans and beyond, Aubrey was sure the magical suppressors had a ready market.

'This may be possible,' he said, while thinking of how to deliver apparatus that looked like fully functional magic suppressors but would fail when used. 'What do you want them for?'

'Is it the usual procedure for your firm to make such an inquiry? I thought discretion was part of what you offered.'

'Of course, of course. It is simply that magic suppressors are so new, so complex, that your people may need training.'

'Ah.' She pressed her hands together and scowled. 'This may be so.'

Aubrey was relieved. Extemporising spells was one thing, but ad-libbing smuggling deals was another. 'Do you need to consult your colleagues again?'

She shook her head decisively. 'No. I am empowered to make such decisions. And I will.'

'Excellent. But with these developments, I'm afraid I must know who we are dealing with. We must be sure that we cover ourselves.'

'I understand.' She took a deep breath. 'I belong to a secret society.'

George snorted. Cake crumbs flew. 'And who doesn't, these days?'

She fixed him with an impenetrable look and then handed him a napkin. 'That may be true. But this society is centuries old.'

'You're one of the Goltan groups?' Aubrey hazarded.

'No. We are the Ancient Order of Enlightened Ones.'

The name rang a very faint bell. 'You're enlightened?'

'It's an unfortunate name. It tends to raise expectations.' She sighed. 'Our secret order was founded by a fifteenth-century Venezian scholar. We are dedicated to repairing damage done by indiscriminate magic.'

'Wait.' Aubrey put a hand to his forehead. 'Indiscriminate magic? What on earth do you mean?'

'You have magic. You must have seen what happens when spells aren't well constructed.'

Aubrey nodded. He'd seen many different results of badly constructed magic – spells exceeding their expected duration and spread, spells fizzling like damp squibs, spells that simply didn't work at all.

But they all had something in common. 'Residue.'

'Even the best spells leave behind magical vestiges. Poor spells throw off residue like a snake sloughs off a skin.'

'I know. Forensic magicians rely on this.' Aubrey had done some work with forensic magicians belonging to Craddock's staff. He liked their intensity, their focus.

'And what happens to the residue?' Madame Zelinka asked meaningfully.

Aubrey started. He'd never really thought about it. 'It just disappears. Evaporates, I suppose, once it loses its efficacy . . .' His voice trailed off. His speculation didn't sound convincing, even to him. 'That's not right, is it?'

'In most cases, it serves. Our scholars think that, in reality, the residue doesn't disappear. It is absorbed, becomes part of the surroundings – and not always to the benefit of these surroundings. If our order had the time and the personnel, we would neutralise each and every instance of magic residue, but that is a pipe dream.'

'So to what *do* you devote your time and personnel?'

'Major events. Magical disruptions of the highest order. We had to spend some time in your country recently, underground, in the heart of your Trinovant.'

Aubrey took a sharp breath, but Madame Zelinka was too involved with her memory to notice it, or the look that passed between Aubrey and George.

'We lost Ambrose, and Gustave,' she said softly.

'Your work is dangerous?' Aubrey asked.

'Our magic workers have particular skills, but it leaves them exposed. I have only minor magic so I support them as they do their work, counteracting the effect of the worst magic left lying about.'

George picked up his empty coffee cup and put it down again. 'This all sounds like jolly good work. So why is your group so secretive?'

Madame Zelinka put her hands together. 'We have found that many countries, many people, wish to control us, to have our learning and expertise for them alone. Their greed and self-interest has meant that we keep to ourselves and deal with whoever we can to do our work successfully.'

'Cleaning up other people's messes,' Aubrey said.

'That's one way to put it.' Again, she chose her words carefully. 'At this time, it seems we're cleaning up one person's messes more than any other. More than any other single person in our order's history.'

Aubrey knew the answer but asked anyway, for form. 'And who would that be?'

'Your countryman. Dr Mordecai Tremaine.'

'The man who used to be Albion's Sorcerer Royal?' He continued playing his role. 'I thought he was dead.'

'He is very much alive, spreading mischief, here in Holmland.'

'Fancy that. Sounds like a man to keep away from.'

'He is not a man to have as your enemy.'

'So you don't confront him. You just clean up for him.'

'He is powerful – vastly powerful – but reckless. If we didn't do our work, it would be a calamity for everyone.'

'Can't have magic residue lying around all over the place, can we?' George said.

'Not unless you want to suffer the consequences, as Holmland currently is.'

Aubrey was alert. 'Holmland is suffering? It doesn't seem so. It appears prosperous enough.'

'One mess that Tremaine left behind has been causing harm.' She took a deep breath. 'It has spawned a magical field that is disrupting souls.'

Aubrey rocked back. He felt as if he were in a boxing ring with multiple opponents – blows were coming from all directions.

'Ghosts,' he said. 'And ghost hunters.'

'You've seen them?' Madame Zelinka grimaced. 'Holmlanders are having their souls splintered, and the ghost hunters have sensed this. They are drawn to the disruption like moths to a flame.'

'We bumped into a few,' George said. 'Scruffy types.'

Madame Zelinka nodded. 'Dr Tremaine cast a spell earlier this year, a powerful spell – something to do with Urbomancy – and the residue has festered, breeding on itself and on the remains of other spells Dr Tremaine has cast. It has become a source of disruption, shattering troubled souls and casting off what – to some appearances – are ghosts.'

'And where is all this magical mess lying about?' George asked, giving Aubrey some time to think. 'Surely Tremaine would notice it, especially if it was festering away as you say.'

'It was in a house, north of the city, where he stayed when he first arrived in Holmland. A few days after he cast his spell, the place went up in flames. He has enemies.'

'And a good sense of when not to be home, I'll warrant,' George said. 'He wasn't harmed?'

'No. But the place was ruined and he hasn't returned. He lives in the city now. Near the Assembly Building.'

'Of course.' Aubrey scratched his chin, thought it didn't look dignified enough, and dropped his hand. 'So you need the magical suppressors to assist you in quelling this magical outbreak? This disruption?'

'We've had several of our people track down the source of the disturbance. They're frightened by what they've found.'

'Frightened?' George said. 'That doesn't sound good. Frightened of what?'

'We're not sure. The last of my colleagues to report from the place died before he could give us any details. We've interdicted the area.'

'The ghost spawning grounds,' George muttered, glancing at Aubrey.

'Spawning grounds? A good description.' She stood. 'Now. I must leave, so you must go. I fear I have remained in one place for too long, but as you can see, we need your machines.'

'You're in danger?'

Her smile was wry, and not without humour. Aubrey found himself liking the brisk, detached woman. 'Who isn't in danger in Fisherberg? And ever since we've become involved with your Dr Tremaine, danger seems to come our way more often . . .'

When they left, Madame Zelinka was packing. Aubrey was silent all the way down in the lift as he tried to put this new information into perspective and he tapped the Beccaria Cage meditatively, which was beginning to become a habit. While a mysterious order of itinerant, altruistic magicians was useful to know about, more important was the havoc Dr Tremaine was wreaking. Was he aware of this? And where would it lead?

Evening was falling. The embassy was full of lights by the time they were admitted by the guards and Aubrey was grateful for the warm cheeriness of the place, but was surprised when Hollows, the ambassador, caught them just inside the entrance hall.

'Where have you been? I've been looking for you.'

'Out, sir,' Aubrey said, automatically keeping his cards close to his chest.

'Yes, yes, that's what von Stralick said.' The ambassador looked up the stairs. Aubrey thought the man looked flustered. 'We have visitors. Unexpected visitors.'

'Ah. I had hoped Miss Hepworth would present herself. Has she brought her mother?'

'No. I mean yes, they're here, but that's not who I meant.' He glanced toward the stairs again. 'Prince Albert has arrived early.'

Twenty

$\mathcal{J}$N WHAT WAS DELIGHTFULLY CALLED THE SWAN Room, a large west-facing drawing room, Aubrey and George found not only Prince Albert, Caroline and Mrs Hepworth, but Lady Rose. All were speaking at once and nobody noticed when Aubrey and George slipped in.

Quentin Hollows looked harried and Aubrey felt for the man. Having the heir to the Albion throne arrive a week ahead of schedule was enough to try anyone. Hollows was in charge of the embassy, this little patch of Albion, and it was his duty as a host and as a diplomat to take care of his future king.

The room was a long and narrow space broken by three square marble pillars, and decorated entirely in black and white. The walls were papered in dramatic stripes, while the floor was carpeted in dizzying black-and-white squares. The furniture was ebony, angular chairs and tables.

Aubrey wasn't surprised when his mother beckoned to them, then made her way to meet them at the door. 'Caroline and her mother both seem well disposed to you, Aubrey, for which I suppose I should be grateful.'

'It means I haven't done anything foolish,' Aubrey said. 'More foolish than usual,' he added.

'Caroline and you seemed to have worked out some sort of arrangement.'

It wasn't a question, but it was definitely an invitation for further comment.

'We have. All's well.'

His mother studied him closely for a moment. 'I'm not so sure about that, but let it rest for now.' She smiled. 'Hello, George. Aubrey hasn't brought down the Albion Empire yet, has he?'

George responded gallantly, Aubrey decided, if one ignored the flaming blush that sprang to his cheeks. 'No, Lady Rose. Not today.'

'What a superb answer,' she said with a quick smile. 'He's lucky to have you as a friend.'

George's blush deepened, he coughed, looked away, tried to speak, and then took out a handkerchief to blow his nose. Aubrey loved his mother for the way she ignored all of this. She glanced over her shoulder to where Caroline, Mrs Hepworth and Prince Albert were chatting. 'Well, we have a knotty situation on our hands here, don't we?' she said to Aubrey. 'That's why poor Hollows is looking so distracted, I imagine. A week earlier in Holmland? A week extra in the worst possible place for the heir to the throne of Albion?'

'Bertie's convinced he can do something to avert the war,' Aubrey said softly.

'And can he?' his mother asked.

Aubrey studied the Prince. Habitually serious, he was smiling in a perplexed manner at something Caroline was telling him. 'He'll certainly do his best. The Elektor will listen to him, that's certain. But whether the Elektor will be convinced, and whether the Elektor can do anything.' He sighed. 'Well, that's another matter.'

The Prince looked in their direction and immediately rose to his feet. He crossed the floor. 'Aubrey! George! I was beginning to think that you'd gone off to sample the delights of Fisherberg without me.'

He shook their hands in turn. 'Your highness,' Aubrey said. 'We've been busy.'

Prince Albert turned to Caroline, who – with her mother – had followed. 'I always begin to worry when Aubrey says that. It hides a multitude of sins.'

'Sins?' Caroline offered her hand to Aubrey. 'I'm not sure about sins, but in Aubrey's hands, a polite phrase certainly becomes an tool of subterfuge.'

'Caroline. It's good to see you, too.'

And it was. After only a short period of not seeing her, Aubrey couldn't deny how his heart beat faster in her presence, how his eye tended to linger on her, how he was acutely aware of her words, her attitudes, her nuances, and – more importantly, perhaps – how eagerly he wanted her to think well of him.

She had had her hair done, he was sure, lifted a little higher at the back. It seemed, too, that she and her mother had stopped in Lutetia on the way over, for she was wearing a new outfit that was undeniably Gallian. A jacket and skirt ensemble of some kind, in a deep, arresting blue.

'Hello, George,' Caroline said. 'I'm assuming that you and Aubrey have been involved in important matters? The symposium?'

Caroline's artful pause spoke volumes. *I want a full report on what you've been up to*, it said, *as well as a chorus of heartfelt, abject apologies for not including me.*

Aubrey was prepared to comply, glad as he was to see her.

'Symposium?' George said.

'Preparations are well under way,' Aubrey cut in smoothly, promising himself to tell Caroline about the afternoon's events as soon as possible. 'Ah, Mrs Hepworth. You're exhibiting during the symposium, aren't you?'

Mrs Hepworth was still in her oriental phase. Her gown was long, flowing silk while she wore a headdress that shimmered like beaten bronze. She smiled and extended her hand. 'And presenting a paper. "The role of the landscape in the Albion imagination." I think they're expecting something quite dull, so I'll make sure to surprise them.'

Caroline rolled her eyes. 'She does like making a scene. Just remember, Mother, we're guests here.'

'Of course. And a guest's duty is to be entertaining. At least, that's how I see it.'

Aubrey caught the eye of the Prince. Leaving Mrs Hepworth to quiz George about Sophie Delroy, his special Gallian friend, they strolled over to an elaborate marble fireplace, where Hollows was earnestly speaking with an embassy official. Both Caroline and Lady Rose found George's rambling responses amusing, and they were doing their best to contribute.

'Now, Bertie,' Aubrey said to the Prince, after Hollows had dismissed the official. 'What's all this about arriving a week early? Spontaneity isn't exactly your strong suit, you know.'

'I know.' The Prince stood with his hands clasped behind his back. 'Blame that on a regimented upbringing.'

'You have a busy life, your highness,' Hollows said.

'Quite,' the Prince said. 'But I must apologise again, Hollows. I haven't done this just to get you and your staff into a flap. Although I seem to have done just that.'

'I'm sure we can cope,' Hollows said and Aubrey saw that the ambassador had recovered his poise. His opinion of Hollows rose a notch.

'The early arrival wasn't my idea,' the Prince said. 'It was Leopold's.'

'The Elektor?' Aubrey said.

'He spoke to me on the telephone. Very excited, he was. He told me it was the first time he'd ever used the device.'

'I'm sure that wasn't what he called you about.'

'No, once he calmed down he told me that he was worried. "Frightfully concerned" was how he put it.'

'About the tension between Holmland and Albion?'

'In part. He was more anxious about the Chancellor. Wanted to know if I had any tips for dealing with a head of government.'

'Ah. Tricky stuff, that. The head of government is the embodiment of the will of the people.'

The Prince smiled. It wasn't a cynical smile, Aubrey thought, but it was a knowing one. 'Yes. And we kings and princes are simply outmoded relics of the distant past.'

'That means you have centuries of experience to draw on. And unrivalled family connections.' Aubrey stared into the distance for a moment, thinking. 'The Elektor wants to talk to you.'

'He says he doesn't trust anyone apart from his nephew Josef, who spends most of his time touring about, being patriotic, so is hardly around to talk to.'

Hollows nodded. 'Duke Josef is currently visiting his cousin, the Tsar, and doing his best to keep Muscovia happy with Holmland.'

'Wise man,' Aubrey said. 'So, Bertie, you wanted to spend some time with the Elektor?'

'Before the symposium, if possible. Chancellor Neumann has Leopold at centre stage as often as he can next week. Full pomp and regalia.'

'And how is the Security Intelligence Directorate feeling about this?' Aubrey asked Hollows.

'The . . .?' Hollows snorted. 'Ah, the cloak and dagger squad? Forgive me, your highness.'

'No need, Hollows. Craddock and Tallis are good men, but they do seem to enjoy the clandestine world, rather.'

'They sent a crack team with the Prince,' Hollows said. 'Fifty men and women commanded by a colonel. My head of household is having a heart attack trying to quarter all of them.'

'A dozen of the operatives are specialist magicians,' the Prince said. 'They appear to be ready for anything, Aubrey, but I do feel happier with you around.'

Aubrey was touched by the Prince's confidence. He didn't imagine many failed assassins were welcomed into the royal inner circle. 'You can count on me. And George.'

'Of course.'

'And Miss Hepworth,' Hollows added slowly, 'since Tallis let me know she's still on special detachment.'

Aubrey hadn't been sure about that, but decided that Tallis's team would be better off for it.

Another embassy official entered the room and made directly for Hollows, who saw him coming, apologised, met him halfway, had a brief, intense conversation, and then returned looking relieved. 'Dinner is ready,' he announced and Aubrey had an immediate appreciation of the difficulties of the ambassador's job. Day-to-day diplomacy was one thing, but he also had to organise a complete little world within the walls of the embassy – including such mundane matters as feeding unexpected guests.

Hollows ushered them to the grand dining room and Aubrey was impressed once again. The tables, the table settings, the flower arrangements and the hordes of waiting serving staff looked as if they had been organised months ago.

Over the course of the evening, Lady Rose and Ophelia Hepworth exchanged scandalous stories that shocked George and brought wry smiles of recognition to the faces of the ambassador and the Prince. Aubrey did his best to keep up with Caroline as she wove in and out of the conversations that flowed around the table. He'd always fancied himself as a dab hand at chat, but Caroline ran rings around him this evening. Not that he minded. Having her running rings around him was a vision that filled many of his daydreams, if truth be told.

When the dinner broke up, amid much laughter at the conclusion of a George story about matching wits with his journalistic nemesis at college, Aubrey was taken aback when he caught the time on the clock over the fireplace. It was much later than he thought.

'I'll walk you home,' he said to Caroline and Mrs Hepworth.

'Thank you, dear boy,' Mrs Hepworth said, 'but I'm sure we don't need an escort on such a brief journey.'

Caroline caught her lower lip with her teeth, then raised an eyebrow at him. 'I'd appreciate it, Aubrey. Thank you.'

When Mrs Hepworth rolled her eyes, Aubrey saw where her daughter got that gesture from. 'You are a contrarian by nature, Caroline. I'm sure that if I'd agreed to Aubrey's request, you would have insisted he stay here.'

'No I wouldn't,' Caroline said, and that was enough for more laughter, a delicately smothered yawn from Lady Rose, a wistful look at the empty chocolate platter from George and for the ambassador to guide them downstairs to the door.

'The gate is guarded all night,' he said to Aubrey after farewelling the Hepworths. 'You'll be let in.'

Nearly midnight, but the streets gave no sign of being desolate. They were well illuminated by bright gaslight and many Fisherbergians were strolling along the pavements. Cabs were doing good business, both horse-drawn and motor.

Aubrey was glad that the city architects and town planners of Fisherberg worked on generous proportions. The streets were wide, the pavements substantial, the way well lit. This meant that he could walk alongside Caroline instead of having to trail behind the Hepworths like some sort of flunky. He did, the three of them walking side by side for some time. They told him about their earlier times in the city, the places they'd enjoyed, the delights it had to offer.

Then Mrs Hepworth quickened her pace a little, striding ahead a dozen or so steps, just at a time when Caroline slowed. Aubrey, of course, matched her pace.

'Mother is discreet,' Caroline said softly. 'I didn't even have to ask her.'

'I beg your pardon?' Aubrey said, confused.

'She knew I'd want to find out what you've been up to since leaving Albion. She's giving us a chance.'

Aubrey admired Caroline's mother, and was thankful for her modern outlook. As well as being an outstanding artist, she was a famous free-thinker, one of the most progressive women in Albion. Her views on raising her daughter were generally thought of as scandalous, but she never cared for public opinion.

And, Aubrey had found, she treated him well – better than he probably deserved.

'Right,' he said. 'We started on a train.'

Aubrey was conscious of Mrs Hepworth leading the way, not far ahead, and he kept the report as concise as possible. Caroline was shocked when he told her of Manfred's reappearance, and she gasped when he described his plummet from the train. She wrinkled her immaculate brow at the details of the brigand encounter, but the near-fatal raft trip through the gorge only made her smile.

'It wasn't funny,' he said stiffly. 'Not at the time.'

'It's not that.' Without looking at him, she patted him on the arm.

His heart was butter, and melted. 'What is it then?'

'I was wondering why you didn't burst through a wall of flame, right at the end.'

'You've lost me, I'm afraid.'

She ticked items off on her fingers. Aubrey had always loved her hands. Elegant, dextrous, beautiful. 'You fell through the air, went into the bowels of the earth, then careered through water. Of the four elements, only fire was left. It was unlike you not to complete the set.' She smiled a little. 'Not all that funny, really.'

Maybe not, he thought, *but I'll listen to you for as long as you'll let me.* 'Clever, though.'

'Don't be patronising,' she said, but grinned. 'I've warned you about that before.'

'Sorry. You're the last person I want to be patronising to.'

She held his gaze for a moment, then looked away. She began walking a little faster. Aubrey kept up and soon they were alongside Mrs Hepworth again. 'And tomorrow, Aubrey,' Caroline said, 'are you free? I have some unfinished matters.'

'Unfinished matters?' Aubrey repeated, despite his intentions never to parrot her. Instead of listening, he'd been looking at how the light from the gaslamps caught her eyes, conscious of a special moment having passed. 'Ah, yes. Of course. Happy to help.'

'I hope you've made some progress in this area already.'

'Certainly, certainly. We've been talking to ghost hunters.'

Caroline gave him a look that promised serious consequences if he didn't fully explain this when they were alone. 'That's good.'

'Ghost hunters?' Mrs Hepworth said. 'I thought they'd vanished years ago. What are you after them for, dear boy?'

'Research,' he said, grasping for an explanation that was true without going anywhere near the heart of the matter.

'Research,' she echoed. 'How Lionel loved his research.'

She put a hand to her lips and Aubrey desperately sought for something to change the topic away from the late Professor Hepworth. 'And this friend that you're staying with,' he said to Mrs Hepworth as they waited for an omnibus to roll past before they crossed the road. 'You've known him for a long time?'

'The baron? Absolutely ages. He spent some time in Albion years ago.'

'Well travelled, is he?' Aubrey asked, unable to stop himself from accumulating information. One never knew what would prove useful. Of course, sometimes it was a fine line between subtle intelligence-gathering and outright inquisitiveness . . .

'He's a man of the world. Rather too much of it, sometimes.'

'He's a businessman,' Caroline said. 'Extraordinarily rich.'

'It's a pity,' Mrs Hepworth said. 'He was a fine sculptor in his youth.'

The street began to trend upward. 'Businessman.' Aubrey's curiosity gave him another nudge. 'What sort of business?'

Mrs Hepworth laughed. 'When you're as rich as Siegfried, your business is just about everything. That's why every Holmland government in the last thirty years has wanted him in their inner circle. He's had enough of that sort of thing, apparently. Retired from the world of politics.'

Alarm bells started ringing so loud in Aubrey's mind that he actually looked around for their source. 'He's a politician, too?'

'Anyone who's anyone in Holmland is either involved in politics, or wishes they were.'

'Just like Albion, really,' Caroline said, but for once Aubrey let this impish jibe slide right by.

'This baron of yours . . .'

Another laugh. 'He's hardly mine, dear boy. Although, at one time – before I met your father, darling – we were close. Ah, here we are.'

It wasn't the largest castle Aubrey had ever seen, but as a private residence it was definitely remarkable. Sited on the top of the hill and surrounded by a massive wall, it loomed over the Empire Gardens and the Istros River like a citadel.

'It's more comfortable than it looks,' Mrs Hepworth said. 'Siegfried's given Caroline and I the east wing. He is most generous.'

Aubrey stared at the two square towers, the hundreds of windows. 'Siegfried is your baron.'

'Of course. Siggy is Baron von Grolman.'

Aubrey contained his shock by the novel method of imitating a stunned goldfish.

The Hepworths were staying with Hugo von Stralick's mysterious mentor.

Twenty-one

THE NEXT MORNING, EARLY, AUBREY AND GEORGE stood in front of Baron von Grolman's residence. In the daylight the edifice was even more impressive. Once, Aubrey thought, it must have dominated the whole area, squatting on top of the hill like a great beast. Even though housing had swallowed up most of the approaches to the castle, it was still the most prominent building in the area, almost a suburb in itself, tucked behind its thick stone walls. Aubrey imagined it having its own postal service, its own police force.

A bell at the gate was connected to a cunning speaking tube which Aubrey sensed, with interest, was magically enhanced. After being admitted, they set off toward the distant buildings. Crunching along well-kept, perfectly clean gravel, he kept wondering about the careless show of wealth behind the speaking tube. It was good, discreet magic – and that was costly. The Law of Attenuation, inverted? Or a novel application of the Law of Similarity? Mulling over the possibilities kept him busy during their trek along the driveway.

After mounting the broad stone steps, they were met at the front door by an officious fellow, somewhat more than a butler, somewhat less than a chamberlain. He looked down his impressive nose at them while they explained they'd arrived to meet Caroline Hepworth. He made them wait in the daunting entrance hall for an uncomfortable time, probably from some sense of necessity. It gave Aubrey and George a chance to become acquainted with each of the six suits of armour standing in the hall, and also to find out how uncomfortable antique Holmland furniture could be.

Eventually, Caroline appeared from one of the arched doors that opened off the entrance hall. 'Aubrey, George. The baron wants to see you.'

She looked fresh and excited. Aubrey knew it was the prospect of a day's adventuring that invigorated her and, wistfully, he longed for her to feel that way about him. On the other hand, he was willing to settle for hoping that his presence didn't actually detract from her good spirits.

'The baron? He's in?'

'I didn't realise it, but he arrived late last night,' Caroline said. 'He's invited you to breakfast, with mother and me. And his guests.'

'Guests?' Aubrey said. He straightened his jacket.

Caroline did her best to hide a smile. Aubrey found the effort fascinating. 'You'll see.'

It was a baronial dining hall. It was so much a baronial dining hall that Aubrey imagined all the other baronial dining halls in the world getting together and talking about how they'd like to be like the von Grolman baronial dining hall when they grew up. Lashings of stone and dark timber. Narrow arched windows high in the walls. Lofty ceiling somewhere high overhead, past the age-blackened beams. Coats of arms and intricate heraldic banners hanging from the walls, interspersed with crossed pikes, swords, halberds and other cunning implements of destruction. The aroma of a savoury breakfast was possibly the only thing not hundreds of years old.

At the head of the long table, a broad-shouldered man rose to his feet when they entered. He waited patiently with his hands behind his back while Caroline, Aubrey and George crossed the mile or two between the door and the table. As they drew closer, Aubrey guessed that he was in his late sixties or early seventies, but his bulk and ruddy complexion gave every indication that he was in good health. His head was bald apart from a slight fringe of grey on either side, a reminder of the past. His moustache made up for the lack of hair on his head, however, being long and defiantly pointed, jutting out an inch or two on either side of his cheeks. Aubrey imagined he could be a danger to bystanders if he turned around quickly.

'Baron von Grolman,' Caroline said. 'This is Aubrey Fitzwilliam and George Doyle.'

The baron made a noise – half snort, half chuckle – that Aubrey took as a good sign. He held out his hand, then saw that he still had a white linen napkin tucked into the neck of his jacket. He barked a full, throaty laugh this time, removed it and shook Aubrey's hand then

George's. 'Come,' he said in good Albionish, 'come, join us. We eat, we talk, all goes well.' He gestured. 'You know my other guests.'

Mrs Hepworth smiled at Aubrey, but he wasn't surprised when he saw the other two guests, small worlds being what they were.

Von Stralick leaned back from the table. 'Sit, Fitzwilliam and the other fellow. Close your mouth or put some food in it. You look most foolish gaping like that.'

Next to von Stralick, Kiefer looked up, blinked, nodded at Aubrey and George then went back to his plate of bacon and eggs with all the appearance of someone with more important things on his mind.

'You managed to find the baron this time?' Aubrey asked von Stralick.

'I did. Through the novel method of visiting his home. I should have tried it earlier, but it lacked the sort of deviousness that I aspire to.'

By the time Aubrey had found a seat – strangely enough, next to Caroline – George was already helping himself to the dishes on the table, right under the approving eye of the baron. Von Stralick was sitting opposite, next to Kiefer, at the end.

Aubrey busied his hands with arranging his napkin and keeping himself from tangling with the stony-faced servants as they piled his plate with food. He hardly noticed what he was taking, because he was trying to fit these developments into some sort of framework.

It was von Stralick who took pity on him. 'Fitzwilliam, what is there to look so anxious about? Lovely ladies, a generous host, good friends and fine food. Could a day start any better?'

It could if I knew what was going on, Aubrey thought. 'I'm sorry. Your presence here is unexpected. I thought you were staying at the embassy.'

'Ach, no. We are doing some work for your Ambassador Hollows, but we are now staying with the most excellent Baron von Grolman. Much safer here. True, Otto?'

Kiefer lifted his gaze from his plate. Aubrey was startled at how pale he looked, with dark circles under his eyes. 'Fisherberg is a dangerous place,' Kiefer said, then turned his attention back to his breakfast.

'Do not mind him,' von Stralick said. 'He has had no sleep. Researching all night, he tells me, in the baron's library.'

'You're lucky to have such a patron,' Aubrey said carefully.

'Von Stralick is one of my best people,' the baron said down the length of the table. 'I do what I can to help him.'

Von Stralick nodded at this and caught Aubrey with a significant look. 'The baron has withdrawn from politics –'

'For the moment,' the baron interjected.

'For the moment. But that doesn't mean that he is without influence.'

'What can I say?' The baron spread his hands. 'People feel compelled to repay the many favours they owe me.'

I can imagine how they feel compelled, Aubrey thought. The baron was a jovial host, but Aubrey had the distinct impression that he was a man accustomed to getting his own way.

Again, von Stralick caught Aubrey's eye and the look he gave him convinced Aubrey that von Stralick knew what he was thinking – and he agreed. 'The baron has had news about a certain Dr Tremaine,' von Stralick went on. 'He is up to something.'

Aubrey bit his tongue. When *wasn't* Dr Tremaine up to something?

'He has a plan for this symposium of the Elektor's,' the baron said with some relish. He seemed to be enjoying his role as holder of information as much as he was enjoying his breakfast, where he had moved from an enormous plate of eggs and tomatoes to an equally large platter of assorted sausages. Even George was impressed by the baron's trencherman talent. The baron speared a sausage with his fork then looked up. 'It is your prince he's after, you know. Tremaine knows that he has arrived in Fisherberg early.'

Aubrey had to put a hand on the table to stop himself from leaping to his feet.

Caroline was horrified. 'No. He wouldn't dare move against the Prince.'

George had frozen with a forkful of omelette halfway to his mouth. He glanced at Caroline. 'That's right. Not when the Elektor himself invited him.'

'And the Chancellor promised safe passage,' Aubrey added, but he couldn't help reminding himself that Dr Tremaine was a law unto himself.

'Ah, but that is Tremaine's genius,' the baron said. With some reluctance, he put down his knife and fork. He placed both hands on the table in front of him, in an effort to appear grave and trustworthy, Aubrey guessed, but the way his eyes kept flicking to the plate of sausages in front of him tended to ruin the pose. 'He isn't going to kill your prince. He's going to control him. Your prince will be Tremaine's puppet.' He waved a hand. 'Or so I have heard.'

'He can do it,' Aubrey said, and everyone at the table turned to him. He remembered how Dr Tremaine had turned him into a mindless assassin. 'If he can get his hands on the Prince, Dr Tremaine has the spells to control him at a distance. Utterly.'

'Tremaine will do it, that is all you need to know,' said the baron. He picked up his fork and jabbed a piece of sausage that disappeared into his mouth. He chewed on it as if he wanted every last iota of flavour from it. 'And he will do it *before* the symposium.'

Twenty-two

*A*UBREY EXCUSED HIMSELF FROM THE BREAKFAST AS soon as he politely could. It caused an exodus. Kiefer hurried off, saying he had still much research to attend to. Von Stralick watched his cousin go, thoughtfully, and then made his excuses as well. Aubrey wondered if von Stralick was having some pangs over his mentoring role for the young magician. It looked as if it was proving harder than he'd expected, with Kiefer's changes of mood. The young man was driven, there was no doubt about that, but Aubrey wondered if revenge or ambition were proving the stronger motivation.

Caroline was keen to go as well, but George looked mournfully at his plate before joining his friends.

Aubrey promised himself he'd treat his friend to a fine meal – when they had time.

Back at the embassy, Aubrey accosted the first official he saw. 'Where's the Prince?'

The man gaped. 'The Prince?'

Aubrey saw Quentin Hollows descending the stairs. 'Never mind. Hollows, where's the Prince? He's in danger.'

Hollows looked alarmed. 'He's gone to visit the Elektor. I say, what's going on?'

'He's taken his bodyguard?'

'Only a pair of them. He's visiting the Elektor, after all.'

Aubrey grimaced. The last place you'd expect an incident is exactly the best place for someone to plan one. 'Send a squad around to the Elektor's palace straight away. Is a motorcar ready?'

'Of course.'

'Good. Can you telephone ahead? Let them know to expect us?'

'I can.' Hollows frowned. 'Can't you tell me what's going on?'

'Remember the attempt on the Prince's life? The one we were sure wasn't going to happen? It looks as if it could be under way.'

The motorcar trip was rapid and probably illegal, thanks to George's sitting in the front seat next to the driver and brandishing a gold ten-mark piece whenever he slowed down.

At the palace, a troop of Imperial Household Guards was waiting for them. George put his arm over the back of the seat. 'Not quite the welcome we were expecting, old man?'

'Not quite. But let's see.'

The officer in charge clicked his heels, but Aubrey noticed how he kept his hand on his sabre. Even though the uniform was laden with gilt and crimson, the sabre looked rather more than ceremonial. 'Mr Fitzwilliam?' the officer said in passable Albionish. 'You will come with us, if you please. And your friends.'

'Sorry, but we must see the Elektor. Or Prince Albert.'

'You will come with us,' the officer repeated and it was clear that the invitation had moved from a request to a demand.

Aubrey sighed and touched the Beccaria Cage. 'If you wish.'

They were taken to an office. It had been renovated reasonably recently, but its origins as a room in the original baroque palace were clear in the remaining cornices, where cherubs peered down at them from among plaster clouds and sunbeams.

A beefy man was looking out the window, over the parade grounds. 'The new Werner lorries have arrived,' he said without turning. 'The best in the world, you know.'

His Albionish was harsh, but fluent. He was wearing a dark suit of conservative cut. When he turned, the first thing that Aubrey saw was the truly impressive set of muttonchops that swelled down his cheeks to reach the corners of his mouth, as if two skinny cats were lounging about on his face.

His head was mostly bald, which made his broad brow seem even broader. The whole effect was a man who was top heavy, especially since he was tall and large framed.

'Chancellor Neumann?' Aubrey said.

The chancellor frowned, then nodded. 'You must be Fitzwilliam. You have the look of your mother about you.' He studied Aubrey for a moment. 'And your father.'

He bowed to Caroline. 'Miss Hepworth. I welcome you and your mother back to Holmland.'

'Your Excellency.'

'And Doyle.'

'Sir,' George said, startled to be recognised.

Chancellor Neumann studied them for a time in a silence that soon became uncomfortable. He didn't scowl – not quite – but Aubrey saw him committing them to memory. Eventually, he waved a hand – an impatient, peremptory gesture. 'What is it you want?'

Aubrey glanced at his friends. They couldn't trust the Chancellor, but could they save the Prince *without* trusting him?

It was time for subterfuge.

'The Prince's medication,' Aubrey said. 'He left the embassy without it.'

The Chancellor's impressive eyebrows shot up. 'Medication? For the Prince? I have heard nothing about this.'

'Oh.' Aubrey did his best to look torn. 'It was meant to be a secret.'

Caroline came to his side. 'You can't keep it hidden, Aubrey. Not now. He could die.'

The Chancellor's eyes narrowed very slightly, while he shook his head with evident concern. Aubrey knew then that the trick had worked. The Chancellor was filing this titbit of information away. Prince Albert unwell? Needing life-preserving medication? Useful. 'You have it with you?'

Aubrey touched his appurtenances vest and was rewarded with the satisfying 'clink' from a tiny bottle of ink he'd stowed earlier. 'Right here.'

The Chancellor held out his hand. 'I will take it to him.'

That wasn't the result Aubrey was after. He froze with his hand on his chest. 'I . . .'

The door opened. The Chancellor stiffened. 'Your highness.'

A young man stood in the doorway, and Aubrey was startled at the family resemblance to Bertie. He was tall, slim, dark haired, dark eyes, with a razor-sharp moustache. He was younger than Aubrey had thought, too, lucky to be thirty. He wore the dark blue uniform of the Holmland navy.

'Neumann,' the Elektor said, his expression open and curious. 'Who are these people?'

The Chancellor worked his jaw. It was apparent to Aubrey that the last thing he wanted to do was make introductions, but he had no choice. 'Your highness, this is Miss Hepworth, Mr Fitzwilliam, and Mr Doyle.'

The Elektor brightened. 'Fitzwilliam? Aubrey Fitzwilliam, the Albion Prime Minister's son? Bertie has told me so much about you!'

Aubrey seized the opportunity so hard that he was in danger of throttling it. 'It's Prince Albert, sir. He's unwell. I have to get his special medicine to him straight away.'

'Bertie is here?' The Elektor frowned. 'You didn't tell me this, Neumann.'

What is going on here? Aubrey thought. *The ambassador said Bertie had gone to see the Elektor!*

'He hasn't been here long, your highness. I was about to inform you.'

The Elektor clicked his tongue with exasperation. 'And where is he, then? Quickly, man!'

The Chancellor hesitated for only an instant, but Aubrey knew calculation when he saw it. The Chancellor was sorting through possible answers before arriving at one that he was obviously unhappy with. 'The Prince is in your laboratory. He asked to see it.'

'This way,' the Elektor said to Aubrey.

A strangled noise came from the Chancellor. Aubrey was startled to see that he was sweating, a fine sheen appearing on his forehead. 'I don't think that's wise, your highness. We have word that an intruder is loose in the palace.'

'An intruder? Why wasn't I told?'

'The matter has just come to light, your highness.'

'I will take guards.'

The Chancellor stood rigidly, his jaw clenched tightly. 'I will go, your highness. It may not be safe.'

'Not safe in my own palace with my own guards? Nonsense! I will find Bertie while you organise the search for this intruder. Now, quickly Fitzwilliam!'

'I have always been interested in magic and in science,' the Elektor said as they hurried along the corridor. The four guards trailing them jingled as they jogged.

Aubrey was interested, despite wanting to find Bertie as soon as possible. The Chancellor's obvious evasiveness was ominous. 'You have good equipment?'

'The best.' The Elektor smiled wryly. 'Many of our companies give it to me. They think it a good way to ensure support from the government.'

Aubrey was about to query this when the Elektor

stopped at a solid iron door. 'My laboratory is through here. I had it built attached to the east wing.' He shrugged. 'I never liked the east wing.'

Aubrey wrinkled his nose. The smell of ozone was creeping from under the door. Electrical experimentation, at the very least, was going on in there. 'Best to wait here,' he said to the Elektor. 'With your guards. Just in case the intruder is inside.'

The Elektor looked thoughtful. 'In that case, you should have the guards.'

Caroline stepped forward. Her pistol gleamed in the gaslight. 'We're well equipped, as well, your highness.'

The Elektor's eyes went wide. He looked from Caroline to the pistol and back again. He swallowed. 'I believe you are,' he said faintly.

The door opened onto a short flight of stairs that were poorly lit by a single electric bulb. Aubrey led the way. Immediately, he was grateful, because Caroline put her hand on his shoulder and followed close behind. George's heavy footsteps echoed as he brought up the rear.

The stairs took them into a chamber that was larger than Aubrey had expected. Chains hung from the rafters a good twenty feet overhead. Electric cables snaked through them and carbon lamps hung from them like exotic fruit, but they couldn't dispel the shadows that hung in the corners of the vast space.

Large cabinets took up most of the room between work benches that were laden with glass and metalwork. The cabinets were heavy industrial make and all of them had thick electrical cables connected to them – sometimes more than one. A low, unsettling hum shook the whole laboratory, a sound Aubrey could feel in his bones.

He paused, frowning. Short, sharp bursts of magic came to him from the installations on the other side of the laboratory and Aubrey was immediately alert. This was powerful magic that slid over his exposed skin – the back of his hands, his face – with a raw bitterness that made him hiss with disgust.

This sort of magic wasn't the tinkering of an amateur. It was directed, intricate magic, with a flavour he knew too well.

Caroline looked at him. He grimaced. 'Magic,' he whispered. 'Tremaine.' She narrowed her eyes. Aubrey pointed in the direction it came from. George nodded, then eased to the left along the wall, peering ahead. They followed his broad back as they crept through the clutter of the laboratory, the noise of their passage masked by the sudden eruption of electrical arcing. Bright light sparked and jumped, making the shadows wheel and swoop overhead – and making them hurry.

They rounded a large cabinet that hummed as they passed, and more brilliant white light crackled. Aubrey had to throw up a hand to protect his eyes. When he brought it down, purple spots danced in his vision, but that wasn't what worried him most. He worked his mouth, trying to dislodge the sound of metal being rubbed together. As he rubbed his ears and tried not to hear colours, George tapped him on the shoulder and pointed to the right, then hurried off, bent nearly double to take advantage of the cover provided by the overladen benches.

Caroline came to his side. 'Are you all right?' she whispered urgently, cutting through the spitting of more electrical discharges – and the prickle of more magic on the back of his eyeballs when he nodded in response to her query.

A tall figure was standing in front of the machine that was the source of the electrical discharges. He was wearing heavy leather gloves, almost gauntlets, extending to his elbows. He wore goggles on his face, tinted glass, Aubrey assumed, but he was surprised to see the man had a shovel in his hand.

The machine was about eight feet tall, and about ten feet or more across. Two large ceramic insulators extended from the top, jutting at angles and looking like piles of dining plates. Four massive cables hung from the rafters and connected to the machine, as well as a six-inch pipe that ran along the stone floor.

The front of the machine was a mass of switches and dials, with three large hatches.

A mound the height of the man was heaped up on the left side of the machine. As they watched and crept closer, the operator stooped and shovelled from the mound into the hatch on the left. When it was full, he closed the door and dropped the shovel onto the mound. He flung a series of switches, and the result was the by now familiar burst of light from the top of the machine – and Aubrey felt the magical excess as slightly sweet on the tips of his fingers.

Heart beating faster, he dropped and crawled closer.

The operator of the machine seized hold of the middle hatch and pulled. The door opened and a long tray slid out. The operator studied it for a moment, then made a sound of disgust. He reached in, scraped around with his gauntleted hands, and then he hurled the contents away in a fury.

Aubrey and Caroline huddled together as glassware crashed around them. A large lump landed on the stone floor near them and came to rest against the leg of the bench. Aubrey waited a moment until the operator started filling the hopper again with the shovel, then he scurried over on all fours, retrieved the lump, and hurried back to Caroline.

He stared at what he'd found. It was about the size of his fist, heavy, orange-brown and misshapen. 'Clay,' he breathed and he darted a look at the machine. 'We must hurry.'

'What?' Caroline said. 'Why?'

'I think he's making a golem.'

'Here? Whatever for?'

'To substitute for Bertie.'

Ever since the baron's revelation, Aubrey had been worrying about how Dr Tremaine was to achieve his end of having a puppet on the throne of Albion. His initial thought was that he would use the same method that he'd use to turn Aubrey into an assassin, but after pondering it for some time, he'd discarded this. The mind control spell had worked, in a fashion, but Aubrey hadn't acted normally. George and Caroline had quickly seen that he was behaving very strangely and were rightly suspicious. Besides, Aubrey hadn't been any good for anything else. He had one task, one mission; his whole existence had been centred on killing the Prince. He had no mind for anything else.

No, the mind control magic couldn't be used to keep a replica Bertie in place, convincing all those around, conducting itself through the thousand and one duties of the heir to the throne.

But Dr Tremaine was master of another sort of magic – one that could produce a perfect replica, and one that could operate with a degree of autonomy while still being under total control of its master.

A golem.

The clay-based magical creatures were difficult for most magicians to make, and so their use was generally limited to simple tasks. But Dr Tremaine, as Aubrey knew well, was no ordinary magician. And, to judge from his efforts with the Glauber golem and with the cloudy stormfleet, his powers were growing.

But where was he?

Aubrey gestured to Caroline. They waited their chance, then scuttled closer to another bench, only a few yards away from the machine. Aubrey lifted his head to peer across the bench, but his eyes widened when he saw what was lying there. He snatched it and lowered himself again.

Caroline stared at it. 'I don't want to ask,' she whispered, 'because I think I know – but whose jacket is that?'

He nodded, the confirmation turning his stomach to ice. 'It's Bertie's.'

The machine crackled again and white light battered them. Aubrey peeped over the edge of the bench to see the masked operator dragging more clay from the drawer, spitting curses as he cast the clay over his shoulder.

The process wasn't a straightforward one, it seemed. They may have some time.

Movement caught his eye. Aubrey looked up and he nearly leaped to his feet. George was climbing through the rafters, negotiating his way through the chains and cables like an arboreal ape through the vines of a jungle.

Aubrey clenched his jaw so tightly that his teeth hurt. Those electrical cables looked well enough insulated, but if George even brushed a bare wire while he was touching just about anything else, he'd be doomed.

Caroline saw him looking up and followed his gaze. Her eyes widened, then she took our her pistol. For a bizarre moment, Aubrey thought she was offering to shoot George, but then he understood that she was suggesting a shot at the golem machine – or the operator.

Aubrey was pulled between choices and, as had been his recent custom, he touched the Beccaria Cage to help him think – but in the gesture he bumped the small bottle of ink in his appurtenances vest.

The idea bloomed even as he thought of it. He leaned close to Caroline. 'Do you have any paper?'

She raised an eyebrow and whispered back. 'Where would I keep paper?'

'Wherever you keep your pistol.'

She shook her head, but carefully reached up onto the bench. 'Here.'

It was good quality foolscap, obviously meant for note-taking. Aubrey signalled his grateful thanks and then set about folding it. With a few quick movements, he had just the sort of paper glider he wanted.

Caroline watched silently as Aubrey scrabbled for a shard of the shattered glassware on the floor. With caution, he ground it under the heel of his boot, then scooped up a teaspoonful – wincing as the dust cut his fingertips – and deposited it in the folds of the paper aircraft.

Then he popped his head up. 'Over here!' he yelled and he launched the paper glider.

The machine operator straightened and, his goggles catching the light, he peered in their direction – which is exactly what Aubrey wanted. He rattled out a spell which used the Law of Attraction. The paper glider, which had been veering wildly, suddenly changed direction as the glass embedded in it was strongly attracted to the glass in the man's goggles, thanks to Aubrey's calculations. As the glass tugged at the paper, the glider lost its shape, unfolding and fluttering through the air before it struck the bewildered man and wrapped around his head.

With an oath he dropped his shovel and staggered around, clumsily trying to tear the clinging paper from his face. Aubrey stood and, for good measure, uncapped the bottle of ink and chanted a variation a spell based on the Law of Propensity. The ink leaped from the bottle and flew straight at the flailing man and his paper-wrapped head, Aubrey having stimulated the ink's natural tendency to bond with paper.

The man let out a wild shout as his vision, which must have been quite obscured by the paper, was now blackened by the spreading ink.

Then Caroline appeared in front of the blinded man. With a graceful movement, she snapped the heel of her hand up under his chin. He toppled like a tree.

Aubrey hurried to her side. She looked at him, wide-eyed. 'I didn't like the sound his head made when it hit the floor.'

Aubrey hadn't either, but he liked the shape of the back of the man's head even less, especially its flattened look.

A huge thump made them both whirl, only to see George landing on top of a crate. He eased himself down to the floor and dusted his hands together, looking disappointed. 'A few more minutes and I would have had him.'

'I'm sure you would have,' Aubrey said. He knew he'd acted hastily in the end, but he hadn't wanted George to do anything dangerous. He smiled ruefully when he realised that they were all doing dangerous things all too often. Still, if he could reduce the risk for his friends by taking more on himself, he was willing to do that. He owed them.

Aubrey went to the golem-making machine. Three doors, two of which they'd already seen. The third then, logically, should . . .

He took the handle and heaved. Another long drawer slid out on metal bearings. It was identical to the middle drawer, except this one was occupied.

'Is he all right?' George said.

Prince Albert lay in the cold, hard confines of the drawer. His eyes were closed, his skin was waxy. He was naked.

'I dearly hope so,' Aubrey said and the groan that came from the drawer was the most rewarding sound Aubrey had heard for some time.

The Prince blinked, then opened his eyes. 'Aubrey?'

'Bertie,' Aubrey said. 'Easy now. Don't make any sudden moves.'

'Your highness,' George said, 'what do you remember?'

'Remember?' He shivered. 'Rather chilly here, isn't it.' He lifted his head and stared. 'Good Lord. Where are my clothes?'

Aubrey and George struggled to help the Prince out of the drawer until Caroline came to their aid. George coughed. 'We're fine. Really. Perhaps you should see to that other fellow.'

'He's dead.' Caroline faltered, but gathered herself and went on. 'And don't be such a prude, George. I've seen more life models while Mother has been painting than you've had hot dinners.'

Aubrey was startled by this, but concentrated on helping the Prince to the bench where Caroline and he had found the royal clothes. It was only a few yards, but by the time they'd reached it the Prince was already insisting that he was strong enough to walk by himself, really.

To give the Prince some privacy – although once he'd gathered himself he'd behaved as if being naked in a laboratory was an everyday matter – they went to the unmoving body of the machine operator.

'He's not dead.' Aubrey squatted alongside the unmoving operator.

'He must be,' Caroline said. She had her arms crossed on her chest, but the way she moved her mouth told Aubrey she wasn't unaffected by what had happened. She was unwilling to look steadily at the unfortunate, either, glancing at him and then looking away. 'His head's crushed. He's not breathing.'

Aubrey squinted and touched the man just behind his ear. 'I don't think he ever breathed. Not properly.'

He lifted an inert leg. When he let it drop it cracked on the stone floor.

Caroline jerked her gaze back and shuddered. 'What did you say?'

Aubrey pointed. 'His foot just fell off.'

George nudged it with the toe of his boot. 'It's hard.'

'A golem to tend a golem-making machine.'

'It's a golem?' Caroline said softly. She swallowed, hard.

'A masterly creation.' It was more than that. It was the most human-like golem Aubrey had ever seen. Dr Tremaine's craft, already great, had grown even more potent.

Aubrey tilted his head and peered at the machine, wondering how it worked. No golem could wield magic – human consciousness was required to work the magical power wrested from the universe – so the machine must have spells embedded in it. Such an extraordinary blending of machinery and magic could have come from only one man.

Again, Aubrey itched with the feeling of Dr Tremaine's presence. He shook it off with difficulty and busied himself with stripping off the creature's goggles.

It had the appearance of a well-built man in his fifties – clean shaven, heavy features, dark blond hair – but the face was rapidly cracking like poorly glazed porcelain.

'Anyone you recognise?' Aubrey said.

'That's Stern,' the Prince said. He'd come up behind them unnoticed during their inspection. 'Used to be the Holmland ambassador to Albion. He was recalled a few months ago because he was too sympathetic to us.'

Aubrey had just begun feeling pleased at having foiled a plot to replace Prince Albert, but the business at hand had suddenly grown murkier. 'I don't think he's sympathetic any more.'

Suddenly, from the shadows, came the whipping crack of a rifle – then two more. The bullets crashed into the golem machine and made it ring like a bell. George threw himself to one side, dragging the Prince with him. Caroline ducked and rolled against a nearby bench. Even though Aubrey was crouching, still next to Stern's duplicate, he felt exposed and he scrabbled his way to join Caroline.

'Do not try to escape,' a Holmlandish voice boomed through the laboratory. 'Come out and put your hands in the air.'

'Neumann?' Prince Albert called. 'Is that you?'

'Bertie!' another voice cried. Aubrey recognised it as the Elektor's. 'They said you were dead!'

Within seconds, the laboratory was a milling mass of politicians, royalty, adventurers and confused Imperial Household Guards. Aubrey dusted his hands, watching the Elektor and Prince Albert greet each other. It appeared to Aubrey that the Elektor was genuinely moved to see that the Prince was unharmed, and he bumped him up on his 'Possibly To Be Trusted' scale.

The Chancellor, on the other hand, was less than moved. He had a rifle in his hands. He gave it to one of the guards then stood, phlegmatically, watching the Elektor and the Prince exchange reassurances.

Aubrey approached him. 'What happened?'

The Chancellor shrugged. 'In the shadows, I thought your prince was the intruder.'

'It's good you missed.'

The Chancellor looked askance at him. 'Most fortunate.'

George ambled over, hands in pockets, but then he stopped and sniffed. 'What's that smell?'

Caroline hissed. 'Smoke. It's coming from the golem maker.'

At that moment, a fountain of sparks belched from the machine, spraying from the bullet holes like fireworks. The Elektor gaped, horrified. 'We must leave. Quickly!'

'What is it?' Aubrey said over the hissing crackle of electrical discharge.

'One of von Grolman's machines. I haven't had time to study it, but it requires much electricity. We could be in great danger.'

The guards crowded around the Elektor and hustled him to the door. George and Caroline did likewise with Prince Albert, which left Aubrey and the Chancellor. 'After you, Fitzwilliam,' the Chancellor said.

Aubrey hesitated. A sharp metallic clanging came from the golem maker and more sparks flew from the bullet holes. He could smell burning and he knew that the workings of the machine were destroying themselves. Nothing would be recovered, further investigation would be useless.

Then he remembered his father's telling him about the Chancellor's past.

He'd been a rifleman. More than that, a sharpshooter.

As they stumbled away from the conflagration, Aubrey stared at the Chancellor, who kept glancing back with a look of grim satisfaction.

I don't think you missed at all, Aubrey thought. He threw up an arm as a side of the golem maker peeled back with an awful screech. *I think you hit exactly what you aimed for.*

Twenty-three

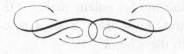

AUBREY SPENT THE REST OF THE MORNING WITH AN abiding sense of relief. While the Prince had a battle on his hands to convince Quentin Hollows that he was all right and that he shouldn't be heading straight back to Albion, Aubrey was able to stay in the background and be thankful that he'd managed to thwart Dr Tremaine's plans. He shuddered whenever he thought of what strife would have followed if the rogue magician had been successful in placing a puppet on the throne of Albion.

Aubrey, Caroline and George were interviewed by both the ambassador and Major Vincent, which gave Aubrey time in his room, alone, to reflect on the affair. Stretched out on his bed, he turned over the stones of the day's happenings to see what crawled out.

It was clear that Dr Tremaine had access to the highest places in Holmland. His position as the special adviser to the Chancellor ensured that. He could easily have slipped into the laboratory and set events in motion.

But what about Baron von Grolman? Was the golem-making machine really a product of his company? But why, then, would he divulge Dr Tremaine's plot to Aubrey?

And what about the Chancellor? At first, Aubrey had thought that the Prince was the target, but with the Chancellor's background there was no doubt he was shooting to destroy the golem maker. His story about an intruder, too, must have been a ruse to hide his involvement in the scheme.

Aubrey decided it was time to revise his reading of the situation. The Chancellor was proving to be remarkably bold in moving against Prince Albert – in the Elektor's palace, too, of all places. That sort of arrogance was a worrying sign with the prospect of imminent war.

Aubrey rubbed his forehead. He could feel a headache coming on, and he had a ghost to catch. It wasn't a good combination.

Aubrey, Caroline and George had barely entered the Blue Dog when Bruno Fromm descended on them.

'My friends,' he said while steering them back outside, 'your timing is good. Bruno Fromm can take you to this ghost, right now.' He went to move off, then he stopped and squinted at Caroline. 'And who are you?'

Aubrey jumped in. 'She's a trusted friend. Caroline Hepworth. Caroline, this is Bruno Fromm. Ghost hunter.'

Fromm leaned toward Caroline. 'Bruno Fromm is not

just any ghost hunter. Bruno Fromm is the best ghost hunter in the world.'

Caroline didn't flinch. 'And Bruno Fromm is far from his home in Nordmarsch.'

Fromm stared, cocked his head, then bellowed a laugh that echoed through the empty tavern. 'You hear Nordmarsch in Fromm's voice, clever one?'

'The northern lakes are still thick in your throat.'

Fromm chuckled, then slapped Aubrey a mighty blow on the shoulder. Aubrey had been readying himself for such an expression of approval and managed not to stagger. 'This one is smart. She will be good value.' Fromm laughed again.

Aubrey let out a sigh of relief when Caroline didn't take the ghost hunter to task, but the look she gave him clearly said not to pursue Fromm's notion of good value.

'Ah,' George said. 'Here's von Stralick.'

Aubrey turned to see the Holmland spy standing at the doorway, outlined against the midday sun.

'Where's Kiefer?' Aubrey asked.

Von Stralick tugged on his gloves and grimaced. 'Busy.'

'I thought he was red-hot in this Dr Tremaine business,' George said.

'So did I,' von Stralick said. 'But all of a sudden, his historical studies are important. Books, documents, libraries, he has cartloads of them delivered to his rooms.'

Aubrey was quite grateful that Kiefer was busy. He wasn't the ideal member of a dangerous expedition team. But his lack of interest was intriguing. It seemed as if a chance for advancement was taking precedence over Kiefer's longed-for revenge. Had he lost sight of it completely, or had he merely postponed it while he chased material success?

And the abandonment of his work into catalysts was equally intriguing. What had prompted the renewed interest in historical studies? Aubrey had come to accept that Kiefer was erratic, but was there more to his changes than that?

Fromm clapped his hands together and Aubrey's thoughts snapped back to the here and now. 'So we are all ready? Good.'

Aubrey expected ghost hunting to involve a furtive journey, lurking along laneways, flitting from shadow to shadow, sniffing the air and whatnot, but Fromm confounded him. He took them to a cart that was waiting down a lane alongside the Blue Dog. While a sceptical grey gelding in the traces studied them, Aubrey did his best to take in the sight of the ghost-hunting conveyance.

The cart was blue, brightly painted. It was decorated with what looked like extreme whimsy, with fine swirls of lighter paint weaving along every flat surface. In between the painted ribbons, shapes were cut in the wood – diamonds, crosses, ovals. To add to the spectacle, irregular shards of mirror were glued to the sides of the cart and flashed in the sun.

Just to add an auditory note to the bizarre display, hundreds of tiny bells were tied to the spokes of the wheels. Silent while the cart was stationary, Aubrey quickly decided they rendered the cart useless for night-time smuggling runs.

Fromm beamed with pride. 'Is beautiful, no?'

Aubrey nodded, slowly. 'It's distinctive.'

'Traditional ghost-hunting cart,' Fromm said as he stroked the muzzle of the gelding. It looked at them with wise eyes. Aubrey wondered what it had seen in its time. 'We decorate, all of us, in our own ways.'

'The ghosts will hear us coming,' George pointed out.

'Ghosts are hard of hearing,' Fromm said. 'Now, ready? Bruno Fromm is a busy man.'

Fromm insisted that Caroline sit next to him on the driver's seat. Aubrey, George and von Stralick took the benches that ran on each side of the cart, behind Fromm. Aubrey felt absurd, as if he were going to a picnic rather than chasing a soul fragment that belonged to the sister of the greatest enemy of Albion. He took some comfort, however, in seeing that von Stralick looked even more uncomfortable than he felt. If it was possible to squirm while sitting absolutely still, that's what the well-dressed Holmlander was doing.

George, on the other hand, was completely relaxed, draping an arm over the sideboard of the cart, as if he were on his way to a country fair.

Fromm kept up a commentary as they rolled alongside the river. He pointed out the many barges and riverboats that were plying their trade, coming from long distances, with exotic cargoes and with raw materials for the hungry Holmland industries: iron ore, coal and – Aubrey noticed with interest – a large open barge that they could smell from where they were.

'Guano,' George said knowledgeably at the eye-watering reek. 'For fertilizer. And explosives.'

They skirted the Academy, which was abuzz. Aubrey noted dozens of carpenters' wagons and was impressed by the extent of the setting-up activity. He felt a little guilty at having left his mother, but Quentin Hollows had promised a squad of embassy staff to tote crates for her.

Soon, they left the heart of the city behind and climbed the gentle rise that led to more residential parts of Fisherberg – Liseburg, and Gret overlooking the river. Aubrey could make out the imposing bulk of Baron von Grolman's castle on its hilltop a few miles away and again appreciated its defensive position, so useful in days of offensive neighbours.

In a neighbourhood of discreet wealth – signalled by the size of the detached houses, the utilitarian nature of the walls and gates, and the sort of abundant greenery in gardens that only came from decades of good tending – Fromm slowed his horse at the top of a cul-de-sac that sloped down to a dead end. The sun was warm and the breeze was half-hearted, wafting a little and then giving up and resting for a while.

'Down there.' Fromm pointed. 'Yesterday, after leaving you, Fromm did his work. Fromm found it wandering around.' He reached into his pocket. 'Here.'

With an expression of distaste, Fromm dropped the Tremaine pearl into Aubrey's palm and then wiped his hand on his jacket.

'Are you sure it's still there?'

Fromm climbed down from the cart. He held out his hand to help Caroline, and she surprised Aubrey by taking it. 'Yes. It's a lingerer.'

Aubrey joined them on the pavement, as did von Stralick and George. 'Lingerer?' von Stralick asked Fromm.

'Some of these soul fragments roam about, lost, nothing to hold them anywhere. They're hardest to find.

Others mope around a place, anchored to it. That's a lingerer.'

'And why do they linger?' Caroline asked.

'Sometimes it's a place that meant something to them in their past. Sometimes it's just a place that catches their attention. They get stuck to it, like flies to flypaper.' He flexed his shoulders, then pushed his hands out in front of himself, stretching his arms. 'We go now.'

Aubrey felt exposed as they walked along the pavement, following the burly Fromm. He would have preferred some sort of disguise, perhaps tradesmen, or merchants delivering goods, but Fromm wasn't fazed at all. He marched along, assessing the houses on either side with an appraising eye.

Aubrey imagined the good folk in the houses peering past the curtains. The ghost hunter's garb was unmistakeable. Would they see him as bringing shame to the neighbourhood, as the presence of a ratcatcher announces an infestation of vermin? Or would he be seen as a godsend, bringing relief?

He glanced at von Stralick, looking for an answer, but the Holmlander's appearance surprised him. He was pale, his face tense and strained. He wiped his face with a hand and frowned at Aubrey's regard, but before Aubrey could question him, Fromm stopped abruptly, holding up a hand. The end of the street was thirty or forty yards away. For a moment, Aubrey caught von Stralick's tension. The air felt still, the breeze having died away completely. The houses on either side of the street took on a brooding aspect, silent and watchful. No birds sang, no dogs barked, no sound of gardeners at work with hedge shears or lawn edgers. Uneasy urban silence had enveloped them.

Look for fear and you will find it, the Scholar Tan had written, but Aubrey felt a moment's irritation with the ancient sage. Although his words were wise, they weren't much practical help at the moment, apart from prodding his uneasiness toward outright nervousness.

Fromm hissed unhappily, then he edged along until he stood right underneath an oak that overhung a formidable garden wall. Cautiously, he tilted his head back and stretched up on tiptoes. He sniffed the air, nostrils flaring, his hands at his side making tiny grasping motions. 'She is still there.'

Aubrey sniffed, following Fromm's lead. All he could smell was a faint hint of lilac, from a tree cascading its purple blossoms over a wall on the other side of the street.

'No?' Fromm's gaze was bright on Aubrey.

Aubrey shrugged.

'You let plumbers do your plumbing,' Fromm said. 'Let ghost hunters do your ghost hunting.'

He went to set off again, but George grabbed his arm. 'Someone's down there.'

With impressive speed, Fromm faded back under the branches of the oak. Shielded by the shadows, all five of them waited in a line, backs to the wall.

Fromm shrugged. 'Intruders. It's not unusual in such places.'

'You've been here before?' Aubrey said.

'No.'

'I have,' von Stralick said. 'On the night of the fire. Most of Fisherberg was here, watching.'

'Fire?' Aubrey said. *Enough is enough*. 'What do you know, von Stralick?'

Von Stralick touched a hand to his forehead. 'Down there is all that remains of Tremaine's residence. The one he took up after he fled your country. It burned down last year.'

'It's more than that.' Fromm seemed to be enjoying von Stralick's discomfort. 'Your ghost? The person it came from grew up here. That's why it lingers.'

Aubrey stared, and put a hand against the wall to steady himself. He added this information to Kiefer's revelation that Dr Tremaine was born in Holmland. He tried to picture Dr Tremaine as a little boy, but had difficulty imagining the manipulator of whole nations in short pants. 'So this could be the Tremaine family home.'

'Ah.' Von Stralick rallied. He adjusted his cuffs. 'Then we should prepare. It may be Tremaine himself who is down there.'

'Tremaine?' George said. 'Why on earth would he be here?'

'His sister's soul fragment,' Aubrey said. 'He may have sensed it.' Von Stralick nodded.

'Good,' Caroline said. 'If Tremaine is down there, we have him.'

It was George who put into words what Aubrey was thinking. 'Not wanting to put too fine a point on it, but are we ready to take him now?'

'I have a revolver,' Caroline said.

Aubrey raised an eyebrow. 'Are you always armed?'

'I make sure of it whenever I go out with you, Aubrey.'

Aubrey began several answers, but before he could come up with anything intelligible, von Stralick chipped in. 'I, too, am armed.' He patted his left breast.

'I'm starting to feel a bit left out,' George said. 'I don't suppose a clear mind and a pure heart count for much?'

'Against Dr Tremaine?' Aubrey said. 'I don't think so. And I'm not sure how much use firearms are against him, either.' He remembered the encounter Caroline, George and he had had with Dr Tremaine in the vaults of the Bank of Albion. Caroline had shot at him from a distance of no more than ten paces, but he had escaped unharmed.

Aubrey listened with half a mind as Caroline, George and von Stralick argued about the efficacy of various weapons, while Fromm looked on with amusement. Aubrey's other half mind was busy rattling through spells to use if it came to a confrontation with Dr Tremaine, and sorting through the items he'd stowed in his appurtenances vest.

'All I have are some nuisance spells,' he announced finally. 'If I had more time, I may be able to construct something useful.'

'We should strike now.' Caroline's eyes were flat and hard.

Aubrey could see disaster rolling their way like barrels down a ramp. He knew that if he tried to argue her out of confronting Dr Tremaine, he'd lose. She'd simply ignore him and go her own way. It was time for an outflanking manoeuvre.

'We can't just barge in on him,' Aubrey said. 'We have to scout the terrain, see what's going on.'

Caroline gazed at him for a moment. Then she nodded. 'Very well.'

Aubrey lay on his stomach, unmindful of the effect the leaf mould and dirt was having on the fine wool of his jacket and trousers. Inch by inch, he wormed his way through the untended greenery.

After scrambling over the wall and finding themselves in a garden that had gone wild, he'd managed to persuade the others that he should go on ahead, by the simple expedient of demonstrating his spell-assisted belly crawl.

Ever since the adventure in Lutetia, where – in a moment of manic invention – he'd levitated a whole medieval tower and sent it sailing across the rooftops of the Gallian capital, he'd worked, sporadically, on refining the weight-cancelling spell that had enabled this dramatic mode of locomotion. He'd had the notion of writing a paper on the subject for the *Albion Journal of Magic*, but he'd wanted to sort out all the derivatives and variations first. Publication in a prestigious journal like the *AJM* meant he'd be on display, subject to scrutiny, and to criticism, from some of the best magical minds in the world, so he wanted to make sure he had everything correct.

All in all, it was a pleasure to be fiddling with minor, very practical applications of the spell he'd been working with so closely. In this instance, he was simply easing his weight a little so he wouldn't make a sound on the dry leaves underfoot. Or underbelly. It worked, and he fancied he slithered like a particularly deft snake.

Ahead, closer to the site of the ruined house, he could hear at least one person. They made little effort to hide their presence – *just like Tremaine*, he thought – and he lay there trying to sort out the tramping. One person or two? Or was it three?

He edged forward, keeping his head down, and parted a heavy, but thankfully thornless, bush.

Just in time to see an old man claw at the air and disappear into nothingness.

Horrified, Aubrey scrambled to his feet and shouted for the others, just as another stranger climbed out of the charred beams and rubble of the ruined house.

'Mr Black!' she cried.

Caroline burst through the foliage. She'd changed into her black silk fighting suit and she had her revolver at the ready. 'Aubrey!'

George was hot on her heels. 'Old man?'

Von Stralick and Fromm were more cautious. They pushed aside branches and edged through the greenery, then stood eyeing the woman who had climbed from the ruins. Her face was smeared with black and she was wearing riding trousers under a black leather coat. 'Do not go over there!' she called.

George froze, to the extent of having one foot in the air. 'Over where?'

'There.' Aubrey pointed to a spot halfway down the side of the ruin, about four or five yards from what would have been a wall. 'Where the old man disappeared.'

'Merikanto,' the woman whispered. She held onto an upright beam, careless of the charred timber. 'He was trying to stop it.'

'Madame Zelinka?' Aubrey said. 'What's going on? Where's Dr Tremaine?'

'Tremaine?' Madame Zelinka looked around in horror. 'Is he here?'

'Apparently not,' Caroline said. She stood with her hands on her hips. 'Aubrey, are you going to introduce us to your friend?'

Von Stralick grinned at Aubrey. 'Do, Fitzwilliam. Be a gentleman.'

Aubrey sighed and did the formalities, finishing with, 'And you know George Doyle. I mean, Mr Evans.'

Madame Zelinka was pale and shaken, but she gathered herself. 'He has two names? As do you? Which is it, Black or Fitzwilliam?' She looked exhausted. 'Who *are* you?'

'Good question,' Aubrey said. He spun his story carousel, looking for a solution to the sticky situation he'd dropped himself in. Perhaps he could invent *another* persona, one that was pretending to be two different people because of an identity stealing spell . . .

Caroline elbowed him. 'Simple would be better, I believe.'

He swallowed, and told Madame Zelinka the truth.

In the end, it was a relief. Madame Zelinka listened carefully. Aubrey was sure she would become angry at his deception, but she simply nodded. 'You were good, Fitzwilliam. And you, Doyle. You had me convinced.'

'Later for this,' von Stralick said. 'What about this old man that you say disappeared? Are we in danger?'

She touched her forehead. 'Merikanto.'

'What was he doing?' Aubrey asked.

'He was trying to quell the disruption that Tremaine left behind.' She trembled. 'It reached out from the basement and took him.'

'He's in pieces, now,' Fromm said. He spat on the ground. 'Like dropping a glass on a stone floor. Shattered, he is, and blown to the winds. Fromm felt him go.'

Madame Zelinka stood in the ruins and her equanimity crumbled. She began to cry, tried to stop it, but then was seized by her distress.

Automatically, they all went to her. They had to pick their way through the ruins, crunching through ash and burned wood, stepping carefully over tumbled-down stones. Aubrey felt glass crushing underfoot and noted the bright frozen rivulets where lead from the roof had melted and run.

Caroline put an arm around the distraught woman while von Stralick and George looked on helplessly. Fromm sidled to Aubrey. 'She's here, you know.'

'Sylvia?'

'She retreated when the old man was broken apart. But she's here.'

'What about this disturbance Madame Zelinka is talking about?'

Fromm snorted. 'Her crew are always finding problems. They are troublemakers.'

'You know them?'

'Ghost hunters know much.'

Which wasn't an answer, but Aubrey let it go. 'You don't think it's a problem?'

Fromm spat on the ground again. 'Could be. Can't you feel it?'

Aubrey glanced at him. Fromm looked back placidly. Aubrey shrugged, closed his eyes, and extended his magical awareness.

It struck him like a gravel flung in a gale, a sharp, painful spattering of loose magic. He winced, but concentrated on making sense of the sensation.

It was wild, unshaped by a restraining spell. It roared like an out-of-control fire in a forest. Assaulted by a jumble of sensation, Aubrey reeled. He heard harsh, bitter tastes, while he smelled blinding white light that rippled and shifted. He bit down on roughness like sandpaper in his mouth and nearly gagged.

He opened his eyes. Caroline and George were both frowning at him. 'It's in the basement. And it's growing. We have to stop it.'

Aubrey had felt something like it before, and that knowledge gave him no pleasure. Some aspects of the magic's wildness were like the raw flame of power that Dr Tremaine had built in tunnels under Trinovant in his effort to destroy the city. This magic, however, was even more unformed. It was as if a brew of noxious chemicals had seeped into a swamp, combining to create something hideous. The soul fragmentation was its work of the moment, but who knew what it could give rise to if it was allowed to grow?

'I have to go down there,' Aubrey said. 'Dr Tremaine has left spell residue to fester and it's getting stronger.'

'Merikanto was trying to stifle it with our usual methods,' Madame Zelinka said. 'He was afraid, because it was stronger and stranger than anything we'd ever encountered before, but he tried anyway. We had no magic suppressors,' she added and her eyes were accusatory.

'I've had some experience with its likes,' Aubrey said, remembering the spell he'd used to quell Dr Tremaine's wild magic in the tunnels underneath Trinovant.

'And you think you can do something about it?' Madame Zelinka said.

'I can try.'

'Good.' She studied him carefully, her dark eyes intent on his face. 'I'm glad you're not a weapons merchant after all.'

'Ah?'

'I deal with them because I must. They all have had their hearts removed and replaced with stones.'

'Oh.' Aubrey blinked, and took a deep breath. Madame Zelinka's concentrated attention was forceful, to say the least. 'What's the best way down to the basement?'

Caroline took his arm. 'Is this a good idea?' She let his arm drop and looked abashed. 'I mean, couldn't you wait for help?'

Madame Zelinka shook her head. 'I have no-one else to call on, not in Holmland.'

Aubrey was heartened by Caroline's concern. He tried to tell himself that it was the simple feeling that she would have for anyone about to risk his life, but another part of him couldn't help but see something else in it. 'It's getting worse. Something needs to be done now.'

'And you think you're the one to do it,' she said.

'I tend to, I know. Sometimes I'm right.'

'And that's the extraordinary thing,' Caroline said. She turned away. 'Very well. I'll leave you to it and go and help George and Hugo.'

'What?' Had she called him extraordinary? 'What are they up to?'

'They're helping Fromm. He's on the trail of the ghost.'

Twenty-four

THE BASEMENT WAS ON THE EASTERN SIDE OF THE house where the floor had given way, leaving it open to the sky. Aubrey crept gingerly around the gap, looking down, and he could see the remains of stone walls and pillars. He counted three arched openings that dived into the blackness beyond and he studied them grimly.

The others were busy with Fromm and Madame Zelinka. He felt a pang, for he did appreciate having George's steadiness with him in a tricky situation. And, all things said and done, he would rather be with Caroline than not.

Even though he hadn't truly extended his magical awareness, he could feel the power pouring from below. It pulsed irregularly, raw and chaotic, and it set his teeth on edge. The fate of poor Merikanto was testimony to its power; Aubrey didn't want to put Caroline and George in such danger.

He, on the other hand, was feeling prepared. The Beccaria Cage was a wonderful asset in any soul-risking situation. After a shaky start, it had proved its worth. Since he'd freed it from Dr Tremaine's influence, he'd suffered none of his accustomed debilitation from his disrupted soul. He'd had no episodes requiring expenditure of will and effort to keep his soul united with his body, efforts that, in the past, had left him sapped of energy.

It was what he'd been striving for ever since his stupid experiment with death magic. Whole, united, much as people were meant to be – and feeling strong enough to risk it against rogue magic that was capable of shattering souls into fragments.

Foolhardy? Reckless? Imprudent? He shook his head and spied a stairway leading downward. He approached it with care.

He knew he had to test himself. He couldn't sit at home, avoiding all danger. He had to know his capabilities, for he had plans. His future depended on knowing how much he could achieve and how far he could extend himself.

The stairs hadn't been damaged by the fire. Cracked by falling beams, they were treacherous but not impossible. Aubrey started down, leaning into the buffets of magic coming from the depths.

He heard someone above, calling his name, but he needed to concentrate in the swirls of magic. He ignored it and pressed on.

The basement was a wasteland, the place where most of the house ended up after the fire. The debris would take an army to clear, but Aubrey thought he could see a way through. Keeping close to the wall, he squeezed between fallen beams and splintered, charred flooring, moving with delicate care over broken furniture, window frames, and – most painfully for Aubrey – the scorched, ruined corpses of hundreds of books. Aubrey hated to see books mistreated, and the loss of whatever library Dr Tremaine had assembled hurt him deeply.

He tested each footfall before committing, never resting his weight against anything other than the stone wall, and ignoring the way his heart hammered as he approached the arched openings.

Then the wooden floor gave way beneath him.

Aubrey flung out his arms, clutching for a handhold, but found nothing. He fell, and did his best to twist and protect his head. Before he could utter a sound he struck the floor shoulder first, and he went tumbling, skinning the heel of his hands on rough stone.

For a moment, half-stunned, he sprawled there, doing his best to remember how to breathe while raw, wild magic rolled over him like storm-driven breakers.

He flinched, grunting as the jumbled, chaotic confusion of magic pounded him. It was like being pelted with wads of clay – as long as the clay was imbued with colours (reds, browns and something that was a nauseating off-white) and smells (a dizzying mash of industrial smells and the sickening, cloying smell of boiling sugar mixed up with faint hints of things barely smelled – glass, stone, snow).

He closed his eyes and tried to make sense of the shifting mess of magic, but the rawness played havoc with his magical senses. It grated on him, and he immediately had a headache the size of a football.

Grimly, Aubrey sifted through this torrent of sensation, looking for its origin. He wasn't surprised when he found, at the core of it, a trace of tightly constructed magic that could only be the work of Dr Tremaine.

He grunted as a shift in the welter of magic made him dizzy for a moment, then he concentrated on examining the remnants of Tremaine's spellcraft.

Clearly, it was an experimental spell gone wrong, and was probably what had brought the house down. Aubrey probed a little more, tasting the elements of the spell, and was sure that the spell had something to do with the making of golems.

A step toward the sort of improved golem that could replace a prince? Aubrey thought.

He gritted his teeth. Raising himself on all fours, he ignored the pain from his skinned hands, and he opened his eyes.

The real world came rushing back in. He could see the rough stone flags, the cracks between them filled with a combination of ash and dirt. The sharp tang of scorched wood rasped at his nose. His own breathing was loud and hoarse.

He was glad he hadn't asked Caroline and George to come with him.

He couldn't stay where he was. Still on all fours, he closed his eyes for a moment and regretted it. Colours swirled in his mouth and his ears were filled with a startling peppermint sensation that made him flinch. The pounding in his head redoubled.

It was enough to get him moving. He braced himself, then climbed to his feet. He swayed there for a moment as he took in his surroundings.

The ceiling of the sub-basement – the floor of the upper basement above – wasn't far overhead. He wouldn't have been able to stand upright when this sub-basement was new – and Aubrey was grateful. It had meant his plunge had been painful but not fatal. The walls were roughly finished stone, as was the floor and the rudimentary slabs for stairs. The entire effect was of age and crudity, as if the place had been constructed by primitives.

The notion made Aubrey shiver. How long had it been here? What magics had been practised here over the centuries? And when had a young Mordecai Tremaine found the place?

Light coming from the Aubrey-shaped hole above showed that the basement was cluttered with rubbish – papers, reagent bottles, lengths of copper wire – the detritus of magical experimentation. On the floor, he wasn't surprised to see the blurry chalk outlines of re-straining diagrams, dozens of them.

After taking this in, Aubrey steeled himself, closed his eyes and turned in a circle, trying to locate the source of the magical eruption. The walls on all sides fairly radiated unformed magic, the leftover residue splattered the same way a maniac cook would splatter a cake batter if he beat it too fast.

He hissed, and staggered, putting a hand to his chest where he felt the comforting shape of the Beccaria Cage. He grunted at the impact and opened his eyes, searching in the gloom. There, by the stairs, was the concentration of magic that he'd been looking for.

He took a step closer, then stopped himself. Keeping a distance seemed like a good idea, at least until he'd discovered what he could.

Which I'd do if I'd remembered to bring a lantern, he thought. He glanced up. The light coming from above was enough to make really good shadows, but that was about all. If he took more than a few steps, he'd be swallowed by darkness.

Aubrey crouched and swept around, looking for something to help. Wood shavings and scraps of paper, some of which he stuffed in his vest for later scrutiny, were good fuel sources, but – of all the things – he'd forgotten to stow matches, even though he'd brought two candle stubs along.

He bit his lip, feeling the malignant beating of the magical residue. The Beccaria Cage on his chest began to feel warm and he swallowed. The magic was testing the strength of his bond between body and soul; the cage was responding.

He shifted his weight and something tinkled. He cocked his head and saw his boot had disturbed some broken glass, the remains of a bottle, to judge from the tattered label.

At that moment, Aubrey had an odd, familiar sensation. It was as if he were moving out of himself. His body continued to function – he picked up a piece of the broken bottle, held it up, admired the clarity of the glass – while his mind was bounding ahead like a hound that had caught wind of an exceptionally desirable fox.

Glass. Focus, he thought. *Lens. Concentration.*

He turned the glass over in his hands. It was a sizeable chunk, most of one side of the bottle. It was first rate, too, not wavy, very few bubbles. For moment he wondered what Dr Tremaine had kept in it, then his mind caught wind of the fox again.

Light. Heat. Law of Intensification.

He held the glass up to the light and turned it, first concave, then convex. Peering through it, he saw his hand as larger. Only slightly, but it was enough for him to smile.

He'd caught his fox.

He scrabbled for one of the candle stubs in his vest. Clutching it in his left hand, he held the glass shard between it and the light. Then he raced through a spell to intensify the light coming through the glass, magnifying it – and magnifying the heat.

A bright spot landed on the floor. Aubrey adjusted, moving the glass until the spot fell on the candle wick. In seconds, the wick began to smoke. He grinned, held the glass steady, and the wick sprang into flame.

Pleased with himself, Aubrey slipped the glass shard into one of the reinforced vest pockets and held up the candle. *One little light dispels all the dark*, he thought and realised he had a metaphor on his hands as well as dripping wax – but no time to ponder it.

Armed with light, he advanced into the face of the magical outpouring.

At first, he was surprised that the candle didn't flicker and he had to remind himself that the disturbance he felt was magical, not physical. It was only apparent to magical senses, not impinging on the physical world.

Not yet, he reminded himself.

'Aubrey?'

George's voice came from above and Aubrey stopped in his tracks. 'Stay where you are.'

'Need any help, old man?'

It was a well-meant question, but Aubrey didn't need the sort of help that George could provide. A crack team of specialist magicians, trained in dealing with high-intensity magical residue, would be more than useful, but he doubted that George had such a thing in his back pocket.

'Not at the moment,' he managed to reply without looking around. 'But if you back away a little, and stay handy, I'll make sure to call if I need you.'

'Ah. You're messing about with magic again.'

'Not for long.'

'How long?'

'Just long enough to stop it from destroying us all.'

A pause.

'Right. I'll let you get on with it, then.'

'Capital idea.'

Aubrey was pleased that the light was steady. It meant that the candle was burning well and unlikely to go out, and it also meant that his hands weren't shaking.

It was the curse of having too much imagination and too much knowledge. He knew enough about wild magic to understand what it was capable of, and his imagination was quite happy to race ahead and supply all sorts of details about messy transmogrifications, arbitrary changes and long, lingering, painful deaths.

If he were alone, it may have been different, but in the immediate vicinity were two people he cared for, and three others he wouldn't wish ill on.

Steady-handed, he advanced in the face of the howling magical storm.

When the candle light fell on the wall, his ordinary sense of sight told him a patch of moss or lichen was growing there. A dark, unhealthy green-grey, it was an irregular shape splashed on the stone, about as large as a dining table. If he hadn't the evidence of his magical senses he would have ignored it and kept searching for the source of the magical disturbance.

And the way it ripples is a bit of a giveaway, too, he thought and rehearsed his method of attack.

When Aubrey had been able to disrupt Dr Tremaine's spell casting under Trinovant, the rogue magician had abandoned his scheme but had left the magical flame running amok, out of control, more dangerous than ever. Aubrey's experiences with magical suppression devices, and the parlous situation of his friends, trapped close to the runaway flame, had sharpened his mind wonderfully, to the extent that he was able to craft a spell under great duress, a spell that achieved the same end as magical suppression devices – it quelled and negated the magical flame, snuffing it out completely.

So he inspected the residue with as much coolness as he could summon, glad for the hand-steadying, gut-settling confidence that comes from having done something before.

He leaned forward, slowly. Close up, he decided, it didn't look so frightening. Even when he closed his eyes, the tumult that assailed him was rather less disconcerting now that he knew that it emanated from something that looked as if it would be at home in an unsanitary bathroom.

Time to clean you up. A faint, dissenting thought flitted through his mind, something about famous last words, but he ignored it.

He'd been rehearsing the quelling spell as he approached, recalling it and taking the opportunity to polish some of the roughness, the understandable awkward phrasing that had come from trying to formulate an intricate spell while bound by copper wire to a possibly living mechanical construction in the face of a magical flame that was threatening to wipe out the largest city in the world.

He tightened the elements for distance and duration, estimating the area of effect by eye. He rearranged the order of the elements that controlled the negation, the anti-magic heart of the spell, to speed up its efficacy. No sense in letting it rampage any longer than it needed to.

He rolled the long, complex string of elements backward and forward, settling them in his mind, ready to go. He adjusted his stance, squarely facing the belligerent patch of dross. Then he gathered himself and began.

The spell came to him as easily as a well-rehearsed speech on opening night, each element falling into place with the sort of solid certainty that was the mark of a well-crafted piece of magic. He was pleased. His focus, his concentration was absolute – the rest of the world had gone away. He was in the realm of magic, shaping and wielding the power that humanity had struggled with since time immemorial. It was the Great Test, taking the mystical energy that arose from the interaction of human consciousness with the universe itself and using language to control and direct it.

He was doing magic.

A smile came to his lips as, only a third of the way through the spell, the patch of residue quivered, as if struck. He kept his focus, working on the Principle of Negation, taking the magic, appraising it, and applying the equal and opposite to make it disappear.

About halfway through the spell, however, he wished he could spare the effort to wipe his brow. He'd begun to sweat. Things weren't going as smoothly any more.

The problem was the shifting nature of the residue. The unpredictable coming together of many cast-off spell fragments had created something that was so raw that it defied categorising. Aubrey was finding it hard to pin down, to construct the precise opposite needed to negate it. The residue was a many-headed beast, a hydra made of slippery magic. When he'd clamped down on one aspect of it, another oozed out on the other side, malignant and ready to do mischief.

But he'd coped with this sort of thing before, he reassured himself. The flame under Trinovant had been much larger and much more menacing. This was puny in comparison.

It had, however, been strong enough to shatter souls across Fisherberg.

Aubrey gritted his teeth and ploughed on. He spat out the elements one after the other and was grimly satisfied to see that the residue was losing its shape and colour. And was it smaller?

Shortly, he was certain that was the case. The residue was shrinking. While he continued chanting, it contracted unevenly, a jelly having scoops taken out of its edges, definitely growing smaller. No longer the size of a dining table, it had shrunk to the size of a sideboard. Even as he watched, it dwindled until it was only as large as a hall table, but before he could compare its diminishing with any other items of household furniture it shrank quickly, drawing in on itself until it was a fist-sized circle just as he finished with his signature element on the spell.

Then, in a desperate last effort, it lashed at him.

A solid extrusion jumped from the remains of the residue, an arm as thick as a tree trunk. It struck Aubrey in the chest, hard, with a blow that was both magical and physical.

Dimly, he felt himself toppling backward. Then it was a numb, painful, cracking sensation that was probably the back of his head – but it was distant and almost unimportant. Most of his being was taken up, absorbed, by an assault on his senses.

The world was a whirlwind of experience where colours, aromas, textures, sounds and flavours were shredded, combined, recombined, layered and mixed together in a chaos that defied shape and meaning. He was being twisted, contorted, disassembled, remade.

Some time passed before he understood that his eyes were open, and that he was looking up at the charred and splintered ceiling of the sub-basement.

I've fallen over, he thought. His head throbbed. His chest hurt.

Hands on his shoulders. They weren't his, he decided, because he could see his in his lap as he was propped up.

Bone grated in his chest and he hissed, mumbling a smothered oath.

'Broken ribs?' George said brightly.

Aubrey nodded, which was a bad idea. He swore again, which was marginally better.

'Take your jacket off,' Caroline snapped.

He considered this. 'Can't.'

'I see.' She came into his vision. She was holding her mother-of-pearl-handled knife. 'Don't move,' she said unnecessarily.

She disappeared. He felt a tugging from behind. It hurt, but not too badly.

'Lean forward,' Caroline's voice said. He couldn't see her and it took a few seconds to realise that she was doing something. Something to his jacket?

He leaned. This time, it hurt. His jacket separated and fell apart into his lap. He considered protesting about the damage, but decided to save his energy. And his protesting. He might need it later.

More tugging. His necktie fell and joined his suit remnants in his lap. He pondered it philosophically. He didn't like mulberry anyway.

The sound of rending cloth came to him from somewhere nearby. His shirt became two half shirts. 'Tear it into strips, George,' Caroline said. She scrooched around and put her face close to Aubrey's. He tried to smile, but his mouth was wobbly. 'We're going to strap those ribs,' she said. 'They'll still hurt but we'll be able to get you out of here. You'll have to take off that vest, too.' Then she stared, wide-eyed, at his chest. 'What happened to your cage thingy?'

Aubrey looked down. The action made him grind his teeth but what he saw nearly made him forget about it.

The Beccaria Cage was gone. Only a vivid red mark on his chest showed where it had been.

'Where's Sylvia?' Aubrey asked. The trunk of the tree he was sitting against was rough. He tried to make himself comfortable. It was a mistake, as his ribs told him in no uncertain terms, but it was balanced by the unaccustomed pleasure of having Caroline's arm around his shoulder supporting him. It meant she was kneeling, close and warm. As he studied the ruins of the Tremaine house, he could feel her breathing.

Madame Zelinka looked at Fromm. 'Sylvia?'

Aubrey went to answer but was forced to bite down on the grunt of pain. Caroline, who looked fetching in her black fighting suit, put a hand on his chest. 'Sylvia was the name of the ghost we were looking for. She lived here.'

Fromm touched his nose and looked at the ruins speculatively. 'She has no presence here any more. Your magic has dispelled the eruption, cast out the ghost.'

'Dead?' Aubrey gasped.

Fromm shook his head. 'It was close at hand. But before Fromm could snare it, it was whisked away to its home.'

'Home?' George said. 'What do you mean?'

'Reuniting with the other soul fragments, in the husk of a body they left behind.' He pointed. 'There, in the city.'

Other soul fragments. Husk of a body. Aubrey would have groaned if he had been able. *Nothing* was straightforward.

'Can you take us to her?' Caroline asked.

'Ghost hunters hunt fragments, not body and souls united. Fromm doesn't know where the body is. This fragment streaked past, back to the city, but then was gone.'

'The pearl,' Aubrey croaked. He reached for the vest Caroline had folded neatly on the ground, but he nearly fainted. His ribs were a sharp, red pain slashing along his side.

'Here,' Caroline said. She bit her bottom lip, endearingly, as she concentrated on finding the pearl while still supporting him. Aubrey found her efforts fascinating.

Fromm took the pearl and eyed it unhappily. Then he put it to his nose and inhaled.

'All gone.' He held the pearl up to the light. 'Empty now.'

Aubrey was concentrating on breathing. George asked the obvious question. 'Where?'

'With all the other bits. To the body it left behind. It was the magic, in the basement. You reversed it.'

Through gritted teeth, Aubrey asked, 'All of it?'

'Most of it.' Fromm sniffed the air. 'Ghosts are coming together, all over. People will wake up soon, whole again.' He slapped his chest. 'Not much work for Fromm, now. Time to leave the city.'

'Sorry,' Aubrey mumbled, and Caroline shushed him.

Fromm chuckled. 'It's not so bad. People will need us, sooner or later.' He rubbed his hands together. 'Money?'

'What?' George said. 'You didn't find our ghost.'

'Fromm brought you to it. You let it go.'

Von Stralick haggled, for form's sake more than anything else, it appeared to Aubrey. While the dickering was going on, with some trepidation he took some time to assess his condition.

With the ease that came from plenty of practice, he closed his eyes and turned his magical awareness on himself, only to be shuttled from bafflement to disbelief to dawning hope.

Ever since the unfortunate experiment that had torn his body and soul apart, whenever he inspected his condition he always saw a fractious, unhappy state. His soul, loosened from the normal bond with his body, was being tugged by its golden cord, summoned to the portal behind which lay the true death. The spells to delay or impede this had various degrees of efficacy, but it was only the Beccaria Cage that had endured. With it gone he fully expected the mortal tug-of-war to resume, and he was already trying to construct variations on spells that had had some success in the past.

Instead, he saw an entirely different state of affairs.

His perspective was the usual out-of-body view, as if he were hovering a few yards over his own form. He could make out the others in the shade of the shrubbery as they talked and argued, but dimly, as if they were fish in a poorly lit aquarium. His magical awareness was not suited to observing everyday things.

His body was motionless in the shade. His soul was an almost transparent duplicate nestled inside, snugly. The left hand of the soul-self was holding a golden cord. The other end was looped around the wrist of his body-self. They were united, bonded as body and soul should be. Automatically, Aubrey looked at the soul-self's right hand, but he couldn't find the dangerous golden cord there, the one he'd become so used to seeing. It was a shock and he turned his attention around, looking for the portal to the true death, the doorway that had been hovering near him ever since the experiment.

It was gone.

This change was so fundamental, so dramatic that Aubrey had some difficulty in taking it in – and it took him some time to realise that something else had changed.

His body was encased in a fine silver mesh.

He concentrated and brought his attention closer, using his magical senses to inspect the shimmering web that was hovering on the edges of perception. Probing it, he detected powerful magic, magic of a patient and enduring sort, a spell that was made for lifetimes – and perhaps more. It had a flavour, too, that he was familiar with.

The Beccaria Cage.

As soon as he realised it, he saw that the silver mesh *was* the Beccaria Cage, but a Beccaria Cage that had expanded and encompassed his whole body in its protection – like a suit of armour. His body and soul were united, joined to such an extent that the golden cord leading to the true death had gone. The portal had vanished, the call of the true death was no more.

He was cured.

Twenty-five

$\mathcal{T}$HE EMBASSY HAD A FINE DOCTOR ON STAFF, AND SHE had a medical magician on call. Together they patched up Aubrey so that his ribs were merely painful instead of a knife in the side. While they worked, Aubrey swooped between exhilaration and a stubborn unwillingness to believe that his body and soul were actually reunited.

In between his mood extremes, he found time to appreciate the irony – that he could be a beneficiary of Dr Tremaine's carelessness in cleaning up after himself. He would have laughed if not for his sore ribs.

Caroline and George were waiting for him outside the infirmary. Caroline was tapping her foot. 'Well?'

'They took good care of me. No lasting damage.'

'That's not what we're talking about, old man,' George said.

'Indeed,' Caroline said. 'We're not oblivious, you know. We saw that something happened in that basement.'

'Something more than cracked ribs.' George studied Aubrey's face. 'You're looking surprisingly well.'

'That's a good way of putting it.' Aubrey rubbed his chin. 'I think I'm cured.'

Caroline gasped, then she smiled, tentatively, and Aubrey forgot any lingering pain. She reached out a hand, then seemed to remember herself and withdrew it. Disappointed, Aubrey consoled himself with hoping that she was holding her hands together as the only way of stopping herself from reaching out again.

'You're sure?' she asked, with the slightest catch in her voice. To Aubrey's delight, she put her hand to her throat and repeated herself. 'You're sure?'

'The Beccaria Cage has disappeared. I think I've absorbed it.'

'What?' George stared. 'When did this happen?'

'Dr Tremaine's residue. Just before it disappeared it lashed out at me. It broke some ribs, but it also affected the Beccaria Cage.' He grinned. 'Random magic sometimes has good outcomes as well as bad.'

'This cage contraption is still working?' George said. 'Protecting you, I mean.'

'My body and soul are bound together as strongly as ever.'

'And this is enduring?' Caroline asked. She looked hesitant, as if unwilling to believe what Aubrey was saying. Not sceptical, but simply unable to trust herself to be pleased.

'Every indication is that it's particularly stable. I'm confident.'

George grinned. 'That's good enough for me, old man. I'm convinced. At least, until the next disaster.'

Caroline nodded. She was standing straighter, Aubrey

noticed, more restrained. 'That's excellent,' she said briskly. 'Your condition has been a concern for some time.'

'Your concern?'

Her lips twitched, just a little. '*A* concern. An issue. Something affecting our tasks. It's much better that you've improved.'

'Much better? In a completely impersonal, objective sense?'

There, he thought. *That was a smile. A knowing smile.*

'Of course.'

Aubrey eased himself into an armchair in a cosy drawing room toward the front of the embassy. George disappeared in search of a late lunch. Caroline took up a chair opposite Aubrey. She frowned at him without saying a word.

Aubrey let this arrangement stretch out for some time. Partly because his ribs were aching a little, but partly because it gave him a chance to gaze at her. He was trying to work out a way to tell her how much he appreciated her company when Lady Rose and Prince Albert rushed in, followed by Quentin Hollows.

'Aubrey. You're hurt.' Lady Rose glared. 'What happened?'

'Ribs,' he said, 'but that's not important now.'

George appeared with a large tray in his hands. 'Ah. Sorry. I've only scrounged up enough food for three.'

George disappeared again but was soon back with another tray piled high with sandwiches. In the meantime, Aubrey had sketched out the events of the afternoon, without mentioning his improved condition – the secret he'd only shared with George and Caroline.

Prince Albert sat back in his chair. He studied the ceiling for a moment. 'Strange times in Fisherberg.' He pursed his lips before going on. 'I've just come back from seeing the Elektor. Leopold is horrified at the prospect of war, and he thinks many Holmlanders are on his side.'

'But I thought the Elektor was a warmonger,' George said. 'At least, that's what all the Albion papers say.' He grinned. 'I actually just said that I believed what the papers say, didn't I?'

'Beating the patriot drum is always a good way to sell more newspapers.' Aubrey touched his chest. The mark the Beccaria Cage had left had already been fading by the time he'd reached the infirmary, but it still itched a little. 'How widespread do you think this opposition is, Bertie?'

'It's hard to say. Leopold's probably more than a little out of touch with the man on the street. He actually called them peasants at one stage in our conversation. With affection.'

'So where is the impetus for war coming from? Apart from Dr Tremaine,' Lady Rose asked.

'The Chancellor,' Aubrey said.

'And many of the aristocrats,' Caroline put in. 'There is a culture of bullyboy bellicosity among them.'

'Bullyboy bellicosity? Nicely done, Caroline,' George said. 'Can I steal that for a headline?'

'Of course,' she said, with a solemn tilt of her head.

'It's neat, but what does it actually mean?' Aubrey asked.

'I remember,' Caroline said, 'when we were living here, how both Mother and Father would talk of the way so many of the barons and counts and dukes spent hours poring over battles in Holmland's glorious past, how they loved inspecting new warships, how they adored a uniform. Even as a young thing, I thought it was frightening.'

'Frightening?'

Caroline shook her head at the memory. 'Count Horstein was someone who was working with Father on Indeterminacy Theory. I always thought he was a nice man, but once he told me that he hoped I'd grow up to marry a soldier, as there was nothing more glorious for a young girl.'

The image made Aubrey extremely uncomfortable. 'So that's the sort of people we're dealing with.'

Lady Rose stood and made her way to the door. Prince Albert accompanied her, but before leaving, she stopped and turned. 'Aubrey. I need some assistance tomorrow preparing for my lecture. If it's not too much trouble, I'd like you to help me.'

'Tomorrow?' Aubrey's plans to locate the rest of Sylvia looked precarious.

'I have people to meet, papers to organise. You'll be well enough, I'm sure. Light duties only.' She turned her attention away from him. 'Caroline. You're free, aren't you?'

Caroline looked at Aubrey, then George. 'I . . .'

'Excellent. What about you, George?'

George glanced significantly at Aubrey. 'I'd like to, but I have to find someone here in Fisherberg.'

'A female person, if I know you,' Lady Rose said.

'An acquaintance,' George said. 'A friend of a friend, so to speak.'

'As long as it's not someone that the lovely Sophie Delroy should be jealous of.'

George coloured and picked up a suddenly fascinating teaspoon. 'No, I think I can assure you of that.'

'Tomorrow, then, Aubrey, Caroline.' Lady Rose tapped Prince Albert on the arm. 'They think they're being very mysterious and careful, but it's obvious that something is afoot.'

The Prince wrinkled his brow. 'I'm not sure I know what you mean.'

'Conspiracies, plots, shadowy negotiations.' She regarded them all with a sceptical eye. 'You're probably all set to save the world again. Just don't mess things up.'

With a warning shake of her finger, she swept out. The Prince shrugged and followed her.

Hollows frowned. 'Is there anything I need to know?'

Aubrey looked at George and Caroline. They looked back at him, then at each other. 'I don't think so,' Aubrey said.

'No assistance I can give? No equipment?'

'Thank you, sir. We'll ask if we can think of anything.'

Hollows stood. He shook his head. 'Your father wrote to me, you know, telling me about you. About all of you.'

I'd love to see that letter, Aubrey thought. 'I hope we're not disappointing you, sir.'

'No, that's not it at all. I'm astonished, to tell you the truth, at some of the things he told me. Strictest confidence and all that.' He paused. 'But just as your father wrote, seeing young people like you makes me think that the future is in good hands.'

The ambassador left.

'Quite the diplomat,' George said.

'Oh?' Aubrey managed to say.

'Yes. Very diplomatic of him, not pointing out how much you looked like a codfish, flapping your mouth like that after he told you what your father wrote.'

'Now,' Caroline said. 'Aubrey, you must rest before tomorrow.'

'Rest? I'm well enough.'

Caroline's eyes widened as she looked past Aubrey's shoulder. 'Why, it's the Elektor! Your highness!'

Aubrey twisted around to see the unexpected visitor, and let out a yelp as his ribs reminded him that twisting was a bad idea at the moment.

No-one was there.

Carefully, with one hand pressed against his ribs and doing his best not to show any pain, he turned back to his friends.

'You're quite well, are you?' Caroline asked sweetly.

The next morning, before breakfast, George was waiting for Aubrey in the corridor outside his room. He broke off from his studying of an Albion oil painting (a landscape with more haywains than could possibly be good for it) and took Aubrey's arm.

'Look, old man, you know that von Stralick isn't my first choice for adventuring companion.'

'Hello, George. Didn't you sleep well?' Aubrey had. Restful, composed, and the medical treatment — both magical and non-magical — had worked startlingly well. He had no pain from his ribs at all.

'I volunteered to go with him so you could go with Caroline. You need to spend some time with her.'

Aubrey shook his head. 'You're a fine friend, George, and I don't deserve you. But I'm afraid it's a hopeless case.'

'Hopeless case? What's this? I've never heard you give up on anything.'

Aubrey paused, chewed his lip for a moment, looked at his shoes, then answered: 'If I've learned anything in the last year or so, it's that I'm not infallible. And that I have strengths and weaknesses.'

'Caroline being one of your weaknesses.'

'In a sense. In a few senses. In every possible sense of the word.'

'Listen, Aubrey,' George said. 'I'm not going to say that you two are right for each other, destined to be together or any of that twaddle. But I will say that you two seem happiest when you're getting on – adventuring, bantering, planning outrageous deeds. And when you two are on the out and out, you're both extremely difficult to be with.'

'She seems happy enough at the moment.'

'What? Are you serious?'

'What do you mean?'

George shook his head. 'I worry about you sometimes, old man, I really do. And not just when you're about to do something remarkably foolhardy. I actually have confidence in you then.'

'Implying that you don't have confidence in me when . . .'

'When you deal with people. Some people.'

'I see. Any sort of people in particular?'

'Female people. In general. And one in particular.'

'Hmm. I thought I was improving on that front.'

'You were. Lately, though, you've gone backward.'

'I can't tell you how uncomfortable that makes me feel.'

'Glad to hear it. What you need is some decent adventuring. Sharpens your mind, it seems.'

'Little chance of that. I'll be at the Academy all day with Mother.'

'And Caroline. Don't forget her.'

'Yes. An uninterested Caroline.'

George rubbed his temples with both hands. 'You can be obtuse, can't you?'

'What do you mean?'

'I mean that Caroline isn't uninterested. She's doing her best to appear so, but she isn't.'

'And you can tell, can you?'

'I think you might be the only one who can't.'

'Not that slide, Aubrey,' Lady Rose called from the stage of the lecture theatre. 'That's a guillemot, not an auk.'

'Sorry.' Aubrey moved the brass carriage of the diascope, took out the offending slide, banished it for eternity and substituted another. 'How's that?'

'Well, that's definitely an auk. But an upside-down auk simply won't do. Come now, concentrate.'

'I'm trying,' he mumbled, but it was easier said than done. Caroline was sitting entirely too close. The other side of the lecture theatre would have been too close, to tell the truth, but that was another matter. Caroline squeezed alongside him in the tiny projection booth was enough to make his head swim.

'Let me, Aubrey,' Caroline said. 'You look flushed. Are your ribs playing up?'

'No, tip-top. Projector's just throwing off a bit of heat. Diascopic projectors tend to do that.'

'Ah.' Caroline adjusted the focus on the lens tube. Then she peered at the image on the screen behind Lady Rose and made a tsk of disgust. She took out a handkerchief and dabbed at the lens until she was happy. 'As opposed to episcopic projectors, I take it.'

'Of course, of course.' Aubrey was sweating. To cover his awkwardness, he waved a hand and nearly knocked over a box of slides that probably represented hundreds of hours of collation. 'Not to mention the more complex epidiascopic projectors, which are prone to breaking down.'

'I see,' Caroline said. 'You are so wise in the ways of projectors and in the manner that episcopes work by reflected light and diascopes work by passing light through an object.'

'They do?' Aubrey blinked. 'I thought diascopes were just bigger than episcopes. Or the other way around.' He concentrated on sliding the carriage smoothly. He squinted at the screen. 'How's that?' he called.

Below, Lady Rose scrutinised the image with her hands on her hips, head back. 'That's a fine example of a Little Auk. Well done, Caroline.'

Aubrey turned to his projection comrade. 'Well done, Caroline?'

'I took the photograph when Lady Rose and I went to the Arctic last year.'

'Ah. When I was interdicted.'

'Because of your appallingly manipulative behaviour.'

'Which I apologised for, renounced and have been doing my best never to repeat.'

'With some success.'

'Really? I thought you hadn't noticed.'

'I notice.' Caroline busied herself with the slides. 'Here's the next. A pair of nesting auks.'

Aubrey wasn't about to let this go. 'Then you've noticed that I've been abiding by our compact. The one where we agreed to be good friends of a jolly platonic sort.'

'I remember. Nothing to get in the way of our studies and the like.'

Aubrey sniffed. 'What's that smell?'

'Your sleeve. It's starting to burn. Move it away from the projector.'

He did. 'No time for frivolities of a romantic sort, that's what you said.'

'Or words to that effect. New slide. A flock of auks.'

Aubrey took the slide offered and jammed it into the carriage. 'What about other frivolities?'

'One must always find time for frivolities.'

'But any frivolities with a whiff of romance are to be avoided.'

'Sadly, I fear so.'

Sadly? Aubrey took a sharp breath. She met his gaze evenly, with a cryptic smile. He was lost, all over again.

'Hello?' Lady Rose's voice came from the stage. 'It's rather too quiet up there.'

'Sorry, Mother. Just fixing up a few things that have gone wrong.'

A few hours passed while Aubrey and Caroline helped Lady Rose sort through the slides for her lecture. Aubrey marvelled how elastic time was. A short period of time spent in a boring classroom could seem like days while a few hours in confined space with Caroline Hepworth could pass in an instant.

Lady Rose eventually insisted that they leave her, suggesting that they had better things to do. The thoughtful look she gave both of them gave Aubrey pause. He knew she felt protective of Caroline, seeing her as almost a protégée, and he was reasonably secure that she cared for him, exasperated though she was on occasion, but he couldn't come to a conclusion as to how she viewed the two of them. Her attitude oscillated between alarm and approval, with much of this variation due, Aubrey had to admit, to the way he treated Caroline.

At Caroline's suggestion, they decided to wander around the Academy. The grand, forbidding building with its medieval corridors and gothic architecture was a stonemason's dream, but it was far from a quiet and studious environment on this day. Too many savants, professors and scholars in diverse fields were fussing about and trying to ensure their display would be perfect, or their lecture theatre well ventilated, or the quality of their chalk first-rate. Aubrey found it easy to tell the Academy staff from the visitors – the Academy staff had long-suffering expressions, a mixture of professional patience and resignation as they listened to complaints and requests.

'Reminds me of putting on a show,' Aubrey said when they passed a porter who was attempting to explain to an extravagantly bearded visitor that there were no tigers to be had in the city, for love nor money.

'Chaos, puffed-up egos and no idea how it's ever going to be ready before opening?'

'Exactly.'

'I was seeing it as like embarking on one of your lunatic adventures.'

'Lunatic?'

'In the kindest sense of the word.'

'Ah. Go on.'

'Well, just like your adventures, I imagine this place is full of that heart-in-the-mouth feeling, not knowing how it's going to turn out, but with the anticipatory thrill of doing something important and exciting.'

Aubrey walked on in silence for a moment. They ignored a pair of squabbling academics who looked as if they were about to come to blows outside a lecture theatre.

'And that's how you feel about our adventures?' he said eventually.

'Mostly.'

He glanced at her. Caroline's expression was thoughtful. A hint of a frown touched her brow.

'And you're willing to endure our misunderstandings?'

'*Our* misunderstandings?'

'Ah.' He rethought. 'You're willing to endure *my* misunderstandings then?'

'Aubrey, you wouldn't be you if you didn't misunderstand some things.'

'That may be true. What sort of things?'

She considered this. 'Your comprehension is astonishing when it comes to magic, or politics, or espionage. You show a truly devious mind at times.'

'It's a gift. I've learned to live with it.'

She glanced at him.

'I'm joking,' he said.

'I know. Such a mind indicates that you understand how subtle people can be.'

And here comes the 'but', he thought gloomily.

'On the other hand,' she said, charming him by confounding him, 'you have an enormous blind spot when it comes to matters of the heart.'

'It's not a blind spot,' he protested. 'It's just a complete and utter failure to understand you at all.'

'Are we talking about me?' she said as they rounded a corner in the cloisters. 'I thought we were talking about you.'

'I think it might be us I'm talking about.' He stopped walking. 'Wait a moment. Act naturally.'

'Instead of acting unnaturally? Whatever do you mean?'

He resisted the temptation to look around for an alternative route. It was too late. Several of the people ahead had noticed them. 'Follow my lead.'

They'd come to one of the more outlying parts of the Academy. The lecture theatres, display halls and demonstration laboratories had given way to workshops and storage rooms. Just inside a pair of open double doors was a knot of people arguing. The argument, however, looked significantly different from those they'd wandered past in the central parts of the Academy. Aubrey recognised one of the participants, and while the rebel leader had done his best to look inconspicuous in the city, his long hair and moustache made him stand out from all but the most eccentric academics.

Rodolfo was talking, earnestly, to two men who clearly weren't scholars. They were businessmen. Everything about them, from their restrained neckties around high, starched collars to their highly polished shoes to the identical briefcases they clutched, announced that they were from the world of commerce rather than the world of academia.

They were standing in front of a large crate.

He picked up his pace. 'Rodolfo!' he called. 'You disappoint me. You couldn't wait for my people to get in touch?'

Rodolfo blinked, rubbed his face with one hand, squinted at the businessmen – who had turned their bland countenances on Aubrey so that he could see them already trying to work out how to make money from him – then he scowled. 'Mr Black. Good. We'd rather buy our necessities from you anyway.'

From the corner of his eye, Aubrey had the great pleasure of seeing how alarm made itself evident on the faces of the business negotiators. It was a tiny tightening around the eyes and an infinitesimal shift in stance that probably came from a slight clenching of the buttocks. For a moment, Aubrey thought about turning his hand to professional gambling and using such observations to gain immense amounts of money.

'Allow me to do the introductions,' one of the businessmen said. 'I'm Mr Shaw. My colleague is Mr Treece.'

Aubrey was glad to have the names, even if they were bound to be aliases. He added them to the notes he was preparing for Tallis. The men were interchangeable to a great extent. Middle-aged, round faces, red cheeks, dark hair parted on one side.

And they were Albionites.

'My name,' Aubrey said, 'is Black. And this is my colleague, Miss Brown.'

Caroline rose to the occasion. She regarded the businessmen impassively. 'Don't we have anything better to do, Mr Black?'

Aubrey smiled. 'Miss Brown is impatient. Please forgive her, but she is the one who controls the money in our organisation.'

Rodolfo rolled a melancholy eye in Caroline's direction and brightened a little. He bowed. 'You, my dear, are very beautiful, and very young for such an important position.'

Caroline turned a frosty gaze on him. 'It suits us to look young. Surely Mr Black told you that.'

Aubrey was impressed. In one swoop Caroline had justified their young appearance and also hinted at mysterious magic. It was nicely done. 'I didn't feel it was important.' He sighed. 'Now, Rodolfo, what is this about? You're not reneging on our deal, are you?'

'We have many irons in the fire, as you say. We had a message that someone wanted to talk to us about our cause.' He shook his head. 'An insult, it was. He wanted to hire us as if we were mercenaries.'

'Oh?'

'He wanted us to fight overseas, far from our cause, to secure a supply of guano.'

Aubrey's uninterest suddenly did a handstand and he became very interested indeed. 'Guano?'

'Bird dung,' Rodolfo said with disgust. 'I cursed him and sent him on his way. But the trip has not been wasted. Shortly afterward, I met these gentlemen, who offered to help me.'

Shaw and Treece smiled with bland confidence. 'We represent a significant supplier of sought-after merchandise,' Shaw said.

Caroline tsked. 'That may be one of the vaguest statements I've ever heard. What's your measure of significance? Who's seeking it? What sort of merchandise?'

'That's between our client and ourselves,' Treece said. He glanced at the crate looming over him. 'Unfortunately, he has ordered it, now he doesn't want to pay for it.'

Rodolfo shook his head as if the businessmen had just informed him of a family tragedy. 'That's not it. You want me to take it now, so I feel it's right to take our transportation costs into account.'

Shaw smiled. 'I don't think so. If you're not willing to pay, we won't hand it over.'

'I'm relieved to hear that.'

An expression of mild surprise crossed Shaw's face. 'You don't want our merchandise?'

Rodolfo extended a languid hand in Aubrey's direction. 'Not now that Mr Black is here. I'm sure his firm can help us.'

Aubrey found himself the centre of both Shaw and Treece's attention. 'Really?' Treece said. 'And who do you represent, Mr Black? I didn't catch the name.'

'Names mean nothing,' Aubrey said smoothly. 'Our firm is new, with none of the old-fashioned processes of the more established suppliers in the area.'

'And his firm is cheaper.' Rodolfo knew a bargaining lever when he saw one. 'Much cheaper.'

Shaw and Treece were impassive. Then Shaw nodded. 'My colleague and I will need to discuss this for a moment.'

'Discuss away,' Rodolfo said. 'Take your time.'

Shaw and Treece withdrew to the far end of the workshop, where Aubrey saw a large metal door standing open and the street outside. The businessmen stood with their backs to them, but to judge from the handwaving and finger pointing, the discussion was a lively one.

'Right, Rodolfo,' Aubrey said, 'what is it exactly that you're trying to buy from these people?'

Rodolfo crossed his arms and gazed longingly at the crate. 'I don't really expect you to be able to sell us one. These men represent the only firm in the world who makes them. But if you play your part here, and they take something off their price, I'm sure I'll have more business for you soon. Consider this taking care of a customer.'

'We won't be dummies in a bidding war,' Caroline said firmly. 'If you don't tell us what's in the box, we're leaving.'

Steady, Aubrey thought, *don't push too hard*. 'We can't afford not to know,' he said, supporting Caroline. 'Too dangerous for us not to.'

Rodolfo blew out a breath through his moustache. 'It's a golem maker.'

Aubrey stared at Rodolfo and then at the crate. It was about the same size as the machine they'd encountered in the Elektor's laboratory. 'What makes you think they have such a thing?' he said, keeping up his persona.

'I heard rumours of such a machine some time ago,' Rodolfo murmured, his eyes on Shaw and Treece, who were still talking in furtive tones. 'Eventually I was contacted, given a demonstration, and was convinced.'

'You've seen it in action?' Aubrey asked.

'A month ago, those two,' Rodolfo gestured at Shaw and Treece, 'met me in a warehouse here in Fisherberg. I watched as clay was shovelled in one end of the device, then Shaw placed his own cat in a chute. Electricity was connected and the thing was turned on.' He glanced at Aubrey. 'The hair all over my body stood up, then they released the cover. On my mother's grave, a perfect replica of the cat sat up and stared at us.'

This was vital information. Aubrey could already see himself writing an extensive report for the Security Directorate. Who was making these machines? 'You have need for such a device?'

'We have several uses in mind.'

'How much were they asking?' Caroline asked.

'One hundred thousand marks.'

'One hundred thousand marks,' Caroline repeated, eyes wide.

'You see why I'm interested in reducing their price.'

'Don't bother,' Aubrey said. 'Tell them that you're no longer interested, and I'll save you fifty thousand of those marks.'

'Fifty thousand? How?'

'Our firm also produces golem makers. But thanks to our superior technicians, we can offer one to you for fifty thousand marks. As long as you're prepared to wait for two months.'

'Two months?' Rodolfo pursed his lips and Aubrey could see the two months versus fifty thousand marks equation on his face. Then the rebel chief brightened. He stuck out his hand. 'Done.'

Aubrey shook. 'I suggest you leave now. Let me deal with Shaw and Treece.'

Rodolfo grinned. 'My pleasure. You'll contact me?'

'Of course.' Aubrey paused and had a sudden, unwelcome thought. 'The man who tried to hire you as mercenaries. Tall fellow, was he?'

'With a pointed beard and a nice, fresh black eye. I'll warrant that he got it in a bar brawl, not fighting for a cause.'

Manfred. 'Where did you last see him?'

'Near the library. He left, but he said he would be back tomorrow if I reconsidered. I have half a mind to come back and thrash him.' Rodolfo left, whistling a moody tune.

Shaw and Treece hurried over. 'Where is he going?'

'To talk to his bankers,' Aubrey said, 'but don't worry about that. How would you like to make an extra twenty thousand marks by selling your machine to me instead?'

He hoped Hollows had a large account for 'miscellaneous expenses'. And a place to store a golem maker.

After a delightful lunch in a café on the edge of the Founders' Park, and some more time helping Lady Rose with her preparations, Aubrey and Caroline were in high spirits as they made their way back to the embassy. Aubrey was already formulating the report about the golem machine, and trying to work out how to ship it back to Albion. Simply knowing that such a machine existed could steer Albion's magical experts in the right direction. But having a working device to study would be even better.

He'd spent long nights wondering about the rights and wrongs of helping build powerful weapons. It didn't seem right to make devices that could harm and kill, even if he was helping his country. On the other hand, not doing so could leave his own family and friends vulnerable if war broke out and other nations had no such qualms.

It was a moral quagmire. While not sure he was entirely right, he didn't like the idea of Albion being attacked. He was determined that wouldn't happen.

The success of the impromptu espionage was exhilarating, but Aubrey was doubly elated because of Caroline. As they walked, she recounted every detail of their double-handed swindle. Her eyes were bright, her cheeks brushed with colour, and Aubrey couldn't help notice the way she touched his arm to emphasise particularly important points.

It was wonderful.

So when they entered the embassy only to find George and von Stralick arguing in an office off the entry hall, Aubrey saw this as a minor hiccup in an otherwise successful day. He motioned to Caroline to wait while they caught the direction of the argument.

'I should have known,' von Stralick was saying. He was sitting behind a large desk and brushing the crown of a stylish black hat with a sleeve. 'Your lack of imagination doomed our enquiries the moment we set out.'

George was leaning against the wall, his arms crossed. Aubrey recognised that his normally even-tempered friend was well on the way to the sort of anger that made him a formidable foe. 'My lack of imagination?' George growled. '*You* insisted that we try to find Fromm again. Did you think he was lying about leaving the city?'

'His type always lie.' Von Stralick sniffed. 'It's a way of life for them.'

'That's the sort of unhelpful comment that meant we spent the whole day running around in circles.'

'Ach. It's not as if you had any better ideas.'

George advanced on the desk. He put his fists on it and leaned toward von Stralick. 'You didn't listen to my ideas.'

Von Stralick put his hat on the desk. 'You are a follower. Not a person of intellect. You must know your place.'

Aubrey winced at that, and with the chance that actual physical violence was just around the corner he decided it was a good time to intercede. He stepped into the office. 'George, von Stralick! No luck, I take it?'

Instantly, von Stralick adopted a pose of casual boredom. 'Ah, Fitzwilliam! Luck is something that was in short supply for us today. This Sylvia Tremaine is elusive. Our enquiries were fruitless.' He bowed to Caroline. 'Caroline. I must compliment you on your exquisite dress. It suits you.'

'Thank you, Hugo,' Caroline said. 'But it's a shame about Sylvia.'

'All may not be lost. Sometimes the simplest approaches work best,' Aubrey said. 'George, is there a telephone directory anywhere in this place?'

While George was searching the shelves, Aubrey sat opposite von Stralick. He picked up the telephone. 'Let's look at this logically. Sylvia has been in many parts ever since whatever her brother did to her, correct?'

Caroline nodded. 'And those parts were sent on their way to reunifying after you neutralised the eruption at the Tremaine home.'

'Exactly. According to Fromm, the parts will be drawn back to the body, the most significant remnant of the original person. But where is it? Alive, but not responding, it must have been taken care of for years.'

'True,' von Stralick said, 'but not terribly helpful.'

'Oh, but it could be.' Aubrey took the telephone directory from George. He leafed through it, found what he was after, and – in his best Holmlandish – asked the operator for a number. 'Western Hospital? I'm a medical student from Greythorn University in Albion. That's right, I'm here in Fisherberg for the symposium. Yes, it's a wonderful occasion. Now, I have a special interest in long-term coma patients. Would you have any in your hospital that I could visit? You do? What are their names?'

Aubrey struck gold on the third telephone call. 'Her name is Sylvia Jesperson? And she's twenty-two years old? Tragic. And how soon can I visit?'

Aubrey scratched an address on a notepad George thrust on him. 'Tomorrow? I'll be there. And I'm able to bring some colleagues? Splendid.'

He replaced the earpiece, then sat back and crossed his arms on his chest. 'I love modern technology.'

Von Stralick snorted. 'How do you know this is the woman we're after?'

'She sounds a good deal more likely than anything we were able to turn up today,' George said.

'You are correct, Doyle, if labouring the obvious. I apologise for wasting the day.'

George looked at him suspiciously. 'You do?'

'I do. And for baiting you. I found it amusing, at first, but I now realise you are taking it seriously.'

George didn't look convinced. 'Don't you have anything better to do than to make trouble?'

Von Stralick put a hand on his chest. 'But I am a professional troublemaker! Can I help it if my hobby is the same as my vocation?'

'That's enough,' Aubrey said. 'We're not going to get anywhere if we're on at each other like this all the time.'

'Quite,' von Stralick said. 'Most unproductive. Now, where does that leave us?'

'We still have the means to lure Tremaine to where we want him,' Caroline said fiercely.

George made a face. 'True, but where do we want him? We haven't really spoken about the details of actually taking him.'

'That would be my job, I suppose.' Aubrey pushed his hair back. It was getting long. He should have it cut. 'I need to think about this.'

Even as he said it, though, plans were presenting themselves. The connection, the tenuous, fragile connection he had with Dr Tremaine. Perhaps he could do something with it. The more he thought about it, the more certain he became. The connection was a potential conduit, a magical link that could be the conductor of more than just an awareness of each other.

Could it be used to bind the most powerful magician in the world?

Twenty-six

THE NEXT DAY, VON STRALICK WAS WAITING FOR them in front of the Western Hospital, a grand brick building that took up a whole block in Barnstadt, a busy commercial part of Fisherberg. 'Hello, everyone,' he said as he tucked his newspaper under his arm. 'I had intended to bring Otto along to help you with any magic, Fitzwilliam, but the scamp insisted that his preparation for his symposium paper was at a crucial stage.'

'What happened to his obsession with Dr Tremaine?' George asked.

'I asked him the very same thing. He simply scowled at me, so I assume that he hasn't forgotten.'

'I should hope not.' Aubrey studied the entrance of the hospital. 'Now, remember that you're all medical students. Take notes, look serious, nod at whatever the real doctors say.'

'I brought a stethoscope.' George pulled it out of a jacket pocket. 'Pilfered it from the embassy infirmary.'

'I have one also,' von Stralick said. 'I know someone who works for a surgeon.'

Aubrey was grateful he wouldn't be carrying the single most clichéd item of medical equipment. He caught Caroline's eye. She was stifling a grin. 'Caroline and I will have to do without, it seems.'

'I'm sure we could scout up a pair, old man,' George offered.

'We'll content ourselves with looking knowledgeable and full of anatomical learning,' Caroline said.

'Exactly,' Aubrey said.

The nurse at Reception was polite and had been apprised of their visit. She handed them on to a hospital orderly, who took them to the fourth floor. The orderly was a voluble fellow, middle-aged, a few wisps of sandy hair, and Caroline managed to find out that he'd worked at the hospital for over thirty years. He remembered the arrival of the patient they were going to see, and the ministrations of her brother, a wealthy benefactor to the hospital. Somehow – and here the orderly's knowing smile hinted that he knew the workings of the world – this had ensured the comatose woman had a private room with the best of care.

Caroline coaxed a description of the brother from the orderly, and the details were enough to make Aubrey very satisfied with his telephonic detective work. Dr Tremaine was a memorable figure.

In front of an impressive pair of glass doors, the orderly handed them over to the senior doctor in charge of the Neurological Ward.

'I am Dr Gottfried,' he said in Albionish. He was well dressed in an expensive blue suit under his white coat. He had a silvery spade-shaped beard and rimless spectacles that made his eyes appear slightly larger than they were. 'You are the foreign medical students?'

Aubrey made the introductions. Dr Gottfried was courteous, interested and his Albionish was very good indeed, which wasn't what Aubrey wanted at all. Why couldn't they get a perfunctory official who'd simply leave them to get on with their business?

Frustratingly, Dr Gottfried made a point of enquiring about their studies. 'Ah, the fine Greythorn University. I spent some time there, years ago, in my training. I know many scholars there.'

'Well.' Aubrey sensed a sticky situation looming. 'There has been much movement in the last year or so, people coming and going, retiring . . .'

'Dying,' George put in helpfully.

'Is that so?' Dr Gottfried looked troubled. 'I had heard none of this. Still, relations between our two countries have not been the best of late.' He looked at them with a degree of speculation. 'Foolishness, though, you know. This is the modern world. We should be above all that.'

With that, Dr Gottfried strode off, leaving them to follow in his wake, and for Aubrey to reflect on the nature of people.

They were led through a long ward. Their feet echoed on the hardwood floor, but the noise was comforting, filling a silence that would otherwise have been daunting.

A few nurses were present, but they seemed to have taken on the quietness of the patients; they moved about the ward like moths.

Dr Gottfried took them to a room at the end of the ward. 'Remarkable case, this is. Requires very little tending or turning. She manages most of her own bodily functions. Even eats when food is placed in her mouth.'

Aubrey paused at the door. 'But doesn't wake.'

'No. We noted a magical component to her condition, of course. But our finest medical magicians have been unable to make any headway. It's a hopeless case, I'm afraid.'

'And her relatives?' George asked. 'Did they shed any light?'

'There is only a brother. He still comes in to see her.'

Caroline took the doctor's elbow. 'He does? When?'

Dr Gottfried looked down. 'A strong grip for someone so charming, young lady.'

Caroline blushed and took her hand away. 'I'm sorry.'

'She wants to know everything about this patient,' von Stralick said. 'You never know what may be important.'

'I see,' Dr Gottfried said, even though it was plain that he didn't. 'In any case, the gentleman in question isn't bound by routine. He comes and goes. Sometimes we don't see him for months. At other times he is here nearly every day.'

'And lately?' Aubrey asked.

'He was here yesterday, I think. I'd have to check with the nurses.'

Aubrey resisted an impulse to whirl around and check if Dr Tremaine were creeping up on them. His presence was suddenly very, very real.

'Thank you, Dr Gottfried,' he said. His mouth was dry. 'Can we see the patient now?'

Dr Gottfried nodded and opened the door. He stepped inside, then reeled back, stifling a most unprofessional oath. Ashen-faced, he clutched both sides of the doorway and stared at what lay within.

'What is it?' Aubrey cried, trying to see into the room.

Dr Gottfried let his hands drop. He lurched into the room. 'I do not believe it,' he whispered.

From a doorway that was suddenly full of people, Aubrey stared.

The young woman in the bed glared at them. 'What are you looking at?'

The voice was hoarse, but she was unmistakeably Sylvia Tremaine. She was identical to the presence they'd encountered inside the pearl – apart from the liveliness in her face.

She waved a hand. It was limp, and the effort was clearly a strain, but it did have a modicum of grace. 'Close your mouths. You look foolish.'

Aubrey had been prepared for almost anything, but he hadn't taken this into account. The reintegration had clearly been achieved. The soul fragments had found their way home. They had joined their pale, incomplete presences to recreate something that was definitely greater than the sum of the parts. While Sylvia didn't appear in the absolute peak of health, she was alert and coherent. She was pale and thin, her eyes were red-rimmed, but she looked like someone with a bad cold rather than someone who had just emerged from a coma that had baffled doctors for years. And she seemed to have a spark that was absent from the presences in the pearl.

It reminded Aubrey of her brother.

'Remarkable,' Dr Gottfried kept saying as he fussed around his patient. 'Remarkable.'

'Don't keep repeating yourself, doctor,' Sylvia said hoarsely. 'It's becoming irritating.'

Doctor Gottfried took her wrist, for the lack of anything better to do. 'Do you know where you are?'

She frowned. 'I'm in the hospital, of course. I've been here a long time.'

'Ah. Yes. Yes you have.'

She looked around the room solely by moving her eyes, as if her head were too heavy to lift. 'Where's Mordecai?'

'Your brother? He's not here.'

'I can see that. Send a message to him, straight away. I need him.'

Doctor Gottfried opened and closed his mouth. He looked at Aubrey, Caroline, George and Hugo. 'I . . .' Then he pushed past them and hurried out of the room.

'Foolish man,' Sylvia said.

Aubrey stepped to the bedside. 'Hello, Sylvia. My name is Aubrey Fitzwilliam.'

She studied him with fever-bright eyes, but her countenance was pale, not flushed. 'I know you.' She flicked her gaze around the room. 'All of you.' She swallowed and a hint of pain touched her face. 'It wasn't a dream,' she added, almost to herself.

'No, it wasn't,' Aubrey said. 'Your soul was in pieces.'

'And you helped free them.'

'I did?'

'At my family home.' She frowned. 'And another place I didn't recognise. Grey.'

Caroline came close. 'You were aware of what was happening?'

She took some time to answer and for a moment Aubrey thought she had fallen asleep. 'I knew. In this room, at my home, in the grey place, wherever my pieces were. It was blurred, but I was aware of them all.'

'Even in the pearl?' von Stralick asked.

'In the pearl?' She rubbed her forehead and sighed before letting her hand fall once again to the bedclothes. 'What pearl?'

Aubrey reached into his vest, and was glad that George had prevailed on the embassy's housekeeping staff to mend it overnight. 'This one.'

Sylvia gasped. With some effort, she propped herself up on one elbow.

'I gave it to him.' She stared at it with hungry eyes. 'A long time ago.' She closed her hand around the pearl and dropped back onto the bed. 'I'm thirsty.'

George appeared at the bedside with a glass of water. 'Here.'

Caroline cradled her while she drank – only a few sips, but it seemed to refresh her. She lay back on the pillows with a little more colour in her cheeks, but that simply emphasised the paleness of the rest of her face. 'The grey place. Part of my soul was in the pearl?'

'Quite a few fragments,' Aubrey said. 'The rest was lingering at your home, it appears.'

'I was scattered.' She shivered. 'But it was only because Mordecai tried so hard to make me better.'

'You were unwell?' Aubrey asked.

'Dying.' She said the single word with the practised ease of someone who had come to terms with death a long time ago. 'A wasting disease. I had made my peace, but Mordecai couldn't bear it. He wrought great magic and stopped it.'

'But shattered your soul in the process,' Aubrey said. He couldn't imagine what that would do to a person. And Tremaine? The man accustomed to having nature itself bend to his bidding? To fail so spectacularly? 'He did his best,' he found himself saying. He patted Sylvia's hand.

A voice came from the doorway, low and full of amusement. 'I'm glad to have your approval, Fitzwilliam.'

Dr Tremaine leaned in the doorway. He was wearing a full-length fur coat and a rakish, wide-brimmed black hat. He had a walking-stick in one gloved hand and a generous cravat around his high-buttoned collar.

Von Stralick was the first to move. He was standing to one side of the door, his back to the wall, and he lunged, swinging a roundhouse blow at Tremaine.

It was hard to follow what happened. A flurry of movement ended in Dr Tremaine still standing in the doorway, not even breathing heavily, while von Stralick lay unconscious at his feet. 'He almost surprised me,' Dr Tremaine said and he nudged von Stralick with his foot. 'I don't think his jaw is broken.'

George was standing next to Aubrey at the foot of the bed. He steeled himself but Aubrey put a hand on his shoulder to restrain him.

Sylvia struggled to sit up. 'Mordecai!'

Dr Tremaine closed his eyes. He trembled, then opened his eyes. 'Oh, Sylvia. I didn't dare believe.'

In an instant he'd crossed the room, ignoring Caroline, who sat on the edge of the bed, next to the pillow. Aubrey and George may as well have been tree stumps for all the notice he took of them.

Dr Tremaine sat on the bed and, with eyes only for his sister, he reached out and took away the pistol that had appeared in Caroline's hand. It vanished into the folds of his coat.

He held Sylvia's hands and Aubrey noticed that he didn't remove his gloves first. 'How do you feel?'

Carefully, Aubrey turned toward the door. This wasn't the time and place of their choosing. 'We'll just leave you two alone.'

George took the hint. He edged away. 'Family reunions should be private.'

Caroline didn't move. She was only a few feet away from the rogue sorcerer. Hands clenched in her lap, she was breathing heavily, her nostrils flaring. Her eyes were hammered steel. 'My father died because of you.'

Tremaine flicked a glance her way. 'Oh, it's the Hepworth girl. Still on about that, are we?'

'You must pay for what you've done.'

Dr Tremaine kissed his sister's hand. For an instant, it looked as if he might cry. 'I have no doubt about that. But you're not the one who's going to make me pay. And don't look at Fitzwilliam like that. He's not going to do anything either.'

'You're a dangerous man, Tremaine,' Aubrey said, then he winced, for he knew he'd left himself wide open.

'Ah, you've mastered a cliché!' Dr Tremaine said. 'Well done, boy. Keep it up and they'll let you write speeches for your father soon.'

I deserved that, Aubrey thought. He gestured at Caroline with a minute twitch of his finger, but she ignored him. With rising nervousness, he knew she'd attack Dr Tremaine in an instant if he didn't do something.

He patted his appurtenances vest. Multiple use paraphernalia, nothing suitable for major magic – and major magic was what would be required to take on Dr Tremaine. He'd learned a number of things since their first encounter.

But not now. Not now, not unprepared.

A wise commander chooses his battlefield, the Scholar Tan said. It was the most quoted of his apophthegms. But Aubrey knew, because his father had drummed it into him, that the Scholar Tan then went on to say: *But the wiser commander makes do with what he has.*

And what did he have? He had George and Caroline, and an unconscious Hugo von Stralick. He had a hospital room.

And he had himself, with his magical connection to the man they had to defeat. He also had the ability to weave magic, to construct spells that were new and different, that were unexpected.

If he could prevent Dr Tremaine from casting a spell, that would be something. It would remove the man's most powerful weapon, but it still wouldn't leave him powerless. His formidable hand-to-hand combat skills were one thing, but now he also had a pistol.

Von Stralick groaned. Painfully, holding a hand to his jaw, he struggled to his feet, glaring. Then he staggered toward Dr Tremaine.

As a distraction, it was enough. George hesitated then

launched himself at the rogue magician, just as Caroline lunged along the length of the bed.

Dr Tremaine sprang to his feet. With one hand, he used his prodigious strength to push the massive hospital bed to the wall. Then he stood between it and his attackers, keeping them away from Sylvia, who cringed, weakly batting with a hand, while the other shielded her face.

Aubrey knew he wouldn't have long for spell casting, so he opted for containment. It was simpler than trying something destructive, and it could buy them some time.

It helped that he had the perfect prison close by – the pearl in Sylvia's hand.

The pearl had already been used as a place of containment. Feverishly, while the four-way brawl raged – Dr Tremaine a colossus standing in front of the bed, lunging, striking, twisting in a blur of motion, blocking Caroline's advance by shoving George at her, heaving von Stralick sideways, recovering to meet Caroline's panther-like leap with his shoulder – Aubrey was able to work up a spell that drew on the Law of Propensity to access that aspect of the pearl. Having once been a prison, it was ready to be a prison again with only minimum magic. A short series of Akkadian syllables and the pearl was prepared. More than ready – the magical power blossomed over it like stardust, feeling like aniseed and sounding slippery.

Even in the middle of grappling with George, Dr Tremaine saw what Aubrey was up to. 'No!' he cried, but then he doubled over when Caroline punched him right in the solar plexus. Instantly, he straightened, flinging off

Caroline and George, then he knocked von Stralick to the floor with a tremendous uppercut.

He locked eyes with Aubrey. Aubrey swallowed, grateful for the three or four yards' separation between them.

Dr Tremaine smiled. 'I think it is time to see you off, Fitzwilliam.'

It was a moment that called for a pithy retort, or a confident gesture, but Aubrey decided otherwise. He raced straight into pronouncing his signature at the end of the spell.

Dr Tremaine stared at his sister with horror, then at Aubrey with utter fury. 'No! You haven't! You couldn't!'

He reached for his sister. She took his hand then cried out. Together, it was as if they gradually turned to smoke. Within seconds, they had lost all solidity, becoming insubstantial, wavery forms that looked as if they would dissipate in a gentle breeze. Then they curled, twining, spinning, spiralling as one, like water going down a drain.

There was a soft rush of air into a suddenly vacated space, and then the tiny noise of the Tremaine pearl falling to the bedclothes.

They were gone.

Aubrey was left panting and trembling, his heart threatening to rebreak his ribs with its battering. Caroline, George and von Stralick untangled themselves.

Caroline turned her head, looking for Tremaine. 'Where . . .?' she began, then she saw the pearl. With a hesitant hand, she reached for it.

'Stop!' Aubrey cried. He lurched for the bed and winced at the pain in his side. 'I haven't finished yet.'

Dr Tremaine wouldn't be trapped inside his own creation so easily. He knew the ways in and out of the magical pearl. But not if Aubrey could do something about it quickly.

Aubrey drew on his study of the Beccaria Cage. Its function was sustaining, but also protective. It kept his soul in his body, locking it in.

He aimed to use some of the same principles to put a layer on the pearl, keeping Dr Tremaine – and Sylvia – inside.

He chanted the spell as quickly as he could while maintaining utter clarity in the proto-Latin language he used. He bit off each syllable, each element clearly and with precision, until he was done. He hoped he'd been fast enough.

Then he sagged to the bed, perfectly aware that he was experiencing a textbook example of the expenditure of effort required by a series of challenging spells.

'Finished now?' George stared at the pearl with suspicion, as if it could explode at any moment.

'One last thing,' Aubrey panted. He searched for the magical connection between Dr Tremaine and him, to ensure that the sorcerer was trapped in the pearl. So close, he should be able to detect it.

He extended his awareness, but grimaced when it was swamped by the magic of the pearl and the protective layer he'd placed on it. He couldn't find the connection.

I'm tired, he thought.

He promised himself he'd check again later, and he picked up the pearl with a hand that trembled slightly. Absurdly, he was expecting it to be heavier than it was earlier, and he was oddly disappointed when it wasn't.

He'd saved Prince Albert from being supplanted and

he'd defeated his arch-enemy. He knew he should feel triumphant, but instead he felt strangely deflated. Unable to help himself, he was already reviewing the last few minutes and found – of all things – that he was wondering about Dr Tremaine's strangely foppish clothing. A high collar? Gloves? And a cravat, of all things.

'They're both trapped inside?' Caroline said, and Aubrey's thoughts about male fashion instantly evaporated. She was looking intently at the pearl too, but not with suspicion – with calculation.

He nodded with more conviction than he actually felt. 'It worked.'

Von Stralick limped over. One side of his face was swollen. 'I think it may be prudent to leave now. The nurses have fled, but they're sure to be back with reinforcements.'

Twenty-seven

𝒯HAT AFTERNOON, AUBREY EMERGED FROM HIS meeting with the ambassador to greet Caroline and George. 'The pearl is in the embassy safe and we'll be able to take it back to Albion once this symposium is over. Hollows is already in communication with the Security Intelligence Directorate to let them know what's happened.'

Caroline was standing at the window, gazing out at the passing traffic. Her face was thoughtful. 'And Dr Tremaine will face trial?'

'Certainly.' Aubrey had worked through his fatigue. Now he was feeling satisfied and found it difficult to keep from smiling. Triumph on triumph, success on success. How could Caroline not be impressed? 'Craddock's people will work on keeping him powerless until his time in court. Magical suppressors should hold him, I expect.'

'What about Sylvia?' George said gruffly. He was sitting in an armchair, lingering over a large slice of layered apple and almond pastry.

'I don't think there are any charges against her. On her release she'll be free to return to Holmland, or stay in Albion, whatever she likes.'

George dusted some crumbs from his lapels. 'Could you really have used her as a lure?'

Aubrey dropped into a seat opposite George. 'I thought I could.' He poured himself a cup of tea. 'You know, become all callous and calculating, greatest good for the greatest number, ends justify the needs, all sort of rationalisations like that.'

'I wanted to.' Caroline joined them but declined George's offer of tea. 'I wanted to take Tremaine, but not like that.'

'I thought you were determined to use her,' Aubrey said.

'And I thought you were.'

'Von Stralick was happy to do it,' George said. 'And Kiefer would have been, too, if he'd have been around.'

Aubrey was silent for a moment. 'People behave differently in groups,' he said finally. 'We do things we wouldn't when we're alone.'

'That's right,' George said. 'People stand around waiting for someone to say "Hold on a minute" and when no-one does, they go ahead and commit awful deeds.'

'Large groups of people are called nations,' Caroline said.

Aubrey steepled his fingers in front of his chin. 'Perhaps this is the time when we need a few more people to stand up and say "Hold on a minute".'

'They are, Aubrey,' Caroline said. 'But their voices aren't heard over the din of the warmongers.'

'The warmongers drown out the voices of reason,' he said, 'and the masses in the middle move in their direction.'

'No need to be so gloomy,' George said. 'We've struck a blow here for the cause of righteousness, so to speak. You've saved the Prince from a horrible fate. And without Tremaine's manipulating and scheming, Holmland's plans will be knocked into a cocked hat.'

Aubrey sipped his tea. 'Amazing man, really. Not afraid of getting his hands dirty, but a master strategist at the same time.'

He felt uneasy at that thought, but shook it off when Caroline pursed her lips. 'Don't sound so admiring of the man. He's evil.'

'So it seems,' Aubrey said.

'And tucked away safely,' George said. 'We survived the worst he could throw at us. Now all we have to survive is the symposium.'

Aubrey groaned. After their adventures, the prospect of enduring hours of esoteric lectures was less than appealing.

Prince Albert and Lady Rose came in, chatting. 'Sit, sit,' the Prince said as all three came to their feet. 'Any chance of a fresh pot of tea?'

Aubrey rang for a maid. 'Been on the social round?'

The Prince smiled. 'That's why I'm here.'

'We've been at lunch with the Elektor.' Lady Rose raised an eyebrow. 'And the Chancellor.'

'Among dozens of other dignitaries,' the Prince added. 'A garden party in honour of tomorrow's symposium opening. Rather jolly, it was, in the best Holmland manner. An admirably energetic brass band kept going forever without seeming to draw breath.'

'It's bound to make a fascinating report,' Aubrey said. 'Er. I assume you've been told that's the sort of thing you have to do while you're here.'

Lady Rose made a face. 'After we refresh ourselves here we both have to dictate our observations to a secretary.'

'Father will pore over them,' Aubrey said. 'And what about the Chancellor? I'm sure he was suitably apologetic for the incident in the Elektor's laboratory.'

'Of course.' The Prince smiled grimly. After reading Aubrey's report on the incident, his anger had been coldly furious, and had hardened into an icy determination not to run away. 'He was doing his best to be affable, but I'm not sure if it comes naturally to him,' Prince Albert said. 'Gave me a detailed explanation of the investigations he'd instigated, that sort of thing.'

'I didn't like the way the way he managed to bring Holmland industry into any conversation,' Lady Rose said. '"We made these plates in our new ceramics plant in Wissebard." "I like your dress. We have four new factories making similar fabric in Stahlbord."'

'He's an advocate for his country,' Prince Albert said as a maid brought in a new tea tray. The Prince helped himself, shaking his head when George offered him a slice of pastry. 'You can't criticise a leader for that.'

'I suppose not.' Lady Rose scowled. 'I wish this whole symposium were over and we could head back home.'

Aubrey thought this an opportune time for his surprise. 'We can relax a little now. You especially, Bertie. We've captured Dr Tremaine.'

The Prince was stirring his tea. He jerked, nearly sending his cup spinning away. 'You did what?' he said after he put down the cup and mopped at his sleeve with a monogrammed handkerchief.

'We had a plan, you see,' George said.

'But it went topsy-turvy,' Caroline said.

Aubrey nodded. 'So while George and Caroline were wrestling with Dr Tremaine –'

'At the hospital,' Caroline put in.

'At the hospital,' Aubrey repeated, 'I managed a bit of magic that trapped him in a pearl. With his sister.'

'As neatly as that.' Lady Rose looked from one face to the other. 'I have the distinct impression that that was the merest outline of an outlandish affair. You've left out any incriminating parts, I take it?'

Aubrey shrugged, even though he knew the non-committal answer wouldn't escape his eagle-eyed mother. 'The pearl is in the embassy safe. We'll take it back to Albion when we go.'

'I'm sure Craddock will be happy to take it off your hands,' the Prince said. 'And we can deal with this blackguard, once and for all.'

'I hope so,' Aubrey said and wondered why he felt as uneasy as he did.

The opening of the symposium was a gala affair. An annex of the Academy Hall had been given over to a trade display, with exhibitors from all over the Continent. Every display was bright, shiny and full of promise. Aubrey wasn't surprised to see that Holmland industries dominated, with displays from chemical manufacturers, ironworks and some particularly cheerful armaments companies. Aubrey and his mother strolled through the aisles, inspecting the booths. Aubrey saw this as the legitimate commercial aspect of the symposium, the daylight version of the sort of dealing Rodolfo was conducting in the far reaches of the Academy.

He brought himself up short as he came to a small booth. Inside, it was composed of tall, narrow bookshelves crammed with ancient books. A tall, spindly man was unpacking a trunk and peering at the shelves, looking for places for these new arrivals.

'Books, Aubrey?' his mother said.

'Antiquarian books, I believe,' Aubrey said. 'Hello, Mr Thomson.'

The man at the stand straightened from writing in a ledger and, seeing Aubrey, smiled in a sickly manner. He adjusted his glasses. 'Hello, young sir. Have we met?'

'You are Thomson, of Thomson and Sons, Antiquarian Books?' Aubrey said. 'From Trinovant?'

Mr Thomson bowed. 'Trinovant, Lutetia and Fisherberg.' He chuckled, but Aubrey thought it forced. 'As well as any other continental cities where there is a love of fine books.'

Lady Rose entered the booth and ran her eye over the nearest shelf. 'Ah. You have one of Professor Hepworth's works.'

The angular Mr Thomson hopped over. 'Oh yes. *The Matter of Matter*, first printing. Quite valuable.'

'I'll take it,' Lady Rose said. 'For Caroline,' she said to Aubrey.

He was chagrined. He should have thought of getting it for her.

'So you travel a great deal,' Aubrey said to the bookseller as he made out the receipt.

'Hither and yon,' Mr Thomson said. He placed the small book carefully on some best brown paper. 'Backward and forward. I'm only here for a week or two before going back to Albion with a shipment. Busy, busy, busy.'

'Really?' Aubrey said. 'Going on the Transcontinental?'

Mr Thomson snapped a length of string and tied the parcel with a flourish. 'Of course. The Transcontinental is the best way to get about the Continent.'

'Naturally,' Aubrey said faintly. His mind was racing off in unexpected directions.

His mother took the parcel and tucked it in her bag. Then she spied something interesting at a booth opposite. 'Look, Aubrey. Lutetian velvet.'

While his mother chatted in Lutetian with the fabric makers, Aubrey studied the program he'd picked up at the entrance to the Academy. It was a sterling production, displaying the best of Holmland printing and typography, and no doubt would have warmed the Chancellor's heart.

His eyes opened. 'Mother, did you know that Professor Mansfield was going to be here? She's presenting on early magical languages.'

His mother turned with a length of rich purple in her arms. 'Anne? I thought she was still in Aigyptos.'

'So did I. She hasn't been in touch with you?'

'No. I must make a point to find her. I haven't seen her in ages.'

Caroline and George made their way toward them through the crowd. Aubrey's heart leaped to see Caroline.

She was dressed in a stylish grey suit – long skirted, smart jacketed.

'Your lecture theatre is set up,' George said to Lady Rose. 'After the opening, it's Professor Heinz this morning with *Forest Fungi of Farnsland*, then lunch, then your show.'

'We'll make sure we get there during the lunch break, just to make sure nothing has been disturbed,' Caroline said.

'Wise,' Aubrey said, 'but we have those opening addresses to get through first.'

'I'm looking forward to hearing the Elektor speak,' Lady Rose said. 'He said he'd been working on his speech for months.' She studied the program. 'And the Chancellor has some time as well. That should be interesting. More about bootmaking machinery or slate production, I should think.'

'No doubt,' Aubrey said, but his startled attention was on a familiar figure hurrying toward them.

'Lady Rose,' Hugo von Stralick panted. 'If you'll excuse us, I must speak to your son. Privately.'

'Of course,' Lady Rose said. 'As long as your "privately" includes these two, for they look determined to be part of whatever conspiracy you're hatching.'

Von Stralick glanced at the hovering Caroline and George. He pushed back his uncharacteristically unkempt hair. 'Naturally.' He took Aubrey's arm. 'Quickly, we must find somewhere to talk.'

'The lecture theatre,' George suggested. 'The one where Lady Rose is going to talk.'

Von Stralick refused to say anything while they struggled through the crowds, out of the door and then down the cloistered walkway. Half of Fisherberg appeared to have descended on the Academy and the old buildings were echoing with excited conversation.

George held open the door and they slipped into the dimly lit, slightly dusty lecture theatre. It smelled of floor polish and chalk.

'Now, what is it?' Aubrey asked as von Stralick made sure the door was shut. His voice echoed from the hard wooden floors and the banked rows of empty seats.

Von Stralick was grim. 'It's Otto, the fool. I went to his rooms. I wanted to give him the good news about Tremaine.'

'I hope he was pleased,' Caroline said.

'He was, but in an absentminded sort of way.'

'I would have thought he'd be overjoyed,' Aubrey said.

'So did I. But he just smiled a little, congratulated me, and insisted he had to get back to his work.'

'His work?' George said. 'And what is this important work he's been so obsessed with? I thought he was going to be of some use here in Fisherberg.'

'This prize he's won. Because of it, he's presenting a paper.'

Aubrey shrugged. 'He told us that.'

'But he neglected to mention that it was part of the opening ceremony.'

Startled, Aubrey whipped out the program. 'I didn't see his name anywhere.'

'You are correct. But look at the item straight after the Chancellor.'

'A Presentation from the Chancellor's Prize Winner.' Aubrey looked up. 'That's what he was talking about.'

'Apparently.'

'A lot of money, is it?' George asked.

'Otto wouldn't say. But he was very pleased with himself and his prospects, it seemed.'

'Quite a lot of mystery about this,' Caroline said. 'Surprise presentations, special prizes.'

Aubrey's uneasiness was threatening to skip disquiet and grow straight into outright alarm. He clamped down on it. 'So Kiefer is going to give a paper. Good luck to him.'

'Heaven help us if he delivers it,' von Stralick said, 'because if he does, the world will be at war within a month.'

Von Stralick delivered this with a flat tone of voice, devoid of drama, which only made it all the more chilling.

'This is the same Otto Kiefer we're talking about?' George said. 'All knees and elbows? Makes a good scone but not much use otherwise?'

'Once he was awarded this Chancellor's Prize, he became obsessed with old documents from all over Fisherberg,' von Stralick said. 'He told me how he'd been digging in archives in the old Imperial Palace, and in private collections, and even in the records in the oldest churches. Once he finished one last bit of research, he was ready, he said, ready to claim for what was owed to him. He was babbling, words tripping over each other, and it looked as if he hadn't eaten for a month.'

'But what's he on about?' George asked. 'Owed to him?'

'His father was promised riches if he worked with Dr Tremaine on catalysts,' Aubrey said, 'but when he died, the family got nothing.'

'Otto has always felt wronged,' von Stralick said, 'and always wanted what was due to him.'

'But exactly what has he been researching?' Caroline asked.

'It was hard to make out, but it had something to do with your Prince Albert.'

Aubrey's unease decided to put on lead boots and dance a little. 'He wasn't talking family history, was he?'

Von Stralick darted a venomous look at Aubrey. 'He said you'd know. He promised it would be the making of his career, thanks to Schweiger, the man who'd prompted him to look into this area.'

'Schweiger?'

'I'd never heard of him and, given Otto's fawning attitude when he mentioned the man, I was suspicious. I asked for a description.'

'Tall, pointed beard? Very dextrous? Black eye?'

Von Stralick sagged and sat on one of the first row of desks. 'How did you know?'

'I didn't. I worked it out. Schweiger is Manfred.' Manfred's part in events was nagging Aubrey – mainly because such machinations suggested the involvement of someone altogether more dangerous.

'Yes, Manfred is helping him,' von Stralick said. 'You see why I hurried to find you. I do not have a good feeling about this.'

Nor do I. Aubrey started for the door. He flung it open. 'We were all convinced that Dr Tremaine was after the Prince. We forgot about feints.'

'Calm down, Aubrey,' Caroline said. 'One thought at a time.'

'That's the point. You can't keep one thought at a time with Dr Tremaine.'

'Steady on, old man,' George said. 'Dr Tremaine is harmless, locked up in a pearl which is locked up in a safe.'

Aubrey stood still, one hand on the door knob. 'That may be,' he said. 'But by now his plans have a momentum of their own. They can move ahead without him.'

'But *what* was he planning?' George said. 'Surely he was after something.'

'We know he wants war. It's how he's going to achieve it that's the puzzle. But it's pretty clear that here he had a great deal invested in Kiefer giving this paper, whatever is in it. Look at the effort he's gone to in order to throw us off the scent.'

'So we have to stop Otto reading this paper?' Caroline said.

'I'd say so. Generally, thwarting Dr Tremaine's plans is an excellent idea for everyone except Dr Tremaine.'

Twenty-eight

THEY SPLIT UP. IN THE CROWDS THAT WERE THRONGING through the Academy it was the only sensible thing to do.

Aubrey decided to head for the library, the obvious place for Kiefer to do last-minute research. Kiefer wasn't an evil person, he reminded himself as he pounded along the cloistered walkways of the Law Faculty, glad that the crowds had thinned this far away from the Academy Hall. But he wouldn't be the last who'd be duped by Dr Tremaine, either.

The rambling collection of stone buildings that was the Medical Faculty led Aubrey directly to his destination, but he skidded to an abrupt halt when he saw the two people in earnest conversation in the forecourt of the library.

Handing Manfred an envelope was Mr Thomson, of Thomson and Sons, Fine and Rare Books.

Plots, plans and suppositions ran together in Aubrey's mind and smashed into a million pieces. Frantically, he sorted through them, discarded most and started building a new whole theory.

The Security Intelligence Directorate wouldn't have found anyone coming to the Trinovant bookshop to collect the secret documents because the *owner* was the one who the documents were for. Here he was in Holmland handing a suspiciously similar envelope to the suspiciously ubiquitous Manfred. Aubrey could see that in a short time, Holmland agents would be making a move on the precious guano cargoes.

He smiled. Tallis's reworking of the document would mean the information may not be as helpful as Manfred thought.

Regardless, Thomson's business was a perfect cover. Moving back and forward between Albion and the Continent, managing shipments of books and documents. Thomson would have plenty of opportunity to ferry useful information to whoever he was working for.

Another peek and Aubrey saw that Manfred and Thomson were moving off together, Manfred with a small leather suitcase in one hand. Aubrey chewed his lip, glanced in the direction of the prominent clocktower overtopping the Academy Hall, and set off after them.

After only a few minutes, they reached a laneway between a service building and the Biology Department. Aubrey crouched behind a large rose bush and almost groaned when Manfred and Thomson shook hands and parted. Thomson took the lane that led to Fransman Street and the city, while Manfred marched off toward the Academy Hall.

Indecision, then decision. Aubrey would make sure to get a report to the Security Intelligence Directorate about Thomson. The only books he'd be seeing when he got back to Albion would be in a prison library.

He'd follow Manfred.

Manfred strode through the campus. His suitcase swung like a pendulum and Aubrey was certain that nothing would have changed if the way had been packed with people. Manfred was a man of purpose, a man on a mission. He would have ploughed through them.

He reached the Academy Hall. The forecourt was still crowded with Holmland's finest edging along, filing through the massive arched doors.

The crowds actually made Aubrey's job of following Manfred easier as he could hide in the numbers, but he was conscious that time was growing short. Surely the Elektor and the Chancellor would be arriving soon, and that would be the signal for proceedings to begin.

Manfred surprised Aubrey by veering wide and heading along the outside of the Academy Hall. Aubrey was forced to ease his way through an untidy garden bed to keep the man in sight as the way narrowed to a service lane sandwiched between the long side of the Academy Hall and the Physics Laboratory. Manfred pressed on, past rubbish bins, piles of wooden boxes and the assorted debris of countless academic functions. When the laneway reached a brick wall, Manfred didn't pause. Relentless, he climbed on top of an old, broken handcart and then vaulted over the wall. He landed on the other side with a grunt that Aubrey could hear from his position in a clump of acanthus.

The sound of the assembled multitudes in the Academy

Hall was like the buzzing of the world's largest bee hive. Aubrey stared at the brick wall, then at the hall, then back again. He rubbed his side and wished for more time.

Five more minutes. He'd follow Manfred for five more minutes and then he'd have to find Kiefer.

Aubrey ran through the garden bed, bent almost double. When he reached the cart he bounded, barely touched the wall and was over.

Only to see Manfred, waiting and smiling coldly at him. 'What took you so long?'

Aubrey took a step backward and found how close he was to the wall when he had no more room to move. He felt a drop of sweat slide down his throat and disappear under his collar. 'Manfred.'

Manfred clicked his heels together and bowed. The whole performance was heavy with irony. 'I knew you were following me. Dr Tremaine warned me about your persistence.'

Aubrey was grimly satisfied when Manfred's words confirmed what he'd been thinking. Manfred's shadowy involvement in affairs was connected with the master of conspiracies, Dr Mordecai Tremaine. 'He'll betray you in the end, Manfred. He's using you and then he'll spit you out.'

Manfred shrugged. 'He pays well, though. I'll take his money for as long as I think it's safe. Then I'll get out.'

Aubrey nearly laughed. Greed tended to cloud one's sense of timing.

'But I have you now,' Aubrey said. 'One less henchman to help Dr Tremaine.'

Manfred picked up his suitcase. 'You might be able to hold me. And then again you might not. So I prepared a little insurance.' He pointed. A brown paper package was sitting against the rear wall of the Academy Hall. 'A compressed spell. It's due to go off at any minute, taking your Prince down with this place. You can stop me, or try to stop it. You can't do both.' He shook his head sadly. 'You shouldn't go up against him, Fitzwilliam. You don't know what he is capable of.'

Aubrey was about to retort, but at that moment, Manfred hurled his empty suitcase. It spun straight at Aubrey, and he had to duck to stop it hitting him in the head. When he straightened Manfred was sprinting in the opposite direction, and was already halfway along the rear of the hall.

Aubrey was left alone.

The package looked harmless, a brown paper parcel such as one would see under the arm of a happy shopper. It looked as if someone had dropped it while hurrying to an appointment.

With urgency hammering at him, he closed his eyes and readied his magical senses. He had visions of the compression giving way at any second, but he steeled himself – and tried to ignore the way his heart was racing. Carefully, with as much delicacy he could summon, he extended his awareness.

With his magical pseudo-sight, the package blazed like a sun. It was so overwhelming that Aubrey didn't know where to start. After taking a deep breath in order to steady himself, he imagined his magical senses as a thin needle, the better to probe the package. His lips drew back from his teeth as he edged his awareness closer, with as much gentleness as he could, looking for a spot of weakness in the magical inferno.

There, he thought, and he was in.

He hissed, then cut it off. He knew this magic. The texture, the construction, the signature. It was typical of the ex-Sorcerer Royal's arrogance, not disguising his efforts, confident that the outcome would obliterate all traces of the origin of the spell – after it had obliterated much, much more.

Inside the package was a coil of compressed weather magic. And unlike the weather magic spell that Aubrey had encountered in Albion, this was a perfectly constructed, expertly compressed magical object, a perfect example in a fiendishly difficult area. The weather spell in Albion had erupted prematurely, and Dr Tremaine had mocked Rokeby-Taylor for it. This one was an example of how to do it right.

He opened his eyes. The sunburst of magical power disappeared and he was once again looking at a nondescript brown paper parcel.

He rubbed his hands together slowly, trying to stem a rising tide of panic.

He'd learned who had constructed the spell – and he was determined that it wouldn't be the last thing he learned. The spell was beautifully refined as well as being tightly controlled. It wasn't the sledgehammer approach of an entire thunderstorm. It took a single aspect of a storm and concentrated it, singling it out and intensifying it, winding it up and packing it tightly, then meshing a timing component among the compression layers so that it would erupt at the appropriate time.

Lightning. A dozen or more individual lightning bolts had been twisted together and packed into a brown paper parcel that was about to give way.

But even with this imminent danger, Aubrey's curiosity wouldn't give up. He probed a little further and was puzzled to uncover a number of complex limiting elements in the spell. If he was interpreting correctly, this was an intricately *shaped* spell. When released, the lightning bolts would erupt solely in a vertical plane.

He looked up. The bulk of the clocktower soared overhead – in the direct line that the unbound lightning bolts would follow.

The clocktower would be blasted. Destroyed, almost certainly, with some damage to the Academy Hall itself – but this spell wasn't intended to slaughter the assembly inside. It would be noisy and highly destructive, but not the lethal weapon that it had appeared at first.

Then what was it for?

Aubrey slapped himself on the forehead. The spell was a sower of discord. The people inside were Holmland's most important, most influential. If they experienced, first hand, an attack that would no doubt be blamed on Holmland's enemies, they would be galvanised behind the Chancellor and his plans.

So I have another reason to stop it, Aubrey thought with a slight trembling in his knees, *apart from a desire not to be blown apart myself*.

He took a deep breath and shook himself, as if he could dislodge the fear that was doing its best to take hold of him. He locked his knees, the better to stop them trembling, then relaxed them.

It's simple, really, he thought. All he had to do was either reinforce the compression, delay the release of the compression, or render the tightly-packed lightning inert.

I'm spoiled for choices. He looked along the length of the rear of the Academy Hall, but he was still alone. No help within earshot, no police constable, no convenient corps of genius magicians, no-one.

It was up to him.

Tinkering with a compression spell that had already been set was a delicate affair, somewhat akin to shaving a tiger, especially if that tiger had particularly sensitive skin. He couldn't use magic suppression – no magic was actually in action yet. The compression spell and the timing spell were inert, passive magic that would release the lightning in an instant. He could try casting the suppression spells as soon as the spells let go, but they needed time to work and he was sure the lightning wasn't about to wait around.

He gnawed his lip. He knew that a theoretical approach existed. He'd read about it in a biography of Harland James, a Caledonian magician who died a horrible – and quite spectacular – death. The trouble was that James's theoretical approach was the cause of his demise and, sensibly, no-one had ever tried it again.

The principle was sound, though. Cast another spell that would latch onto the end of the existing spell. The new spell would contain variables that would alter the effects of the original spell, extending the time before the release of a timing spell, for instance. Naturally, casting a spell to attach to a spell that had already been cast some time ago meant including some sort of temporal inversion constant. In other words, the tricky little appending spell had to send itself back in time to grab onto the compression spell at the moment of its utterance. And in this case, it had to avoid all notice by the original spell caster and blend itself seamlessly, doing its good work unseen and undetected.

All in all, it struck Aubrey as about as simple as teaching a goldfish calculus. On the other hand, the alternative was being crisped by an angry lightning bolt, so he didn't have much to lose.

While his body went through the physical symptoms of fear – churning stomach, dry mouth, propensity for his feet to want to take the rest of him well away from this undeniable source of danger – he concentrated on constructing a taut, well-defined spell and not on imagining the results of a suddenly uncompressed lightning storm. Not knowing when the compression spell was due to release added a certain urgency to his deliberations, but he needed to do it right. If he didn't, he was likely to trigger the compression spell and release the lightning himself. In fact, he realised, there was a number of ways for him to come to a messy, charcoaled end here, and only one way not to.

He had to cast a perfect spell.

Duration was simple – he wanted to add a few days to the release of the lightning, enough to allow for safe disposal of the package. Range, dimensions, intensity, all these factors were easy to put into place. The tricky part was the temporal inversion component.

He had to define the temporal inversion so that, once the spell was cast, it would effectively disappear, fold itself back into time and attach itself to the compression. He could use the signature element from the compression spell – Tremaine's signature – splice it into his spell so that the inverted spell would be able to track the compression spell to its source, the same way a bloodhound would use a scrap of cloth from a burglar to track the villain to his den. Straightforward, in a rather twisty way.

Aubrey opted for Sumerian. He was comfortable with it and its circumscribed vocabulary left little room for ambiguity, which was always helpful when time elements were concerned.

He ran through the spell twice, then a third time, before readying himself to pronounce it aloud.

He paused for a moment. The lane was silent. The hubbub from inside the hall was a far-off drone, business, diplomacy and simple human interaction going on oblivious to the imminent disaster that was taking place not far away. Aubrey spared a moment to smile wryly over how much that was like all of human history, then he pressed his hands together.

A few mildly curious pigeons looked down from the roof below. Aubrey decided they'd have to take their chances. He began.

The elements marched from his mouth like well-drilled soldiers. It was a long spell, as he'd spared no detail in trying to get it right. Dimensionality, duration, range of effect all fell into place one after the other and his hopes rose. He felt confident in his delivery and his final, signature element was firm and steady.

The package tilted.

Aubrey took a step back and waited to be blasted out of existence.

Then he patted himself. He glanced at the pigeons, who hadn't moved and were giving him a look of 'What was *that* all about?', decided he was still in reasonable physical shape, and reassessed. The parcel hadn't moved at all. He'd simply had the *impression* that it had tilted. It had shifted its existence, but not in a physical way. He waited a moment, savouring the feeling of not being charcoal, then probed the parcel with what was becoming his customary delicacy.

The compression spell was nailed down tightly. Probe as he might, he could find no signs of weakness, no signs of release, nothing that indicated destruction was a heartbeat away.

He sighed. With a hand that was only slightly trembling, he touched his brow. Then, his control lapsed for an instant and his body reasserted itself, relief warring with the desire for immediate flight from danger. The result? He felt like throwing up. He sagged, as if all the air was being let out of him by way of a valve in his heel, and had to steady himself against the wall. He let his head rest on the brickwork.

This can't do, he thought, eventually. He straightened, and then realised how tense he'd been, because every muscle protested as if he'd been in the gym for hours. He shook himself, then he bent and picked up the parcel.

Now, he thought as he limped off, *to find Kiefer*.

Twenty-nine

OUTSIDE THE ENTRANCE TO THE ACADEMY HALL, Aubrey found a police officer herding the crowds. He pushed the parcel on him, explained in a few words what it was, watched the police officer blanch and rush off, then he went off to try to get backstage.

He did his best to slide through the crowd that was emptying from the trade annex. Hundreds of people had apparently realised, simultaneously, that the opening ceremonies were about to start and they were all seeking their seats.

Aubrey was distracted from his quest for an instant when he saw a tall, dark-clad figure standing near one of the ornamental columns in the foyer of the Academy Hall. He was startled, for he hadn't known that Craddock was going to be present, but it made some sense. He assumed Quentin Hollows had let Craddock know of the developments in Fisherberg. Craddock would have lost no time crossing the Continent once he heard the details of the plot against Prince Albert.

It was an explanation that needed following up, but it didn't account for the extremely familiar manner in which the habitually taciturn Craddock was talking the sublimely beautiful Madame Zelinka.

Aubrey would have been gobsmacked if he'd had time. As it was, he had to postpone his amazement for another time – but he promised himself he'd have an explanation from Craddock before too long. The man was actually laughing!

Aubrey's plans to get backstage, however, were dashed when he was turned away from the wings by a pair of commissionaires. They were older men, but sharp-eyed and straight-backed, obviously ex-military, and serious about their job of keeping riff-raff away from the important speakers who were gathering offstage.

'I have an important message for Mr Kiefer,' he said in his best Holmlandish. 'It's urgent.'

'We'll take it to him.' The larger of the two commissionaires eyed him suspiciously.

'Sorry, but I've been honour bound to place it in his hand. I must see him.'

'You'll have to wait until after the speeches,' the smaller one growled. 'What did you say your name was?'

'Von Stralick,' Aubrey said without hesitating. He looked over the auditorium. It was filling rapidly – the rows and rows of seats had few gaps. 'Are you sure I can't see him?'

'He's busy, Mr von Stralick,' the larger one said. 'You'd better find your seat. Speeches are starting soon. You wouldn't want to miss them.'

Aubrey saw Caroline slip into the auditorium through the large rear doors. She stood at the rear for a moment, gazing about. Aubrey eased past a muttering dignitary and then hurried down the middle aisle.

'Have you found him?' Caroline asked.

'He's backstage already.'

'Do you have any ideas?'

Aubrey looked up to see George on the other side of the hall, up on the balcony. At the same time, George saw him and shrugged. Aubrey shook his head in exaggerated fashion only to meet George's pointing across the auditorium. Von Stralick was arguing with the commissionaires and he appeared to be having as much success as Aubrey had. Then the commissionaires went to grapple with him. Von Stralick twisted, then hurried off.

'What happened there?' Caroline asked.

'I hope he wasn't trying to assume someone else's identity. These officials take a dim view of things like that.'

Von Stralick joined them, at the same time as George had made his way down from upstairs. 'I'm off to see the baron.' The Holmlander brushed himself off. 'He may be able to do something.'

'Isn't he here?' Aubrey said, scanning the audience.

'He said he couldn't be dragged to the symposium.'

'Hush,' Caroline said. 'They're starting.'

'Time to find our seats.'

They left von Stralick. The three friends worked their way to their row, second from the front. Lady Rose nodded at them from her seat, but refrained from asking any questions. Prince Albert was in the front row, just in front of Aubrey. He was sitting next to the Chancellor and the Elektor.

With the ominous sense that comes from a half-glimpsed outcome, Aubrey took out his program. The grey-haired, gowned fellow who was tottering toward the lectern on the stage was apparently the President of the University.

As he spoke, Aubrey was impressed. The President apparently appreciated his role was to take up as little time as possible before the important speeches, so he confined himself to a vague welcome and then quickly introduced the Elektor.

The Elektor was wearing the uniform of the High Admiral of the Holmland Navy, which had enough gold trappings to open a moderately sized jewellery shop. A gold sword on his hip made his walking awkward as he made his way to the lectern.

Aubrey, having a politician for a father and a famous scientist for a mother, was accustomed to being part of an audience. He was also a connoisseur of applause and he judged that the acclamation that greeted the Elektor was genuine and heartfelt. The Elektor stood at the lectern and gathered his papers while the clapping rolled around the hall. After some time he was forced, with a smile, to hold up a hand to bring it to an end, then he launched into his welcome.

As a speech, it was solid but uninspired. Well-meaning was the best description Aubrey could give it. The Elektor wasn't a natural orator, but his earnest delivery carried weight with his audience. He spoke of the importance of scholarship and his hope that it could contribute to understanding between all nations.

Even though Aubrey's mind was elsewhere wondering what Kiefer had planned, he saw how the Elektor gradually warmed to this topic. At one stage he forgot his notes and addressed the audience directly, unfolding his vision for a rational world of peace and understanding for an appreciative audience. Then Aubrey saw that the Elektor's attention was diverted by someone off stage. With a minute stiffening, he slowed, then dropped his gaze to the lectern. Soon, he'd returned to his prepared speech. With a handful of the usual platitudes his speech wandered to the point where he officially declared the symposium open.

The applause was as warm as that which greeted the Elektor and Aubrey was heartened that such a call for understanding had fallen on receptive ears. Admittedly, the audience at an academic symposium may not represent the nation as a whole, but it was reassuring nonetheless.

But his curiosity was engaged wondering who had been able to curtail the Elektor's enthusiastic outline of a better world. Who could cut short the ruler of the country?

The Elektor fumbled for a piece of paper. He stared at it for a moment then, quite obviously, read it word for word. 'I have much pleasure in introducing a special speaker. An extraordinary man has been behind this symposium. It was his idea, and the organisation and implementation of this complex occasion has been entirely overseen by him.' He paused. 'The special adviser to the government of Holmland, Dr Mordecai Tremaine.'

For a moment, Aubrey felt as if his brain had been scooped out and replaced with a lump of putty. He couldn't move, he couldn't think, all he could do was stare as the rogue magician strode onto the stage, clad in a stylish black coat, and shook the noticeably hesitant Elektor's hand before he made his way to the wings.

Didn't I trap you in a pearl? Aubrey thought, dazed. Dimly, he realised that his arm was in the process of developing five neat bruises, right where Caroline's fingers were gripping him. He glanced at her, but her attention was locked on Dr Tremaine as he took his place at the lectern.

Kiefer was forgotten as Aubrey actually felt dizzy. *What is going on?*

Mundane senses only told him so much, so, with great trepidation, he focused his magical awareness with as much will and as much force as he could muster.

And with his magical senses, he sensed it. He ground his teeth, he wanted to leap to his feet and shout to the assembly that the man in front of them was a liar, a manipulator, a thief and a murderer, because he sensed it – and it confirmed what had happened.

Aubrey's magical awareness showed the silvery, insubstantial thread that curled and twisted – passing right through solid objects, undisturbed by the physical world – and connected Aubrey Fitzwilliam and Dr Mordecai Tremaine.

Then he knew that he'd been hoodwinked. Despite having been witness to Dr Tremaine's trickery at Banford Park, in Lutetia, under Trinovant, he'd been duped again. How could he believe that he could trap Dr Tremaine so easily? The creature that he'd cast into the pearl was a fake, a substitute. It was no wonder he hadn't been able to detect a magical connection with it.

Pieces fell into place. It had to be a golem – and if that was the state of Dr Tremaine's golem-making art, then the world had a great deal to fear.

I should have realised, he thought, but at the time he'd been too rushed – and also, he had to admit, too pleased with himself to doubt, too sure of his talent to observe, too carried away to worry.

He shook his head. He hadn't heard a word of Dr Tremaine's speech, but it didn't seem to matter. When Aubrey came to himself, the sorcerer paused and looked directly at him.

And he winked.

It was so brief that Aubrey knew no-one else could see it but him – and it struck him like a blow to the chest. Aubrey flinched, and immediately, Dr Tremaine made an odd movement, reaching out and patting his pocket while he went on, echoing the sentiments of the Elektor.

Automatically, Aubrey did the same and he wondered at the deft, subtle magic involved when he felt something in a pocket that he'd known was empty just a few moments before.

He took it out and unwrapped the small package. Dumbly, he stared at his stolen pocket watch. The Brayshire Ruby glowed warmly, set in the gold cover.

Nonplussed, he eventually realised that the paper wrapping was written upon.

I return your family trinket, for you returned my sister to me – a treasure beyond reckoning.

But did you really think you could out-manoeuvre me? it

said. *You've been a useful decoy. Take some satisfaction in that and accept that you cannot match me.*

It was like a blow to the chest. He found it hard to breathe as he remembered the chaos in the hospital. Despite his efforts, there must have been a window, a tiny opportunity for Dr Tremaine to whisk Sylvia out of the pearl from a distance.

He went to screw up the paper, but Caroline plucked it from his hand. When she looked up, her cheeks white with shock, Dr Tremaine was already concluding his address, notably not thanking anyone else.

Aubrey felt like a puppet and even glanced overhead, looking for the strings and the puppet master, so he nearly missed it when Dr Tremaine introduced Chancellor Neumann before he bowed, made a half-salute in Aubrey's direction and exited, stage right.

Immediately, Aubrey wanted to leap up and follow, but a cooler part of his brain told him that Dr Tremaine had organised events beautifully. By the time Aubrey could push his way to the end of the aisle – if he was prepared to create an unseemly disturbance on such an august occasion – Dr Tremaine would no doubt be through the wings and out via a backstage entrance.

There was no point pursuing him. Besides, Kiefer hadn't appeared yet – and Aubrey couldn't leave before he heard what he was up to.

Dazed, Aubrey had trouble concentrating on the Chancellor's speech. It was punctilious, the work of many underlings, Aubrey assumed. While he worked through welcoming the important guests, the Chancellor's mighty bald head began to sweat. Without any embarrassment, he mopped it with a red handkerchief, and lumbered through his official duties with dogged determination. His role, as far as Aubrey could tell, was the official welcome to Holmland and he discharged this conscientiously, but Aubrey felt that his monotonous tone of voice would have been the same if he were speaking in the Assembly, ordering a meal at a restaurant, or giving the eulogy at a funeral.

When he finished, he held up both hands to acknowledge the applause, which was, to Aubrey's learned ears, definitely polite rather than wholehearted. Aubrey took the time to look around, trying to see into the wings to spy Kiefer.

His head whipped back, however, when the Chancellor pointedly paused, then uttered a single word – a word Aubrey guessed had never been used in the Academy Hall, and certainly not with such satisfaction and relish: 'Guano.'

The Chancellor visibly enjoyed the effect this had on the audience. Muted expressions of disgust rippled around the auditorium while the Chancellor shuffled his notes, doing little to hide the smile on his face. When the reaction had lessened, he looked up, eyebrows bristling. 'Holmland's industry is the finest in the world.'

This was much more to the liking of the audience, but the connection was clearly puzzling. The Chancellor waved a hand placatingly. 'While our industry is the finest in the world, it has been hampered by a number of issues. Procurement of guano is one of these. While many countries have access to great quantities of this precious substance –' he bowed slightly in the direction of Prince Albert '– Holmland's munitions and fertilizer producers have been hamstrung, held back in their efforts. But not any more.'

Aubrey was stunned when the Chancellor actually grinned before going on. It was a broad grin, an expression of total satisfaction.

'Thanks to one of Holmland's finest industrial magicians, we are free of this dependence on imported guano. Advances in the areas of –' the Chancellor peered at his notes '– catalysts and pressurised vessels have enabled the artificial production of unlimited amounts of ammonia.'

While polite bafflement ruffled the audience, Aubrey sat astounded as the implications battered at him.

The Chancellor went on. 'This, of course, means unlimited supply of nitrates for fertilizer, leading to substantial increases our crop yields. And,' he added, almost as an afterthought, 'unlimited nitrates for our munitions and explosives industries.'

This is what Aubrey had feared, and to judge from the consternation on Bertie's face, the implications weren't lost on him either. An increase in production of Holmland munitions was the last thing the world needed. Controlling Holmland's armament build-up by controlling its guano imports was no longer an option.

And how easy would it be to sabotage guano shipments heading to other countries? Aubrey wondered, remembering Manfred's interest in the stolen shipping documents.

The reaction from the assembly was electric. Delight, pride and excitement greeted the Chancellor's announcement as the audience took it as a sign of Holmland's correct place in the world. Of course Holmland was leading the world in such industry. Doesn't it lead the world in all important things?

Eventually, the Chancellor signalled for quiet, then went on. 'But enough of such things. This symposium is about more than the finest industries in the world – it is about the speakers.' He cleared his throat again. 'And I have much pleasure in introducing a special speaker, a gifted young man whose talents lie in two distinct areas. His advances in industrial magic led to my announcement, and his historical research has resulted in his being the recipient of the inaugural Chancellor's Prize. With his prize-winning essay: Mr Otto Kiefer.'

Amid polite applause, Kiefer stumbled onto the stage. At first, he looked both bewildered and angry, gaping at the other side of the stage in the direction Dr Tremaine had gone. Then he seemed to remember where he was. He stared at the audience, then at the papers he clutched in his hands. The Chancellor took him by the hand and shook it in a firm and masculine manner, muttering some encouraging words. Kiefer was instantly wide-eyed, being so close to the leader of his nation. Gradually, he straightened and grinned sheepishly. Neumann smiled tolerantly, warmly, and swept a wide hand to beckon Kiefer to the lectern. Once Kiefer was there, Neumann moved to the edge of the stage. He stood for a moment and beamed, as if Kiefer were a pet dog he'd trained to perform a difficult trick, then he marched off stage – in the same direction Dr Tremaine had exited.

Aubrey braced himself, as if he were sailing into a hurricane, ready for what Kiefer had in store.

'Ladies and gentlemen.' Kiefer's voice was shrill with tension. Aubrey wondered if it was simply stage nerves or whether it was foreknowledge of what was to come. 'Ladies and gentlemen,' he repeated, 'my paper is titled:

"Some Genealogical Findings on the Lineage of Some of Our Royal Families".'

Aubrey had been hoping that he'd leaped to the wrong conclusion about Kiefer's research, but the title of his essay let him know that he was right – horribly right. Kiefer was about to drop a bombshell that would reverberate across the Continent all the way to Lutetia and then across the channel to Albion itself.

Kiefer pushed his spectacles back on his nose. He looked at his notes, then at the audience. He blanched a little at the polite attention that awaited him from Holmland's rich and powerful, and dropped his gaze back to his notes, where it remained as if nailed.

'As is well known,' he began, 'the throne of Gallia has been vacant for over a century, ever since the events of the Gallian Revolution.'

Aubrey's fears were about to be realised.

Much of Kiefer's speech was hesitant, full of names and relationships, thickly littered with academic terms like 'consanguinity' and 'morganatic marriage', which strained Aubrey's Holmlandish. Painstakingly, Kiefer traced branches of family tree after family tree, pointing out where names were similar or repeated, which was common, the Gallian aristocracy having a profound lack of imagination when it came to names.

The audience had descended into a diplomatic state of boredom, where impatience was expressed by shuffling of feet, uncreasing and creasing of programs, coughing that was immediately infectious. It was only after nearly half an hour of speaking that Kiefer stopped, coughed himself, then looked up. After an instant's faltering when he saw the audience looking back at him, he went on.

'With the extinguishment of the Gallian royal family in 1793 it was assumed that no legitimate claim to the throne could be found. But new evidence has recently come to light which suggests an astonishing development.'

The shuffling in the audience immediately stopped. Programs were forgotten. Respiratory complaints underwent miraculous recoveries. *This* was something interesting. Rumours of missing heirs to the Gallian throne had kept people entertained for a hundred years or more, but they were always in the realm of the fairytale. Something concrete, however, would be delicious.

Kiefer dropped to his notes again, but this time he had the attention of the entire audience. After another fifteen minutes pursuing a sidetrack into minor Gallian peers, he launched, without warning, into an examination of the Albion royal line.

A murmur hurried around the hall. Aubrey saw Bertie stiffen and he wished he could see his friend's face.

Lady Rose leaned over. 'Do you know anything about this?' she whispered.

Aubrey made a half-shrug, half-wave that he hoped was inconclusive. He glanced at his mother to see that she knew exactly what he was doing. 'I'll expect a full account later,' her expression said.

As Kiefer blundered on, closer and closer to his conclusion, the auditorium was so full of bated breaths that Aubrey had genuine fears the hall would explode when everyone exhaled again.

He began to experience a dreadful sense of inevitability, the inexorable approach of a disaster. It was like watching someone trying to walk across a frozen lake, knowing that each step was taking him closer to his doom.

Kiefer, however, was mistaking the tension in the hall for acclaim. He began to look up more frequently, and he even started adding jaunty gestures of emphasis, abandoning the death-grip he'd had on the lectern.

Oh, don't smile, Aubrey thought when Kiefer peered outward again, but his silent plea went unanswered. Kiefer attempted a raffish grin, which slid into a grimace before finally coming across as a demented smirk.

Aubrey could see that they were on the downhill slope now. He thought of trying to stop Kiefer by casting a spell, then he looked around and he realised how well Dr Tremaine had set up this manoeuvre. Aubrey couldn't interrupt the ceremony. Any attempt to do so, here, in the heart of Holmland, would be an undeniably hostile act. And by the son of the Albion Prime Minister? That way lay diplomatic horror.

Aubrey could almost imagine the whistling sound as the bombshell came closer and closer. Kiefer paused, pursed his lips and, with a confidence hitherto unseen, gazed over the audience. For a moment, he was a scholar, a holder of incontrovertible evidence, imbued with authority and gravitas far beyond his years. It was his moment, and he savoured it.

'And so,' he said gravely, 'it is indisputable that the late Count de Vere of Carleon was the rightful King of Gallia.' Kiefer gestured. 'As he died with no brothers, and only one daughter, that means his grandson, Prince Albert here, is the heir to that throne as well as that of Albion.'

The bombshell exploded and, to Aubrey, it sounded like the laughter of Dr Mordecai Tremaine.

Thirty

A WEEK AFTER THE EXTRAORDINARY EVENTS OF THE symposium opening, a launch pulled alongside the HMS *Invulnerable* with commendable sureness, given the choppy sea. Aubrey watched from the bridge as his father came onto deck looking neat and trim. He took his time to greet the captain and his officers, even though it was apparent to Aubrey that he'd rather be on his way to meeting Lady Rose. It was subtle – the duration of the handclasp, a touching of his hand to the brim of his hat – but Aubrey knew his father well. He was sure that every man on the *Invulnerable* would remember the Prime Minister's visit and how he talked with them about their particular duty.

'I'm surprised he could get away,' George said. His sandy hair ruffled in the wind as they walked down the passageway from where the captain had let them watch their arrival into Imworth harbour.

'It would take more than chaos in Gallia to keep him away,' Aubrey said. Almost unconsciously, he touched his chest – where once the Beccaria Cage had nestled – and then put his hand to his pocket to feel the comforting weight of his pocket watch. He was glad to have it back, even if its return simply meant it was *more* difficult to fathom Dr Tremaine and his motives.

Kiefer's announcement had caused such an uproar that the symposium had been abandoned. While Prince Albert was ushered out safely, pandemonium ruled. Academics and analysts gathered and argued about the political implications of the revelation, diplomats hurried out to spread the news, curious guests surged about trying to glimpse the young man who could soon be the ruler of two countries. Within an hour, the only people left were trade exhibitors, who were glumly packing up their displays and counting the costs of the lost opportunities.

Fisherberg exploded with gossip and speculation. In packed coffee houses and tense meeting rooms, Albion's ambitions were dissected, international treaties discussed, and plans were redrawn.

The Albion Embassy was besieged. Prying journalists, countless petitioners and the simply inquisitive had trapped Prince Albert, Lady Rose, Aubrey and the others for days – time which Aubrey used to probe what had happened when the chaotic magic interacted with the Beccaria Cage. The way that it had fused his body and soul together was baffling, but it showed no signs of deteriorating. The events of the Fisherberg trip had been mixed in their outcome, but this looked as if it was undeniably positive.

He really was cured.

They found a ladder and went below to the next deck. He peered over the rail to see a large group of able seamen grappling with a large crate. In the days of chaos after Otto Kiefer's speech, Ambassador Hollows had done well to organise the payment and shipment of the golem maker to the *Invulnerable*. Craddock was below, supervising the loading of the crate onto the same launch that had brought Sir Darius. Aubrey was sure the arcane machinery would be whisked into the lowest reaches of the Darnleigh Buildings, home of what used to be the Magisterium. He could imagine magicians in the employ of the military rubbing their hands in anticipation, ready to deconstruct it.

Before leaving Fisherberg, Aubrey caught up with an angry Hugo von Stralick. Betrayed and bitter, von Stralick dropped a number of broad hints that made Aubrey very suspicious about the origin of the golem-making machinery. Aubrey was keen to examine the apparatus itself to see if he could find anything to connect it to a certain Holmland industrialist. If they were, the events in Holmland were even more complex than they seemed. Baron von Grolman was a player who needed further analysis.

Seeing Craddock reminded Aubrey that he hadn't questioned him about how he knew Madame Zelinka. Since the symposium, he'd learned that Craddock and Tallis had indeed caught an emergency dirigible flight to Fisherberg as soon as news had made its way back to Albion about the plot to replace Prince Albert, but they'd barely spoken to Aubrey – apart from insisting on his compiling a detailed report. Their attention was on ensuring that the Prince – and Lady Rose – were safely escorted from Holmland.

Tallis was waiting for Aubrey and George on the deck below. He was standing, arms behind his back, eyeing the sea with the suspicion of the true land dweller. 'Thomson the bookseller,' he said without any preliminaries. 'Hollows sent your report on to my department.' He scowled. 'We've investigated further. You may be right.'

'You've taken him into custody?'

Tallis turned away from the sea. He smiled. 'Hardly.'

'He's given you the slip?' George shook his head. 'Cunning chaps, those booksellers.'

'We'll keep a good eye on him,' Tallis said, ignoring George, 'and use him to feed false information to his masters. It may prove invaluable.'

'And Stafford Bruce?'

'He was mortified,' Tallis said. 'Resigned immediately. The Opposition is disarray. Some analysts in Foreign Affairs are saying that this could have been the actual plan in the first place.'

Aubrey saw the shifting movements of international intrigue all over again, the shadows under the surface of the sunny world. Complex, tortured, tangled, the unseen armies already at war.

They met the others in what had been the officers' dining room but had, out of necessity, become a debriefing room. The room itself was well lit, with many ports allowing light in from the outside, and it was surprisingly well appointed. A number of round tables with heavy, starched tablecloths were surrounded by heavy-based chairs that swivelled – a sensible arrangement for heavy weather.

Caroline and Lady Rose were already there. Caroline waved to him as he entered and Aubrey's heart was hers.

He wasn't sure if she knew it, but he wouldn't have been surprised if she did. She was anything but unperceptive. If she chose not to acknowledge it, Aubrey had decided, it must be her sense of responsibility again, laying as heavily on her as his did on him. She was determined to pursue her studies, her career and her wider ambitions in the world. Aubrey had had the tantalising hint from her that politics was something that she was thinking of. And then there was this adventuring, which she had thrown herself into in a way that only increased her appeal to him – if that were possible.

With such aspirations, Caroline's firm view that single-mindedness of outlook was paramount meant that any personal dalliances were seen as unnecessary uses of time. The optimum route to success called for dedication and couldn't countenance anything frivolous.

But had he detected some thawing in Caroline's attitude? He was aware of how easy it was to misinterpret such things. Acutely aware. He swallowed at the multitude of memories that presented themselves, evidence of his inability in this area. They made him hesitant to conclude anything, but could there be some hope?

He greeted Caroline and his mother, then sat next to Caroline. She didn't object, and even patted his elbow absently as she craned her lovely neck to look toward where the captain was entering via another door.

I can always hope, Aubrey thought and vowed to be content with this.

Sir Darius strode into the room. Immediately, he found his wife and crossed to her side.

Aubrey had grown accustomed to warm displays of affection between his parents. It set them apart in a society where decorum was the norm and Aubrey loved them for it. The genuine feeling that had brought them together was as strong as ever, unaffected by the censorious eyes of the world.

Lady Rose stood. Sir Darius swept his wife into his arms and held her tightly. She put her head on his shoulders and closed her eyes. They said nothing.

Having seen this before, Aubrey discreetly watched Caroline. She smiled at Sir Darius and Lady Rose. Aubrey thought her smile was wistful, and the way she rested her hand on her cheek added to the contemplative cast of her face. Or did it? Perhaps she was simply tired. Or thinking of something else.

I have no idea, Aubrey admitted to himself, and he sighed.

'Something wrong, Aubrey?' Caroline asked.

'Apart from Gallia questioning their alliance with us and thereby providing an opportunity for Holmland to start aggression?'

'No need to be so testy.' She patted his arm again. 'You did well.'

Aubrey had never had fireworks go off inside his skull, but he imagined that this is what it would feel like. 'I did?'

'You did, old man.' George leaned across the table. 'Don't you think that Dr Tremaine would have actually taken the Prince, even if that wasn't his main aim for the symposium?'

Lady Rose smiled. 'Aubrey, dear boy. You can be hard on yourself. Take some pride in what you've achieved.'

Aubrey sat back, surprised. Ever since their precipitous departure from Fisherberg, he'd been kicking himself for not anticipating Dr Tremaine's plot within a plot within a plot. Even now, warming to the praise, he wondered if he'd missed a plot or two.

Craddock entered. He took his hat from his head and beat it against his leg. Behind him was Tallis and Prince Albert, who was accompanying Caroline's mother. The Prince saw the party at Aubrey's table, waved and escorted Mrs Hepworth across the room.

Requisite greeting, bowing and curtseying completed, the Prince waited until Mrs Hepworth was seated before taking a place himself. 'Have you heard the news? Your friend Kiefer has disappeared.'

'Not exactly a friend,' Aubrey said, with a pang. He'd liked Kiefer, despite his eccentricities, and he hated seeing the way Dr Tremaine used people and then discarded them. 'An acquaintance.'

Tallis glanced at the open notebook he held. 'Hollows's people report that he's not been seen in any of his old haunts since his speech.'

'The poor boy who made the speech at the symposium?' Ophelia Hepworth said.

'The poor boy who seems to have helped Holmland to the secret of ammonia synthesis.' Aubrey stopped and blinked. 'He was studying pressure containment magic while he was at Greythorn. I'll warrant that Dr Tremaine organised his placement here to facilitate that.'

'Used and then thrown away,' George said.

'He's not the only one who's missing,' Craddock said. 'I believe you know Professor Mansfield? Ancient Languages at Greythorn? She was meant to present at the symposium but didn't appear. Our Holmland operatives think she's been abducted.'

Lady Rose put a hand to her mouth. 'Mercy. Anne.'

Sir Darius took her other hand. 'We'll do what we can?'

Tallis made a decisive note. 'Of course.'

Ophelia Hepworth looked puzzled. 'I'd still like to know why poor Kiefer's work on ammonia is so important. I thought his revelation about the Prince was far more interesting.'

Aubrey went first. 'Explosives. Munitions. Holmland's war preparations have been hampered by uncertain supplies of nitrates – which can be extracted from guano.' He paused. 'If you don't have guano, you have to get it from ammonia, and that process has been hideously expensive.'

'Until now,' the Prince said.

'Oh dear.' Mrs Hepworth folded her hands on the table.

Sir Darius touched his moustache. 'Our best estimates have said that the Holmland armed forces only had three months' supply of bullets, for instance. Not enough for a serious war.'

'But that's all changed now,' Aubrey said. 'Cheap ammonia means plenty of bullets. Plenty of bombs. Plenty of torpedoes.' He shuddered at the prospect. 'I'm starting to think war is inevitable.'

'That's depressing,' George said.

'Is Dr Tremaine behind this?' Caroline asked.

'If it was just him, I think we'd have a chance of doing something. But after seeing the state of play in Fisherberg . . . Too many important Holmlanders seem to think war might be an opportunity.'

'War as an opportunity?' Lady Rose said. 'What a depraved notion.'

Sir Darius shrugged. 'They see it as a chance to expand Holmland's borders, to seize resources, to become the dominant nation on the Continent.'

'And don't forget profit,' George pointed out. 'War's good for business, if you're in the right business.'

George's suggestion suddenly threw light on something that had been nagging at Aubrey. 'That's it, George. Baron von Grolman. That's what he's up to.'

'The consummate businessman,' Caroline said softly, immediately following Aubrey's lead. She clenched a fist. 'He's not against war. He just wants to be in a position to make the most money from it.'

'That would explain why he was interested in getting rid of Dr Tremaine,' George said. 'Tremaine was keeping the baron away from power.'

'Sorry, Caroline,' Aubrey said. 'Sorry, Mrs Hepworth.'

'Ophelia, Aubrey dear. And no need to apologise. Siggy has changed. I was glad to leave him behind.'

Aubrey slipped away as the others pulled apart the revelations. He was pleased when Caroline and George followed.

Together, they stood at the rail and watched as the great ship edged its way toward the dock. The pretty town of Imworth was perched overlooking the harbour, white-washed houses cheery in the sunlight.

'Well, George,' Aubrey said. 'I suppose our adventure had left you with enough to fill a few newspapers?'

'I'm not sure if the papers would be after the sort of thing I want to write.'

'Meaning?'

'I wouldn't mind writing about the Holmland people, the ordinary folk, not the politicians. Good sorts, they are.'

'Sounds as if you're talking about a book.'

George looked alarmed. 'A book? Steady on, old man. An essay is the sort of thing I was thinking about. Find a place for it in one of the journals, perhaps.' He put his hands in his pockets. 'Speaking of such, I'm heading down to talk to some of the sailors. Get their opinion about things, their view of what's going on.'

Whistling, he strolled away, leaving Aubrey and Caroline alone.

'He did that deliberately,' Aubrey said.

'I know. He's very well-meaning.'

'To a fault.'

The breeze ruffled Caroline's hair. Aubrey thought it was the most wonderful thing he'd seen since he last looked at her.

'Let's just see what happens,' she said suddenly.

'I beg your pardon?'

'You were going to ask about us.'

'I was?'

She smiled. 'Your need to know everything is one of your most appealing and most infuriating traits.'

The ship sounded its horn as it neared the dock but Aubrey didn't hear anything over the roaring in his ears.

Appealing?

Some response was necessary. 'We should let things take their course?'

'It sounds like the most sensible idea.'

'Sensible. I like sensible.'

'I thought you would.'

'And you won't get irritated, or upset, if I press my suit?'

'Press your suit? What a charmingly old-fashioned way of putting it.'

'Charming? I can see it's working already.'

'Don't get your hopes up. I reserve my right to be irritated, or upset, at any time.'

'I'll endeavour never to give you cause, then.'

Caroline gazed out at the welcoming sight of Albion waiting for them. 'I'll be interested to see how that turns out.'

As will I, thought Aubrey as they made their way, at last, into a safe harbour.

THE LAWS OF MAGIC

❦ MOMENT OF TRUTH ❦

The unthinkable has happened: Albion is at war. Aubrey and George are swept up into the military – but not in the way they expect. With Caroline drafted into the Special Services, Aubrey is sure the combination of his magic, George's practical skills and Caroline's fighting secrets will make them a formidable team. But what if the military hierarchy has other ideas?

When Aubrey's top secret espionage unit is sent to Gallia to investigate mysterious magical emanations, what they discover is intelligence gold. Holmland is about to unleash an unstoppable horror upon the world. It could win the war within weeks. Aubrey is in a dilemma: should he obey orders and simply observe, or should he and his friends do their best to stop a bloodbath?

**Book Five: *Moment of Truth* is available at
all good retailers in August 2010**